Praise for F. Paul Wilson's Repairman Jack

"*Ground Zero* is not only packed with action and revelations but told so well that fans will want the next two books *now*. . . . Wilson's writing has never been sharper, with the story really focused on the main problem at hand, all leading to a climax where even Jack seems to be powerless with what he has to face. It's truly going to make his fans giddy."
—*Bookgasm*

"There are some writers who, once they settle into an ongoing character, become complacent and happily just write and rewrite the same two or three books over and over again. And then there's F. Paul Wilson, whose Repairman Jack series seems to get better as its hero gets closer and closer to his ultimate fate."
—*Fangoria* on *Crisscross*

"Wilson remains in top form with *By The Sword,* which receives my highest recommendation." —*FearZone*

"Sinuous plot twists and shocking revelations abound, but Wilson [ties] them dexterously to the series' overarching chronicle of a battle between occult forces in which Jack serves as a reluctant but responsible warrior. Like its predecessors, this novel shows why Jack's saga has become the most entertaining and dependable modern horror-thriller series."
—*Publishers Weekly* on *Bloodline*

"Part hard-boiled detective novel, part *Matrix,* and all fun, Wilson's latest and, perhaps, greatest kept me up all night. A pulse-pounding novel that grips you by the throat and doesn't let go even when it's over."
—Eric Van Lustbader on *Harbingers*

ALSO BY F. PAUL WILSON

REPAIRMAN JACK*

The Tomb
Legacies
Conspiracies
All the Rage
Hosts
The Haunted Air
Gateways
Crisscross
Infernal
Harbingers
Bloodline
By the Sword
Fatal Error

YOUNG ADULT*

Jack: Secret Histories
Jack: Secret Circles

THE ADVERSARY CYCLE*

The Keep
The Tomb
The Touch
Reborn
Reprisal
Nightworld

OTHER NOVELS

Healer
Wheels Within Wheels
An Enemy of the State
Black Wind
Dydeetown World
The Tery
Sibs
The Select
Virgin
Implant
Deep as the Marrow
Mirage
(with Matthew J. Costello)
Nightkill
(with Steven Spruill)
Masque
(with Matthew J. Costello)
The Christmas Thingy
Sims
The Fifth Harmonic
Midnight Mass

SHORT FICTION

Soft and Others
The Barrens and Others
Aftershock & Others

EDITOR

Freak Show
Diagnosis: Terminal

*See "The Secret History of the World" (page 435)

F. PAUL WILSON

GROUND ZERO

A REPAIRMAN JACK NOVEL

A TOM DOHERTY ASSOCIATES BOOK
NEW YORK

GROUND ZERO: A REPAIRMAN JACK NOVEL

A Tor Book
Published by Tom Doherty Associates, LLC
175 Fifth Avenue
New York, NY 10010

www.tor-forge.com

ISBN 978-0-7653-6279-7

First Edition: September 2009
First Mass Market Edition: October 2010

Printed in the United States of America

0 9 8 7 6 5 4 3 2 1

GROUND ZERO

AUTHOR'S NOTE

You hold the antepenultimate Repairman Jack novel.

That's right: I've decided to end the series with number fifteen (though Jack will make his final appearance in *Nightworld*).

I've always said this would be a closed-end series, that I would not run Jack into the ground, that I had a big story to tell and would lower the curtain after telling it.

The end of that story draws nigh. (There's a highfalutin phrase.)

And if you've been following along, you've noticed that the recent novels do not tie up as neatly as the earlier ones. I've always kept longer story arcs running from book to book, but I used to be able to bring each installment to a distinct conclusion. That, I'm afraid, is no longer the case.

As I move people and objects into place and set the stage for the events that will tip all of humanity into *Nightworld*, the final chapter, this sort of incremental closure has become impossible.

So I ask you to bear with me. You may have noticed that *By the Sword* began shortly after *Bloodline*, and *Ground Zero* picks up a couple of months after that.

Two more Repairman Jack novels remain, the last ending just before *Nightworld* begins. Along the way we'll be reprinting the remainder of the Adversary Cycle, synching the releases of *The Touch, Reborn,* and *Reprisal* with Jack's timeline. (See "The Secret History of the World" at the end of this book for the sequence.)

The post-*Harbingers* installments of Jack's tale have become what the French call a *roman fleuve*—literally, a "river novel," with one story flowing from volume to volume. As a result, each new installment is going to feel richer, deeper, and make more sense if you've read the ones before.

Hang in there, folks. It's been a long ride, and we've still got a lot of wonder, terror, and tragedy ahead. I promise you'll be glad you made the trip.

—F. Paul Wilson
the Jersey shore

ACKNOWLEDGMENTS

Thanks to the usual crew for their efforts: my wife, Mary; my editor, David Hartwell; Elizabeth Monteleone; Steven Spruill; the indispensable Becky Maines; and my agent, Albert Zuckerman. Special thanks to David J. Schow for the guided hajj to hallowed Bronson Canyon and its infamous "caves."

Surreal, he thought as he watched the twin towers burn.

His rented boat rocked gently on the waters of New York harbor, a thousand feet off the Battery. The morning sun blazed in a flawless cerulean sky. But for the susurrus of the light breeze and the soft lapping of the waves against the hull, the world lay silent about him.

A beautiful, beautiful day . . .

. . . unless you were anywhere near those towers.

He tried to imagine the pandemonium in the streets around them—the Klaxons, the sirens, the shouts, the confusion, the terror. Not a hint of that here. The towers belched black smoke like a couple of chimneys, but all in silence.

He checked his watch: nearly ten o'clock. The plan was to allow an hour or so of chaos after the Arabs completed their mission. By then, though fear and terror would still be running high, the initial panic would have subsided. The situation would be considered horrific and tragic, but manageable. The second jet had hit at 9:03, so the hour mark was almost upon him. Time to initiate the second phase—the real reason for all this.

From a pocket of his Windbreaker he pulled a pair of gray plastic boxes, each the size of a cigarette pack—one marked with an S *for the south tower, the other with an* N *for the north. He put the* N *away for later. After all, the south tower was the important one, the reason for this enormous undertaking.*

He extended an aerial from the S box, then slid up a little safety cover on its front panel, revealing a black button. He took a breath and pressed the button, then watched and waited.

The vast majority would blame the collapse on the crazy Arabs who hijacked the planes and the Islamic extremists who funded them—the obvious choice. A few would notice inconsistencies and point fingers elsewhere, blaming the government or Big Oil or some other powerful but faceless entity.

No one, absolutely no one, would guess—or be allowed to guess—the truth behind the who and the why of this day.

MONDAY

1.

Diana stared at herself in the mirror. She did that a lot. Maybe too much. No, definitely too much. But she didn't have much else to do.

She hated her life. So *boring.*

Mainly because she was so lonely. Not that she was alone. She shared this big house with three men—grown men, sworn to protect her with their lives—but they weren't friends. She could talk to them, as in have conversations, but couldn't really *talk* to them about things that mattered. She chatted online all the time, but that wasn't the same as having another flesh-and-blood fourteen-year-old girl in the same room.

But that flesh-and-blood girl wouldn't stay long once she got a look at Diana's eyes.

She stared at the reflection of those eyes now. With their black pupils, black irises, and black everything else, they looked like ebony marbles stuck in her sockets. Sometimes she wanted to rip them out. Yeah, she'd be blind, but at least then she could go to school instead of having tutors. And she'd have a true excuse for wearing wraparound sunglasses all the time instead of lying about a rare eye condition.

She guessed it wasn't a lie. It was rare—only a few Oculi left around the globe—and it was definitely a condition.

So she was an Oculus. Big deal. These black eyes were supposed to allow her to see things regular eyes were blind to, warnings from Outside.

Alarms.

She'd yet to experience one.

Not that she was complaining. She'd seen her father when he'd received Alarms and it didn't look pleasant. In fact, it looked awful.

Why was she thinking of Alarms tonight? She hadn't—

Something flashed to her right. She turned to look but it flashed again, still to her right. She realized it wasn't in the room, but in her eye. A scintillating scotoma. She'd looked it up. The flashing lights always preceded her migraines. This wasn't the sparkle she usually saw, more like wavy lines, but she knew the sooner she dug out her bottle of Imitrex and took one, the better.

And then the room tilted. For an instant she thought earthquake or tsunami, but then the pain stabbed through her head—much, much worse than a migraine—and the lights flashed brighter and longer and fused to blot out her room as her knees gave way and she dropped to the floor.

As she lay there shaking, shuddering, writhing with the pain that suffused her, a tunnel opened through the light, revealing . . .

. . . a man in a loincloth, standing on an old-fashioned scaffold and carving a huge block of stone more than twice his height into some sort of thick pillar or column . . . his hammer striking the chisel again and again but making no sound . . . all eerily silent . . .

. . . the same man carving strange symbols into the side of the pillar . . .

. . . and others . . .

. . . and carving a cavity, perhaps three feet across and five feet deep, into one end of the pillar . . .

. . . and suddenly she is grabbed from behind and bound hand and foot . . .

. . . forced into the cavity . . .

. . . sealed over with a stone plug, plunging her into darkness . . .

. . . as she struggles for air she feels the pillar tilt as it slides into a deep hole in the earth and is covered over . . .

. . . she thrashes in the small space until her air runs out and darkness claims her . . .

. . . and then . . . a spark in the distance . . . growing . . . swelling . . . to become a glowing egg . . .

. . . the egg fades and darkness regains control until a booming voice splits the silence . . .

IT HAS AWAKENED!

. . . and then the egg reappears and a spot of darkness materializes within it . . . growing . . . growing until . . .

. . . it bursts free . . .

. . . a strange, formless, flickering, alien being . . .

. . . and as it emerges, an odd word forms in her mind . . .

Fhinntmanchca . . . Fhinntmanchca . . . Fhinntman-chca . . .

The vision faded, and with it the pain, replaced by beckoning oblivion. Diana fought the draw of the temporary reprieve it promised and forced her eyes open. She pushed herself off the floor and staggered to her bedroom door. She had to tell them . . . she had to go to New York.

She had to tell the Heir. She had to find Jack. But where was he?

2. For an instant her fingers froze over the keyboard—surely no more than a heartbeat—before she forced them to keep typing. But they were typing gibberish now.

The man seated by the door was watching her, she was sure of it.

The cybercafé was small but tended to be only half full at this hour—the reason she timed her visits for this time of day. She didn't want anyone too close while she typed.

She made a practice of rotating among a long list of cafés, coffee shops, and libraries that offered laptops and computers for public use. The list was numbered and she used a random integer generator to choose which one she would visit on any given day. The only time she did not follow the generator's choice was if it happened to produce the same number twice in a row.

On some visits she would simply surf through her list of blogs and Web sites, blocking and copying pertinent passages and storing them on her flash drive. She never posted on surfing visits. And she never surfed on posting visits.

Today was a posting visit. She'd typed out her posts

last night and this morning, then stored them on her flash drive. That way, when she reached a computer, all she had to do was plug in her drive, block and copy the posts onto the various forums or into the appropriate blog comments sections, then be on her way.

She was just finishing up—no more than ten minutes at the keyboard so far and maybe two to go—when she noticed the man get a call. He spoke briefly on his cell, then began scanning the room. After studying everyone, his scrutiny settled on her.

She kept her face toward her screen but watched out of the corner of her eye. He had a bit of a Eurotrash air about him. Maybe it was the hair—bleached blond and short, combed forward for a Caesar look. A well-preserved fifty, tanned, muscular, with strong cheekbones. She didn't know the country of origin of his clothing, but it was not the U.S. All in all he seemed just a little too well put together to need to rent a laptop in a cybercafé. He looked more like a BlackBerry type.

He was discreet, pretending every so often to stare off into space as if composing his thoughts, but she'd caught him eyeing her. Certainly not because she was attractive. She had no illusions about her appearance. After Steve's death, it had ceased to matter much. She'd let herself go somewhat—gaining weight, dressing in baggy warm-ups designed for comfort and little else, letting her hair grow out and wearing it in a styleless ponytail. In fact, if her frumpy looks deflected attention, so much the better.

No illusions about her mental state either. Maybe a bit paranoid. She might have been pushing evasive measures to the extreme.

Or not.

You weren't paranoid if people were really out to get you, but she couldn't be sure. If the wrong people were reading her posts, they might—*might*—care. And if they did care, they might—*might*—want to stop her.

If they thought she was a threat.

A big if. Who frequented these Web sites besides weirdos and nutcases? But the weirdos and nutcases were on to something. They were ninety percent right about everything except who and why. They were pointing fingers in the wrong directions.

Everything was either political or religious or cultural to them. They couldn't see that the real reasons were much darker, more sinister, and more dangerous and threatening than their wildest nightmare scenarios.

Only one man was listening—or at least not dismissing her as a kook as were most of the others.

When the kooks think you're a kook, maybe it's time to reassess your position.

No. Not when you're sure you're right.

And she was sure. Well, pretty sure. As sure as you could be about these things when—

There. He'd looked at her again. Her gut tingled with alarm. No question: He was watching her.

How could they have found her? Her practice of switching log-in locations guaranteed a different IP address every time, and her random choice of location made it impossible to predict where she'd be.

Well, not literally impossible, but virtually impossible.

She'd sensed they might be looking for her, but never dreamed they were this close.

The café, already small and cramped, seemed to shrink.

Her practice was to situate herself in a rear corner with her back to a wall so no one could read over her shoulder. But that was working against her now. She wished she were closer to the front, nearer the door.

Keeping her fingers moving and her head perfectly still, she flicked her gaze back and forth. The coffee bar sat against the far wall; to her right, the restroom—"Customers Only"—and an "Employees Only" door leading who knew where; the front door to Amsterdam Avenue lay all the way across the café to her left. Through the windows she could see people whisking by in the bright July sunshine.

"Another?"

She jumped at the voice, then realized it was the waiter. Where had he come from? She glanced up at him—certainly no older than his late teens. He looked underfed and overtired. A college kid maybe?

She forced a smile as she nodded. "Why, yes. I do believe I will."

She liked to indulge herself in these cafés, usually with a mocha latte—she was expected to buy something, so she might as well enjoy it—but only one. But today a second cup might prove useful. Make it look as if she intended to stay awhile.

While she waited, she put the time to good use by uploading the rest of her posts. She'd just hit ENTER on the last when the waiter returned.

"Hang on," she said as he placed the cup on the table. She handed him a bill. "Here. I may have to leave on short notice. Keep the change."

He looked at it, then her. "This is a twenty."

"I know." She understood his confusion: The tip was more than the coffees. "You look like you could use it."

He gave her a self-conscious smile. "Yeah. Thanks."

As he wandered away, she glanced into her virtually empty bag. She kept no ID of any sort on her person. Cash, a few toiletries, a pay-as-you-go cell phone, the keys to her three front door locks—that was it. No one could be allowed to know where she lived, because that was where she kept her proof, all the documentation for what she knew to be true. It had taken her years to assemble it and she doubted she'd ever be able to do so again. She couldn't allow it to fall into the wrong hands.

With a start she noticed her stalker rise from his seat and amble her way. She stiffened as her heart rate jumped. What was he doing? Was he going to speak to her?

No, he passed without a look and stepped into the restroom.

The not-looking was a giveaway. A casual patron would have glanced her way. Or would he?

She sighed and slumped in her seat. Maybe this was all in her head. God knew she'd been told often enough she was crazy—starting in her teens and continuing through the rest of her life. Maybe they were all right. Maybe—

No. She couldn't allow herself to think like that. She knew some of the truth and had to put what she knew out there, to stimulate others to help her look for the rest of it.

She also knew that blond man had been watching her. Her second cup of coffee had lulled him into thinking he could take a bathroom break.

Wrong.

She straightened and rushed through her routine of deleting cookies and erasing her browser history. It wouldn't stop anyone really serious about finding out what she'd been up to, but would foil run-of-the-mill snooping. She pulled her flash drive from the USB port and shoved it into a pocket. Normally she'd delete everything, then fill the drive to capacity with junk—overwriting all the memory—then delete all that to make sure none of her original files were recoverable, but no time for that now.

She rose and hurried toward the door.

Outside she paused and looked around. The air-conditioning in the café had been set a little too high for her and the hot air on the sidewalk felt good. The nearest corner lay to her right so she headed that way at a trot. The sooner she was out of sight of the café, the better.

She'd broken a little sweat by the time she rounded the corner. Out of shape. Well, what else could she expect from a sedentary life spent reading from either a page or a monitor?

She glanced back. No one following.

She slowed her pace. Had she lost him? Had she truly had anybody to lose?

Even if she'd been wrong, she'd just had a good drill on staying alert. She couldn't allow herself to become complacent. Not with what she knew.

Another glance back and she almost tripped over her own sneakers as the blond man rushed into sight at the corner. He stopped, looking around. His movements seemed jerky, almost frantic.

As if desperately looking for someone.

She wasn't imagining it. He was after her.

Panicked, she ran blindly. She cut toward the street and felt someone grab her arm.

Another!

She twisted free and increased her speed. If anything happened to her, her brother would check her house and read the note . . . the note that told him to contact Jack.

3.

"All right, lissen up."

Jack stood on the Lexington Avenue sidewalk with a dozen typically scruffy Kickers and pretended to pay attention as Darryl gave them their marching orders. Darryl's scraggly brown hair had grown longer as he'd grown progressively thinner over the past couple of months. He didn't look well, but he was as enthusiastic as ever as he handed out the sample chapters of Hank Thompson's bestseller, *Kick*.

Jack always saw him around on his regular visits to the

Lodge. Hadn't ever spoken to him, but he didn't seem a bad guy. Thompson's gofer. Kind of the Jar Jar Binks of the local Kicker enclave.

His first encounter with Darryl had been in the basement of the Kickers' borrowed clubhouse back in May on the night all hell had broken loose. Jack had been clean-shaven then and had had a foot planted in Darryl's back. No way he'd ever recognize him today.

"Now," Darryl said as he scratched his arm with his free hand, "I think you've all been here before, so you all should know the drill. But just in case one of you's a newbie, here's how we play it. We're gonna go across the street and stand in front of the Dormie building there and hand this sample chapter of the boss's book to anyone going in or coming out."

Jack stared at the art deco front of the Dormentalist Temple on the far side of Lexington and scratched his new beard. Relatively new. It had filled in nicely since he'd stopped shaving a couple of months ago. He'd needed to change his appearance and it had worked. With his hair cut short—not much longer now than his beard—he looked like a different person.

Thompson, the Kicker leader, was the reason. Their last meeting had not gone Thompson's way. Nothing he'd like better than to extract a little payback from Jack's hide. He'd probably spread his description among his followers, so Jack wasn't taking any chances.

He glanced down at the faux tattoo on the thumb web of his left hand.

Thanks to Gia's deft touch with a black Sharpie, he looked like a true-blue, dyed-in-the-wool Kicker.

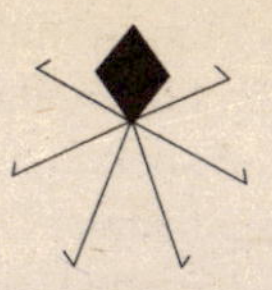

"You can't miss the Dormie members," Darryl was saying. "They got the Michael Jackson jackets on."

"Faggots," said Hagaman, a long-bearded, barrel-chested biker type to Jack's left. "Just like their boss man."

"Former boss man," Jack said.

Indelicate photos involving Luther Brady, the Dormentalists' disgraced Supreme Overseer and Acting Prime Dormentalist—now *former* SO and APD—had surfaced last fall. He was awaiting trial on a variety of charges, sexual misconduct the least of them.

Hagaman sneered. "Bet the new one's a faggot too." He squinted at the entrance to the temple. "And what's that bullshit over the door? I seen it a dozen times but what the fuck's it mean?"

> *The desires of the worthless many are controlled by the desires and knowledge of the decent few.*
>
> Plato

Jack shrugged. "It's Plato. And Plato didn't always make a lot of sense."

He'd never understood how anyone had ever bought into that shadows-on-the-wall stuff.

"Yeah," Hagaman said with a derisive snort. "What can you expect from Mickey Mouse's dog?"

Jack laughed, then noticed Hagaman's sharp look. "You were kidding, right?"

"No."

"*Play*-toe—the philosopher."

"Oh, yeah. Sure. Him. What's his first name again?"

"He's just known as Plato."

"Just one name? Who's he think he is—Madonna?"

Jack turned away and spotted a couple of Dormentalists walking toward their temple. Their steel-gray, double-breasted jackets were buttoned all the way up to their high collars. Some wore military-style cords draped across the front or around a shoulder. He was pretty sure they weren't going for the Michael Jackson look. Maybe Sergeant Pepper.

"We'd like to convert the members," Darryl was saying, "but we're most interested in the ones going in and out who ain't in uniform. Those are recruits. And we want to get them before the Dormies do. We want them to be Kickers instead of Dormies. All they gotta do is read that chapter and they'll want to read the book. And once they read the book, they're ours. So concentrate on them." Darryl grinned. "And if the Dormies give you any trouble, well, you just give it right back. Got it?"

The Kickers cheered, Hagaman the loudest.

Jack knew the possibilities for some rough-and-tumble were what drew these guys up here. Most of them were bunking at the Kicker HQ downtown and it gave them a chance to earn some Kicker "community service" points in exchange for their keep.

For Jack it was a chance to stay in touch with the group. He sensed they'd coalesced around Hank Thompson for some purpose. They themselves didn't seem to know what that was, but he wanted to be nearby when they found out.

As they trooped across the street, a dreadlocked Kicker who Jack knew only as Kewan—and who knew Jack only as Johnny—sidled up to him.

"Hey, Johnny, got a light?"

A smile creased his deeply pocked cheeks . . . a face like the surface of the moon—the dark side.

"Sure." Jack fished out his Bic and handed it to him.

Kewan grinned. "Great. Now, got a ciggie?"

Jack had guessed that was coming. A lot of these guys had little cash, so he always made a point of carrying a pack of Marlboro Reds. Kewan had lit up by the time they reached the other side.

They split into two groups of a half dozen each and flanked the doors. As the universally smiling and pleasant Dormentalists emerged or approached, the Kickers pressed them to take the sample chapter and read it. To a man and woman they refused. They knew they were being watched from inside.

Last year Jack had become involved with the Dormentalists—he wasn't alone in thinking of it as a cult rather than a church—and knew what went on behind the walls of this tightly controlled, globe-spanning organization that touted its costly programs as steps toward self-realization. By contrast, the Kickers were a loose organization of disparate types brought together by a bestselling book.

The so-called Kicker Evolution that Hank Thompson touted in *Kick* embraced all socioeconomic strata, but the lower echelons seemed to return the clinch with the most fervor. Many of them—including their leader—had had brushes with the law.

The Dormentalists had been in long-term competition with the Scientologists—known in Kicker circles as "L. Ron Hubtards"—over who could cull more depressed and lost sheeple from the human herd for fleecing. Then Hank Thompson had appeared on the scene with his *Kick* manifesto, urging people to "dissimilate" from society and join the Kicker Evolution. Millions had responded, decimating the ranks of both the Dormentalists and Scientologists. But Thompson wanted more. Right now another group of Kickers was over on West 46th Street at the

Scientology building handing out chapters and spoiling for a fight.

After ten minutes of harassing the Dormentalists, Jack checked his watch. Any second now . . .

Sure enough, right on time, a group of Temple Paladins spilled from the entrance. Their military jackets were a deep burgundy instead of gray. Known as TPs, they functioned as the cult's security force.

"All right, you Wall Addicts. How many times do we have to tell you? Move away from the door!"

"We've got as much a right to be here as anybody!" Jack shouted, for the simple purpose of establishing his presence among the Kickers.

The usual pushing and shoving match began. Soon the NYPD would arrive and break it up. Jack always made it a point to be gone by then.

A super-size TP, looking like a grape Kool-Aid pitcher, appeared in the doorway carrying a cardboard box.

"Attention TPs!" he bellowed. "They've been declared 'In Season.' Come and get 'em!"

In Season . . . Dormentalese for an enemy of the cult who was to be eliminated by any means necessary.

The TPs surrounded the new guy and pulled billy clubs from the box. Then they charged. The Kickers outnumbered them, but the Kickers were unarmed.

A TP with short blond hair and bad skin took a diagonal swing at Jack's head. Jack shifted to the side and grabbed the guy's arm as the baton went by. He pushed it farther in its present direction and brought his knee up against the back of the elbow, hyperextending it. The TP screamed and dropped the nightstick. As Jack grabbed for it, he saw another TP taking a grand-slam swing at him.

Why was he so popular? Because he'd shouted?

He pulled the first TP into the path of the blow, hearing him grunt as it hit his shoulder. He picked up the first's nightstick and rammed it into the second's solar plexus, doubling him over. Then he jabbed him in a kidney. The guy went down.

"Hey, you're pretty good with that."

He looked around and saw Hagaman grinning at him. Behind him on the street he saw someone step out of his car and raise a camera.

He ducked his head and handed Hagaman the baton.

"Let's see what you can do."

Time to move.

As Hagaman charged into the melee, Jack turned and strode off. The Kickers would remember him as someone who spoke up when challenged and gave better than he got in the fight. His Kicker credentials were reconfirmed. No need to be on camera or present when the cops arrived.

Time for a beer. He'd earned one.

4.

Ernst Drexler ended his phone call and turned to find someone standing in his office.

No, not someone. The One.

He shot to his feet and broke out in a sweat as he always did in the One's presence. The man—no, he was something more than a man—frightened him to the core, especially the way he entered and left rooms without warning whenever he pleased.

"You've located the troublemaker," the One said—a statement, not a question. "Who is he?"

"Surprisingly, it was a woman."

"What is her name?"

"We, um, don't know yet. But she won't be bothering us anymore. That I can guarantee."

"Nothing is guaranteed."

"Yes, sir."

In apparent deep thought, the One wandered the office. Ernst observed him as he waited for him to speak. His appearance had undergone subtle changes lately. His frame seemed smaller, his skin tones just a shade darker, his features softer, the brown of his hair deeper. All incremental, nothing dramatic, but right now he could pass for Hispanic. Ernst wondered why. Some reason beyond vanity. The One was anything but vain.

Although he did seem to enjoy good suits. He wore dark blue silk today, with a white shirt and a maroon tie. He tended to look like a businessman.

Ernst preferred the opposite. As a young man he had begun wearing white, three-piece suits, no matter what the season, and had continued the practice into his sixties. He did not feel his age, knew he did not look it, and was glad of that. He confessed to a modicum of vanity.

Finally the One turned to him.

"The Orsa is awake."

The news startled Ernst.

"It is? I had no idea. I was going to check on it later when—"

"I sensed it awaken a few hours ago. We must waste no time. The *Fhinntmanchca* process must begin as soon as possible."

"Yes, of course. This is wonderful."

"It won't be truly 'wonderful' until the *Fhinntmanchca* successfully completes its task."

"Of course. The Order—"

"I am not leaving it up to the Order. The High Council consists of seven egos who will have to agree on how to proceed. I want no delay. The Septimus Order deserves untold credit for its efforts so far." He jabbed a finger at Ernst. "But I am putting *you* in charge. You personally, Ernst Drexler."

"I exist to serve."

As Ernst bowed his head, he fought to keep his knees from buckling. He had assumed that, as actuator for the High Council, he would do most of the work, but would share responsibility with the council. But now the One was laying responsibility for the successful creation of the *Fhinntmanchca*—something that had never been done before—entirely on his shoulders. Should he fail . . .

He did not want to think about that.

He hesitated, then cleared his throat. "Existing lore is vague on the precise purpose of the *Fhinntmanchca*. If I may be so bold to ask—"

"You may. Should you succeed in your task, you shall have your answer. Should you fail, it will not matter to you."

Ernst swallowed. He did not like the sound of that.

The One stepped to the window and looked out. "One of these Taints should provide suitable raw material."

Ernst moved to his side and saw the usual group of Kickers clustered outside the Lodge's front entrance.

Taints . . . the archaic term for people like the Kickers. And they should indeed provide ample raw material. After all, the Ancient Fraternal Septimus Order had loaned Hank Thompson and his followers the use of this Lower East Side Lodge. He was surrounded by Kickers.

The question was: Which one fit the requirements?

He looked around.

The One was gone.

5.

His sister didn't answer his knocks, so he tried his keys. He heard the latch snap back as he twisted it in the last of the three locks on her door, but he didn't push it open right away. He was afraid of what he might find.

She called every day at six P.M. sharp. But not today.

He didn't always answer the six P.M. call. She didn't expect him to. All he had to do was recognize her number on the caller ID and he'd know she was okay. Any other call he'd answer, but the sixer was just her way of checking in.

No call today.

His older sister—older by less than two years—was a loony bird but a punctual one. Her looniness had a compulsive component. She wouldn't skip the call. Something was wrong.

Earlier he'd been overcome by an uneasy feeling. He hadn't had a clue as to why, but he'd felt as if something awful were about to happen. Then he'd glanced at his watch and seen that it read 6:07.

She was late. And she was never late.

So he'd called her home and heard only her voice-mail message. He'd called her cell and heard the same.

Something was most definitely wrong.

So here he was, outside her door, fearing what he'd find on the other side. Not violence. The door showed no sign of damage or tampering. Not that he expected to find any—ever. His sister's fears that someone might come after her for what she knew were as unfounded as her wild conspiracy theories.

His concern was more for her health. She didn't take care of herself.

Strange how time had changed them. As kids she'd been the slim, picky eater and he'd wolf down anything that didn't wolf him down first. Now he carefully watched what he ate while she lived on takeout.

She wasn't forty yet, but that didn't mean she couldn't have a heart attack. Or a ruptured aneurysm. She could be lying on the floor in a coma. Or worse.

Taking a breath, he turned the knob and pushed against the door.

It opened.

He didn't know if that was a good sign or not. She had a steel bar she kept across it when she was home. No bar meant she might not be in.

He entered, calling her name.

No answer.

He wove among the piles of junk—what she called "research"—and walked through every room, searching. He hadn't been here in a long time. The place hadn't changed much except that the junk piles had grown.

Nothing. An empty house.

Where could she be? She'd been off her meds for years. Was she finally off the deep end and wandering the city in some sort of fugue state? The possibility terrified him. Anything could happen to her.

He headed back to the door but stopped short when he saw the paper taped to the inner surface. He'd missed it on his way in.

If I'm missing
Don't call the police
They can't help
Get in touch with Jack
Please honor me on this
Our Jack can find me

Then she'd written a phone number and the URL of a Web site called repairmanjack.com.

Jack? *Our* Jack?

Who the hell was she talking about?

6. If the damn book weren't so valuable, Jack would have tossed it out the window months ago. But the *Compendium of Srem* was one of a kind and priceless.

And frustrating. Because all its pages were out of order. He'd been searching for references to the Lilitongue of Gefreda and had come across another of the so-called "Infernals"—an odd-shaped contraption called "the Cleaner." He reached for a bookmark but by the time he turned back, the page had changed.

He slammed the cover shut and shoved it across the round top of the oak table, then rose and stalked around his apartment. Not much stalking room with all the old furniture, so he sat back down and opened the book again.

"I can't believe I fell asleep."

He turned to take in the slim blonde standing in the doorway to the bedroom. She wore beige panties and was fastening her bra behind her. He loved her sleek thighs and the swell of her hips.

He added a swagger to his tone. "Well, Miss Gia, I guess I must've worn you out."

"I guess you did. But still . . ."

Sex had been especially hot tonight, and Gia had dozed off afterward, something she rarely did. She was almost back to normal after the hit and run. Her fine motor skills had returned and she was doing commercial art—mostly book covers—full-time and eking out some time for her own paintings. She'd even let Jack see some of her new stuff.

After she finished with the bra she padded over to the wingback chair where she'd left her sundress, a crazy turquoise pattern that did amazing things to her blue eyes. She slipped it over her head and was fully dressed again.

"Well, after being lifted to countless peaks of almost unendurable pleasure that shattered worlds and turned whole universes inside out—"

She laughed. "And turned your prose purple."

"—and clove the earth beneath you—"

"Clove?"

"Past tense of cleave, right? But anyway, after countless peaks of—"

"I don't know about countless."

She stepped closer and slipped into the pair of sandals she'd left by the table.

"You were counting?"

She smiled. "I always count."

"You do?"

She stood next to him and ran her fingers through his hair. It felt delicious.

"Well, sometimes I lose track."

He glanced back at the *Compendium*. "Not like I lose track of these pages."

"Still shuffling?"

He nodded. "I found something on the Infernals, but before I could dig in . . ." He shrugged.

"I'm glad it wasn't doing that when we were looking up the Stain." She caressed his nape, sending tingles down his back. "Still wondering about Tom?"

"Yeah."

His missing older brother . . . where in the world was he? Jack had a feeling he was gone from this world. Gone for good.

"Me too." Her fingertips moved to his beard. "I think I'm getting used to this."

That was good news. She'd hated it at first.

He slipped his hand under her dress and ran his fingers up her silky inner thigh.

"You know . . ."

She stepped away. "It's late."

"I could be quick."

She laughed. "Now *there's* an offer."

"Come on. Or we could just sit and talk. We didn't get much chance earlier with you in Siestaville."

Jack still hadn't told her the truth about the hit and run—that it had been no accident. Maybe tonight . . .

"Wish I could, but I'm trying out Courtney Love as a babysitter and I'm not sure how she'll work out."

"Yeah, well, she can't turn out worse than that Iggy Pop guy."

"Seriously, I've left Vicky with this girl after school a few times and they get along beautifully. This is her first night gig and I don't want to get on her mother's bad side by getting her home late."

He slapped his thighs and rose. "I know when I'm beaten."

Some other time for the truth.

Yeah, right.

Coward.

7.

After finding her a cab on Columbus Avenue, Jack returned and seated himself before his computer instead of the *Compendium*. He accessed the Web mail from his site. After sifting through the Cialis and penis-enlarger offers, he found an e-mail that had come through the site's Contact function.

The subject line read: *my sister is missing.*

A missing person. Swell. The last missing person he'd looked for had been Timmy O'Brien's teenage niece and that had led him into the worst days of his life.

No thanks.

But he opened it anyway. Just for a look.

Dear Jack—

I left you voice mail, now I'm trying this. My sister disappeared today. She left a note saying not to call the police but to get in touch with you instead. She said "Our Jack can find me." I have no idea what she means by that but I'm honoring her wish. Please contact me ASAP.

EPC

He'd left a phone number at the bottom of the message.

Jack reread it with a growing sense of déjà vu. The words sounded chillingly familiar. And then he remembered . . .

About a year and a half ago a guy named Lewis Ehler had contacted him about his missing wife. Melanie had told her hubby not to call the cops but to call Jack and only Jack because he was the only one who would "understand."

That hadn't ended too well either. In fact, that had started the souring of almost everything in his life.

He checked the date on the message: less than an hour ago. That meant this guy's sister had been gone less than twenty-four hours. Too soon to call the cops anyway.

Our Jack can find me . . .

He had no idea what that meant either, and didn't particularly want to find out. Question was: Should he contact the guy and blow him off, or simply ignore him?

His instincts urged the latter course, but the "our Jack" thing would follow him around until he found out a little more.

He logged off and checked his voice mail. He had three accounts and found the guy's message on the second, saying basically the same thing.

Oh, hell. Nothing better to do . . .

He dialed the number. Voice mail picked up on the fourth.

Swell. Voice-mail tag.

"This is Jack. You left me a message. Now I'm leaving you one: Be on the southwest corner of Columbus Avenue and Eightieth Street at noon tomorrow and we'll maybe talk about your sister."

Julio's wasn't right for this meet, especially since he wasn't guaranteeing he'd talk to the guy. If he didn't like his looks—assuming he could pick him out of the other pedestrians—he'd leave him waiting there.

The guy could go to the cops or find his sister on his own.

TUESDAY

1. "Enough, already," Abe said. "My ears. Oy."

"One more."

Jack loaded another steel ball into the pocket of his slingshot, stretched it back to his chin, aimed, and let fly. The shot smashed into the piece of half-inch plywood twenty feet away with a shower of splinters and a bang that echoed through the cellar like gunfire.

Jack walked up to the board and inspected his marksmanship. He'd placed ten of a dozen balls within the six-inch target circle. The first few had lodged in the wood until struck and punched through by subsequent shots. Much of the wood originally within the crudely drawn circle lay in pieces on the floor.

Jack nodded. His aim was improving all the time. "SBD."

Abe, dressed in his uniform of half-sleeve white shirt and black pants, came up behind him.

"And that means?"

"Silent But Deadly."

"I prefer a suppresser on a twenty-two."

Jack shrugged. "That's because a slingshot requires physical effort."

The slingshot appealed to Jack—not simply because it was so retro, it was practical too. He saw it as a long-range sap. He could put someone down from a couple of dozen feet away. Plus it had great potential as a harassment tool.

He collected the shot from the floor and replaced them in their leather pouch. He'd found a ball-bearing company that made big bearings and talked them into selling him some one-inch steel balls.

He said, "After I sweep this up, I've got a gift for you upstairs."

Abe rubbed his pudgy hands together. "Edible?"

"Yep."

"Sweep shmeep. I'll take care of it later."

Jack hid a smile as he folded the sling's wrist brace. "Okay. If you're sure."

"I'm sure already. Let's go."

He followed Abe's rotund, bustling form past neatly stacked rows of every weapon imaginable and up the narrow staircase to the ground floor of the Isher Sports Shop. Once in the store proper Abe ensconced himself in his usual spot, perching atop the high, four-legged stool behind the scarred rear counter.

Jack produced a Krispy Kreme bag he'd hidden on the way in and placed it before Abe.

"Voilà."

Abe pulled a chocolate donut from the bag and inspected it like a paleontologist with a newfound raptor tooth. Parabellum, his baby-blue parakeet, fluttered down from the ceiling to perch on his shoulder. He cocked his head back and forth, eyeing the donut with naked hunger.

Jack had brought four—a pair each of the chocolate cake and sour cream models, both glazed—for a mid-morning snack.

"Nu . . . what's the catch?"

Jack leaned against the far side of the counter and shrugged as he scratched his beard.

"They're my white flag. I've surrendered. How long

now have I been bringing you stuff you don't want to eat? Does it do any good? No. I've decided it's futile for me to care more about your health than you do."

Abe put a hand over his heart. "I'm hurt. To the quick you've cut. So easily you give up?"

"It's been *years,* Abe."

"And you think I'm unmoved by these caring gestures?"

"Doesn't matter. They haven't changed a thing. And I confess my motives have been purely selfish: I don't want to have to look for a new armorer."

In truth, Abe was his best friend—not counting Gia—and he wanted him around as long as possible. Simple as that. No need saying it. Abe knew.

"And you should lord your diet over mine? You who thinks Cheetos is a dairy product and who considers a box of Pringles a serving of vegetables."

"Yeah, but I *move*. I work all that off. You, on the other hand . . ."

"I had no idea of your deep feelings for me." He sighed. "I'm touched. And because I'm so touched, a supreme effort I'll make. Just for you."

Jack watched in amazement as Abe replaced the donut in the sack, rolled the top, and slid it to Jack's side of the counter. Even Parabellum's beak gaped in wonder.

"Yeah, right."

"It's true. A new leaf I'm turning. As of right now."

They stared at each other for maybe half a minute, then Abe grabbed the sack and tore into it.

"Tomorrow. Tomorrow I'll start."

Jack had to laugh as he was reminded of the sign over Julio's bar: FREE BEER TOMORROW . . . Abe's diet was always starting mañana.

Which was why he was built like the Liberty Bell.

Then he sobered. "Think heart attack, Abe."

Abe chewed his first bite thoughtfully as Parabellum hopped onto the counter and policed the crumbs.

"I have, Jack. And I've decided I don't care. If I drop dead tomorrow, it's okay already."

Jack knew he wasn't overstating. Abe's wife was dead, his daughter hadn't spoken to him in years, and he had very few friends—Jack perhaps the closest.

"Nothing to live for?"

Abe shrugged. "I'm not saying that. Do I want to die? No. But if I go, I'm gone. No regrets."

"Worse things than dropping dead. You could have a stroke and wind up paralyzed."

Abe pointed at the floor. "For that I've got a basement full of solutions." Then he pointed to Jack. "And a friend who'll help me cut short any unseemly lingering."

"Swell."

Offing Abe. He couldn't imagine it.

"So enough already with the morbid talk." Abe flattened his copy of Long Island *Newsday* on the scarred counter and took another bite of his donut. "I need to know what happened in the world whilst I slept."

Jack sighed and pulled the *Post* from the stack of papers. He turned to the sports section. The Mets were in a hitting slump. Again.

"Nu," Abe said after a moment. "Here's an interesting story. Yesterday this doctor's house burned to the ground in Monroe."

"That's interesting? I mean, I'm sorry for the guy and all, but houses burn every day."

"If you'd let me finish, you might know why it's interesting."

Jack glanced at Abe. He usually wasn't cranky in the morning. He hadn't finished his first donut yet, so maybe his blood sugar was low. But that didn't mean Jack would cut him any slack.

"You don't need to finish. If it happened in Monroe, it's automatically interesting."

Weird little town, Monroe. Really weird. If Jack never saw it again, he wouldn't miss it.

"You want to hear or not?"

Mimicking his accent, Jack gave an elaborate Abe-style shrug and said, "So speak already."

"Turns out he was invaded by current patients and people who wanted to be his patients."

"And they burned down his house? Why? He forget how to spell oxycodone?"

"No. They thought he could heal with a touch."

Jack's glazed sour cream donut stopped halfway to his mouth.

"Whoa-whoa-whoa! Heal with a touch?"

"That's what it says. I remember reading something about him in *People* not too long ago."

"You read *People*?"

Jack didn't know why he was surprised. Abe read everything.

"I should spend my days not knowing who's pregnant and by whom? Anyway, the article interviewed some of his patients who said they'd been healed by his touch."

"And what did he say?"

" 'No comment,' I believe."

The story sounded too familiar. Walt Erskine from Jack's hometown had been rumored to be able to heal people with a touch, but he'd kept pretty much to himself. And wore gloves all the time, even in summer. Jack vaguely remembered an incident with a woman with a deformed baby—

He stiffened. Wait a sec. Back in the spring . . . the paper had said Walt had died . . . in Monroe.

Abe's eyebrows rose. "Nu?"

One guy who supposedly could heal dies and then

another guy in the same town develops a similar rep. Coincidence, or . . . ?

"Nothing. Just thinking."

Abe bent again to his *Newsday*. "Thinking is good . . . to a point."

Abe started on a second donut; Jack bit back a remark. He'd given it his best shot. Time to back off. He flipped toward the front of the paper and stopped when a column header caught his eye: *CULTure WARS.*

"Tsk-tsk-tsk. Looks like those mean old Kickers and Dormentalists are still at it."

A photo of yesterday's melee—Jack was relieved to see that he'd ducked out of frame before it was taken—was followed by an article on the ongoing conflict.

"So I read," Abe said. "But the real war is online. The Kickers have been hacking all the Dormentalist sites and either crashing them or changing the content."

"Changing the content how? Somehow having Dormentalism make sense?"

"No, more like posting pictures of naked adolescent boys."

Jack frowned. "Ah. The Luther Brady connection."

"Yes. It's getting ugly. The Dormentalists are recruiting fewer and fewer new shnooks and keep on losing existing shlemiels to the Kickers, and the Kickers are rubbing their faces in it."

Jack nodded. "And since the Kickers are far less centralized, they're harder to strike back at."

"Exactly. Especially since they're anti-Internet."

"Does anybody see a contradiction here? They say they're anti-Internet, but they have hackers who can breach the Dormentalists' firewalls. What's up with that?"

"You want I should explain these people? Why they don't like the Internet, I have no idea."

"Well, according to the book, the Kicker goal is to become 'dissimilated,' which has something to do with 'kicking free' from society. Maybe they see the Internet as something that assimilates everything."

"I don't know about assimilating," Abe said, "but it connects everything and everyone who wants to be connected. Even some people who don't want to be connected, I imagine."

Jack glanced at the clock on the wall behind the counter. "Speaking of connecting, I'm supposed to meet some guy to tell him I can't help him."

"You could do that on the phone."

"It's more polite in person."

"Polite? Since when you're polite?"

Abe's fingers were edging toward a third donut. Jack snatched it up before they could reach it.

"Uh-uh. Mine."

Abe pouted. "See what I said about polite?"

"I need it more than you. I have blocks to walk. I need the fuel."

"It's not *that* far."

Jack took a big bite and headed for the door.

2. "All hostilities must cease immediately," the dude in the white three-piece suit said in his oh-so-lightly accented voice. Sounded like German.

Darryl stared at him in disbelief. Who did this guy think he was?

"Hey, you can't come into our house and talk to Hank like that."

Hank, seated beside him, gave him a rough elbow nudge. "This is *his* house, remember?"

Darryl suddenly felt like a fool. Right. The Ancient Fraternal Septimus Order owned this big old fortress of a building—their downtown lodge—but they'd been letting the Kickers use it since the winter. Couldn't blame him too much for getting confused. He'd been living here lately. Only natural to think of it as home.

"Oh. Yeah. Sorry."

The guy in white—Mr. Drexler—didn't bother to look at him. Like Darryl wasn't worth it. An older guy with an eagle-nosed face, black hair slicked straight back, and eyes like ice-blue lasers that could bore holes right through you.

Drexler was the point man for the leaders of the Order, the High Council of Seven that no one ever saw. Darryl wondered if even Drexler ever saw them. He'd called this meeting in the basement of the Lodge and Hank had dropped everything to make it. Darryl hated seeing Hank run whenever Drexler whistled. Hell, he was leader of the Kickers, man. Shouldn't have to answer to nobody.

"I required the presence of you and Mister McCabe," Drexler said to Hank. "I don't recall authorizing anyone else."

"Darryl's okay," Hank said. "Not much he doesn't already know." Darryl felt his chest puffing until Hank added, "Besides, we may need coffee or something."

That's me: trusted gofer.

Well, at least he got to hang with the Kicker Numero Uno.

His right arm started to itch. He scratched it. Damn rash.

The fourth guy at the table was Terry McCabe, the Kicker Evolution's spinmeister. Drexler himself had brought him in, and McCabe was the guy responsible for the "hostilities" in the first place.

"They've provided a valuable distraction," McCabe said. "Because of them, the press has forgotten our link to the horror show on Staten Island. As a result, so have most people. And the few who do remember think the Dormentalists were to blame."

Drexler steepled his fingers and nodded. "Even though they were not involved in the least. All well and good, and rather entertaining in the short run. But the brawls and this ongoing Internet assault are beginning to have a deleterious effect on the Church's abilities to fulfill its purpose."

" 'Church'?" Hank said. "They're a bunch of money-grubbing fucks whose 'purpose' is to fleece anyone they can grab. Their members are seeing the light and coming over to us."

"Yes. Too many of them."

Hank slammed his hand on the table. "Never too many! I won't quit till every one of them becomes a Kicker."

"You . . . will . . . stop . . . *now,*" Drexler said, his blue eyes glittering. "The Dormentalist Church is under our guidance and—"

"Yours? The Septimus Order's connected to them?"

"The lower echelons do not realize it, but yes, we helped fund them in the early years until they became self-sufficient. They are involved in a project the Order has been guiding for millennia."

McCabe frowned. "Millennia? As in thousands of years?"

"It's called Opus Omega. You need know nothing beyond its name. I can tell you that it is near completion, but your too-successful assaults on the Church are distracting it and forcing it to direct its dwindling resources in directions other than Opus Omega. For that reason, you must back off."

Scratching seemed only to worsen the itch on Darryl's arm. He pulled up the sleeve of his black Polio T-shirt and examined the purple splotch. They'd been popping out on his skin for months. He had about a dozen now.

"What is *that*?" McCabe said, pointing to Darryl's arm.

Darryl yanked down the sleeve. "Just a rash."

"Well, get it looked at." McCabe leaned away. "It looks kind of funky."

"Funky?"

"Yeah. Like something catching. You—"

Drexler picked up his black cane and rapped it against the table. "Can we stick to the matter at hand?" He turned back to Hank. "Inform your followers to cease and desist, do you understand?"

Hank slouched and drummed his fingers on the table. "You know, we appreciate you letting us use this building and all, but we can't let you Septimus people call the shots for Kickers. The reason for the Kicker Evolution is to get folks to break from the crowd and call their own shots."

Darryl forgot the itch as he fought an urge to jump up and cheer.

You tell 'em, boss.

Drexler didn't react. He simply kept his cold gaze fixed on Hank as he spoke. "On the night of your debacle in Staten Island, do you recall a visit from a rather unusual man?"

Hank jerked up straight in his chair. "How the hell do you know about that?"

Darryl's gut twisted as he remembered that guy. He'd looked kind of wimpy at first, but his eyes . . . next to his, Drexler's were like a warm, loving grandma's. And he'd done something to Darryl and Hank that sort of paralyzed them.

Drexler's thin lips twisted with what might have been amusement. "He is in contact with me from time to time. When he speaks, I listen. And when I relay word from him, you would be wise to listen."

"All right, I'm listening," Hank said. "What's the word—and who is he, anyway?"

"Who is he? You would not understand. And you are better off not knowing. He goes by many names, none of which would mean a thing to you. Call him the One. But his 'word,' as you put it, is to cease and desist."

"How do we know that?" Darryl blurted. "This could be your idea and you're just saying it's his."

Drexler kept his eyes on Hank. "Would you like a personal visit from him?"

The words hung in the air for a few heartbeats, then Hank turned to McCabe. "Okay, Terry. You heard the man. We'll back off the temples and leave the Dormies' Web site alone."

McCabe nodded. "I'll get on it as soon as we're finished here."

"You are finished here now, Mister McCabe. Get to it immediately." As McCabe rose and headed for the door, Drexler pointed to Darryl. "And take this fellow with you. I have something special I wish to discuss with Mister Thompson."

"Darryl stays," Hank said.

Darryl could have kissed him—not that he'd ever really kiss a guy.

"It is a sensitive matter."

"Darryl stays."

Darryl sensed that because Hank had given in on letting up on the Dormentalists, he wasn't going to budge on this.

"Very well. But he must be sworn to secrecy, as must you, Mister Thompson. What I am about to reveal must remain secret from everyone, including your most trusted followers. Do you agree?"

"Yeah, sure," Hank said. "I won't breathe a word." He turned to Darryl. "You cool with that?"

"My lips are sealed. Like with Krazy Glue."

And he meant it. If Hank wanted tight lips about whatever this was, that was what he'd get.

Drexler nodded. "This is quite serious. Even though this nondisclosure agreement is not on paper, it is binding. Do you understand?"

They both nodded, then Hank said, "Let's get to it."

"One more thing," Drexler said. "The gentleman we were discussing a moment ago suggests you allow the council to guide you into other areas of endeavor that will speed your goal of universal dissimilation."

Darryl remembered the scary guy saying something about that.

Wouldn't you like to see everyone on the planet dissimilated—every man, woman, and child an island? . . . That works into my plans as well. I may be able to assist you toward that end.

"And just what would those areas be?" Hank said.

"I've learned to avoid second-guessing him or the council, so I'll stick to what I know, and . . ." His eyes seemed to glow as he smiled—the first real smile Darryl had ever seen on this guy's puss. "What I am about to reveal is *wonderful,* in every sense of the word."

"I can hardly stand the suspense," Hank said in a bored tone. "What is it?"

"It would be almost impossible to explain." Drexler rose from his seat. "So I will show you."

"Better be close by," Hank said. "'Cause I've got things to do."

"Very close by. No more than thirty feet away."

Hank looked around. "Where?"

Drexler pointed to the floor. "Straight down. Directly beneath our feet."

"Nothing down there but rock."

Drexler's grin broadened. "*Au contraire.* There's a subcellar, and it is occupied."

3. Someone—no, two people were sitting at Jack's table.

Right now they appeared as a pair of lighter splotches against the dark rear wall. He stood inside the door and waited for his eyes to adjust from the late morning sun.

Julio appeared. "They showed up half an hour ago. The guy handed me his pistol. I checked him and he's not carrying a backup."

Julio, short and muscular, had let his usual pencil-line mustache expand to a goatee. Jack didn't think it was inspired by his own beard, but who knew.

"What about the other guy?"

"That's not a guy. That's a girl. A kid."

"And you gave them my table?"

Julio shrugged. "They been here before, meng. You know them."

As his eyes adjusted, Jack recognized Cal Davis, back to the wall, looking his way. And next to him . . . Diana.

He hadn't seen these two since January; he hadn't left Cal and his fellow yeniçeri on the best of terms.

He looked around the sparsely populated bar. No surprise, seeing as it was pre-noon, and only the heartiest digestive tracts dared eat at Julio's.

"Any noobs?"

"Nah. All regulars."

Jack went to the window and checked out the street. No sign of any yeniçeri. He stepped back toward Julio.

"They say what they want?"

"What else they gonna want? Talk. You gonna?"

"Yeah, I guess so."

"You gonna want coffee?"

"Yeah. I think I'm in the mood for a double mocha latte with extra whip cream."

Julio gave him the finger over his shoulder as he walked away.

Jack approached the table. Davis rose but didn't extend his hand, so Jack simply nodded. He did however offer his hand to the girl.

"Hello, Diana. This is a surprise."

Despite the dim lighting, she wore large sunglasses. She'd changed some since Jack had last seen her, losing a bit of her baby fat, maybe a little taller.

She gave his hand a quick, light shake—more of a finger tug. "For me too."

"How old are you now?"

She lifted her chin. "I just turned fourteen."

Poor kid. Teen years were hard enough without being a bona fide freak.

He turned to Davis. "I assume this wasn't your idea."

He was dressed in a black suit and tie over a white shirt. His black fedora sat on an empty chair.

He glanced at Diana. "I was and still am opposed to coming here."

"Well then, let's do what we can to get you back to where you'd rather be and that's my seat you're sitting in."

Davis offered a tight smile as he moved to another. "I know. I was keeping it warm for you."

Jack took his usual place as Julio arrived with a cup of coffee that appeared to have a small turd floating in it.

"What is that?"

"As close as we get to mocha, meng." And then he was gone.

Jack spooned out the object: a baby Snickers bar. He ate it, then sipped his coffee.

"So . . . still in Nantucket?"

Davis nodded. "What's left of us. Just me and Grell and Novak now. Lewis, Cousino, and Geraci lit out after you that night and never came back. Finan and Dunsmore quit a couple of weeks later."

He knew Davis was talking about his fellow yeniçeri, but Jack had no faces for the names.

"I thought all you yeniçeri dedicated your lives to guarding the Oculus," he said with a nod toward Diana.

"Some more than others." He gave Jack a hard stare. "What did you do to those three? They vanished without a trace."

"The guys in the Hummer? You might want to drag the harbor."

His eyes widened. "How—?" He shook his head. "Never mind. Diana has something to tell you."

Jack turned to her. "You've had a vision?"

She nodded. "An Alarm, yes. My first."

Oh, right. Oculi called their visions Alarms.

"Do I want to hear this? I mean, considering what your father's last Alarm led to."

Diana paled and Davis's right hand balled into a fist.

She said, "I'm so sorry about that. I—"

"Not your fault. Not even your father's fault." He glanced at Davis. "But I can't say the same for some of the yeniçeri."

"We were being used," Davis said through his teeth. "We were all being used. We're *still* being used."

Jack sighed and leaned back. "Yeah. I suppose we are."

"And you got your revenge—in spades."

Jack remembered that time. He'd really lost it.

"Revenge only in one case. The rest was preemptive. You gonna sit there and tell me you blame me, that if positions were reversed you wouldn't have done the same?"

Davis looked away. "No. Still, a lot of them were friends."

Jack dropped it. The past was past. No use rehashing it. But he and Gia and Vicky would live the rest of their lives with the fallout from that last Alarm. And Emma . . . Emma wasn't living at all.

He turned to Diana. Might as well get to it.

"What did the Alarm show?"

As she related her vision Jack realized she was describing the carving and burial of an ancient Opus Omega column.

"You're nodding," she said. "You know about this?"

"It's been going on for thousands of years. Those columns are buried around the globe in a specific pattern."

Davis frowned. "To what end?"

"When they finish the job, they believe it will give the Otherness the edge to change the world."

Jack also knew that every insertion of one of those columns into the ground was a knife in the back of the Lady with the dog, and left a scar. Was that the purpose—hurt her? Was she some sort of barrier between the Otherness and Earth, and if they weakened her enough the Otherness could make the leap?

He wished he knew. So many things he wished he knew.

"Are they crazy?" Davis said. "Don't they know what that will mean? Hell on Earth."

"Not for them. They believe participants in the Opus Omega will be given special treatment and privileges in the new world order."

Davis snorted and shook his head. "Privileges or not, they'll still be in hell. Ignorant dumbasses." He turned to the girl. "Sorry, Diana."

She didn't seem to have heard, or care if she had. She sat twisting her fingers together.

"But in the vision they sealed me in the column—alive—and then buried it."

"Apparently it's not enough simply to stick a body in the column. Someone has to die *inside* it."

"It was horrible. But then the strangest thing happened. A glowing egg appeared and hatched something . . . something I couldn't see . . . a dark shape that seemed to suck in the light around it."

Jack tried to grasp that and failed. Could that be the goal of Opus Omega—create a cosmic egg with some sort of black hole within? He turned to Davis.

"You must have heard about a lot of these Alarms over the years."

He nodded and glanced at the girl. "From Diana's father, yes."

"Did they tend to be pretty much true to life, or more metaphorical?"

"From what he told me, true to life. The Alarms showed either what would happen if we didn't interfere, or what we should make happen. It wasn't always clear which. They could be ambiguous at times, but definitely true to life."

True to life . . . a big egg hatching something. Sheesh.

"But that's not the strangest part," Diana said. "The thing that came out of the column . . . it might have been human, but I don't think so. If it was human, it wasn't a normal human."

More vagueness. Couldn't anything be clear-cut?

"So you didn't get a good look at it."

She shook her head. "It was blurred, almost flickering, as if it was flashing in and out of existence. And then a word sounded in my head: *Fhinntmanchca*."

"Say what?"

"*Fhinntmanchca*. Don't ask me what it means. I have no idea."

Davis said, "Don't look at me. I've never in my life heard the word, or anything even close to it."

"I think it refers to whatever came out of the egg."

That seemed a reasonable assumption.

"Did the egg crack open?"

Another shake of her head. "No, this just sort of *emerged* from it. One second it wasn't there, and then the next it was moving toward me." She looked at Jack. "*Fhinntmanchca* . . . you've never heard of it?"

"No." He didn't even know if the word applied to the egg or the thing that hatched from it. "Why would I?"

"I don't know. The Alarm . . . at the end it was clear that I had to tell someone who could do something about it."

"And you chose *me*?"

"Well, the Sentinel would have been best, but no one knows where he is, do they?"

The Sentinel . . . that was what these folks called the point man in the war against the Otherness. Others called him the Defender. They ascribed all sorts of power to him, but he was just a man now, an old one. Jack knew his real name, but the old guy preferred to go by the name Veilleur.

"So, since I couldn't tell him," Diana was saying, "it seemed pretty clear I should tell his Heir. And that's you."

Yeah, he thought. Me. Lucky, lucky me.

What was he going to "do" about something he'd never heard of?

He'd have to wait until he could ask Veilleur about it, but he seemed to have dropped off the face of the Earth the past couple of months. Maybe the *Compendium* had heard of this finnymacaca or whatever it was. But even if it was in there, could he find it? Worth a try.

"Got an idea," he said. He rose and retrieved a pen and a napkin from the bar. "Okay. What's this thing called again?"

Diana repeated the name and Jack spelled it phonetically: *fint-MAHNCH-ka*. One weird word. Didn't seem to fit any language he'd ever heard.

Suddenly Diana shot from her seat.

"He's here!"

Jack saw Davis instinctively reach for his empty shoulder holster. They both looked around, wondering what she meant.

"I feel him!" she cried.

The whole place was staring at her now. Someone at the bar said, "Hey, you can feel me too! Anytime you want."

Jack shot a look toward the bar, searching for the comedian. Couldn't tell so he turned toward the front window and saw Veilleur's face peering in. An instant later he was gone.

"He's outside!"

She rushed toward the front door. Davis tried to grab her arm but missed, so he rose and followed on her heels. Jack held back. He wanted to see Veilleur too, but had to let him go.

Diana stepped outside and peered up and down the street. Finally she gave up and came back in.

"I know it was him," she said with a despondent look as she dropped into her chair.

Jack knew the answer but felt obliged to ask. "Who?"

"The Sentinel. He was right outside. I *felt* him."

"Are you *sure*?" Davis said.

"Of course I'm sure," she snapped. "Sometimes you just know things, and I know he was out there." She looked at Jack. "Why didn't he come in? If I can sense him, I'm sure he can sense me. Why would he avoid me when I could tell him about the Alarm?"

For all Jack knew, Veilleur could have been stopping by to see him after all this time. He certainly understood why he wouldn't want an Oculus and a yeniçeri to see him in his present condition.

"Maybe he already knows," Jack said, realizing it sounded lame.

She shook her head. "I don't understand. It feels like everything is slipping away. The Adversary seems to be getting the upper hand, and the Sentinel does nothing."

Because he can't, Jack thought. Because he's not the Sentinel anymore. There *is* no Sentinel. Just an old man and his supposed Heir.

But he couldn't say that. No one could know, or even suspect—especially the Adversary . . . the One . . . Rasalom.

"I'm sure he has a plan."

"Well, if he does, he'd better act soon, because there's not much time."

She pulled off her glasses and he had a glimpse of her startling, all-black eyes before she covered them with her hands and sobbed.

Jack wanted to reach over and hug her against his side and tell her it was going to be all right. But she knew too much to believe that anyone could promise that. And how convincing could he be when he didn't believe it himself?

He saw Davis's stricken look and knew he felt the same way.

"Did you see anything else?"

"No," she said without looking up. "But I had a dream after the Alarm, and it was what I *didn't* see then that scares me."

Jack knew immediately what she was talking about.

"You mean the future?"

She nodded. "I saw the Nantucket house in the summer as it is now. And then in autumn with the leaves falling. Then covered with snow. Then the trees budding.

Then . . ." She lowered her hands and leveled her black gaze at him. "Then nothing . . . nothing but blackness."

Jack held her gaze. "I know."

"You *know*? How?"

"You're not the first to see that. Over the past year I've heard exactly the same thing from a couple of other sources."

The late Charlie Kenton for one. And during her coma, Gia had experienced something similar to Diana's dream.

"Then that means the Adversary is going to win," Diana said. "And if that's true, then all this is for nothing."

"Not necessarily."

She squeezed her eyes shut as tears rolled down her cheeks. "I'm never going to be fifteen."

Jack grabbed her hand. "I have it on good authority that what you're seeing is how it will be if we do nothing. But we aren't going to do nothing. We're going to stop him and the Otherness."

He didn't know why, but he needed to give her hope.

"How?"

"The Sentinel—once he's alerted to the danger, he'll act. He'll come charging in and make the Adversary wish he'd never been born. He's kicked Otherness butt before and he'll do it again. That's why the Adversary is being so sneaky. He knows if the Sentinel gets wind of his schemes, he's cooked."

Jack marveled at how easily he mixed lies and truth. And Diana seemed to be buying it.

"But why doesn't he do something *now*? I have an awful feeling about this *Fhinntmanchca,* whatever it is."

"I'll look into it," Jack said.

If he couldn't find it in the *Compendium,* maybe Veilleur would know—if Jack could find him. Damn, he wished he knew where he lived.

The three of them lapsed into silence and Jack glanced at the PBR clock over the bar. Noon was approaching.

Diana took a slow, shuddering breath and pointed to the black orbs of her eyes. "I don't want this."

"Diana," Davis said softly. "You were born to it."

"Then I wish my parents had never met. I don't want to know what's coming. I don't want to look like this. And I *don't* want another Alarm."

Jack had witnessed her father in the throes of one and it hadn't looked pleasant.

"Painful?"

"You wouldn't believe." She replaced her sunglasses. Her voice edged toward another sob. "I didn't ask for this."

"That makes two of us."

She leaned toward Jack. "You're the Heir. You're supposed to be itching to take on the Adversary."

Jack held back a laugh. "You're kidding, right? I've met him, and believe me, that's the last thing I want to do."

"But you're supposed to be noble, a hero."

Teenagers . . .

"I don't know who's doing all this supposing, but it doesn't change who I am. I'm just a guy from Jersey who's learned a few tricks. This is the only way I know how to be."

"But how . . . how will you defend us if your heart's not in it?"

"Defend you?" Jack looked at her, then Davis, then back to her. "I don't know you well enough to put my life on the line for either of you."

"She was talking about the rest of humanity," Davis said.

"Hey, I know the rest of humanity even less. But I do know a couple of people in this town I will die for if I have to. So if you wind up benefiting from my defense of them, then lucky you. But you won't have to thank me, because I'll have done it for them."

Diana shook her head. "I don't believe you. You're better than that. You're the *Heir*." She said the last word as if repeating it would somehow morph him into her preconceived image.

"So I'm told. Be nice if someone had checked with me first."

"If you're the backup," Davis said with a sour expression, "then let's wish the current Sentinel continued long life and good health."

Jack raised his coffee cup. "I'll drink to that."

4.

"What is *that*?" Hank said.

Drexler had led them to a closet in a small room off the main basement space, and pulled up a trapdoor in the floor. He'd explained that all the Order's lodges were built with subcellars and escape routes. "Just in case."

Down a wrought-iron spiral staircase to a dark, dank space that echoed like a cave. Then Drexler hit a switch somewhere and the place lit up.

Yeah, kind of cavernous, with a domed ceiling strung with hanging lights. Then Hank saw it. How could he miss it?

A big, oblong thing, like a huge, blunt-ended football that needed some air, lay on its side at the far end of the space. He guesstimated its size at maybe ten feet long and four feet high. Light from the overhead incandescent bulbs reflected dully from its surface.

"Yeah," said Darryl at his side. "What is it, man? Looks like a giant booger."

Hank had to smile. Darryl had pretty much nailed it—like a transparent football filled with snot.

"How quintessentially you," Drexler said.

Darryl shrugged. "How'd you get it in here without any of us noticing?"

"You never noticed because we moved it in long before a single Kicker set foot in the building."

Hank didn't see any door big enough to fit it through. "What you do—bring it in in pieces?"

"No, that would have been quite impossible. The task required a bit of demolition and subsequent reconstruction, but we succeeded."

Hank had noticed signs of repair on the rear wall of the Lodge, and now could see signs of the same in the roof of the chamber.

"You must have wanted it in here really bad."

"Oh, we did, Mister Thompson. We did."

"Back to my original question: What is the damn thing?"

"We call it the 'Orsa.'"

"Orca?" Darryl said. "You mean like a whale? Don't look like no whale I ever seen."

"No," Drexler said with a definite edge to his voice. "Or*sa*. It's Latin. It means 'first.'"

Hank stared at it. "What's it supposed to do?"

"Change the world, Mister Thompson. And I believe you know the change I'm talking about."

Hank nodded slowly. He did. His daddy had talked about that change. He'd called it the Plan and it involved beings, the Others, locked out from the world, waiting for ages to return, and a way to help them back in.

But the Plan was all about a bloodline, Hank's bloodline, leading to a very special baby, a baby now living in a teenager's belly, a pure-blooded child who would unlock the gates that prevented the Others from returning to the Earth and reclaiming it.

When they returned they'd reward those who'd unlocked the gates. Or so he'd been told.

"Yeah, I know. But the way to make it happen didn't involve anything like this."

"There is more than one route to that end, Mister Thompson, and all are being pursued. Opus Omega is stalled, at least in this country, due to some unfortunate scandals involving the Dormentalists."

Darryl snickered. " 'Unfortunate,' all right."

Drexler looked like he'd just sucked a rotten egg. "Must he be here?"

"Cool it, Darryl."

Hank stepped closer for a better look. He could see pretty much all the way through it—like looking through churned-up water, only nothing was moving inside. It sat about chest high and he realized it wasn't entirely empty. Through the ground-glass transparency he saw a thick, four-foot-long streak of chunky, brownish powder—looked like dirt—floating near the right end.

Darryl came up and bent at the waist for a closer look at the deposit, so close his nose almost brushed the Orsa. He put his hand out to lean against it but snatched it away and leaped back as soon as he made contact.

"Jesus!"

Wondering what was the matter, Hank touched it himself. It felt soft, rubbery, almost like—

A tremor rippled over its surface and he too snatched his hand back.

"You feel that, Hank?" Darryl said in a hushed tone. "The freakin thing's alive!"

5. Jack arrived at the northeast corner of Columbus Avenue and 80th Street a little after noon. He checked himself in a store window. With his beard and a Mets cap worn low over wraparound sunglasses, he was virtually unrecognizable. So even if this was a setup—he'd royally pissed off more than his share of people over the years—no one would spot him until he wanted to be spotted.

He searched the far side of the intersection as he pretended to wait for the walking green and found a trim, athletic-looking guy with longish sandy hair; he looked about Jack's height and age. He wore a tan suit and stood with his hands in his pockets as he peered about. Could be him. Or just a guy out to grab some lunch.

The light changed and Jack crossed Columbus with the crowd, but the suit stayed where he was, glancing at his watch and still looking around. The odds increased that this was the guy. Jack studied him some more as he waited for the signal to cross 80th to his corner, trying to guess what he did for a living. Good quality suit but not designer. Office job, obviously. Advertising? Wall Street? Lawyer? Whatever, his expression was concerned, maybe even worried.

Afraid "our Jack" wouldn't show?

Another green light. Jack hesitated, then figured what the hell. The guy looked okay—in fact Jack had an inexplicable good feeling about him, and that was unusual. Maybe together they could figure out the "our Jack" thing.

So he crossed and passed him, then turned and stopped just sunward.

"Looking for someone?"

He gave a little jump, then turned and raised a hand to shade his eyes.

"You're Jack?"

" 'Our Jack,' in the flesh. EPC, I presume."

He looked puzzled for an instant, then gave a crooked smile Jack found oddly familiar. "Oh, yeah. The initials. I felt a little queasy about leaving my name."

Queasy . . . that seemed to set off something in Jack's head. Why?

"Smart," Jack said. He pointed east along 80th toward Central Park. "I assume your presence here means you've had no word from your sister, so let's walk."

But the guy stayed where he was. "This is a little too weird. I don't know a thing about you, yet I'm meeting you here on a corner because my missing sister asked me to call you and I don't even know if you're really the guy I was supposed to call."

"Point taken. And the thing is, I probably won't be able to help you, but—"

"What are you? A cop? A detective? What?"

"Just a guy who's curious about how your sister knows me. What's her name?"

"Louise Myers."

Louise Myers . . . didn't ring a bell, even faintly.

"Never heard of her." Jack pointed toward the park again. He didn't like standing on the corner. "Walk a ways and tell me what makes you think she isn't simply on a trip to Maine or somewhere."

As they started to move, EPC reached into the breast pocket of his jacket and pulled out a folded piece of paper. He handed it to Jack.

If I'm missing
Don't call the police
They can't help
Get in touch with Jack
Please honor me on this
Our Jack can find me

If I'm missing . . . That didn't sound good.

"Sounds as if she expected some foul play to go down."

He sighed. "Well, yeah. She did. She always did."

"Did she have enemies?"

He tapped his temple. "Only up here."

"Paranoid?"

He shrugged. "A little, maybe. At first they said she was bipolar, then she was this, then she was that. I've come to the conclusion that Weezy is just . . . different."

Jack's stomach dropped and he stopped so abruptly a woman bumped him from behind.

"Idiot!" she said as she slipped past him.

Jack ignored her and stared at the guy. "Did you just say 'Weezy'?"

"Yeah. That's what we called her growing up and—"

"Weezy Connell?"

His eyes widened. "Yeah. How do you—?" He leaned closer. "Jack? Oh, Christ, it's you! I don't believe it!"

"Eddie!"

They embraced, back slapping, then stepped back and looked at each other.

Now that he knew who he was looking at, Jack could see his boyhood friend, but it wasn't easy. Chubby Eddie Connell had grown into a lean, fit-looking man.

"You know, Eddie, I was looking at you and there was something about you, but I couldn't figure out what it was. I mean, how could I? You've got cheekbones!"

He laughed. "Hey, it's Ed now. And look at you with the beard. Who'd've thought? 'Our Jack.' It all makes sense now."

They both sobered at once.

"Weez . . ." Jack said. "You really think something's happened to her?"

The idea was hard to take. He hadn't seen her since high school, but they'd been soul mates as kids.

"What else *can* I think?"

"But you said her enemies were all in her head."

Weezy had been eccentric as a kid, for a while very much into what she called the Secret History of the World. Come to think of it, Veilleur had said there truly was a Secret History, so maybe she had been on to something. She'd spent time on and off medications for mood swings. Definitely "different," as Eddie-now-Ed had said, but hardly a threat to anyone.

"She's become something of a recluse, rarely leaving her house except to go food shopping and to Internet places."

"No access at home?"

"Yeah, but . . ." He frowned. "Don't ask me to explain it because I can't, but she told me she needs to keep changing her IP address for certain of her online activities."

"Such as?"

"Wouldn't say. Said I was better off—safer—not knowing."

That didn't sound good.

"Could she be involved in anything shady?"

He made a face. "Weezy? You know her. Straight arrow."

"I *knew* her. Been a lot of years. You never know."

"She hasn't changed all that much."

Jack remembered something. "You called her Louise Myers. I gather she's married."

"Was. Married a guy named Steve Myers right after she graduated John Jay and—"

"John Jay? The criminal justice place?"

He nodded. "She has a BS in forensic science."

"Like I said: You never know. The marriage didn't work out, I take it?"

Ed shook his head. "Steve blew his brains out."

6. "It *is* alive," Drexler said.

Darryl watched him run his hands over the surface of the Orsa's flank like he was feeling up a woman. He hadn't liked the feel of the thing, like football hide, but with a little more give. And he especially hadn't liked that little ripple effect when he'd touched it.

"How can it be?" Hank said, looking a little scared.

"It simply is. And over the years it has been most entertaining to watch the transformation."

Entertaining? Darryl thought. Drexler found the weirdest things "entertaining."

Drexler's voice dropped in volume. "But then, in the early hours of yesterday morning, it woke up."

"How could you tell?" Darryl said.

Drexler didn't look at him. "We knew."

"Well, like how?"

Not like it had eyes that opened, or a mouth that could say good morning.

He still wouldn't look at Darryl. Like he thought if he didn't look, Darryl would disappear. But Darryl wasn't going anywhere.

"When it awoke, the Orsa changed from an opaque gray to clear, as you see it now."

Darryl's arm started to itch again. Damn.

"Okay," Hank said, "let's just say I buy that this thing is alive and awake. What does it do?"

Drexler looked at Hank—oh, sure, look at Hank but not Darryl.

"As I said, it will help change the world."

Change the world . . . the Kicker Evolution was supposed to change the world, but Darryl got a real strong impression that they were talking about a different kind of change, and speaking in some sort of code.

Hank didn't look convinced. "Yeah? How?"

He gave a sideward nod toward Darryl. "It's too complicated to go into now."

"Hey," Darryl said, scratching his arm, "I can tell when I'm not wanted."

Finally Drexler looked at him. "Can you now?"

"Yeah. I'll leave and let you get 'complicated.' "

"That would be—" Drexler stopped and stared. "What is that on your arm?"

Darryl tugged his sleeve down. "Nothing."

Drexler stepped closer. "Show me."

"It's nothing. I—"

"Show me."

Didn't look as if the guy was going to give up, so Darryl yanked up his sleeve and exposed the purplish rash. Drexler stared a few seconds, leaned in for a closer look.

"Do you have more of these?"

"Yeah."

"How many?"

"Half a dozen, I guess. You know what it is?"

"How long have you had them?"

Darryl was getting worried now. "A couple months. What is it?"

"I'm not a doctor, but you need that looked at. Have you been having night sweats?"

"N-no."

Not true. He'd been sweating a lot at night, and it was getting worse. Just last night he woke up with his undershirt so wet he could have wrung it out. He'd had to get up and change.

But he didn't know why he'd denied it. Maybe it was the way Drexler was looking at him . . . like he suddenly found him interesting. But not a caring interest. More like a guy who'd found a strange-looking bug.

Maybe he was afraid Drexler would find him "entertaining."

"Be that as it may," he said, pulling out a cell phone, "I'm going to call a doctor I know and get you an appointment immediately. You need a full work-up."

Now Darryl was really scared. "What do you think it is?"

But Drexler wasn't listening. He was frowning at his cell phone.

"Forgot: no signal down here. We must go upstairs."

"Hold on a second there," Hank said. "That can wait. I want to know how this thing's gonna help change the world."

"I'm afraid this cannot wait. This man must see a doctor immediately."

Darryl didn't know what frightened him more now: what might be wrong, or Drexler's concern.

7.

"She calls me every day at six P.M. sharp," Ed was saying.

They'd found a hotel with a bar—the first place they'd tried, the Excelsior, had been shockingly deficient in that amenity—and snagged a booth away from the windows. Jack didn't sit in windows.

"And I do mean sharp," he added. "In years I don't think she's ever been more than five minutes late."

"Why the call?"

"To let me know she was all right—for her sake rather than mine. After Steve's death, she became concerned about living alone. Something could happen to her and no one would know. She could fall and lie there for days, dying of dehydration or starvation, with no one having a clue that anything was wrong. Or someone could come in and attack her and leave her there with the same result."

"So when yesterday's call didn't come . . . ?"

"I called her. When I got no answer, I went over to her place and found it empty with no sign of a break-in."

"Just where is her place?"

"Queens—Jackson Heights."

"So we assume that sometime between six o'clock Sunday night and six o'clock last night she went out—"

"Sometime between dawn and six yesterday. She doesn't go out at night."

The black-jacketed waiter arrived with their drinks. Jack had ordered a Heineken, Eddie a Ketel martini with three olives.

Eddie . . . a martini drinker. Strange.

"Why don't we start off assuming no foul play," he said as Ed took a hefty sip.

"Why assume that? Her note—"

"Because of Occam's razor: It requires the fewest assumptions."

"Well, if there's been no foul play, where would a recluse like her be, besides home?"

"How about a hospital?"

"First thing I tried. I called emergency services and they had no record of ferrying a Louise Myers to a hospital. I even had them check her maiden name, but no hits."

"Then we'll have to try all the hospitals themselves. I mean, she could have felt ill and cabbed to an emergency room."

Ed frowned. "Never thought of that. How many hospitals are we talking about?"

"Lots. But if she lives in Queens we should probably start there and work toward the city."

" 'We'? Does that mean you're going to help?"

"Hell, yes. This is Weez we're talking about."

Ed was staring at him over the rim of his martini. "Just who are you, Jack?"

"I'm the guy who used to whip your ass in *Pole Position*."

He gave a tight smile. "You're also the guy I used to kill in *Missile Command*, but that doesn't tell me why Weezy sent me to you instead of the cops. 'Jack can find me' when the cops can't? What's that all about?"

How to answer that? He'd grown up with Eddie Connell and didn't want to lie to him, but he wasn't about to tell him the truth. As a teen he'd done plenty of things he'd shared with no one, especially Eddie, whose mouth had tended to runneth over.

"I honestly don't know what she was thinking. I didn't have much contact with her after high school. Hardly any. I don't know how she got my number or even knew I was in the city."

"So what are you? Some sort of detective or black ops guy or spook?"

Jack had to laugh. "Not likely. Why would you even think that?"

"Because of the way you disappeared. I got home from college and you were gone. I came looking for you and your father told me you'd walked out of the house and never come back, never called, never wrote. He and Kate were crazy with worry."

Jack took a long slow sip of his beer to buy some time.

Yeah, that had been a rotten thing to do, but he hadn't seen it that way at the time. He'd hit reset. He'd severed all ties with his old self, with his old life, with everyone he'd ever known and everything he'd planned to be. New start. New Jack. New life. He'd been angry, bitter, and a little crazy then—hell, a *lot* crazy—and hadn't thought about the hurt and worry he'd cause. He'd just done it and never once looked back.

Maybe he should have.

"I assure you I am not now, nor have I ever been, associated with any government—city, state, federal, foreign or domestic or intergalactic."

"Then why—?"

"I don't know. We'll ask her when we find her."

He smiled. "I like the way you think. But what do you do?"

"I run a repairs business."

"Appliances?"

Jack blew right past that. "What about you?"

"I'm an actuary."

"An insurance guy?"

He looked a little put off. "I freelance to pension consultants and HMOs and, yes, insurance companies."

"So you crunch numbers all day? Makes sense. You were always good in math."

"It's rated overall the second best job you can have."

"No kidding? What's first?"

"Biologist. Good work environment, good pay, little or no stress."

"Sounds great."

But Jack was thinking, Shoot me first. In the brainstem. With a .454 Casull hollowpoint, please, to guarantee no chance of survival.

"You live in the city?"

Jack nodded. "Yeah." He took a gulp of his beer and hoped Eddie wouldn't ask his address.

"You know the city hospitals?"

"A bit."

Knew more than he wished about some of them.

"Good. I work here, but I commute from Jersey, so it's not my stomping grounds."

"Well, Queens isn't mine. We need to get to a computer and Google hospitals over there—"

"This can do all that," Eddie said as he pulled a Black-Berry or one of its clones from a pocket.

Over the next few minutes he came up with a bunch of hospitals—the ones in Queens seemed mostly animal hospitals—and Jack wrote down the numbers. Then they divided the list and began calling.

"Don't forget to ask about any Jane Doe admitted yesterday too."

Ed slapped the table. "Shit."

"What?"

"I just remembered: Weezy didn't carry ID."

What?

"You're kidding, right?"

He shook his head. "Wish I was. She was afraid someone would steal her pocketbook and learn who she was and where she lived, so she never traveled with credit cards or anything."

"Then we just wasted our time. Call emergency services and see if they delivered a Jane Doe to a hospital yesterday."

Ed got right to it. Didn't take him long—he had the number in his call history. He did some talking, then looked at Jack.

"A Jane Doe was hit by a car yesterday afternoon half a dozen blocks from here. She was unconscious and they took her to Mount Sinai."

Jack rose as he gulped the rest of his beer.

"Let's go."

8. Dawn Pickering stared down at the Jackie Onassis Reservoir in Central Park and felt one of her berserk moods coming on.

She didn't know if being three months pregnant had

anything to do with it, or just the fact that she was totally a prisoner in this apartment. Not just an apartment—a beautiful apartment with every imaginable amenity. Beyond beautiful. A Fifth Avenue penthouse duplex overlooking Central Park. But a gilded cage. She wanted to smash its walls.

She rubbed her swelling belly. She'd popped a few weeks ago and was showing. She realized it was a relatively small bump but it made her feel like an elephant.

Back in May she'd sneaked out and landed herself in terrible trouble. She lived with daily reminders of those days. But she'd gone for a good reason—to abort the baby. She'd never wanted this baby, especially after learning the father's—Jerry's—true identity. And now, as the weeks passed, she was getting closer and closer to the point of no return, where she wouldn't be able to get an abortion.

And it was making her totally crazy.

All Mr. Osala's fault. He said he'd been hired by her mother to protect her and so he kept her locked up here. For her own good, he insisted. Because Jerry was out there, looking for her, looking for his child, and as long as she carried that child he would never hurt her. But if he ever learned that she had aborted his baby . . .

No argument that Jerry was a totally dangerous guy, *but she couldn't have this baby!*

Didn't anyone understand that? She was only eighteen. She couldn't spend the rest of her life in hiding. That would be like seventy or eighty years.

She wanted to throw a knife at somebody.

She turned away from the window and walked past the hot tub, the pool, the gym equipment, and went downstairs toward the living quarters. She was just stepping out of the stairwell when she saw Gilda the housekeeper leaving Mr. Osala's suite. She knew from chitchat with the older woman that Mr. Osala had a bedroom, an office, and his own bath in there—the reason she hardly ever saw him on the rare times he was home.

She noticed that the latch didn't catch as Gilda pulled the door closed behind her. Dawn had long wanted a peek inside, but the door was always locked and Gilda would never let her in—the "Master" totally valued his privacy.

Fine. But he'd taken charge of her life and she deserved to know a little more about him. She had only his word that Mom had hired him, and Mom wasn't around to confirm or deny the story.

Dawn felt her throat tighten. God, how she missed her. If she could have just one more day with her . . . even ten minutes . . .

She shook it off and waited for Gilda's solid form to bustle around a corner. Then she tiptoed to Mr. Osala's door and slipped through. She checked the knob to make sure it would turn, then closed the door behind her. The windows were shaded, so she felt along the wall till she found a light switch.

Shockingly bright overhead fluorescents flared to life, intensified by the stark white of the bare walls. Totally bare. Not a photo, not a painting, not even a scratch or nail hole to suggest that anything had ever decorated them. A big, plain mahogany desk dominated the room, sporting a computer monitor and nothing else. A black leather office chair and a filing cabinet completed the furnishings.

This was it? This was his office? She'd expected dark paneling, lush carpeting, and all sorts of memorabilia.

She moved to the next room and found more bare white walls surrounding a neatly made double bed with a light beige blanket but no spread. Two large armoires dominated the room. She opened one, then the other. Both were racked with expensive suits.

Strange.

But then, Mr. Osala was a strange man.

Clothing appeared to be his only extravagance—that and the rest of the house. But as for his personal quarters, he lived like a monk. And he'd chosen rooms with no view of the park. Not that it would matter with the heavy shades on the windows.

She smiled. Might be evidence that he was a vampire, except she'd seen him standing in full sunlight. So it had to be a privacy thing.

Dawn wandered back to the office area and pulled open one of the desk drawers for a peek. She spotted a driver's license and what looked like a college ID. She reached—

"The Master is a man who values his privacy."

Dawn gasped and looked up to see a thick-bodied woman with gray, bunned hair standing by the door.

Gilda.

"The door was open." She felt her face redden as she slammed the drawer shut. "I was just curious."

"You are trouble," the older woman said in accented English—Eastern Europe somewhere. "You have been trouble since the day he brought you here."

She had been warm to Dawn in the beginning, but then Dawn had made her escape and Henry, Mr. Osala's chauffeur, had suffered for it. Gilda and Henry had been friends. Now Henry was gone, and with him, Gilda's warmth.

"I totally don't mean to be. I'm just so *bored*. Can you understand that?"

She nodded. "Of course I can."

Good. Maybe Gilda was mellowing a little toward her. Dawn needed an ally here. Mr. Osala's new driver was totally unreachable. That left only Gilda.

She didn't know why she was afraid of Mr. Osala. He'd never threatened her, hadn't punished her for disobeying him. He saw to her every comfort, gave her everything she asked for except freedom and communication with the outside world—no phone, no Internet, which meant no MySpace or Facebook. She was totally cut off from everyone she'd ever known. He said that was to protect her from giving away her location. Maybe so, but it seemed totally extreme.

And there were times . . . the way he looked at her . . . no lust or anything like that, just sort of . . . calculating. She would have totally preferred lust. She could handle lust.

She had this feeling sometimes that he wasn't saving her *from* something so much as saving her *for* something.

She stepped closer to Gilda and looked her in the eyes. "Then you won't tell Mr. Osala about this?"

The woman's dark eyes flashed and she smiled, revealing her gapped teeth.

"Of course I will."

9. It took a lot of wheedling, but the hospital finally agreed to allow Eddie a peek at Mount Sinai's latest Jane Doe.

Jack had never been particularly enamored of hospitals, but after Gia and Vicky's ordeal earlier this year, he'd developed a definite aversion. The last time he'd seen the inside of one had been May when he and Abe had visited Professor Buhmann after his stroke. Right here at Mount Sinai, in fact.

The old guy had moved on to a nursing home, and then last month he'd matriculated to the Great Lecture Hall in the Sky. A grieving Abe had dragged Jack to the memorial service.

"They say she's still unconscious," Eddie said.

They stood in a foyer as he waited for security to escort him up to the floor.

Jack nodded. "Figured that."

After all, she wouldn't still be listed as a Jane Doe if she could tell them her name. Jack and Eddie used to play Master of the Obvious as kids. He wasn't going to bring that up now.

Visions of Gia and Vicky inert in their beds with tubes running in and out of them flashed through Jack's brain.

"If it is her, how are you going to prove you're related?"

Eddie shook his head. "Damned if I know. They asked me if I had a picture of her. Are they kidding? Who carries a picture of his sister? Do you carry a picture of Kate?"

"No. But maybe I should."

"Oh, hell, Jack. I'm sorry. I heard about Kate. I should have said something. She was a . . . a wonderful person. And your dad. That was the most bizarre damn thing. My condolences. I would have said so earlier except . . ."

"Don't give it another thought. Let's think about Weez. You have a key to her place, right? If Jane Doe is Weezy, you could match it up with a key in her bag."

"Except this lady's bag was stolen from the scene of the accident."

"Swell."

"Yeah," Eddie said. "What kind of person sees somebody knocked down by a car and the first thing he thinks of is snatching her purse? I'm glad I live in Jersey."

"Right," Jack said, feeling suddenly defensive. "Like that would never happen in Newark or Paterson."

A uniformed security guard arrived then.

"This won't take long," Eddie said as the guy guided him toward the elevators. "All I need is a peek."

"If it's her, you let me know ASAP and I'll come up."

He hoped not. Under any circumstances it would be kind of strange to reconnect with Weezy after all these years. But Weezy in a coma . . . he couldn't bear the thought of that unique, bright mind with the power cut off.

As an elevator swallowed Eddie, Jack wandered around to kill time. He found a Starbucks Kiosk and was going to grab a coffee of the day when he realized one of the patrons—a skinny, shaggy-haired guy—looked familiar from the back. He wandered closer and recognized Darryl. As he looked up Jack quickly turned and wandered away. He wondered what Darryl was up to. He'd noticed a Band-Aid in the crook of his arm. Blood tests? He didn't look happy to be here. In fact, he looked damn scared.

10. Darryl wondered why that bearded dude had been staring at him, then decided he didn't care. He'd looked kind of familiar. Like maybe he'd seen him around the Lodge. Another sick Kicker? Well, who cared? Wasn't going to be able to care much about anything until he got the results of those blood tests.

Weird how they'd told him to wait right here for the results. Whoever heard of getting test results right away?

This had to be real serious.

He had to say he was impressed with Drexler's suck. He'd made his call and next thing Darryl knew he was on his way uptown to a big-time specialist. He'd been ushered right through Dr. Orlando's office and into an examining room. He'd spent fifteen seconds, tops, with the doctor, a bald, round-headed fat guy in a white coat who reminded Darryl of Dr. Honeydew on *The Muppet Show.* He popped through the door, took one look at the rash, rattled off a bunch of medical gobbledygook to his assistant, and disappeared. Next stop had been the lab where they sucked out some blood, and then here to wait.

Why here? Darryl wondered why he wasn't cooling his heels in Dr. Orlando's office. He'd noticed INFECTIOUS DISEASES on the door. That was good, right? Infections could be cured.

"Mister Kulik?"

It took Darryl a second to respond. No one hardly ever used his second name. He was just Darryl to folks. He looked up and saw the doc's skinny, red-haired assistant. Her name tag read B. SNYDER PA.

"Doctor will see you now."

Darryl started shaking as he rose from the chair.

"He's got results? What do I have?"

"The doctor will tell you."

"Hey, if you know—"

"He wishes to discuss this with you himself."

He shook all the way to the office. The walk, the elevator ride—blurs. Eventually he found himself sitting across the desk from Dr. Orlando.

"Well, Mister Kulik," he said as he stared at the printout in his hands, "the stat labs confirm what I knew the instant I saw your skin lesion."

"You mean the rash? What is it?"

"Kaposi's sarcoma."

"What's that?"

"A form of cancer associated—"

"Shit!" Darryl would have leaped from the seat if his legs would have held him. "I got cancer?"

"Yes, but we can keep it under control by treating the underlying cause."

"Which is?"

"AIDS."

It took a while for the word to sink in, and when it did, Darryl felt like he'd turned to stone.

"What?"

"Acquired Immune Deficiency Syndrome, Mister Kulik. Your HIV test came back positive."

He said it like a sandwich guy telling him they were out of ham but he could have turkey instead.

"But-but-but queers get AIDS!" he blurted when he found his voice. "I ain't queer!"

"We prefer the terms 'homosexual' or 'gay,' Mister Kulik. And indeed you need not be homosexual to catch HIV. Heterosexual transmission occurs, but the majority of HIV-positive heterosexuals I see are the victims of contaminated syringes. Are you a drug addict or do you have a history of drug abuse?"

"No way. Never."

Dr. Orlando's tone said he didn't believe him. "Yes, well, be that as it may, I—" He stopped and pointed at Darryl's hand. "Oh, I see you have a tattoo. Contaminated tattoo needles can spread the infection as well."

Darryl looked down at the little black Kicker Man in the web between his thumb and forefinger.

"Aw, no. Don't say that."

"The manner in which you were infected does not affect your treatment options. The fact that you have Kaposi's indicates that you've been infected for some time—years, most likely."

Years? Then it couldn't be the Kicker tattoo. He hadn't had it anywhere near that long. But how then? Darryl couldn't imagine. He'd had a couple of girlfriends back in Dearborn after his divorce—well, okay, before his divorce too—but he'd always used a rubber because they hadn't been the choosiest women.

But right now *how* didn't matter all that much. He had AIDS, man. Fucking *AIDS*!

He listened to the doc go on about staging him and waiting for the results of tests that would take longer to complete and how treatment was so much better these days.

Yeah, sure. Medical bullshit. Everybody knew AIDS was a death sentence. So as the doc rattled on about this and that, tossing out terms like T-cell counts and remission, Darryl rose and forced his rubbery legs to carry him out of the office and back down toward the street.

Dead man walking.

He wasn't a fool. He'd been handed a death sentence.

He just couldn't let anyone else know.

11. Jack spotted Eddie at the far end of the waiting area, motioning him over.

"It's her," he said, relief large on his face as Jack reached him. "Weezy's their Jane Doe."

He pressed a hand over his eyes and for a moment Jack thought he was going to sob. He squeezed his old friend's shoulder.

"At least she's in good hands."

He nodded. "I was so worried. She's nutty as a fruitcake, but I love her to death. She's the only family left."

Uh-oh. Jack had never thought to ask . . .

"Your folks?"

"Gone. Mom from cancer, Dad from a car crash a year later."

"I'm sorry. I never heard a thing about it."

"It's okay. Old news."

"How's Weez?"

"Pretty banged up and still unconscious."

"I want to see her."

Eddie looked at him. "You sure?"

"Hell, yeah. I didn't get involved in this just to locate her and say, 'See ya, bye.' "

She'd been his best friend at one time and he hadn't seen her in ages. He needed to lay eyes on her at least once.

He followed him upstairs to a semiprivate room that seemed oddly familiar. At least it wasn't an ICU or trauma unit. The inside bed was empty. Eddie led him to the one by the window.

"Hey, Weez," he said to the supine figure under the sheet. "You'll never guess who's here."

The figure didn't move or respond as Jack stepped closer and looked down at his childhood friend.

He could see that she'd added a few pounds—picked up some of the weight Eddie had lost, maybe? Her face had rounded out, but he could still see the old Weezy Connell in those features. She'd never been pretty in the classic sense, but as a teen she easily could have been considered "cute." He remembered her dark, dark brown eyes, closed now. Her almost-black hair was shorter than he'd ever seen it and showed minute streaks of gray. Was that unusual for someone in her late thirties? A partially denuded area of her left frontal scalp revealed a stitched-up, three-inch laceration. Her skin was as milk pale as ever—even as a kid she'd never liked the sun.

No endotracheal tube or respirator, just an IV running in from a bag hung high and a catheter tube running into a receptacle slung low. He noticed movement under the sheet where her right hand should be but didn't lift it to investigate.

"Well," Eddie said. "There she is."

Jack felt his throat constrict. He hadn't given her a thought for so, so long. She'd been a year ahead of him in school, but during pre–high school summers they'd been almost inseparable. He'd never paid much attention to her mood swings; that was the way she was, and he accepted it. Weezy was Weezy—a loner like Jack, a free thinker, one of a kind. During high school a doctor began putting her on medication that smoothed out the swings but, in the process, changed her. Things were never quite the same.

He wished she was awake and on her feet now so they could hug and exchange long-time-no-see clichés.

"Yeah," was all he could manage.

"Good day," said a high-pitched, accented voice behind him.

He turned and recognized the tall, lean, dark-skinned man in the white coat. He had a Saddam Hussein mustache and carried a clipboard. Jack checked his ID badge to make sure he was right.

"Hello, Doctor Gupta."

The man looked confused. "I'm sorry. Have we met?"

Jack now knew why the room seemed familiar.

"Yes. I was acquainted with Professor Buhmann." When Gupta shook his head, Jack added, "The guy with the stroke who spoke only in numbers?"

His eyes lit. "Ah, yes! How is he?"

"Gone."

"Yes-yes. The tumor. So sorry. A most fascinating case." He gestured toward Weezy. "I am told you are the brother of our mystery patient?"

Jack pointed to Eddie. "That would be him."

"Her name is Louise Myers, Doctor," he said, stepping forward and shaking hands. "How is she?"

"As you can see, she is comatose from her head trauma. She has a lacerated scalp but no skull fracture. Scans reveal no intracranial hemorrhage or hematoma."

"What's her Glasgow score?" Jack said.

Gupta gave him a puzzled look. "You know the Glasgow scale?"

Jack nodded. His father, Gia, and Vicky had all been comatose at one time or another. He knew more about comas than he wished.

Gupta moved toward the bed. "Well, strictly speaking, her score is eight. She makes incomprehensible sounds now and then, and she responds to painful stimuli. Here. I will show you."

He pulled a little rubber-headed percussion mallet from his pocket and removed a pinlike instrument from its handle. Then he raised a flap of sheet to reveal Weezy's left hand.

"Watch."

He lifted it about six inches off the bed; when he let go it dropped like a piece of meat.

"Now watch."

He jabbed her palm with the pin. Her hand jerked away and her eyes fluttered open for a second.

"Hey!" Eddie said.

But Gupta was already moving to the other side of the bed, saying, "So, that gives her a score of eight. But this does not fit with that score."

He lifted the sheet to reveal her right hand. Its index fingertip was scratching the sheet in a circular motion.

"See? Intermittent spontaneous movement. That should move her above an eight but I'm not sure where. The movement is certainly not consciously directed."

"What's the prognosis?" Eddie said.

"Good, I think."

"When will she wake up?"

"Oh, that I cannot say. It would be foolish of me to predict."

As they talked Jack stared at Weezy's finger where it scratched the sheet. After a moment he began to sense a pattern in the movements. She'd make somewhere between fifteen and twenty loops—her movements were too rapid and small for an accurate count—stop for maybe two seconds, then start again. Almost as if . . .

"Doctor Gupta," he said, motioning him over and pointing to her hand. "Could she be writing something?"

He leaned closer, stared a moment, then straightened, shaking his head.

"It is highly unlikely. The movement is most likely the result of random neuron firings." He started for the door. "I must continue rounds. I shall check on her later. In the meantime, please fill in the nurses on as much of your sister's medical history as you know."

When he was gone, Eddie stepped up to Jack's side and together they stared at Weezy's moving finger.

"Doesn't look very random to me," Jack said.

"You really think she's writing something?"

Jack nodded. "*Mene, Mene, Tekel Upharsin.*"

"What?"

"Nothing." He leaned close to her ear. "Weezy, it's Jack. You told Eddie to call me and he did. If you can hear me, stop moving your finger."

The fingertip kept up its relentless pattern.

"Okay, then, if you can hear me, draw an 'X' with your finger."

No change. The looping motions continued. As Jack watched them, an idea formed. He straightened and turned to Eddie.

"You going to the nursing station?"

"Yeah."

"Good. I'll come with you."

The station lay fifty feet down the hall. While Eddie hunted the head nurse to background her on Weezy, Jack leaned over the counter and got a candy striper's attention.

"Can I help you?" She was all of sixteen and chewing gum with her mouth open.

"I hope so. I need to scrounge a notepad and some carbon paper."

She stopped chewing. "Carbon paper?" She turned and called to another girl who was maybe a year older. "Hey, Brit? Do we have any, like, carbon paper?"

Brit looked at her like she'd just spoken Farsi. "*Carbon* paper? Like what's *that*? Is that, like, a *color*?"

Feeling terminally Triassic, Jack said, "Never mind. How about we try this . . . ?"

Two minutes later he returned to Weezy's room with a yellow legal pad, a black Sharpie, and a roll of quarter-inch adhesive tape. He pulled a chair up to her right side and seated himself before her hand. He taped the Sharpie alongside her index tip so that its point jutted just beyond the fingernail. Then he placed the pad under her finger and let her rip.

At first all he got was an irregular blotch of black scribbles. So he decided to slide the paper along under the tip. And as he did, figures that looked like letters began to appear. He kept working at it, varying the speed until . . .

"What on Earth are you doing?" Eddie said as he returned to the room carrying some papers.

"Trying to find out what she's writing."

"You heard the doctor—random neurons."

Yeah, Jack had heard. But he knew doctors could be as pigheaded as anyone else, refusing to see what was dangling before their noses because it didn't fit their preconceived notions.

"Really?" Jack held up the latest sheet he'd run under her finger. "This look random to you?"

bunnyhouse

Eddie frowned and squinted at it. "'Bummyhouse'? What's that mean?"

"I was hoping for a 'Eureka!' from you. No bells going off, no lightning-bolt epiphany?"

"No."

"Google it."

Eddie handed Jack his papers, then pulled out his BlackBerry or whatever and did a fingertip tap dance. A few seconds later . . .

"I've got 'buy my house' but nothing else."

"Could it be 'bummyhorse'? Was she into horses, OTB, anything like that?"

"No. She'd never bet on anything anywhere. She thought everything was fixed."

"Why am I not surprised? Try it anyway."

In its own nice way, Google told them to go fish.

"Well then, what about 'bunny house'? Did she have a pet rabbit?"

"No. She's never been into pets."

Right . . . she'd never had one as a kid. But that didn't mean she hadn't become a cat lady . . . or a bunny lady.

"You're sure?"

"Absolutely. I was just at her house. I searched it from cellar to attic yesterday and believe me, there's no rabbit hutch there."

"They're usually outside. Did you search outside?"

Eddie hesitated. "No . . ."

"So there could be an old unused hutch there, maybe left over from the previous owner."

"Could be, but—"

"And maybe she's hidden something there."

"Jack—"

"We should go see. Jackson Heights, right? This time of day the subway'll get us there in no time."

Eddie was staring at him. "You're really into this. Why?"

"Because it's Weezy. And my curiosity's up. Paranoid or not, she thought something might happen to her. And something did. Now, it might or might not have been an accident—"

"It wasn't a hit and run, if that's what you're thinking." He pointed to the papers he'd handed Jack. "I got a copy of the police report from the nurse. A lady from Jersey hit her. Said she ran right in front of her."

Jack scanned the report. A couple of witnesses corroborated the driver's story. They also said a guy scooped up Weezy's shoulder bag right after she was hit and took off running.

He handed the report to Eddie. "Okay. So it was an accident—at least that part of it."

"What do you mean?"

"Maybe she was being chased."

"Oh, come on, Jack."

"Was Weezy the type to just step out into traffic?"

"She was the type to get lost in thought. She was also the type to worry about being followed, which might lead her to be watching over her shoulder when she should have been watching traffic."

Jack sighed and nodded. "You're right, you're right. Just playing devil's advocate."

"Oh. Almost forgot." Eddie reached inside his jacket and pulled out a small, flat, metallic rectangle. "They found this in her pocket."

Jack took it from him and turned it over. IMATION was printed on its side.

"Flash drive."

"Right. She was never without one. She had all her posts prewritten and ready to go so she could get on and offline as quickly as possible."

"At these Internet cafés and such she frequented."

Eddie nodded. "Exactly. A little sad, isn't it."

"Yeah, I guess."

She obviously believed that someone was looking for her.

"I wonder if we should—"

"Excuse me?"

Jack turned and saw a swarthy, dark-haired guy stepping into the room. He looked like he'd just shaved but he still had five-o'clock shadow.

"I understand one of you is brother?"

Jack tried to identify his accent. Polish? Czech?

Eddie said, "That would be me."

The guy extended his hand. "Bob Garvey. I was there when your sister hit. I call nine-one-one."

"Well, thank you," Eddie said, shaking his hand. "I appreciate that, and I'm sure my sister does too."

"The least one could do." Bob turned and extended his hand to Jack. "And you are other brother?"

"Just a friend," he said as they shook. He maintained his grip as he asked, "Did you happen to notice if she was being chased?"

Bob's fingers twitched as he freed his hand. "No. Why would someone chase?"

"For her purse. It was stolen from the scene, you know."

"Yes, I heard. Can you believe some people? I was on phone to emergency services when it happened, but my back was turn so I don't see it. When I turn around and people tell me, I could not believe. I just stand there with mouth hanging open. I would have chased but he was gone."

"So you never saw him?"

Bob shook his head. "Unfortunately I did not."

"Why are you here?"

He looked a little sheepish. "Well, you know how it is . . . you help someone, you feel responsible. And because no one know her name . . . I don't know . . . she become this mystery woman in my mind and I just think I look in on her until her family show up."

"That's very kind of you," Eddie said.

Yeah, Jack thought. Very kind of strange.

Something about this guy wasn't ringing true. First off, the name didn't go with the accent.

"I am given to understand her name is Louise."

Whoa.

"How do you understand that?" Jack said.

"I ask nurses if she still a Jane Doe. They tell me she is identified as Louise Myers."

Eddie nodded. "Yes, that's her. We've always called her Weezy."

"Weezy," Bob said with a slow smile. "That is nice."

Fearing Eddie might offer his sister's address and Social Security number and maybe even a dinner date next, Jack blurted, "Where can she get in touch with you, Bob? I'm sure she'll want to thank you when she's recovered."

"Oh, that will not be necessary. I—"

Eddie said, "Oh, she'll never forgive me if I didn't get at least a phone number from you."

"And an address," Jack added. "In case she wants to send a thank-you note."

Bob waved his hands. "It is not necessary."

"Oh, but it is," Jack said. "In fact, we insist."

Bob hesitated, then sighed. "Okay. I do not have card—"

"No prob," Jack said, showing him the blank back of the police report. "I've got paper and he's got a pen."

Eddie pulled a ballpoint from a breast pocket and handed it to Bob. They both watched him scribble an address and phone number.

"Well," he said as he handed everything back, "I must go now, but it is pleasure meeting you and even better knowing that Louise's family has finally found her."

He walked to the door, then did a Columbo turn as he reached it.

"Oh, may I ask if she is New Yorker? Where does she live?"

"Montauk," Jack said, stepping in front of Eddie. "Year round. I don't know about you, but the isolation during the winter would drive me nuts. She loves it, though. Go figure."

Bob smiled, nodded, and left.

"Montauk?" Eddie said. "She doesn't—"

"I know."

"Then why tell him that?"

"Because one good lie deserves another."

Eddie looked baffled. "I don't—"

"Because the only true thing he said was that he was glad to know that Louise's family has found her. I wouldn't be surprised if he stole Weez's bag, or knows the guy who did."

Eddie's eyes widened. "Are you kidding me? You're beginning to sound like Weezy."

Maybe he was, but that guy had had a three-dollar-bill air about him.

"Sometimes a person only seems paranoid. And even paranoids have real enemies. That guy was on a fishing expedition. He knew her name when he stepped in here and—"

"You heard him. He asked the nurses."

"So he said. And maybe it's true. Look, I know this is a silly question, but I have to ask: Is Weezy's phone listed?"

"Of course not."

"Good. Our friend Bob was looking for her address. Came right out and asked for it. Why? Humor me, Eddie. Play along. Why would he want her address?"

He sighed. "Because she's got something he wants?"

"Logical. He didn't get her address from her bag because she never carries ID. So what does he do? He sets up watch on the hospital, hoping friends or family will come looking for her. And when they find her—shit."

"What?"

"Did you give her address to the nurses?"

"Well, sure. Why wouldn't I?"

Damn.

"Okay, then, we have to assume that, one way or another, the guy calling himself Bob Garvey will be able to get her address from the hospital records." He noticed Eddie grinning. "What?"

"All this assumes he really wants to know. But assuming he does, he's out of luck."

"Why?"

"Sometimes paranoia pays off. Her mailing address isn't her house address. She uses a rental mailbox in Elmhurst just the other side of Roosevelt Avenue."

Jack had to smile. He used mail drops all over the boroughs.

"A girl after my own heart."

"Why do you say that?"

"Oh, no particular reason."

He looked again at the scrawl. It sure as hell looked like *bummyhouse*.

House . . . her house seemed to be a focus of interest. Her house . . . but to her it would be *my* house. What if . . .

He took a pencil and drew two lines through the word, then showed it to Eddie.

bum|my|house

Eddie frowned. " 'Bum my house'?"

"I think the first hump there is an *r*."

Eddie's eyes were wide when he looked up at Jack. "'*Burn* my house'? She can't mean that."

"I think we'd better get out there."

This time Eddie didn't argue.

12.

Ernst listened to Kris Szeto's report. The cell connection wasn't good.

"Her name is Louise Myers and she is still in coma."

A name . . . they finally had a name for this nuisance.

"Address?"

"Just mailbox number."

"Did you search the real estate—"

"Not listed."

Disappointing news, but Ernst was glad that Szeto was anticipating him. This was why he used operatives from the Order's European lodges. They were much more on the ball than their Stateside counterparts. He supposed his being born in Austria and spending his early years bouncing around Europe had something to do with it as well.

"How much longer will the coma last?"

"That I do not know. I speak to brother and friend. They look worried. Then they leave."

"Where to?"

"I think maybe to her house."

"Excellent! You're following them, of course."

"Not me. They know my face. I send Max."

"Good."

They needed access to wherever this woman lived—her computer, her files—to find out how much she knew and who else shared that knowledge. Once they eliminated that, they could eliminate her.

"Who's watching the woman?"

"Josef."

"If there's any sign she's waking up, we'll have to take action."

"Of course. A plan is in place. I will keep you informed."

Ernst ended the call. Under normal circumstances, he could understand why the One would be so intent on silencing this woman; but with the *Fhinntmanchca* soon to be a reality . . . why bother?

That reminded him . . . He speed dialed Dr. Orlando.

13.

"Remember that time in the Barrens when that cop locked us in his car?" Eddie said as they bounced and swayed in the Flushing-bound 7 train.

"If he was really a cop. Weezy had her doubts, remember? And remember how you faked being sick to get us out?"

The subway wasn't sub out here in this area of Queens—it ran on elevated tracks over Roosevelt Avenue. The afternoon sun, still high, cut steep, bright, mote-bedizened channels through the air of the not quite half full car.

Jack and Eddie sat side by side on an orange plastic bench. They'd picked up the train beneath Bryant Park and Jack had been watching for a tail the whole time.

Maybe he was having his own bout of paranoia, but something didn't feel right. Weezy's accident appeared to be just that—an accident. Someone running off with her bag—happened all the time. A guy following up on someone he'd helped on the street—not so common. Rare in a city like New York, but not out of the realm of possibility. But something was *wrong* about that guy.

He'd checked out this car and so far it looked pretty good. All but one of the people who'd got on with them was gone, and she was a bent little black lady, eighty if she was a day. But the place to bird-dog someone on a subway was from the car ahead or behind.

As he and Eddie talked, Jack kept flicking his gaze back and forth between the windowed doors to the adjoining cars. Last stop he saw a guy with short, bleached-blond hair peek into their car from the one behind.

Might be nothing, might be something. He'd keep watch.

"No," Eddie said, "*you* got us out. And then you tricked him and that guy in the suit into the spong. That was so cool."

Now that Eddie knew his sister was safe and in good hands, Jack noticed a change in his tone and body language. He'd relaxed some. And with the easing of tension came reminiscing time.

Eddie nudged him. "The three of us had some good times, huh? Flitting in and out of the Pine Barrens on our bikes. Some scary times too."

"Yeah, I suppose."

Jack wasn't much for memory lane. Much of the past was a blur.

"You were always playing tricks on me. I still remember the Rubik's cube scam you pulled. You really had me going for a while. I thought you were a freaking genius."

What scam? Jack tried but couldn't remember.

Eddie leaned back, his eyes unfocused. "I think about those days a lot."

"Really? What for?"

Jack seldom thought about his childhood. He'd flashed back every so often when he'd been with Kate or Dad or Tom during the past year, but for the most part the good old days were a haze. When he'd dropped out he'd divided the timeline of his life and had rarely crossed back.

"Good times," Eddie said. "Free times. No responsibilities other than to have fun. Remember sneaking out at night? We were always on the verge of getting busted for something."

If you only knew the half of it, Jack thought. The three of them had spent a lot of time together, with Jack and Weezy spending even more time as a duo. But Jack had had plenty of alone time when he'd done things on his own, things he hadn't felt free to tell anyone about. His own Secret History.

Enough of memory lane. The past was gone . . . dead . . . so much of it literally dead.

"What's Weezy do for a living these days?"

Eddie shrugged. "Reads and surfs the Internet mostly."

"She gets paid for that?"

"No, she lives off the proceeds of her investments."

"Oh? Her half of the Connell family fortune?"

"Yeah. Pretty much."

Jack had remembered the Connells as being comfortable—their dad had been a well-paid union pipe fitter—but they'd been far from rich.

Jack's confusion must have shown because Eddie smiled and nudged him again. "Life insurance, Jack. My father had this big fear of dying and leaving us destitute. Add his brother, my uncle Bill, who was an insurance agent, and the result is a man with term insurance up the wazoo. Most of his policies paid double for accidental death, so when he hit that bridge abutment, the payout was millions."

"Millions?"

He nodded. "A little over two. To tell the truth, I don't think it was an accident."

Jack looked at him sideways. "Is this Weezy talk?"

"No. I'm not talking foul play, I'm talking . . . you know."

Jack nodded. "Oh."

"The insurance companies had the same thought. It happened a year and a half after my mother's death, during which he'd been very despondent. I don't think he wanted to live without her. His seat belt was off, but he'd left no note, they found no drink, no drugs in his system, so they had to pay."

As the train jerked to a stop at the 74th Street–Broadway station, Jack noticed the blond guy peek again and felt himself go on alert. Could still be nothing, but their stop was next. Decision time approaching.

"How do you feel about that?" he said as he pulled the police accident report from his pocket.

Weezy and her father hadn't been close—he'd given her a hard time during her goth period—but Jack remembered Eddie and his father sharing a keen interest in sports, but only on TV. Eddie, a chunky kid then, had loathed physical activity.

Eddie shrugged. "Weez and I were both grown and out of the house by then, so it wasn't as if he was deserting us. We had no sense of abandonment. We grieved, sure, but he went into such a funk after Mom died."

"So Weez wasn't the only one in the family who had ups and downs."

"I guess not. My dad would never admit to something like that—for his generation, depression was a sign of weakness and personal failure. But in the end, I think I was kind of relieved for him. We'd tried to get him help but he refused. I thought time would bring him around—I'm sure it would have—but he couldn't see any light at the end of that tunnel. Took me a while, but I've accepted it." He looked at Jack. "Your dad, on the other hand . . . that's a lot fresher for you."

Jack nodded. "Yeah. A whole lot."

Just a little over half a year since he'd lost his own father. Hadn't been suicide, but it hadn't been an accident either. Seemed like only yesterday they'd been fighting for their lives in the Everglades.

Eddie gave his shoulder a gentle squeeze. "It does get easier."

"So I've been told."

He shook himself and glanced at the report. Witnesses said that the man who'd run off with Weezy's bag had blond hair. Still could be a coincidence.

Uh-huh.

"So, Weezy's a rich widow?"

"'Rich' is relative. I hooked her up with a financial planner and she's pretty well set. She can't join the jet set but she'll never have to worry about a roof over her head and food on the table."

"Good for her."

"She lives very simply in a plain, no-frills, middle-class house—no trips, no fancy clothes. She doesn't even spend what she gets, so her principal is growing."

A thought had occurred to Jack. If someone wanted to find where Weezy lived, they wouldn't need to tail them. If they had her name, they could find her address on the Internet for a small fee.

"Weezy's house . . . she own it?"

Eddie shook his head. "She didn't want to own. I told her it was the best long-term investment ever, but she insisted on renting—but under our mother's name, of all things."

Jack couldn't help laughing. "I love it! That's my Weez!"

"What—?"

The conductor's voice interrupted, crackling over the speaker to announce Jackson Heights coming up.

Jack said, "Sit tight."

"But it's our stop."

"We may have company."

His eyes widened. "You mean *followed*?"

"Possibly."

"Come *on*. No one's going to—"

"Think about it, Eddie. Your sister's in a coma. Someone stole her bag. Whoever did has keys to her house but doesn't know where her house is because she's not listed anywhere as an owner or a tenant. A stranger was just asking about where she lives. We didn't tell him. So the only way to find out is to follow us."

Eddie leaned back and shook his head. "No wonder you and Weez were such good friends."

As the train slowed to a stop, the bleached blond head appeared again, then pulled back.

Yep. They had a tail. Not the guy calling himself Bob Garvey. Strictly amateur to have a familiar face try to follow, which would have given Jack a certain amount of comfort. Instead he'd sent a second guy.

Which led to the question: How many were involved here? How big was this?

Worst-case scenario for Jack: the government. In most cases, if they wanted Weezy's address they'd just flash a badge at Eddie and demand he tell them. But what if Weezy had stumbled onto some covert operation?

Listen to me, he thought. I'm cooking up a Jason Bourne plot here.

But he couldn't ignore the possibility, because for a guy who didn't pay taxes or even have a Social Security number, feds were, if not a worst-case scenario, then at least very, very bad.

But if not government, then who? And why?

Weezy, my dear old pal, what the hell have you got yourself into?

"What's the plan?" Eddie said as the train lurched into motion again. His tone dripped sarcasm. "Put on wigs and mustaches? Or do we climb between the cars and jump off as it's moving?"

"Do I detect a note of skepticism?"

"You detect a whole orchestra."

"O ye of little faith."

"What do you expect? You're Jack from Johnson, New Jersey, who repairs appliances, and you expect me to believe you've spotted someone following us?" He gestured at the sparsely populated car. "Who? Point him out."

Jack wasn't so sure that was the thing to do. "I said we *may* have a tail. I didn't say I'd spotted one."

"Right. Because there isn't one. These are just regular folks minding their own business. They don't care about us."

Jack couldn't blame him. Were positions reversed, he'd feel the same way.

"Yeah, you're probably right. But humor me, okay? We'll get off at the Elmhurst stop and train back."

"Not as if I have a choice now."

"We can always pull the emergency stop and jump onto the tracks."

Eddie stared at him a long moment, then barked a nervous laugh. "You know, for a minute there you really had me going. I mean, I thought you were serious."

"I was," Jack said, deadpan, then laughed. "Are you kidding me?"

14.

As the train pulled into the 90th Street–Elmhurst Avenue stop they rose and stood before the nearest door. From the corner of his eye Jack saw the blond guy take another peek. When the train stopped and the door panels split, they stepped out onto the platform. One car down, the blond guy stepped out too. As they headed for the stairs down to the street, he followed. But then, he'd do that even if he wasn't following them.

"All we've accomplished is to prolong the trip," Eddie was saying.

"Yeah, I suppose so. But it gives us a little extra time to discuss the elephant in the room we've been ignoring."

"You mean, 'burn my house.'"

Jack had been thinking about it while watching for a tail but could make no sense of it.

"Yeah. What's up with that?"

"I've turned it over and over and upside down and inside out and still can't make sense of it. She loves that house. It contains all her worldly possessions—and believe me, she has a *lot* of worldly possessions."

"I thought you said she lives very simply."

He smiled. "She does. And her possessions are simple, but there's lots and lots of them."

"I'm not following."

"You'll see when you get there. It's easier to show than tell."

When they hit the street they crossed Roosevelt Avenue to the Manhattan-bound entrance. As they reached the turnstiles, Jack stepped ahead of Eddie and swiped his MetroCard through the reader.

"Since I'm the reason you're here, my treat."

Eddie laughed. "Jack, I can well afford—"

Jack made a flourish toward the turnstile, saying, "I insist," and used the move as an opportunity to peek behind them.

The blond guy was standing at the bottom of the stairway across the street looking baffled.

Jack swiped the card for himself, and then he and Eddie climbed the stairs to the platform. Jack guided him to a spot that would put them on the middle of the train. The sun was hot so they stood back in the shadow of the partial roof.

"So you have no idea why she'd want us to burn her house?"

Eddie shook his head. "Not a clue. But I assume it has

something to do with her idea that she'd turn up 'missing.'"

"Well, she *was* missing for a while."

"Because she ran out in front of a car—not because someone abducted her. And not because someone was following her—if you get my meaning."

He gestured around the near-empty platform just as the blond guy emerged from the stairwell and stood thirty or so feet away. Eddie glanced at him but didn't react.

Clueless, Jack thought as he forced a heavy sigh.

"I guess you're right."

The Manhattan-bound train pulled in half a minute later. Jack and Eddie boarded. Uptrack to his left, Jack saw the blond man step on as well.

"Let's stand," Jack said, stopping just inside the door. "It's only one stop."

Eddie shrugged. "Sure."

Jack waited a few seconds, then grabbed the back of Eddie's jacket and yanked.

"On second thought . . ."

"Hey!" he cried as he was pulled through the closing doors. "What are you doing?"

As the train began pulling out, Jack gestured at the empty platform. "Just making sure we weren't followed."

"Jesus, Jack! You're crazy, you know that? You and Weezy always had this . . . this rapport, where one seemed to know what the other was thinking. And now you've bought into her paranoia."

"I don't know about that. But one thing I do know: Your sister was way smarter than I ever was. I think that counts for something."

He remembered his continuing wonder at the breadth of her knowledge and her photographic memory.

"She's still smart—smarter than both of us put together, I'll bet—but that's not going to bring the next train any faster."

Jack couldn't decide whether it would be easier to leave Eddie in the dark about the tail or clue him in. He decided a wake-up call was in order.

"Keep your eyes on this train," Jack said as it gathered speed. "In one of the cars you'll see a guy with bleached-blond hair combed forward. When he spots us out here he won't be happy."

Sure enough, the next-to-last car carried the blond man who stared out at them with an angry, befuddled expression.

"Wave to the nice man." Eddie didn't. Jack began pulling him toward the stairway. "Now walk with me."

Eddie came along but was staring at him with an uncomfortable expression.

"You think that man was following us?"

"Just walk."

He hoped seeing them heading toward the exit would convince the blond guy that Elmhurst had been their destination all along.

"Seriously, Jack—"

"He was peeking at us from an adjoining car all the way out from the city. When we doubled back, so did he. Draw your own conclusion."

Eddie stopped at the entrance to the stairwell. "So it's true? Someone was really following us?"

"Looks that way to me."

"You're . . . you're not an appliance repairman, are you."

Jack had been afraid of this.

"As you said yourself, I'm just Jack from Johnson."

"Yeah, and I knew that Jack, and that Jack would never settle for being an appliance repairman."

"Why not? It's honest work. You have the satisfaction of accomplishing something. You're your own boss, you set your own hours, and you leave the job behind at the end of the day."

Not an untrue word there—except he wasn't talking about himself.

"But how does a simple appliance repairman spot a tail and outsmart him like you just did?"

"Well, maybe I *am* a bit paranoid—after all, I was watching for a tail. And I've read my share of thrillers."

"You were awfully smooth giving him the slip."

"Learned everything I know from Jake Fixx."

Eddie smiled. "You read those novels? Me too, I'm ashamed to say."

"Ashamed?"

"Well, they're just plain silly. And that character, that Jake Fixx, he's preposterous."

"But you keep reading them."

"Yeah, well, there's something about the guy . . . he may be ridiculous but—this is going to sound crazy, but I almost feel as if I know him."

You have no idea, Jack thought.

"Yeah, me too."

Eddie frowned. "But if we really were being followed, that changes everything."

"Ya think?"

"No, seriously. It means—"

"—that Weezy might not be as paranoid as you thought."

"Yeah. Which is not a comfortable thought."

Welcome to my world.

"I agree. But first thing we do is check out her house. And we'll cab it from here. My treat."

15. The cabby dropped them off at the address Eddie had given him.

A narrow residential street, lined with parked cars; quiet as expected on a Tuesday afternoon in summer. The surrounding houses had small front yards sporting lawns and plantings that spanned the bell-shaped curve in terms of care and quality. A couple of Asian kids shot baskets in a driveway a few doors down. A woman in a sari wheeled a little shopping cart up from Roosevelt Avenue.

Jack stood on the front walk and stared at the house: Two stories tall, it sat cheek by jowl with its identical neighbors, with what looked like the original postwar, asbestos-shingle siding painted Broomhilda green.

"She rents Archie Bunker's house?"

Eddie, a few steps ahead of him, stopped and stared for a second, then laughed.

"You know, I never saw it before, but you're right. Not a whole lot of single-family houses around here. This is one of the few blocks that's got any."

Jack had been through Jackson Heights countless times over the years. It sat in northwest Queens—not as far north or west as Astoria where the Kenton brothers lived, but convenient to the Brooklyn-Queens Expressway, and with good subway service in and out of the city. Back when Jack was born, white middle-class folks like Archie and Edith peopled its ubiquitous garden apartments. But then, like Astoria, it morphed into an ethnic polyglot, home of Little India with its myriad South Asian shops and restaurants, and loads of Africans and Latinos as well. And then, as real estate prices began soaring in Manhattan, the whites had started moving back. But not too many yet.

Mostly working folks in Jackson Heights, but gangs

reared their ugly heads every so often. And more and more of those gang members seemed to be wearing Kicker Man tattoos.

Jack noticed Weezy's windows. Heavy sunshades inside the glass screened the interior from view; wrought-iron bars protected all the first-floor windows—not all that unusual. Then he spotted more on the second floor over the front-porch roof.

He did a slow turn to check out the neighborhood again: seemed quiet enough. Why was Weezy's house the only one secured like a jewelry store?

He caught up to Eddie at the front door as he was unlocking the second of three deadbolts.

Okay, Jack had multiple locks on his door too. Nothing wrong with that.

"What's with all the window bars?"

"When you think you might go 'missing,' it's only logical to take precautions, right?"

"True that. Nothing to do with the fact that she appears to be the only Caucasian on the block?"

Eddie gave him a sharp look and his tone took on an acid edge. "You should know better than that."

"That's just it—I don't. I don't know a thing about the adult Weezy."

"Yeah, I suppose you don't. But trust me on this: The grown-up Weezy is very much like the Weezy you knew before they started . . . medicating her. She doesn't notice race—or at least that's not the way she categorizes people. She has her own unique criteria."

"As in the parts they play in the Secret History of the World?"

"Bingo." He turned the key on her last deadbolt and looked at Jack. "Get ready."

"Ready for what?"

"You'll see."

He pushed the door open and an unusual odor wafted from the dark interior. It threw Jack for a second until he recognized it. Old paper—it smelled like an antiquarian bookstore.

Eddie stepped inside and flipped a light switch. Jack followed but froze on the threshold.

"What the—?"

Eddie's comment about Weezy having a *lot* of worldly possessions suddenly made sense.

The walls of the front room were lined—as in spackled—with books, but the shoulder-high piles of newspapers dominated the front room. Row upon row of stacks with narrow passages between forming the equivalent of an English hedgerow maze.

"Amazing, isn't it," Eddie said, navigating a lane toward the rear.

Jack closed the door and followed.

"Well, it's not on the scale of the Collyer brothers—"

"Who?"

"Two recluse brothers who were found dead in their Fifth Avenue brownstone with a hundred tons of junk, much of it old newspapers."

"No junk here, as you will note." Eddie sounded a little defensive. "And everything neatly stacked."

Jack had noticed that. The tabloids were stacked together, as were the full-size papers. They weren't tied into bundles. He wondered if they were in any special order. He stopped and checked out a few. A 1968 *Post* lay atop a 1975 *Daily News*. In the next stack a 1993 *Times* atop—

"Wow. Check this out—a *Journal-American* from nineteen sixty-two. Where'd she get these?"

"God only knows."

"Looks like they're all New York papers."

"They might be. I wouldn't know."

The maze extended into the next room. Yes, she had a dining set, but the table was piled high with papers and more stacked beneath. The same with each of the four chairs. Her china cabinet was stuffed with books.

"It's the same upstairs—the extra rooms, the hallway, even her bedroom."

Jack glanced at the living room ceiling and thought it appeared to belly downward.

"She hasn't filled the basement, but that's not to say she couldn't. It's damp down there and she's afraid the moisture will mildew the papers."

"Well, she could get the walls and floor treated—"

"And let workers in? You must be joking."

"Sorry. What was I thinking?"

"I've begged her not to store anything in the kitchen and apparently she's listened. The thought of an open flame and all these papers . . ." He gave a visible shudder.

" 'Burn my house,' " Jack said, looking around at the astounding amount of paper. "As easily done as said."

"Not that she does any cooking anyway." Eddie stepped into the kitchen. "She lives on takeout and microwaveables."

The kitchen looked more like an office—scanner and printer on the counter next to the microwave, computer on the kitchen table. Jack checked out the refrigerator: Lean Cuisine entrées in the freezer on top; milk, cheese, condiments below.

No beer. Damn. Could have used a beer.

He lifted the shade and peeked out the kitchen window into the wildly overgrown backyard. A well-weathered six-foot stockade fence ran along the perimeter.

"Doesn't she ever cut her grass?"

"Not in back," Eddie said. "I asked her once and she said she never went out there, so why bother?"

No sign of a bunny hutch—a long shot anyway—so

Jack dropped the shade and looked back into the dining room at the piles of papers.

"Why would she want to burn all this? Must have spent half her life collecting it."

"Only the last three years or so, actually. Started some time after Steve died."

Jack shook his head. He'd assumed it was a longtime obsession. How had Weezy amassed this collection in only three years?

"Did she ever give you a reason?"

"She refused to say. As I told you, she said I could be in danger if I knew. She was pretty serious about it."

"Ah. So then it's a good bet that her perceived threat is linked to the newspapers."

"That was the impression I got."

Jack grabbed a copy from the nearest pile and handed it to Eddie.

"Okay, then. We'd better get started. I hope you're an Evelyn Wood graduate."

Eddie gave him a baffled look. "Huh?"

"Speed reading. We've got to go through every one of these to see why she's been saving them."

Bafflement turned to shocked disbelief. "Have you lost your mind?"

Jack held his gaze for a heartbeat or two, then said, "Psych!"

Eddie looked ceilingward and burst out laughing. "Oh, man, does that take me back!"

It took Jack back too. They had put each other on so many times growing up, always ending with *Psych!*

The laughter died and they looked at each other.

Eddie said, "If someone really was following us, it means they're looking for this house." He rolled his eyes. "Listen to me: 'they.' That sounds so paranoid."

Jack hid his annoyance. He understood Eddie's

reluctance to believe and his difficulty letting go of the long-held conviction that his sister was cuckoo, but enough was enough.

"Maybe it's time to stop second-guessing Weezy—and yourself, for that matter—and go with the possibility that she's got something here that somebody else wants. That way we can focus on discovering what it is."

Eddie looked out over the sea of paper with dismay. "But where to begin?"

Jack looked at the computer and remembered something.

"How about that flash drive?"

"Yes!"

He pulled it out of his pocket and seated himself before her computer. He reached toward the power button, then pulled back.

"Hey. It's already on."

"What's wrong with that?" Jack said.

He left his on for days.

"This is Weezy we're talking about."

"Yeah. But this house is like Fort Knox."

Eddie shook his head. "It just doesn't seem like Weezy. A running computer is a hackable computer."

Jack spotted a loose cable beside the box. The big jack identified it as a network cable. He grabbed it and held it up.

"Not if she's cut off from all potential hackers."

Eddie smiled. "That's my sis."

He plugged the flash drive into a USB port. A few mouse clicks revealed the contents: a single text file. Jack leaned over his shoulder as he opened it.

It contained URLs separated by blocks of text. They read in silence for a while, then Jack straightened.

"They don't make a lot of sense."

A little like reading the *Compendium of Srem,* where

the author assumed the reader shared a context. But the *Compendium* had been written millennia ago. These were probably only days old, if that. They were riddled with mentions of the Trade Towers and al Qaeda and conspiracies. They were giving Jack a bad feeling.

Eddie shook his head. "Don't you get the impression she's trying to say something without really saying it?"

"Exactly. Let's try some of these URLs and see where they take us."

"They're not live links," Eddie said as he plugged in the network cable, "so I'll have to block and copy."

He launched Weezy's browser—Firefox—and did just that with the first URL.

Jack winced as a 9/11 Truther blog popped up. He'd been afraid of that.

"Scroll down to the comments on Monday's entry," he said. "See if we spot anything familiar."

Sure enough: A familiar chunk appeared as a comment by "Secret Historian," posted yesterday.

Secret Historian . . . Jack had to smile.

Eddie tried three more URLs and found comments identical to excerpts from Weezy's text file. Each site was a 9/11 Truther blog or conspiracy site, blaming either Clinton-Bush-Cheney if they were on the left, or the New World Order if they were on the right. Nobody was blaming Osama bin Laden except for being a tool of the former or the latter.

"I've seen enough," Eddie said. "She's become a Nine/Eleven Truther." He rubbed his eyes. "This is so sad."

"Could be worse," Jack said. "She could be a Holocaust denier or converted to one of those Wasabi Muslims."

"*Wahhabi* Muslim."

"Or one of them too." He shrugged. "Seriously, though, I've got to say I'm a little disappointed. I mean, this is

Weezy we're talking about—the gal who was wise to the Secret History of the World as a teen."

A sad smile from Eddie. "Remember how she used to talk about that? I wish she still did."

So did Jack—because crazy as she'd sounded then, she'd been right. But he couldn't tell Eddie that.

"I would have expected better from her."

Eddie looked at him. "What the hell's that supposed to mean?"

"Well, most people who pay attention to this stuff—I'm not one of them—seem to think the nine/eleven conspiracy theories are just a new rack for the Kennedy assassination doubters and their fellow travelers to hang their hats. The old-school, grassy-knoll true believers are now in the Nine/Eleven Truther movement, trading in *The Warren Report* for *The Nine-Eleven Commission Report.* Weezy always saw beyond that political crap, because when you come down to it, the political crap is trivial."

"Oh, really? And what's *not* trivial?"

Jack wished he could tell him about the Conflict, the cosmic shadow war waged out of sight and influencing everything, and about the approaching all-encompassing darkness, less than a year away. But Eddie already thought Jack a little crazy. Or maybe a lot crazy. Either way, he'd never understand.

"I'm just saying that I'd have figured Weezy to be delving into something more esoteric and elusive. The nine/eleven theories sound just like the December-seventh theories. Sure, there's lots of circumstantial evidence pointing to FDR and his crew and how they deliberately made Pearl Harbor a sitting duck for the Japs, but after almost three quarters of a century no one's been able to come up with anything definitive. Same with the Kennedy assassination. Almost half a century and nobody's found the second shooter."

"He could have been one of the many strange deaths and suicides connected to the investigation."

Jack shrugged. "Yeah. Could be. I can see where you could maybe cover up an assassination conspiracy by strictly limiting the number of people in the know, but something as massive as what they say went into bringing down those towers—rigging the demolition charges and such . . . too many people had to be involved. The world has changed. There's no code of honor and silence anymore. Someone would be talking. Someone would be on *Oprah,* telling the world and looking for a book deal."

Eddie sighed. "Yeah, I suppose." He jerked a thumb at the monitor. "Should we take a peek into her computer? Would that be snooping?"

Jack looked at him. "She's in a coma, she feared she'd go missing, she wants her house burned, and we were followed after leaving her. What do you think?"

Eddie turned back to the keyboard. "Right. Let's start with her documents."

Her e-mail required a password, of course, but so did many of her folders. And the ones that didn't contained documents that were nothing but gibberish.

"At the risk of being called Master of the Obvious," Eddie said after repeated failures to find anything readable, "it looks like she's using an encryption program."

"Surprise, surprise."

"That's our Weezy." He leaned back. "What now? No way we can sift through all—"

Jack heard a noise from the direction of the front room. He grabbed Eddie's arm and shushed him. He listened and heard it again.

"Someone's on the front porch."

16.

Darryl noticed right off how the chatter on the Lodge's front steps died as soon as he showed up.

As usual a bunch of Kickers were hanging out in front smoking—no smoking inside on order from the Septimus folks, so they gathered out here. Some stared, some didn't look at him.

Did it show on his face how sick he was? All he'd been able to think about on the subway back downtown was his AIDS and what he was going to do with the little time he had left. After all, he had cancer too.

He couldn't go back to Dearborn. What for? His ex hadn't wanted anything to do with him when he was healthy—well, other than his alimony and child support checks, and he'd been skipping those—so she sure as hell wouldn't want nothing to do with him sick and out of work. Same with his ma. Hadn't spoken to her in years, and she had a new husband who wouldn't want him around.

He'd stay here. The Kickers were the only family he had. And it was a good family. They took care of each other. They'd help him out if he was sick, but he couldn't tell them *why* he was sick. They wouldn't understand. They'd think he was queer or a junkie. Didn't want nobody thinking that.

Why now? That was what he wanted to know. Just when he was getting his act together and settling himself in a new life, why'd it all have to get ruined by this? Wasn't fair.

He walked inside and found the usual half dozen or so Kickers hanging out. They got quiet too. Really noticeable in the echoey marble foyer. His footsteps sounded like he was walking down a long, empty hallway.

He spotted Ansari, the unofficial head of security for the building, and caught his eye.

"Hey."

Ansari looked away, then looked back. "Hey."

"What's going on? Seems kinda weird around here."

"You look like crap, man."

That took Darryl by surprise. He knew he looked ailing, but not like crap.

"I love you too."

Someone behind him snickered. "I bet you do!"

That got a laugh, and Darryl spun to see who'd spoken.

"What's that supposed to mean?"

"Word came in you're sick," Ansari said.

Darryl felt his blood turning to ice as he looked back at him. "Word? Word from who?"

Ansari shrugged. "Got a call." He pointed to the phone on the slim foyer table against the wall. "Said you got the virus."

Darryl reeled. Someone had *called*? Who? Why? Wasn't that kind of stuff supposed to be private?

"The virus? What virus?"

"You know. AIDS. How long were you going to live here with us and eat with us and not tell us?" His face reddened. "How many of us have you spread it to, you mother—"

"It's not true!" He'd begun to say he'd just found out, but that would be admitting it. And he couldn't admit it. "Whoever he was, he was lying!"

Who'd called? Had to be someone who knew the doctor. And that left Drexler, the bastard. Why would he—?

"Wasn't a he. Was a her."

Her? Orlando's assistant?

"Yeah, well, it's still not true."

Ansari stared at him a moment, then said, "I might believe you if you didn't look so bad."

"Just been off my feed is all."

"Yeah. And now we know why."

Darryl had no answer for that. He looked around and found everybody—including a bunch of guys who'd come in from the front steps—staring at him. He saw no pity, no caring in those eyes, only anger and distrust.

He turned and fled upstairs to his room.

17.

Jack pointed to the steel door leading out of the rear of the kitchen and whispered, "I'll sneak out the back and—"

"Sorry," Eddie said, shaking his head. "Different keys for those, and I don't have copies."

Jack considered his options. Not many. With all the windows barred, his only choice was the front door.

He motioned Eddie to stay put, then eased through the stacks to the front room. Without moving it, he peeked around a window shade and caught sight of a skinny guy in a T-shirt and baggy jeans tiptoeing past, moving toward the front door. He wore a backpack but his hands were empty.

Quickly, Jack stepped to the door, yanked it open, grabbed the guy by his shirt, and pulled him inside.

"Hey!"

"Hey, yourself," Jack said as he slammed the door and pushed him back against it. He gave him a quick pat down as he said, "You're trespassing."

The guy blinked and cringed. "N-no, I'm not! I'm visiting! Just ask Louise! And who are you?" He looked over Jack's shoulder. "And where is she?"

"She's in the—" Eddie began.

But Jack cut him off. "Not here right now."

With a sob the guy closed his eyes and sagged.

"She said you'd find us if we weren't careful. Please don't hurt me."

Jack wasn't sure what to do. Hadn't expected anyone to show up at the house, and now that he had this guy up close and personal, he couldn't buy that he was connected to blondie on the train. And no matter what, he sure as hell hadn't been expecting this reaction.

"Who do you think we are?"

He opened his eyes. "You're them."

"No, we're us. What 'them' are you thinking of?"

"You're the ones responsible."

Jack could feel his annoyance rising. "For what?"

"You know."

Jack yanked him forward by the front of his shirt, then slammed him back.

"Cut the crap! Who do you think we are?"

The guy winced, then looked past Jack at Eddie. Eddie's face must have given something away.

"Hey, wait. You're *not* them, are you. Then who—?"

"I'm Louise's brother," Eddie said.

Swell.

Jack released the guy, but he kept staring at Eddie.

"You don't look like her."

"Doesn't change the fact. Who are you and why are you sneaking around her house?"

"I'm . . . Ted—"

Jack flipped him around and held him face-first against the door while he removed his wallet.

"Hey!"

"Shut up."

"Jack," Eddie said, "is this really—?"

"If his name is Ted, I'll eat his wallet."

Jack pulled out some credit cards and a driver's license. They all read *Kevin Harris*. Jack handed them to Eddie and released the guy.

"Okay, Kevin Harris, what's up?"

He blinked. "What?"

"Who are you and what are you doing here?"

He looked at Eddie. "Are you really her brother?"

Jack shoved him back against the door. "God *damn* it!"

"All right, all right! I . . . I'm a friend of hers. We've been working together."

"On what?"

"It's private—proprietary."

Jack took a stab. "You mean the nine/eleven thing? She told us all about it."

Harris's eyes widened. "No! She wouldn't! She'd never—"

"Oh, but she did," Eddie said, getting on board—finally. "I'm her brother. She trusts me."

"I don't believe you. Why would she endanger her brother and not me?"

Good question, Jack thought.

"From the looks of you," he said, "I think she feels we can handle the risk a little better."

Harris didn't look happy to hear that, but made no objection. Just stood there chewing his upper lip.

Jack watched him, trying to get a feel for him. He looked like a nerd, but that could be an act. If so, he was the Edward Norton of his organization. He'd been genuinely frightened when Jack pulled him inside.

"Open your backpack," Jack said.

"Why?"

Jack gave him his coldest stare. "Look, either you do it or I do it, but it winds up open."

With a sullen expression Harris shrugged out of it and unzipped the large compartment. He pulled out a thick, oversize paperback—a dog-eared copy of *The 9/11 Commission Report.* What a shock. Jack flipped through it and saw either yellow highlighter or underlining or margin notes on almost every page.

Good chance he was for real. And if so, telling him about Weezy's accident might loosen his tongue. If he was connected to the tail, he'd already know about it, so no harm done.

The rest of the backpack held half a bottle of Poland Spring water, a couple of peanut chocolate chip Soyjoy bars—"fortified with optimism"—along with paper clips, an array of pens and highlighters, and a thick manila folder. Jack pulled it out and was starting to open it when Harris snatched it away.

"Hey, that's private!"

"Between you and Wee—I mean Louise?"

"Damn right. And if she told you all about it, like you said, then what's in here won't be news to you."

The guy had a little fire in him.

Jack decided to let it ride and give Harris an apparent victory. He could take the folder any time he wanted.

"Actually, she didn't tell us everything."

Harris pumped a fist. "Knew it!"

Watching him closely, Jack said, "That's because she was run down by a car before we could get the whole story."

He turned a sickly white and sagged back against the door. "Oh, no! They *did* get her!"

No way Harris was faking that. He hadn't known.

"She's not . . . tell me she's not . . ."

Another point for Harris—that would be the first thing a real friend would want to know.

"She's alive but in a coma," Eddie said.

Harris's eyes narrowed. "How do I know that?"

Well . . . probably time to get back to the hospital anyway.

"Time for show-and-tell. We'll take you to her."

18. "It's her," Harris said, standing at Weezy's bedside and staring down at her. "It's really her."

His devastated expression convinced Jack that he was the real deal. The question now would be: Would he believe Jack and Eddie were the real deal?

The guy had already turned out to be a royal pain in the ass . . .

First, back at the house, he'd started questioning the accident and if there'd really been one. Jack had shown him the police report but that hadn't convinced him because it was all about a Jane Doe.

Harris had wanted to take the subway—more public. Jack hadn't—too public. Before getting into the cab Harris had demanded some ID from Eddie and had questioned why he and "Louise" had different names. Eddie had patiently explained that she hadn't changed back to her maiden name since her husband's death.

Harris had reluctantly accepted that as a possibility. Then he'd asked Jack for ID.

Like, yeah, he was going to see something. In his dreams.

Jack had pushed Harris into the cab and he was a twitchfest the whole trip, asking the driver over and over if he was really a cabby and if he was really taking them to Mount Sinai Hospital.

But now . . . seeing was believing.

"Is she ever going to wake up?" he said, his face full of angst as he turned to them.

"The doctor's not sure," Jack said quickly, before Eddie could speak. "It's touch and go. She might enter a persistent vegetative state."

This earned a questioning look from Eddie that Jack ignored. He'd pulled the term out of his store of unwanted coma lore.

"Like that lady in Florida?" Harris said.

Jack nodded. "Exactly. Terry Schiavo all over again." He hoped Eddie would stay clammed.

Harris turned back to the bed and stepped closer to Weezy. He shook her shoulder as he leaned over her. He spoke in a low voice but Jack caught the words.

"Wake up, Louise. You've got to wake up. I think I've found him. I think I know who he is."

"Found who?" Jack said.

Harris jumped and turned. "Nothing. A private matter." He suddenly looked scared. "I don't care what the report says, I'll bet this wasn't an accident. They found her and got to her. They've finally silenced her."

"We can't let that happen," Jack said, flicking a glance at Eddie. "She mustn't be silenced. I think she knew they were closing in, and that's why she came to her brother here. To continue her quest for the truth."

Eddie cleared his throat. "Yes. I, um, run a small security firm—"

Harris stiffened. "Securities?"

Jack wondered why that word would cause a reaction.

"No," Eddy said. "Security—as in building security. You know, hospitals and such." He nodded toward Jack. "This is one of my employees."

Swell. Now I'm working for Eddie.

Jack said, "Yeah. She told us she thought she might need some protection."

Harris snorted and looked back at the bed. "Some protection."

"She was just bringing us up to speed," Jack said. "She was worried about endangering her brother, so she was very stingy with her information."

Harris nodded, a little more enthusiastic now. "Oh, yeah. That was Louise, all right."

"You said it." Jack looked at Eddie. "Like pulling teeth, right, boss?"

Eddie turned away. It looked like he might be fighting tears but Jack was sure he was fighting off a smile from the "boss" line. When he turned back he was composed.

"Sorry. This is very hard."

Jack said, "Let me be blunt here: I'm thinking that she thought someone wanted her dead. Am I right?"

Harris nodded. "Permanently silenced, yeah."

Jack pressed his case. "Well, it's not permanent, not as long as she's breathing and has a chance to come out of this coma. So that means someone might try again. We can't protect her very well if we don't know who we're protecting her from. That's where you come in."

"Me?"

Jack was already winging it, so he decided to push it a little further.

"She told us about someone special, someone close to her that she trusted, but she wouldn't give us a name." Jack narrowed his eyelids and fixed a B-movie stare on Harris. "I've got a feeling that trusted guy is you."

He nodded. "Well, I was—I mean, I am."

"Then you need to fill in the blank spaces she left us—for her sake."

"I don't know . . ."

Eddie said, "I told you: I can't protect my sister if—"

"—if you don't know who to protect her from. Right-right-right. But you need to know that she didn't tell me much. Only just enough to help her find what she was looking for."

"We'll take whatever you can give," Jack said.

He chewed his lip. "Okay. Is there someplace private we can talk? You know, where we can't be overheard?"

Jack thought about that. Julio's was out—didn't want

anyone tailing him there. Then he remembered that they were right across the street from Central Park.

"How about down by the reservoir? We can find an isolated spot in the open where no one's in earshot and—"

Harris made a face. "Ever hear of a parabolic microphone? Someone could be listening in from a hundred yards away. We'd be better off in a bar or a restaurant." He glanced at his watch. "It's way before the dinner crowd. We should have no problem finding an isolated table in a midscale place."

Jack couldn't argue with that. He'd always linked paranoia to longevity, though Harris was taking it a bit far.

"Okay. Let's do it."

But no way Harris was picking the restaurant.

19.

"I guess this is good enough," Harris said.

As the hostess led him and Eddie toward the pub's empty rear dining area, Jack hung back near the door, waiting to see who would follow them in.

Harris had chosen a Mexican place on Lex but Jack had vetoed that and picked this Irish pub on Third Avenue at random. He'd kept his eye out for a tail on the way over. Hadn't made one, but the streets were crowded with summer tourists—a bird-dogger's dream.

A couple of laughing young girls speaking something that sounded like Swedish popped in five minutes later. He waited another five and when no one followed, he joined the other two at the booth in a rear corner. He had Eddie slide over so he could take the outside seat facing the bar area.

A florid-faced waiter with a big belly stretching his vest to the limits of its tensile strength asked in a brogue if they wanted a drink before dinner. Eddie ordered another martini, Harris a Guinness.

Jack shook his head. "Not while I'm on duty. Right, boss?"

Eddie rubbed his mouth. "We'll make an exception this time."

Jack said, "Well, I don't much like beer but maybe I'll try something I saw on tap as I passed the bar. I believe it's called Smithwick's?" He deliberately pronounced the "w."

Eddie appeared to be trying very hard not to roll his eyes.

Jack turned to Harris as the waiter left. "Okay. What can you tell us? You told Weezy you 'found him.' Who did you find?"

Harris hesitated, then shrugged. "She's had me looking into a particular stock account."

Jack said, "You mean a brokerage account?"

"Right. In this case, a UBS account. Opened in Basel, Switzerland, in July of 2001 by a Spaniard named Emilio Cardoza."

Eddie looked as puzzled as Jack felt. "So?"

"It became active the week of September third—the week before the planes hit the towers."

That brought a hush to the table. Jack broke it, saying, "How active, and what was he buying?"

"More like what he was selling." He paused for some sort of effect but it was lost on Jack.

"Are you going to tell us or what?"

Harris sighed. "On September sixth he purchased puts on American Airlines, United Airlines, Morgan Stanley Dean Witter. Lots of them."

Jack saw Eddie's expression register shock but hadn't a clue as to why.

"What's a put?"

They both stared at him. Jack didn't even attempt to explain why he knew so little about the stock market. A person needed a Social Security number to open a brokerage account, and would be expected to pay taxes on the profits. Jack didn't have an SSN and had yet to file a 1040. So, when reading the paper, he tended to skip to another article at first sight of words and acronyms like Dow Jones and NASDAQ.

Eddie said, "A put is an option, essentially a contract that will allow the holder to sell stocks at a specified price by a given date. A call is the opposite, allowing you to *buy* a certain stock at a specified price by a given date."

Jack's turn to stare. "Okay. Could you try that in English? I never learned Wookie."

Harris said, "Look: If you buy a put on United Airlines stock and the price suddenly drops, you pocket the difference between the higher price of the put and lower price of the stock. Puts are sold in blocks of a hundred. Puts for a thousand shares for a stock selling at a hundred bucks a share will net you twenty-five grand if the share price drops to seventy-five."

Another moment of dead silence as that sank in. Jack didn't like the feeling seeping through him. The jets hijacked on 9/11 had belonged to American and United Airlines. That meant . . .

"So this Cardoza was betting that the stocks of those two airlines would drop?"

"You got it. Plus Morgan Stanley Dean Witter as well."

"Why them?"

"They occupied twenty-two floors of the North Tower."

"Holy shit . . ." Jack leaned back. "He knew."

"Sure looks that way."

The waiter arrived with their drinks and asked if they were ready to order their meals. Nobody wanted anything, and that didn't go over too well.

"If you'll be sitting in the dining area," he said with a stern look, "you'll be ordering food."

Well, they needed the privacy—especially with the bombshells Harris was dropping.

But were they private? The choice of the pub had been as random as Jack could imagine. No one was in earshot. He'd been keeping an eye on the bar area. No one there had shown any interest in them, but bars held countless reflective surfaces. Someone could be scoping them out in a mirrored beer sign. Jack had done it plenty of times himself. But even if they were, they couldn't hear—that was the important thing.

To satisfy the food requirement, they each ordered an appetizer. Jack chose the fried calamari. This being an Irish pub, he figured he'd be dealing with the equivalent of breaded rubber bands, but nobody said he had to eat it. The waiter departed reasonably happy.

When they were alone again, Harris pulled the manila folder from his backpack and shuffled through the papers.

"My guy wasn't alone." He peered at a sheet. "Here. In the week before the Towers attack there was no bad news about air travel in general and no bad news about either American or United in particular. Both were trading in the low thirties. Yet on September sixth and seventh, the CBO—"

"The what?"

"The Chicago Board Options Exchange—it handles zillions of puts and calls. It recorded over forty-seven hundred puts on United and less than four hundred calls those days. The volume on the sixth, the Thursday before the attack, was *two hundred and eighty-five* times the average—an incomprehensible increase."

"All in one account?"

"No. In numerous accounts. The people who knew what was coming were moving to cash in."

Jack shook his head. "You've got to be making this up."

"I'm not. Same thing happened to American Airlines on the tenth, the day before the attack—over forty-five hundred puts. Way, way, way above average. Same with Morgan Stanley: twenty-five times the usual daily average in puts. The stock markets were closed the rest of the week after the attack, but when they reopened on the seventeenth, United dropped forty-three percent and American dropped forty. Morgan Stanley dropped too. The result: Anyone who held puts on those stocks cleaned up."

"But everything dropped," Eddie said. "The whole market tanked. Someone could have simply shorted the indexes and cleaned up."

"Not to the extent our boy did. Relatively, the Dow dropped a mere fraction of what United, American, and Morgan Stanley suffered."

The conversation was making Jack gladder than ever that he kept his money in gold.

Harris said, "At that time, a one-hundred-share put on United was selling for around ninety bucks. He bought a hundred of them for nine grand."

"Meaning he had options on ten thousand shares," Eddie said. "How much did United drop?"

"Thirteen bucks."

Eddie whistled. "He made a hundred and thirty thousand on that one deal alone."

Harris nodded. "Fifteen hundred percent profit. But that's not all. Our boy also purchased calls—meaning he expected the stock price to rise—on Raytheon."

Jack looked at them. "Which is . . . ?"

"I've heard of it," Eddie said. "A defense contractor. They make Tomahawk missiles." He sighed, puffing out his cheeks. "I can guess what happened to Raytheon when the market reopened."

Harris was nodding. "Big jump—thirty-seven percent."

Jack was finding all this . . . incredible. Literally.

"Is this for real? I mean—don't take offense—but we have only your word that any of this went on, and we don't know you."

Harris shrugged. "I know it's a lot to swallow, but it's all verifiable. Look it up yourself. The put-call ratios are a matter of public record."

Well, if so, that raised an obvious question . . .

"Hold on a sec. If this kind of bump in activity was recorded, how come no one else noticed?"

"Believe me, plenty of people have noticed. The SEC even launched an investigation—or at least said it did."

"And?"

"And nothing. Have you heard of any arrests?"

"No, but then I don't pay much attention to—"

"I do," Harris said. "I pay a *lot* of attention. And not a single person has been arrested."

"But how do they explain—?"

Harris shrugged. "They don't. It's been dropped."

"Sounds like *How to Spark a Conspiracy Theory* one-oh-one."

"For sure. And the conspiracy theory is bolstered by the fact that two and a half million dollars' worth of puts remain uncollected."

Eddie leaned forward. "Why do you think that is?"

"I don't think they expected the markets to close so quickly. They probably planned to make a quick transaction the next day, before anyone made the connection between the whacked-out put-call ratios and the attacks, and disappear. But the markets stayed closed all week and after that they didn't dare collect."

"What about your boy?" Jack said.

"With his foreign account, he managed to execute the options and get away with it."

"I gather then from what you said to Weezy that you've been looking for this Cardoza and you've found him."

"Well, yes, and no. There is no Emilio Cardoza—at least, the Emilio Cardoza who opened the account doesn't exist."

"Then you haven't found him."

Harris smiled. "Oh, but I have. Louise assumed it was a false identity and asked me to look into it. She bought me tickets to Basel and Madrid and paid all my expenses. With the help of a bunch of euros—also supplied by Louise—I managed to get my hands on a security photo of Cardoza."

Jack spread his hands. "So he does exist."

"Only on paper. I speak decent Spanish and in Spain I showed his photo around and learned that his real name is Bashar Sheikh, a Pakistani whose last known residence was just outside Tarragona, Spain."

Jack's bullshitometer was redlining. Pass a few euros in Switzerland and get a photo . . . show that photo around in Spain and get a real name. All Jack knew about international intrigue was what he'd read in novels, but whatever the reality was, it couldn't be that easy. And Harris was no George Smiley.

Eddie looked equally baffled. "If this is supposed to mean something, it doesn't."

Harris said, "I don't know what it means either. Sheikh hasn't been seen or heard from since the spring of '04. I've never heard of the man, but he immediately looked familiar. I've seen his face before, but I can't place him. But I knew Louise would recognize him because—"

"—she never forgets anything," Jack and Eddie said in unison.

Harris stared at them, nodding. "Right. I guess you two really do know her."

"As only a brother who grew up in her academic shadow could."

Jack remembered how Weezy always did well in school and could have been number one in her class, year in and year out, if she'd chosen to be. Not only did she have that photographic memory, but she could put all her stored data to use—often in ways that were a little too unique for her teachers. Eddie had had a hard time following in her footsteps. Academically, he'd been the Andrew Ridgeley of the Connell kids.

"So anyway, when I got back yesterday I started calling her as soon as I landed."

"Why didn't you call her from Spain?" Jack said.

Harris gave him a look. "Do you have any idea how closely overseas calls are monitored?"

Jack didn't. He didn't travel.

"Okay. You waited till you got back. You called and got no answer, and became worried."

"Right. I mean, I wasn't worried at first. Sometimes she goes off the grid—turns off her phone and doesn't check her e-mail—but never for more than a day. I thought yesterday was one of those days, so while I was waiting I went through my photo files, looking for that face. But it wasn't there. Today I began calling again and still no answer. *Now* I was worried. So I came over." He shrugged. "And the rest you know."

"No, pal," Jack said. "Not even close. You said there were multiple accounts buying those puts. Why did she choose this particular one?"

"You'll have to ask her."

"Well, since I can't do that, I'm asking you."

"Well, then you're out of luck, because she didn't tell me. She tells me only what she thinks I need to know, and I guess she didn't think I needed to know that. But I have an idea."

"We're waiting."

"Emilio Cardoza was listed as from Tarragona. In July of 2001, Mohammed Atta, the leader of the nine/eleven attacks, visited Spain and dropped out of sight in the Tarragona area. It's widely believed he met with high-ups from al Qaeda to finalize the plan of attack. I will bet—although I have no facts to base it on—that they used Bashar Sheikh's home as a safe house."

Eddie tapped the table. "You said he opened his account in July."

"Yep. Right after Atta returned to the U.S. Atta landed in Miami on the nineteenth, and the Cardoza account was opened on the twenty-third. Seems pretty obvious that Sheikh knew the details and decided to cash in."

Jack tried to put himself in that position and couldn't imagine doing something so damn stupid.

"Idiot."

Harris smiled. "Maybe not an idiot. Maybe just greedy. Isn't greed amazing? Isn't it wonderful? Even sucking up to Allah doesn't immunize you. I love greed. It allows me to *cherchez la moolah*."

Swell, Jack thought. I'm having a beer with Gordon Gekko.

20.

"Max lost them," Szeto said.

Ernst grunted and squeezed the phone as he paced his office. "So we still don't know where she lives. Why wasn't I told before?"

Instead of answering, Szeto said, *"They are back at hospital with third man. Josef followed them to restaurant and watches the place now."*

So . . . he'd delayed reporting Max's failure until he could report that the quarry had been spotted again.

"And the woman?"

"Max watches and—wait." Ernst heard some muffled conversation in Polish, then Szeto was back. *"Max, he overhear nurse say woman is waking up."*

"Then get her out of there. Immediately."

"I will call Josef. We have plan in place. We will move upon his return."

Ernst ended the call and put down the phone. When he looked up, the One stood on the other side of his desk.

"Where will you be taking her?"

Ernst swallowed. "The Order owns space in the Meatpacking District. They will take her there. They will find out where she lives. She will be a problem no more."

The One nodded. "And the *Fhinntmanchca*? You have a suitable candidate?"

"Yes. A perfect candidate. I am working on isolating him now. Soon he will have no one left to turn to but me."

The One didn't smile, merely stared at Ernst with those bottomless eyes.

"And then it begins."

21.

Darryl rose from the bed and stepped to the window. He'd tried to nap, but as tired as he felt, sleep wouldn't come. His mind wouldn't stop racing, running high and hot but stuck in neutral and not going nowhere.

He wasn't thinking about the future because he didn't have one. He had AIDS, man. Fucking AIDS. What wouldn't leave his head was the question of *how*. How-how-how?

He'd lain there, searching through his past, looking for a way the virus could have gotten into his body. And then it came to him. That one summer years ago . . .

Stupid! What a fucking idiot he'd been.

He looked down at the street from his third-floor window. The sun was dropping but still had a good ways to go. He had his window open despite the heat. No air-conditioning in this old building, but he didn't mind. He chilled so easily these days. The place was built like a fortress with thick stone walls that kept out the heat. The open window let some in.

How long did he have? He'd have asked the doc but was sure all he'd get was bullshit, any excuse to fill him with drugs that would only make him feel worse and wouldn't work anyway.

His bladder started complaining so he headed out into the hall and down to the john. Too bad he didn't have his own bathroom, but no one did. No one had been living here until the Kickers moved in. The Septimus Order had used it only as an office building and meeting space for a long time, but they'd offered it to Hank for his use. That seemed generous, but Darryl was sure there was something in it for the Order. They'd told Hank that certain of their goals coincided, but hadn't come right out and said which ones.

He stepped into the bathroom. It had two urinals, a toilet stall, and a shower. He was bellied up to a urinal, relieving himself, when a burly, bearded Kicker named Hagaman came in. He lived down the other end of the hall.

"Shit! What're *you* doin' in here?"

"Drivin' a cab. What's it look like?"

"You shouldn't be in here, man."

Darryl had a sudden bad feeling about what was coming.

"Why the hell not?"

"Because you got the sickness, you got the AIDS, and shouldn't be around, spreadin' it."

"Fuck you!"

Hagaman's face got all red. "Hey, I don't know *who* you been fuckin', but it ain't me and ain't never gonna be!"

Darryl tried to hold back, but he lost it.

"Yeah? Well, how's this?"

He turned in a circle, spraying the room with a yellow stream. If Hagaman hadn't jumped back he'd have caught some.

"Son of a bitch!" he shouted, raising a fist. "If I wasn't scared of catchin' something, I'd break your face!"

Darryl tucked himself back in and started toward him, pointing to his own chin.

"Yeah? Let's see ya try!"

Hagaman backed out and hurried away. Darryl might have chased after him and told him a thing or two, but his throat felt so tight he didn't think he could manage a word.

So instead he hurried to his room and kicked the wall as he fought back a sob.

22.

The appetizers arrived. Jack leaned against the back of the booth as Eddie and Harris sampled their food.

Hell of a day so far.

Weezy Connell had come back into his life—in a comatose state, yes, but he hoped that wouldn't be for long.

He felt as if he'd fallen down a rabbit hole. He'd awakened with 9/11 a distant, bitter memory, but very much alive. Now . . .

Eddie sighed. "Nine/eleven . . . it's been misused and manipulated, and it's paraded out every time the powers that be think we need a little injection of fear. We need to put it behind us and move on."

Jack thought about that day. He remembered standing on his rooftop that sunny Tuesday morning with Neil the

Anarchist and some of his neighbors from the building, all staring south. The towers themselves hadn't been visible, but the drifting gray-black plume couldn't be missed. Some had talked of traveling downtown for an up-close-and-personal look. Not Jack. He found the idea ghoulish. And besides, the city was in full lockdown mode.

And then suddenly the smoke changed—more of it, and a lighter color. Something had happened. They all ran down to the nearest top-floor apartment to watch reruns of the first tower's collapse. And then the second went . . .

He remembered the gnawing in his stomach. Let the pundits and politicos and preachers argue about whether or not foreign policy chickens were coming home to roost. None of that mattered. This was his city. And some slimeballs had attacked it. Rage had consumed him.

But he'd gotten past that. Or thought he had. Today was dredging up a lot of buried feelings. The rage flooded back.

"I agree with you about the fear," Jack said. "Yeah, put the fear behind. It's useless. But keep the rage. Stick it in a back pocket and take it out every so often. A gang of oxygen wasters came into our house and killed some of our family. We *never* forget that. And we don't forgive." He slammed a fist on the table. "Ever."

He noticed the two of them staring at him. The intensity of his feelings surprised him. He'd dropped out, turned his back, and gone underground. He'd refused to participate in the machine. And yet, on that day he'd felt part of the city, of its gestalt. Felt as if *he'd* been attacked. He'd taken it personally . . . still did.

That wasn't like him. But it was the way it was.

Go figure.

"All right. End of speech. Back to Weezy."

Yeah, Weezy. What had he learned? That she'd been interested in the owner of a Swiss account who, days before the attack, had bet on United and American Airlines' stock falling and the Tomahawk maker's stock rising. Obviously Bashar Sheikh had prior knowledge. And if, as Harris said, he'd hosted Atta two months before the attack, that would account for it.

But so what? Yesterday's news. What could that have to do with some shadowy "them" looking for Weezy, trying to tail Jack and Eddie to her home? No reason for her to want to torch her own house.

He tried a calamari ring. Better than he'd expected—rubbery, but not vulcanized. He wasn't hungry, though, so he pushed the plate to the center of the table.

"Help yourselves."

As Harris moved to do just that—his hand descending on the rings like a crane in a toy vending machine—Jack leaned forward. Time to get into tough-guy mode.

"Can I ask you a question, Harris?"

"Depends, but okay."

"Who the fuck are you?"

He dropped the rings, partially missing his plate.

"What do you mean?"

"Where are you from? What do you do? How are you friends with Weezy? Basic stuff like that."

"Oh . . . well, I'm a Florida boy—believe it or not, some people are born there; we aren't all transplants from the north. I went to FSU"—he made a tomahawk chop—"go Seminoles. Majored in computer science. Spent years as a systems analyst for Bear Stearns until they got caught with their suspenders down. Now I write medical-imaging software for a company in White Plains. Mostly I work from home, but if I need to go in I just hop Metro North. It's a pretty good gig."

"And how does all this put you in Weezy's orbit?"

"She came into mine when she began posting comments to my blog on tz9-11truthquest."

A blogger. Well, why not? Everyone seemed to be a blogger these days.

"The 'tz' stands for what? *Twilight Zone*?"

Harris gave him a sour smile. "Ha. Ha. If I had a dime for every time . . . never mind. It stands for Ted Zawicki."

"And who's he?"

"The supposed author of the blog—you don't think I'd put my real name on it, do you?"

"Silly me."

Eddie said, "Why did she choose you?"

He looked offended. "Tz9-11truthquest is my site—a sort of clearinghouse for Truther info. Not the first, mind you, but the oldest still operating. Nine/eleven sites and blogs come and go, but tz9-11truthquest hangs in there. It's the Energizer bunny of the field. My blog on the site has become the touchstone for Truther blogs. Everyone who is anyone in the Truther Movement drops in at least once a day."

"Must get real crowded," Jack said. This earned a glare from Harris but before he could retort, he added, "She must have said something special."

"And how. She raised a lot of hackles when she said we were right about conspiracy and the controlled demolitions, but wrong about the who and why. That we had to look deeper. That we were missing something important."

"What's the 'who and why' in your book?" Eddie said.

"The same people who've been running western civilization for centuries. The families and financial interests behind the UN, the Council on Foreign Relations, and the Trilateral Commission."

Jack felt his eyes roll of their own accord. "The New World Order."

"Yeah," Harris said, his tone defensive. "And their

head-of-state lackeys. A plan of sorts was sketched out in a book from a conservative think tank just a year before. It's called *Rebuilding America's Defenses,* and you can read it yourself. It called for 'a new Pearl Harbor' to get Americans off their asses and start kicking Middle East butt. Well, Bush and Cheney and Wolfowitz and all the rest listened and gave us nine/eleven."

"Who does my sister think is behind it?" Eddie said as he poked disconsolately at his Caesar salad. He didn't seem anxious to hear the answer. Appeared to be dreading it.

"That's just it. She never said. Her posts teased with comments like, 'You've got the right crime but the wrong criminal' and 'It's much, much bigger than an excuse to send America off to war.' " He grinned. "Well, you can imagine how that went over. 'Secret Historian' was branded a heretic and a denier and a confuser sent to sabotage the Truther Movement."

"Did she ever explain the 'Secret Historian' name?"

"No, but she used it on my site and others. She was going around to all the sites, pissing them off and acting as a sort of provocateur, but never enough to get herself banned as a troll, because she obviously knew her subject."

"To what end?" Jack said.

"To nudge them out of their Bush-Cheney-Trilateral Commission obsession and start looking for other villains—the real villains."

"And what's her take? What's she think is the real story?"

"She doesn't know. At least that's what she tells me, and I believe her. She knows she's only one person and can do only so much, so she's trying to enlist others to help. She'd love to put together a coalition of these groups and guide them, use them as an investigative team, but she doesn't want to show her face. She doesn't want to be known."

Jack thought about trying to organize and lead a group of these paranoid types. Herding cats suddenly became a snap.

"But she's known to you. She let you see her face."

Harris smiled. "It took quite a while before we got to that stage—lots of encrypted e-mails passed between us before we got around to meeting."

"Let me get this straight," Eddie said, his expression grave. "My sister doesn't think al Qaeda flew those jets into the Towers?"

"Yes, she does. Bin Laden and Zawahiri and Atef orchestrated the whole thing. And she believes the Bush administration and whoever they're connected to leveraged that into an invasion of the Middle East. But she says that's not important."

Eddie's eyes widened. "Not important!"

"Right. She told me that al Qaeda isn't the end of the trail and that this is much bigger than we think. That there's another organization or cabal or camorra whatever pulling al Qaeda's strings and using it for its own purposes."

"Who?"

Harris spread his hands. "That's the zillion-dollar question."

Eddie looked at Jack. "Can you believe this bullshit?"

Jack said nothing as all the disparate bits and pieces he'd learned over the past few years about the Secret History of the World swirled through his brain.

Yes . . . he could believe it.

23.

They found Weezy sitting up in bed sipping water through a straw.

"Wow," she said as they gaped at her from the doorway. "Three visitors at once. I must be popular."

Jack immediately glanced at Harris to gauge his reaction and saw joy and relief in his eyes.

All right, so the guy really cared about Weezy. Why didn't Jack feel he could trust him?

Eddie rushed forward and embraced her. "Weez! When did you wake up?"

"About an hour ago."

Jack noticed that her IV was still running but her catheter bag was gone. He hung back as Harris moved to her bedside and grabbed her hand.

"Louise . . . I was so worried."

"Kevin." She looked puzzled. "I didn't expect to see you here."

"When you didn't answer your calls—"

"How was . . . Europe?"

"Everything we hoped for."

"Excellent." She looked past him and smiled as her dark eyes focused on Jack's. "You look so different, Jack. I never imagined you with a beard." She held out her hands. "I'd never recognize you except for your eyes. They haven't changed a bit."

Feeling awkward, he stepped forward and grasped her hands. Her skin was smooth and warm. He squeezed. She squeezed back, releasing a flood of childhood memories—school buses, endless bike rides through lazy summers, and the Pine Barrens . . . he could almost smell those trees.

"You . . . you still look like Weezy."

She released his hand. "But more of me than you last saw."

"You exaggerate. You look great."

No kidding. The extra weight looked kind of good on her.

She looked at Eddie. "Did Jack find me?"

Eddie nodded. "Yes, he did."

"I knew he would." She beamed.

"Do you know what happened to you?"

"Car accident, I'm told. I have no memory of it." She pointed to her stitched-up scalp. "But I think I'll have a nice souvenir."

Jack thought her tone seemed a little too light. Was she putting on a show? Hiding fear?

"What about leading up to it?"

She shook her head, then quickly pressed her hands against her temples and closed her eyes. "Note to self: Don't shake head." Opening them again, she said, "I remember leaving the house and heading for an Internet café and that's about it."

"Retrograde amnesia," Jack said. "Happens with head trauma."

"Right. You know about that?"

He winked at her. "I read it."

That had been her mantra when they were kids. She'd spout some tidbit of arcane lore and whenever Jack or anyone else would ask how she knew, that was what she'd say.

But he hadn't read it. Through experience over the past year he'd learned too much about head trauma.

"Were you being followed or chased?" Harris said.

"I have no idea."

"Excuse me," said an accented voice from the doorway.

Jack saw a lean black man in scrubs pushing a gurney ahead of him.

"I must take"—he glanced at a yellow slip in his hand—"Louise for an x-ray. Please step aside."

They complied and watched him wheel the gurney up to the bedside and pull the curtain. They waited, heard a few grunts of effort from her, then the curtain reopened and Weezy, propped up on pillows, was wheeled toward the door. She waved as she went by.

"I think I'm going to head home," Harris told her. "A million things piled up while I was away. Now that I know you're safe, I can concentrate on other stuff."

"We need to talk," she said.

"Do we ever. I'll be in touch as soon as I get home."

When she was gone, Jack turned to Harris. "You might be followed."

He grinned. "If so, I'll lose them. No one's tailing me home."

Jack had said it for effect. He figured if Harris was such a big shot in the Truther movement, whoever was interested in Weezy already knew where he lived. But then again, maybe not.

After Harris shook hands with both of them and left, Jack turned to Eddie.

"Did you give the hospital your address?"

"Not yet, but—"

"Your phone?"

"No, but I will before I—"

"Don't. It can be traced to your home."

"I've got to leave a number. What if something happens?"

"You've got mine. Give them that."

"But—?"

"It's prepaid. No billing address connected."

Eddie nodded and headed for the door. "Good thinking." He stopped at the door. "You're not an appliance repairman, are you."

"You're wasting time."

A few seconds after he left, a smiling Dr. Gupta

showed up with a binder in his hand. "Well, well. We've had—" He stared at the empty bed. "Where is Mrs. Myers?"

"Down to x-ray."

Gupta frowned and flipped through the chart. "That cannot be. I ordered no studies, and besides, her chart would go with her. I have it here."

Jack had started moving on "That cannot be." He ducked out into the hall and checked the elevator area. They would have had to take the gurney by elevator. No sign of her there. Already gone. She wouldn't be making a fuss either. She'd be compliant until she realized something was wrong. By then she'd be out of earshot.

Jack took the stairs as fast as he dared. He lifted his shirt and pulled his Glock 19 from the nylon holster nestled in the small of his back. He tended to keep the chamber empty when he was walking around town. He worked the slide to remedy that now, then returned the weapon to its holster.

They'd want to move her off premises ASAP. They couldn't use the lobby because she'd make a scene. Needed a back way.

The hospital had to have a loading dock for food and medical deliveries. After five now. Probably not much activity in those areas.

Okay, if he were going to spirit someone out of here, how would he do it? How about putting her in a box and loading her on a truck? Good, but someone might want to know what he was removing from the hospital. Could be stealing supplies, drugs.

Better: Pretend to be transporting a body to a funeral home. Perfect. People died all the time in hospitals and they weren't taken out through the front door. The two main entrances were on Fifth and Madison, so most likely the loading area would be on a side street.

But how to get there? The medical center covered three square blocks.

He'd have to ask. He hated asking directions.

When he reached the main-floor level he stopped the first maintenance worker he saw.

"The undertakers are taking my mother's body to the funeral home and I need to catch them before they go. Where do I find them?"

The guy sent him down another level. He had to ask again along the way, but finally reached an open receiving area where he spotted the black guy rolling the gurney off the edge of the dock into the open rear of a waiting panel truck. The guy with the bleach-blond hair was helping him. A black body bag lay on the gurney, held in place by duct tape. Whatever was inside the bag was moving.

What? No security?

And then, to his right, he spotted a portly figure slumped over a desk, blood leaking from his scalp.

Jack looked around for somebody, anybody to intervene. No one in sight. That left it all up to him. It meant exposing himself—something he never wanted to do—but he couldn't let this go down.

He pulled his Glock and kept it pressed against his thigh as he hurried toward the pair. He'd loaded the magazine with alternating hardball and hollowpoint rounds. The top round was always a hollowpoint, so one of those was in the chamber now.

When he came within ten feet he called out, "Hey! I need a word with you guys."

The head end of the body bag lifted and movements within the bag increased to a frenzy. The blond guy looked up. Shock of recognition flattened his features and then he was reaching inside his jacket. Jack was a half dozen feet away now and saw a pistol grip jutting from a shoulder holster.

"Let's not," he said.

Gunfire was the last thing he wanted.

But blondie didn't even hesitate, so Jack raised the Glock and shot him twice in the chest. Then he swiveled and put two into the black guy who was fumbling for something under his scrubs top.

A look back at blondie showed him collapsing backward, his arms outflung, his hands empty. The black guy was ninety degrees into a spin move as he hit the floor.

Neither moved again.

Shit. Why were some people such dumbasses? He'd have to put it in high gear now.

With the terrific din of the four reports echoing through the loading area, Jack returned the Glock to its home and grabbed the weapon from blondie's holster—a Tokarev 9, from the look of it. He had no idea what the rest of the day would bring. No such thing as too many guns.

Then he slid the gurney the rest of the way into the back of the panel truck and unzipped the top of the body bag. Weezy raised her head and looked at him, eyes wide, mouth sealed with duct tape. He pulled the tape off, then jumped out and slammed the rear doors. The truck was running. He slid behind the wheel, slammed into gear, and roared up the ramp.

"Jack!" Weezy cried from behind him. "My God, Jack! What just—ow!"

The acceleration slammed her gurney against the rear doors. He'd neglected to lock its wheels.

"Sorry."

The gurney rolled forward again and struck the back of his seat when he stopped at the street. Only one choice here: left turn toward Fifth Avenue. He had to stop at the red light on Fifth so he used the opportunity to pull out his Spyderco and climb into the rear compartment.

"Jack?" Her expression bordered on panic. "What just happened?"

"You almost got kidnapped."

He opened the bag further and saw that Weezy's arms were duct taped against her sides.

"I know, but—"

"Hush." He cut one of the bonds, freeing her left arm. He saw blood on her skin. "They cut you?"

She glanced at it. "He ripped out my IV. It's okay. Jack—"

"Cut the rest while I drive," he said, handing her the knife. "But stay there and don't touch anything."

He locked the gurney wheels and hopped back into the front just as the light turned green.

"Jack," she said, as he turned onto Fifth Avenue, "I heard shots. Who was shooting?"

Change the subject, he thought.

"Who were those men?" he said.

"I don't know! Thank God you came along. But those shots—the blond man was carrying a gun—I saw it under his jacket when he was taping me up. Did he shoot at you?"

"Um, no."

"Then how . . . ?"

As Jack turned onto the wide expanse of East 96th and headed for the FDR Drive, he heard a thump from the back. In the rearview mirror he saw Weezy extricating herself from the body bag. A few seconds later, wrapped in a sheet from the gurney, she began wriggling over the back of the seat.

"Stay down."

"No. I need to be up here with you."

She landed on the passenger side, then adjusted the sheet around her. She had no street clothes, just the hospital gown and the sheet. She sat there trembling.

"Okay, but don't touch anything. Don't leave any prints."

"They were kidnapping me." Her voice shook as the words tumbled out. "Really kidnapping me. I thought I was going to x-ray but instead I was wheeled into this little room where another man was waiting with these rolls of tape. A memory came back then. I'd seen him before—yesterday, I guess it was—when he followed me from an Internet café. Before I could say a word they taped my mouth shut and wrapped me up, then put me in that body bag. I could barely move and it was hard to breathe. I'd imagined the possibility, but the reality . . ." She shuddered.

"Easy, easy," he said. "They failed. That's the important thing."

She was shaking her head. "This has gotten way out of control. I—" She fixed her dark gaze on Jack. "They *did* fail, didn't they. I heard shots. And then the next thing I know, you're unzipping the body bag."

"I just happened along at the right time."

"No. It's more than that. Jack, are you carrying a gun? Did you shoot those men?"

"You don't mince words, do you?"

"And you don't answer questions. A simple yes or no, please."

Tell her? She seemed to have a pretty good idea what the answer would be. And later on, when she'd inevitably hear about two men shot to death early this evening at Mount Sinai Medical Center, she'd put it all together anyway.

She must have taken his hesitation as a refusal to answer.

She sighed and said, "In all my surfing I've picked up chatter on New York sites here and there over the years about a guy who hires out to fix things. Some people call him 'the repairman,' others call him 'Repairman Jack'—"

"Oh, swell name."

She smiled. "You still say 'swell.' Just like when we were kids. That was out of date even then." Her eyes unfocused for a second, as if she were detouring down memory lane, then she was back. "Anyway, some just call him 'Jack.' But somehow—don't ask me how or why—out of all the Jacks in the world, I knew it was you."

"Me? That's crazy."

"I heard about this guy fixing situations and I flashed back to Carson Toliver's locker and all the tricks someone pulled on him, and suddenly I realized you were behind that. Admit that, at least, will you?"

He shrugged. "Yeah, that was me."

"Why?"

"Because he hurt you."

She closed her eyes and leaned her head back. When he heard a sob he snapped a look at her. A tear squeezed out from behind her closed lids.

"You okay?"

She straightened and wiped her eyes with a corner of the sheet.

"I'm fine. You drove Carson Toliver crazy and made a fool of him . . . for me?"

He reached over and squeezed her hand. "You can't let someone hurt your friends and get away with it. Especially not your best friend."

She looked like she was going to cry as her voice teetered on the edge of a sob. "But why didn't you tell me?"

"Couldn't tell anybody. That would bring a lot of attention, and I wasn't looking for any."

"I found your Web site last year and left you a message. You called me back and I recognized your voice. As soon as I heard it I hung up, but I knew it was you."

Jack vaguely remembered something like that. He'd just assumed the person had changed her mind. Happened now and then.

"But back to the questions at hand: Are you or are you not carrying a gun, and did you or did you not use it back there?"

There she sat in an open-back hospital gown under a clumsily wrapped sheet, bleeding from an IV site, recent victim of an attempted abduction, yet back in control of herself and trying to control the situation.

He gave a mental shrug: What the hell.

"Yes and yes."

For a few seconds she seemed taken aback, then, "You shot those two men?"

"Yes."

"Do you think you killed them?"

He'd hit them twice each square in the chest with both a hollowpoint and a hardball. The hollowpoint would do the most damage, expanding upon impact and shredding lungs, major vessels, and the heart.

"Yes."

"Did they try to shoot you?"

"The blond guy was going for his gun but I already had mine out."

"What about the other one?"

"I didn't see a gun on him. But he might have had one."

" 'Might' have had a gun? You didn't know?"

"No."

"But you shot him anyway?"

"If he didn't have one now, he'd probably have one the next time we met. And he'd probably want to get even for his friend."

"But you didn't know if you'd ever see him again."

He glanced at her. "Whoever's looking for you, I don't think they're going to quit. Do you?"

She looked out the window, then back at him. "No. I guess not."

"Well, I'm going to do my damnedest to keep them from finding you."

"You don't need to be involved."

"But I do. And anyway, the point is moot: I am involved. So therefore my chances of running into a guy who wants to kill me are kind of high. I try to avoid situations like that. Sometimes you have to be proactive."

"So . . . you . . . just . . . killed him."

Truth was, he hadn't thought twice about it. Hadn't thought even once, really. He'd seen them wheeling Weezy away and he'd clicked into expediency mode. The last thing he'd wanted was to shoot anyone—too messy, too noisy. He realized now that he'd instinctively positioned himself so that if a hardball round went through one of them, it wouldn't hit Weezy. They hadn't left him much choice.

Them or us.

But her choice of words irked him.

"Don't say 'just.' There's no 'just' killing someone. And these weren't 'just' someones. They were someones who were abducting you. I don't know what their plans were. Maybe they just wanted to question you. Maybe they were going to question you and kill you. I don't know. I may never know. But I *do* know one of them was going for his gun. And I also know that neither of those two will be trying that again."

"You're not the Jack I knew. You're scary."

"I'm nothing of the sort. I would have been perfectly happy to resolve that little problem without fireworks, but I wasn't given a choice. And once the guns come out, you need to keep firing until no one's shooting back. It's not pleasant, but it's the way it is." He glanced at her. "My turn at twenty questions: Why are they after you?"

She sighed. "It's—"

She winced and cupped a hand over the stitches in her scalp.

"What's wrong?"

She spoke through clenched teeth. "My head. I don't think I'm supposed to be up and about yet."

Jack knew she was right. But he couldn't see taking her to another hospital.

"What do you want me to do?"

She lifted her head and lowered her hand. "It's passed. I'll be okay once I get home. I live—"

"—in Jackson Heights. I know. I've been there."

She made a face. "Ew. Did Eddie let you in? Why were you there?"

He told her about how her finger had been tracing "burn my house" on the sheet.

" 'Burn my house'? Why would I want you to burn my house?"

"That's what we wanted to know. That's why we went out there."

"No way. That's been my greatest fear—that someone would burn all the hard evidence I've collected. If anything, I'd be trying to tell you 'don't let them burn my house.' Maybe only the second half was coming through."

"Well, whatever, it sent us out there and I saw your collection. What—?"

Jack's phone rang then: Eddie, and he sounded upset.

"Jack! Where are you? Weezy's gone and all hell's broken loose here! There's a rumor of a shooting—"

"I've got Weezy. She's safe. But you might not be if you hang around the hospital. Go home and stay there. I'll contact you later."

He hung up and turned off the phone. Little chance of Eddie being followed now. Whoever was behind this probably thought they had Weezy in their grasp, so no need to follow her brother. But that would change once they found out their men were dead.

He glanced at Weezy. "That was Eddie. He'll be okay. But you . . . that's a different story. Who's after you?"

"It's a long, long story."

"I know some of it. I had a talk with your pal Harris. I gather from all this that you know something about the nine/eleven attacks that someone wants kept quiet."

Her lips tightened. "What did he tell you?"

"About the puts and calls in the Cardoza account and how he traced him back to a Pakistani named Bashar Sheikh."

"Is that his name? Bashar Sheikh?" Excitement seemed to overcome her fear. "He found him?"

Jack nodded. "Says he has a photo and the guy looks familiar. He's counting on you to identify him."

"Wonderful!" She clapped her hands. "I hope I can."

"Still have the eidetic memory?"

She nodded. "Sometimes it's a blessing, sometimes it's a curse, but, yeah, I still have it."

Jack reached the FDR and turned downtown, heading for the Queensboro Bridge.

"What do you know, Weez? Why are people after you?"

"That's just it: I *don't* know. Not yet. But I'm getting close."

"To what?"

"To why the Trade Towers were knocked down."

Jack suppressed a groan. "You're not going to tell me it wasn't al Qaeda, are you?"

"Oh, al Qaeda members flew the planes, no question about that. And they did it for all the reasons al Qaeda has stated. They're very up front and honest about that. But I believe someone or some group with another agenda had bin Laden's ear and was pushing him toward those particular targets and that particular method of attack."

"'Another Pearl Harbor'?"

"No. It's not the government. We'd have had dozens of whistle-blowers by now if it were. It has to be a secret organization—or organizations. Though I have no proof, I believe the Dormentalists are peripherally involved, but I'm pretty sure the Septimus Order is in the thick of it."

"The Order? They're pretty tight with the Kickers these days."

"I know, but the Kickers didn't exist back on nine/eleven."

Jack shook his head to clear it. He was falling under the spell of her words.

"What possible reason could the Septimus Order have for bringing down the Trade Towers?"

"That's what I want to know."

"Wait—does this have anything to do with your Secret History of the World?"

"It's not *my* Secret History, Jack. It's *the* Secret History. And I'm surprised you still remember it."

Oh, he remembered it, all right. It had been hanging over his life like a Joe Btfsplk cloud. And he'd met a guy who'd lived through most of it.

"Let's just say I've had a change of heart and leave it at that for now. But what could possibly be worth all those thousands of lives?"

"That's what I'm trying to learn, and that's what someone doesn't want me to find out. But I do know this: It all seems to hinge upon one man, a shadowy, elusive figure named Wahid bin Aswad. I call him The Man Who Wasn't There."

Jack wasn't following. "Well, if he wasn't there—"

"Oh, yes, he was. It's just that a process has been under way for years to erase all evidence of his existence."

Jack took the on-ramp to the Queensboro Bridge. Not far to Weezy's house from here.

"How . . . ?"

"You'll need to see to believe."

Jack leaned back, wondering. Sometimes you had to see in order to believe, and sometimes you had to believe in order to see.

Which would this be?

24.

"Max and Josef dead?" Ernst said. "Both of them?"

Szeto stood stiff and straight, almost at attention, on the far side of the office desk.

"Yes."

This was terrible. They'd had her in hand. And now . . .

"How is that possible?"

Szeto shook his head. "I do not know. Is mystery for now. Security was there and then police come. I was prevented from scene. I stay as long as I dare, then I must leave."

Anger quickly overwhelmed bafflement.

"What did she do? Grab one of their guns?"

"I do not know. Max's weapon was missing. One of our brothers in NYPD tells me each shot twice—two kill shots each."

"That sounds like she's trained."

"Very possible. We have investigated this Louise Myers. Very little is available about her. We know her husband is dead. We find much about him but almost nothing about her. That is suspicious. It means she has kept herself secret. Why do that unless she is hiding something?"

"Like past training?"

"Is possible she is intelligence operative. We had no idea. If Max and Josef did not suspect . . ."

Ernst reined in his fury. "They got careless. I'll bet she grabbed Max's gun. He's done nothing right. He chased her into the path of a car. Then he lost track of her brother. And now he got himself and Josef killed."

He saw Szeto's lips tighten. "We do not know that."

. . . possible she is intelligence operative . . .

If true, this was bad. It made eliminating her much more difficult.

"Who do you think she's with? CIA?"

Szeto shrugged. "We do not know."

"No." Ernst let his voice rise, but not too much. No use letting any Kickers out in the hall know he was upset. "We don't know much of anything, do we?"

"We know that Max and Josef had her and were transporting her to truck. We know both shot dead. We know truck taken. We do not know for sure she took it but we assume."

"So if we find the truck, we find her. Are you looking for the truck?"

Szeto smiled. "No need. We know where is truck."

"Explain."

And he did.

25.

"I can explain all this," Weezy said, gesturing to the high stacks of newspapers all around her. "I haven't got the Collyer disease."

Jack smiled. "Yeah. I'm sure you have an excellent reason for keeping every one of these."

"Believe it or not, I do."

Jack had taken a meandering course through Queens until he was certain he wasn't being tailed. Then, after assuring himself her place was empty, he'd left her there and driven the panel truck out to North Corona. He wiped down anything he and Weezy might have touched, then left it in a lot on 108th Street. He didn't know if the police would be looking for it, but it could go unnoticed there for a while. He took the subway back to Jackson Heights and walked up from Roosevelt Avenue, picking up a six-pack of Yuengling lager along the way.

During the interval Weezy had showered and changed into a sweatshirt and jeans that were a bit small for her. Her black hair was wet and glossy, and she'd combed it to the side, covering her stitches.

"Can we start at the beginning?" Jack said.

Weezy nodded. "Probably the best way. Let's go into the kitchen where we can sit."

Once they were settled, Jack set the six-pack on the table next to the computer, twisted the cap off a bottle, and offered it to her. She took it and sipped.

"Never had this before. Good." She held up the bottle. "The downfall of my waistline: pizza and beer."

"You look good."

And he meant it. The extra pounds enhanced her. She'd been skinny to the point of boyishness in high school.

"I'm fat."

"Women don't know what fat is." How many times had he heard Gia complain about the "enormity" of her perfect butt? "As they say, real women have curves."

"Well, I've got bulges on those curves."

"You're way too hard on yourself."

He cracked a brew for himself and took a long pull. Aaaah.

Suppressing a burp, he changed the subject. "Never had a Yuengling? Please don't tell me you drink Bud."

Her dark eyebrows rose. "My old friend Jack is a beer snob?"

"And proud of it."

She smiled. "No Bud—Coors Light. I tell myself I'm cutting calories as I use it to wash down pepperoni pizza." Her smile faded. "I'm a widow, you know."

Jack nodded. "Eddie told me. I'm sorry."

"I am too. Things were going great. Then, four years ago, he bought a gun, took the train out to Flushing Meadow Park, sat with his back against a big oak, and put a bullet through his brain."

"I'm sorry," Jack said again. And he was. He sensed a deep, lingering hurt. "Did he leave a note?"

"Yeah. 'It's all become too much. I'm sorry. Love, Steve.' And that was it." She sighed. "Never a hint that anything was wrong."

Jack tried to imagine how he'd feel if Gia ever did something like that. He failed. At least Steve had thought enough of her to do it where she wouldn't be the one to find his body.

She sipped her beer, then said, "Anyway, as I was going through his things, I went into his laptop and found lots of bookmarks to Nine/Eleven Truther sites. We've both always been into conspiracies and apparently this one tickled him."

"Could there be any connection between his . . . death and what happened to you today?"

She shook her head. "That's tempting, but no. The police traced his movements—applying for the gun permit, waiting for the background check . . . apparently he'd been planning it for some time. I never had a clue. I still don't have any idea why. I don't think I ever will." She shook her head. "But that's not the story. The story is that as I skimmed a few of the sites I came across a photo of bin Laden and his top two deputies, al-Zawahiri and Mohammed Atef. Here. See for yourself."

She turned to her computer and began typing. Soon a black-and-white photo of three bearded guys in turbans popped up. Jack recognized bin Laden but not the others.

"I kept staring at it, feeling something was wrong. And then it hit me. I'd seen the photo before and was sure there'd been a fourth man in it. So I did an image search, but every time I found it, only the same three were in it. No sign of the fourth."

Jack feigned shock. "Don't tell me the famous Weezy Connell memory hiccupped?"

She stuck her tongue out at him. "Not funny. I was worried it had."

"Nobody's perfect."

"True, but it's never let me down yet. So I went hunting through newspapers and magazines."

"Ah," Jack said, glancing at the stacks that filled the neighboring dining room. "I'm beginning to see."

"I was pretty sure I'd seen it in the *Times,* but I wasn't sure of the date."

More mock shock: "You *forgot*?"

"I never forget what I read, but I'm not always aware of the date when I'm reading it, so my brain doesn't form a connection. Anyway, I bought a bunch of back issues from the immediate post–nine/eleven period and found it."

"Where on Earth do you buy old newspapers?"

"Google 'vintage newspapers' and you'll see." She popped up from her seat. "Here, I'll show—oh!"

Swaying, she clutched the back of the chair.

Jack leaped to his feet and grabbed her arm.

"What's wrong?"

"Just dizzy. Not ready for sudden movements yet, I guess."

"Maybe you'd better lie down."

She shook him off. "No way. But maybe a beer isn't such a good idea."

She left the bottle behind and led him on a winding course through the stacks in the living room. She stopped by one next to the stairs to the second floor, counted down to the sixth issue, and pulled out a copy of the *Times.*

Handing it to Jack, she said, "Check out page four."

Jack did just that, and immediately spotted the photo.

"I'll be damned."

The exact same configuration of bin Laden and his buds, but this one showed an extra man. The fourth was bearded and turbanned like the others but caught in profile instead of face on—as if he'd been turning away from the camera when the shutter clicked.

Weezy was tapping a finger against her temple. "Never forgets."

"Who's the fourth guy?"

"Remember I mentioned The Man Who Wasn't There? That's him. Wahid bin Aswad."

"But what's the point of taking him out of the photo?"

"That's what I'd like to know." She crooked her finger at him as she headed back toward the kitchen. "There's more."

Back at the computer she plugged in her network cable, opened the *New York Times* site, and found that issue. But the photo showed only three men.

Jack blinked. "Somebody hacked the *Times.*"

"Yes. Twice. Because I contacted them—anonymously, of course—and told them the photo had been altered. I watched daily and soon the original was restored. Days later, the doctored photo was back in its place."

Baffled, Jack dropped into a chair. "But what does the hacker hope to accomplish? Copies of the real photo have to be all over the place."

"But they're not. The real, four-man photo exists in newspapers, which are disposable. They wind up either recycled or used as landfill or fish wrapping or on the bottom of birdcages. More and more, people are looking to the Internet for their reading and research. If they blog about nine/eleven and want to include this photo, they snag it from the *Times*'s site or from someone else who previously borrowed from the *Times.* And later on, folks snag it from that blog for some use of their own. And on and on and on. The doctored version of that photo is everywhere on the Web. The original with Wahid bin Aswad . . . is nowhere."

Jack shook his head. "But why?"

"I don't know. But it's pretty clear that since nine/eleven, someone's been trying to rewrite history. Someone's trying to erase evidence that Wahid bin Aswad was with bin Laden and company on that day, or on any day, for that matter."

"What do you mean, 'any day'?"

She started mousing around and opened a photo file.

"I did an image search for bin Laden and collected any in which he appeared to be part of a group photo. Then I traced them as best I could to their origins—almost always online news sources. I bought up a lot of old papers and searched out those photos. I found three more that had been altered. In all instances, a single figure had been removed."

"Let me guess: Wahid bin Asswipe."

Weezy frowned. "Oh, that's mature."

"I have a wide streak of immaturity, Weez. I nurture it. And I have a big problem showing even a flyspeck of respect toward bin Laden and his buddies."

"This is serious, Jack."

"Is it? Why?"

"Because the Internet is becoming the source of record

for all but the most serious and dedicated researchers." She clicked on an icon and the doctored three-shot popped onto the screen. "This is a lie. And it's a lie that's being told again and again all over the Web every time it's copied and posted somewhere else. Tell a lie often enough and it can become the truth. Someone is expunging all photographic evidence of Wahid bin Aswad from the Web. Not mentions of his name—those have remained untouched—just the images."

She wiggled and clicked her mouse again and started a slide show of photos.

"Look," she said, tapping the screen over a figure in a group photo. "Here he is at a meeting in Kandahar—I scanned this from a newspaper." A click and the photo changed. "Here's the version that's all over the Web."

Sure enough, one of the bearded wonders was missing from the second photo. The same was true for the next two pairings.

Jack leaned back. "Now that's weird. Why just the photos? Why not erase all trace?"

"Obviously he doesn't want anyone to know what he looks like."

"Sounds to me like a guy who's planning to reinvent himself as a regular, everyday guy."

"Maybe not a regular everyday guy. Maybe someone a lot of people are going to see, someone who doesn't want anyone making the connection."

"I don't know," Jack said. "These photos aren't the best quality, and one bearded guy looks a lot like another." He ran a hand over his own short beard. "See what I mean?"

She laughed, then hunched her shoulders and grabbed her head. "Oh!"

"What's wrong?"

"Need to remember not to laugh." Whatever it was passed quickly and she looked back at him. "You'll never pass for an Arab. You're—" Her computer dinged and she clicked around until . . . "E-mail from Kevin."

"Harris? You trust him?"

She nodded. "As far as being someone genuinely searching for the truth about this, yes. As for his past, whatever he says about that is a lie—unless he tells you he's ex-NSA."

Alarm buzzed down Jack's spine. "What?"

"Strictly low level, and I believe he was let go because of his nine/eleven beliefs."

"Swell."

"You say that a lot."

"I've had lots of cause today. How do you know?"

She pointed at the monitor. "With a little know-how and a lot of patience, you'd be amazed what you can find on the Web. I even found you, the Man Who *Isn't* There."

Jack didn't like that. If Weezy could find him, so could others. Getting harder and harder to stay under the radar. Why couldn't people shut up? These goddamn bloggers with their incessant nattering, feeling they have to be saying something all the time just to fill the empty space on their blog page, and so they talk about some guy they heard about from a friend of a friend of a cousin of an uncle who met this guy named Jack once who might be real or maybe just an urban legend.

Yeah. Urban legend. Go with that.

And. Then. Shut. Up.

Weezy leaned closer to the screen. "It's got a jpeg attached. He must have scanned his photo of Bashar Sheikh."

"That photo kind of bothers me," he said as she downloaded it. "How did he get it?"

Weezy shrugged. "He still has friends in NSA. Probably got a little help." She glanced at Jack. "His heart's in the right place." She hit a few more buttons. "Now to decrypt it."

Jack said nothing. Maybe she was right. He'd seemed genuinely relieved to find her alive in the hospital.

"Okay," Weezy said. "Let's open the photo."

A head shot of—surprise!—a bearded guy in some sort of Muslim skullcap popped into view.

"Harris told me he looked familiar but—"

"He does. Let me pop him up in another photo."

He shouldn't have been surprised that she recognized him right off, but her perfect memory never ceased to amaze him. One of the undoctored photos she'd run through before appeared and she tapped the screen.

"There he is, standing right next to bin Aswad. He's never been identified, but was obviously one of the nine/eleven planners. Now we have a name for him."

She typed out a response, telling Harris where to look, and sent it off.

"So, you've identified Sheikh," Jack said. "You think he's going to lead you to bin Asswi—" Weezy shot him a look. "Okay, okay—bin Aswad?"

"Maybe, maybe not. But it's one more piece of the puzzle. I—" The computer gave out another *ding!* "Kevin again."

Jack watched as the decrypted e-mail appeared on the screen.

OMFG!!! I recognize him now! That's the guy in the torture video I told you about. We need to talk!

"Torture video?" Jack said as Weezy rapid-fired a response.

Not tonight. Save it for tomorrow.

She straightened and faced Jack. "Years ago someone sent Kevin—via his blog—the URL to a specific video on a site that specialized in torture porn. The sender said he'd find it 'interesting.' Kevin told me he'd tried to watch but lasted only a minute or so. Said it was sickening."

"Why would someone send him that?"

Weezy shrugged. "He has a nine/eleven site and blog—maybe someone thought he'd like to see an al Qaeda suspect being tortured. He said the whole site was devoted to torture videos."

"A YouTube for sadists." Jack added that to the long list of things he didn't understand about his species—before pierced nostrils but after Lou Reed. "You think this Bashar Sheikh might have been the torturee?"

"If I'm reading Kevin right, he was." She shook her head. "I don't think I could handle a torture video on a good day. But tonight, with my stomach already rocky . . . no way."

Jack quaffed the rest of his beer and was reaching for another when he spotted hers, barely touched.

"You're sure you don't want it?"

"I'd love it but I'd better not. Don't let it go to waste."

"Beer? Never." He took a sip and said, "Al Qaeda, the Dormentalists, the Septimus Order . . . you've got some heavy hitters there. You sure you want to be a 'person of interest' to them?"

"I don't want to be a person of interest to anyone, but it might not even *be* them. Maybe we'll get an idea when they identify that blond man."

"You said you saw him in an Internet café?"

She nodded. "I rotate my sites but maybe they had some staked out. I mean, I've used that place before. But I noticed he got a call and then began looking around. They must have traced my IP address after I logged on. He followed me out of the café and I began to run . . ." She touched her scalp. "And that's all I remember until I woke up today." She shook her head. "So weird not to remember something."

"Sometimes forgetting is good."

Her expression turned bleak. "Sometimes I wish I could."

Without warning she stepped closer, put her arms around him, and pulled herself against him, pressing her face against his shoulder. She was trembling.

"I get so scared at times," she said, her voice muffled.

After a few heartbeats, Jack put his beer down and returned the embrace. How could he not? She was Weezy. Not the angular body he remembered from their youth, but this was nice . . . better. They'd kissed a few times growing up, but never anything beyond that, never anything serious. It might have gone further if not for her mood swings, and the medications her doctors tried. They drifted apart, drifted close, then apart again. But always, always remained friends.

"Right now, I think you've got good cause to be."

"But it's not just this. It's my brain. It catalogs everything. But that's not where the trouble lies. It's my subconscious. It's got all that information at its disposal—there aren't many brains that can store and retrieve like mine—and as it filters through the jumble, it starts making correlations, spotting patterns, forming possible explanations for what it sees. Sometimes it tells me, sometimes it doesn't. Most times it's not important—curious at best—but sometimes it's . . . terrifying."

"H. P. Lovecraft once said something about how we'd go mad if we knew the real truth."

"You mean, 'The most merciful thing in the world, I think, is the inability of the human mind to correlate all its contents'?"

"Is that a quote?"

She nodded against him. "Uh-huh."

"Exact, I suppose." He had no doubt.

Another nod. "He also said, 'The piecing together of dissociated knowledge will open up such terrifying vistas of reality, and of our frightful position therein, that we shall either go mad from the revelation or flee from the light into the peace and safety of a new dark age.' My problem is that my brain can correlate all its contents, and it's flashing me glimpses of that terrifying reality, and I wish it weren't."

"Even as a kid you seemed to have an intuition about this stuff."

"I knew there was a Secret History—I didn't know the whole story, or even a fraction of it, but I sensed that much of what people considered true was really an elaborate fiction."

"And what's your subconscious say about nine/eleven?"

"That everybody's wrong. And by everybody, I mean the government, I mean the nine/eleven conspiracy theorists, even al Qaeda—bin Laden himself doesn't know the whole truth. Probably thinks he does, but he's been used just like so many others through history."

"And you *do* know the truth?" he said, thinking, Please don't say yes.

"No, I don't. And neither, I think, does my subconscious. But it knows something is very wrong with the stories out there. It's a perfect example of the Secret History. Bin Laden says—and believes, I'm sure—that he attacked the World Trade Towers to strike a blow for Islam and because of the U.S.'s meddling in the Middle East. That will go down as accepted history. But the Secret History could very well be that a group, some secret society or cabal—through inspiration, insinuation, manipulation, and whatever other means—used him to bring down those towers for an entirely different reason."

Jack couldn't buy it.

"Why on Earth—?"

"I don't know. But when I noticed bin Aswad being erased from the photographic record, my subconscious clicked into high gear and didn't like what it saw. It needed more info, so I began gathering it."

"The papers and magazines . . ."

"Yes. They can't be changed. They may not be true, they may be packed with errors, but those errors and untruths are the same as the day the ink hit their paper. The Secret History is there, hidden behind that ink. If only someone would write it down and give me a copy, I could figure it out. But I don't think it's ever been written down. I think it's passed from generation to generation through oral tradition."

Jack flashed on a certain weird and wonderful book.

"What about the *Compendium of Srem*?"

She pushed away and stared at him. "*The Compendium*? How does a skeptic like you even *hear* of that?"

He was tempted to tell her he had the world's only copy sitting back in his apartment, but she'd drive him nuts to see it. He'd have to tell her eventually, maybe even tomorrow, but better to spring it on her.

"Someone told me a tale about Torquemada—"

"And how he tried to destroy it but couldn't, so he buried it and built a monastery over it. I've heard that one. Well, if the *Compendium* was ever under that monastery—if the book ever even existed—it's not there now. Lots of people have searched for it and come up empty-handed."

"You never know."

She smiled. "Right. Probably shelved in the restricted section of Miskatonic U—right next to the *Necronomicon*."

Jack grabbed his beer and finished it. "Gotsta go."

"Oh, no." Her smiled vanished. "You can't. It's been so many years and we've just reconnected and there's so much to talk about and . . . and I don't want to be alone here tonight."

"You mean, stay the night?"

"Sure. I've got a spare bedroom."

"Not filled with papers?"

"We can move them. Please?"

He understood her fright, and felt obliged to ease it, but still . . .

"I guess I should ask," she said, peering at him as he hesitated. "Are you married?"

"Not officially."

"Then what?"

"Functionally."

"Monogamous?"

He nodded. "Very."

She frowned. "Odd. From what I gathered about you, I figured you'd be more the lone-wolf type."

"Used to be. Spent a lot of years that way after leaving home. It was a blast at first."

"I imagine so. I sense you became a bad boy, and all the bad girls love a bad boy."

He experienced a brief torrent of memories, a flash flood of faces.

"Yeah, they do. But then you find a good woman, and she makes you want to become a good man, or at least a better one. And so you try to be."

She was staring at him. "What's her name?"

"Gia."

"You say it like a prayer."

"I don't pray. But if I ever did, she'd be an answer."

Silence lingered briefly, then, "To feel that way about someone . . . to have someone feel that way about you . . . Steve and I had a bond like that. At least I thought we did. I miss it. You're both lucky. I'd like to meet her someday."

"No reason why you shouldn't."

"So you'll stay the night?"

Another spasm of hesitation, then . . . why not? This was Weezy asking. How could he say no?

"Okay, but I'll have to make some calls."

WEDNESDAY

1. A door swung open down the hall. Jack opened his eyes in the dark and listened.

Earlier he'd walked down to Roosevelt for some Chinese takeout. He called Gia along the way and told her he'd be out all night. That was enough for her. Most times she preferred not to know what he was into, and that tended to work out well for both of them—she worried less, and he wasn't distracted by concern that she was worried. He didn't want to get into the details on the phone; he'd tell her tomorrow.

He and Weezy had talked late into the night about old times, and he revealed some of the schemes he'd worked as a teen in addition to Carson Toliver's locker, culminating with saving Mr. Canelli's lawn.

"That was you?" she'd said, wide-eyed. "I never guessed."

"Good. No one was supposed to."

His first official fix. Up till then they'd all been personal. Mr. Canelli was the first ever to hire him.

The talk faded and they called it a night. After making sure all the locks were engaged, Jack moved the newspapers off the double bed in the spare bedroom and helped Weezy make it up for him. They hugged good night and went to their separate beds.

Jack lay under the sheet, facing the window, fully

dressed except for his work boots. The stolen Tokarev lay on the nightstand, his Glock was a hard lump beneath his pillow. Overkill, perhaps, since whoever was after Weezy didn't know where she lived. The first floor was secure—steel doors, iron grilles on the windows—and the second accessible only via ladder, but he wasn't taking any chances. Overkill had its charms.

He heard bare feet on the floorboards, heading for the bathroom, no doubt. But they stopped outside his door. After a few heartbeats he heard it swing open. A weight settled on the mattress behind him and a warm body pressed against his back.

"Weez?"

"You've got all your clothes on?"

"Weez, what are you doing?"

"I need to snuggle," she whispered. He could feel her breath on the back of his neck. "Is it okay if we snuggle? I've gotten used to sleeping alone, but after today . . . I think I need to snuggle. Do you mind?"

How could he refuse her? Anyway, it was just Weezy.

"No. Snuggle away."

"Thanks."

She spooned against him and snaked an arm around his chest, pulling herself closer.

She sighed. "This is nice. I needed this."

Jack agreed it was nice, and if it gave her some comfort, even better. He was just drifting off into slumber when he felt her hand begin to move against his chest in a gentle circular motion. He waited for her to stop but she didn't. Then she began sliding her palm down along his abdomen.

He grabbed her wrist.

"Weezy, what are you doing?"

"Just feeling a little needy."

"With *me*? This is Jack, remember?"

"I know. And maybe that's why. I mean, Jack . . . after all the years we spent together, all the growing up we did together, don't you think we owe each other one time? Just once? That once probably would be ancient history by now if all those meds they tried on me hadn't messed up my already messed-up head, but I'm clearheaded now and we're here together in the same bed . . ."

"Yeah, but I'm taken."

"We predate her."

"Weez . . ."

"It's because I got fat, isn't it."

How to let her down easy? No way this was going to happen, but he didn't want to stomp on her feelings.

"Cool the fat talk. You're not. And if I was in a different situation, I might think it was a great idea. But with things as they are, we'll both regret it. Besides, you're vulnerable right now—"

"Of *course* I'm vulnerable. I've been scared every day and every night. Then my worst fear is realized—someone kidnaps me. Or tries to. But a figure from the past, my tried-and-true friend Jack rides in with six-guns blazing and rescues me. And after we spend some time together I realize I want him—I want him reeeeeal bad."

"I thought you said I was scary and not the Jack you knew."

"I was upset then, but as we talked later I realized the Jack I knew as a kid would do anything, whatever it took, to help a friend. And that's what you did this afternoon."

"Okay, but not to sound like a broken record, Weez, I'm taken."

"I'm not talking an affair here. I'm talking one time for 'Auld Lang Syne,' a moment, a lightning flash, and then we'll have fulfilled a mutual destiny and it will be over. We'll never speak of it again and she never has to know."

"But I'll know."

Weezy wriggled her wrist free of his grasp and pulled her arm back. But she stayed spooned against him. She didn't move and neither did Jack.

Had he hurt her?

She sobbed.

Damn, he had. He turned toward her.

"You're taking this all wrong, Weez. I—"

"No, *you* are. I'm *glad* you turned me down."

What? She'd always been unpredictable but . . .

"I'm not following."

"It means you haven't changed. The whole world is going to hell and nobody knows what's up or what's down, but here you are in the middle of it all, just as steady and true as you were when you were a kid."

"Oh, I don't know about that . . ."

"*I* do. And I'm just so damn happy there's still someone I can count on in this world." She pulled the sheet off and started to get up. Jack saw she was wearing a long, oversized T-shirt. "I'm sorry I put you on the spot like this. I'll—"

He placed his hand against her back.

"Stay."

She froze. "What?"

"You said you needed to snuggle, so let's snuggle. Just . . . snuggle."

After an instant's hesitation, she lay back down and rested her head on his shoulder.

"That's all I really wanted to do anyway. I was just kidding about the other stuff."

"Just testing me, huh?"

"Uh-huh."

Jack doubted that, but with Weezy, you could never be one hundred percent sure. That was what made her Weezy.

"All right, now," she said, settling against him. "Quit your incessant chatter and let me get some sleep."

Jack smiled and stared at the ceiling until her breathing settled into a rhythmic pattern, then he closed his eyes.

2. The sound of shattering glass tore him from sleep. Then another smash.

Downstairs.

Jack grabbed the Glock from under the pillow and leaped for the door. Dropping to his knees he kept his head low as he peeked into the hallway. Then more glass shattered followed by a pair of *whoomps!* as yellow light lit the stairwell at the end of the hall.

Firebombs.

"Jack?"

She was sitting up in bed staring at him. Flickering light through the doorway lit her terrified features as he found his boots and began pulling them on.

"Your greatest fear is coming true. They're burning down your house and everything in it."

Including us.

"Ohmygod! What do we do!"

"We get the hell out and call the FD."

She darted from the bed, screaming, "My papers! My papers!"

"They're goners. We can't save them."

Leaving his boots untied, he followed her into the hall where smoke was pouring up the stairwell. He saw her disappear into her bedroom.

"Weez, we've got to get out!"

"I'm not going out in just a shirt and panties!"

He entered the room to find her pulling on sweatpants.

He stepped to the barred window that overlooked the front yard and saw two men standing by a white van across the street, watching the flames. The van looked just like the one he'd ditched earlier.

Could it be . . . ?

"Shit!"

"What?"

He turned and saw her slipping into a pair of Crocs.

"Guys out front—either to make sure you don't get out, or grab you if you do."

"Oh, God!" Her voice quavered. "What do we do?"

Jack stepped back into the hall. The stairway was a mass of climbing flame.

"A window—out back."

The two bedrooms were lined up along the south side of the house, the stairway and bathroom along the north. None of those windows were barred. Jack led Weezy to the other end of the hallway and checked out the backyard. A guy stood near the bushes along the rear fence.

Both doors covered, but no matter. The doors were downstairs and downstairs was not an option.

He pulled Weezy into his bedroom. After stuffing his phone and his wallet into various pockets, he stripped the sheet from the bed. He tied knots at both corners along the long axis, then opened the window. He kicked out the screen and motioned Weezy onto the sill.

"What?" She held back. "I can't."

Grabbing her upper arm he shoved her toward the opening.

"We haven't got time for 'can't.' Sit on the sill—everything outside but your butt. Now!"

She complied—shakily—and he steadied her until she was positioned outside the window. He handed her one of the knotted ends of the sheet and looped some of the rest around his hips.

"Grab it above the knot with both hands and hold on for dear life. I'm going to lower you."

"I can't do this!"

"I disagree."

He gave her a shove and she tumbled off the sill with a high-pitched yelp. But she held on, legs kicking the air, as he eased the sheet over the edge. Suddenly her weight released. He looked out the window and saw her sprawled on the ground—she'd let go a little sooner than she had to, but she waved up at him, indicating she was okay.

Jack climbed out and crouched, facing the window with his feet on the sill. He slammed the inside sash down onto the sheet, leaving the knot inside. He looked toward the front and then the back as he prepared to rappel down the wall. Spotted a man with a gun come around the rear corner. Must have heard Weezy's yelp. When he saw her he raised his weapon. His attention was fully on Weezy and he seemed unaware of Jack. And the way he was taking his time, he must have been sure she was unarmed.

But Jack wasn't. Freeing a hand he pulled his Glock and fired two quick shots. The second scored, dropping the guy to his knees as he grabbed his shoulder.

Jack slid the rest of the way down the wall in a controlled fall and hit the ground running, pulling Weezy toward the fallen man. He saw them coming and raised his pistol. Jack shot him in the face; his head snapped back as he slammed onto his back.

"Ohmygod!" Weezy cried and dug in her heels.

Keeping his pistol raised ahead of him, Jack virtually lifted her off her feet and yanked her around the corner into the backyard. A quick scan showed it empty, but for how long? The guys out front must have heard the shots.

He used a high-capacity magazine for his Glock 19—fifteen rounds. He'd expended four at the hospital and three more just now. Hadn't brought a spare mag—a fire fight was the last thing he'd expected today—so that left eight in his main carry. Had eleven rounds in the little Kel-Tec P11 strapped to his ankle. Nineteen rounds should carry him through, but you never knew. Wished he'd thought to bring the Tokarev. He could go back and grab the fallen man's pistol—probably another Tokarev—but didn't want to risk it.

Crouching, he peeked back around the corner—no one coming their way along the south side . . . yet. But they could sneak along the north flank if they chose. Had to get Weezy out of the backyard.

The fire had reached the rear of the first floor; its light flickered through the windows. At the far end of the overgrown yard Jack made out the stockade fence. He'd seen it earlier in the day and remembered it looking old and weathered, gray wood tinged with green patches of moss. Must have been put up by Weezy's neighbor because the posts and crosspieces faced this way.

Had to risk it.

"Follow me," he whispered and charged the fence.

When he closed within a few feet he launched himself at it, aiming his shoulder at a centerpoint between two posts and the upper and lower crosspieces spanning them. The impact hurt like hell but the old wood gave way with a satisfying *crack!* Jack kicked some of the uprights free until he had a decent-size opening, then pushed Weezy through. His first instinct was to follow her but he didn't want any pursuit.

"Find someplace to hide."

"But what about you?"

"Be right back."

He hurried back to the house, found a bush near the foundation, and huddled at its base. He knew the first-floor windows were ready to explode into the yard and he didn't want to be here when they did, but he'd give the guys out front one minute. If they didn't show by then, they probably wouldn't show at all, and he'd join Weezy. If they did, he knew exactly what they'd do.

He rubbed his sore shoulder as he stared at the broken opening in the fence, clearly visible in the firelight from the windows. Yeah, that was where they'd go.

He began counting. He'd just passed forty-five seconds when they charged into the backyard, one to his left, one to his right, both in a running crouch. They did a quick look-see around the yard but the hole in the fence captured their attention. Both made a beeline for it.

Jack jumped up and followed, checking to see how they held their weapons. Both right-handed. That meant the one to his left would have to pivot almost ninety degrees before getting off a shot, while the one to his right could fire cross-body in a fraction of the time.

So he shot the one on the right first, then caught the one on the left in mid-turn. Both center-of-mass hits. He pumped another into each as they tumbled to the ground.

Fifteen rounds left.

As he dove through the break in the fence, the first-floor windows exploded, belching flame and smoke and bathing the backyard in fierce yellow light.

"Weezy! It's me! Let's go!"

She emerged from the shadows. "Ohmygod, Jack! Ohmygod!"

He wished she'd stop saying that. Lights were coming on in the surrounding houses and people were starting to lean out windows.

He turned her and propelled her ahead of him, saying, "Get to the street."

They ran along the side of the neighboring house. When they reached the sidewalk he turned her toward Roosevelt and laid an arm across her shoulders.

"Put your arm around my back."

She complied. "But—?"

"Pretend we're a tipsy couple coming back from a party or something."

She leaned against him. "But Jack, I saw you . . . you shot those two men in the back."

"Well, that was the part of their bodies toward me."

"But . . ."

"But what? That's not right, that's not fair?"

"Well, I guess."

"You really believe you play by rules when someone's out to kill you? Think about that, Weezy. If you lose, you're dead. It's not a game. There's no reset button. No rules, no ref to toss a flag and call a foul, no 'fair' or 'unfair,' just live or die."

"When you put it that way, I guess—"

"You *guess*? They firebombed your house and were waiting outside to make sure you didn't escape. Should I have yelled 'Hey!' to give them a chance to turn around and get off a couple of shots?"

"No, but—"

"No buts in this situation. As a guy once told me, 'If you find yourself in a fair fight, you didn't plan properly.' It's some of the best advice I've ever had."

"Okay. Let's drop it. I feel dumb."

"You're not dumb. Violence gets romanticized and ritualized—boxing, football, jousting knights, whatever. But the truth is it's ugly and nasty and comes down to survival by whatever means necessary."

Weezy sobbed as sirens began to howl. "My house!"

Jack had wondered when the realization would hit. She'd been running for her life. Now reality was setting in. He tightened his arm around her shoulders.

"At least you made it out alive."

"But all my papers, all my proof, everything I own in

this whole world . . . it's gone! All gone! It took me years to assemble all that hard evidence. Now it's ash . . . smoke."

"But you're backed up, right?"

She nodded. "Multiple backups. But I scanned only a fraction of the collection, and I'll never be able to reassemble it."

"So . . . they've won?"

"No." Her voice took on a hard edge. "No, they haven't."

"Good. Hold that anger. Nurture it."

They walked on in silence.

Finally Weezy said, "How did they find me?"

Jack had been thinking about that and didn't like the answer.

"The van. I think I saw it out front."

"But you left it miles away."

"Right. But they may have had a GPS tracker in it."

"But why? They couldn't know you'd take it."

"Lots of people track their employees. GPS doodads are cheap and let you know if your man is where he's supposed to be when he's supposed to be there. Someone could have been tailing us from a mile back. And when we stopped at your house so I could check it out, they could have driven by and seen us. Damn. Never guessed. Sorry."

"No, that was my fault for wanting you to drop me off."

"You were feeling woozy."

"Yes, but I could have—*should* have gone with you."

"Hindsight's great, huh." They were almost to Roosevelt. "We need to get back to the city and find you a hotel."

He could book and pay for it with his John Tyleski identity.

"No. I need to go to Kevin's."

Jack didn't like that idea.

"I don't trust him. He could have fingered your place."

"He could have done that anytime. Why now?"

"I don't know. You said yourself, he's ex-NSA."

"Yes, and 'ex' is the operative word—or prefix, rather. He's devoted to finding the truth about this. Much as I don't want to, I need to see that torture video."

3.

Maybe Harris is all right, Jack thought after studying his expression during Weezy's recounting of the night's events. He'd seemed genuinely horrified.

They'd awakened him by ringing his buzzer in the downstairs lobby until he'd answered. Even though he was a long way from senior status, he lived in a senior citizen high-rise in Coney Island. Jack didn't care enough to ask how. In sharp contrast to Weezy's place, his two-bedroom apartment was small, neat, and uncluttered.

The three of them clustered now in the spare bedroom that functioned as an office.

"What do we do now?" Harris said.

Weezy took a breath. "I'd like to just sit and cry, but we need to watch the Sheikh video."

He made a face. "You sure? I lasted maybe a minute before cutting it off."

She seated herself before the computer, hands poised over the keyboard.

"It was sent to you for a reason. Now that we know he had prior knowledge of nine/eleven, we have to see it. What's the URL?"

"It's gone. The URL is a no go. The Web site's still up, but that video is gone."

Weezy leaned back and closed her eyes. "Aw, no."

"But!" Harris grinned as he held up a finger. "Kevin, who always thinks ahead, downloaded it and burned it to a disk."

He turned to a cylindrical organizer atop a bookshelf, popped the top, and pulled out a disk.

"Here you go," he said, handing it to her.

Weezy dropped it into a slot and the three of them waited, Jack and Harris leaning forward, flanking Weezy in the chair.

What followed was ugly. A bearded guy who could have been Bashar Sheikh—Weezy seemed confident he was—had been stripped naked and strapped on his back to a table. He was bloody, especially in his genital area, and screaming in a foreign language. Jack noticed a date in the lower right corner of the frame: *13/3/04*.

Weezy quickly minimized the screen, removing the video from view but leaving the audio.

"What language is that?" Jack asked.

"Some of it's Spanish," Weezy said, leaning closer to the speaker. "But some of it's Urdu."

Jack looked at her. "You know Urdu?"

She nodded. "And Arabic. I decided I'd need to know them if I was going to get serious about this."

"So you just learned them?"

She glanced up at him and shrugged. "I bought some Rosetta Stone programs and learned in no time. It—wait." She turned back to the computer. "Did you hear that? He just mentioned bin Aswad. Oh, God, this could be important."

She grabbed a pen and a yellow pad from a corner of Harris's desktop, then returned to the video and restarted it. She wrote furiously as she listened to the audio.

After three passes, she swiveled her chair toward them and studied her notes.

"Well?" Jack said. "Anything coherent?"

She nodded. "A lot of it's pleas for mercy. He seems to be the prisoner of some CNI operatives—sort of Spain's CIA—because all the questions are in Spanish. The

March 13, 2004, date on the video is two days after al Qaeda bombed the Madrid commuter trains. Sheikh was involved in obtaining the explosives."

"You're sure?" Harris said.

"Well, he admits it, although he seems ready to confess to anything as long as they stop doing whatever they're doing to him."

"And bin Aswad?"

"He says bin Aswad—and there's no mistaking who he means because he calls him by his full name: Wahid bin Aswad al Somar. He says it was on bin Aswad's insistence that the trains were targeted during rush hour—for maximum terror, maximum body count. He claims bin Aswad was at his house for the final planning of nine/eleven and insisted on the same thing for the Towers. Sheikh swears *he* argued for a weekend strike—they could still make their point but without taking all those innocent lives."

"You believe that?" Harris said.

Weezy shook her head. "Not from a guy who shorted all those stocks, but it's possible. He says bin Aswad insisted on a midweek strike for, again, maximum terror and maximum body count."

Maximum terror . . . maximum body count . . . he got his wish.

Jack said, "This is the guy who's been disappearing from the online photos, right?"

"One and the same."

The same big question remained: Why? Jack still could think of only one reason.

"It's got to mean he intends to go legit, where his face is going to be out in public. Maybe he's going to run for office somewhere in the Middle East, or become a UN ambassador or whatever." Jack scratched his beard. "But then again, all he'd have to do was shave off his beard and no one would recognize him."

Harris shook his head. "In that world a beard is important. Growing it fist length or longer shows a devotion to Islam. He must plan on keeping the beard."

Jack looked at Weezy. "Anything else about this bin Aswad or what you're looking for?"

"Nothing specific, but it convinces me more than ever that he's a member of the larger conspiracy, the group that manipulated al Qaeda into striking the Trade Towers."

"But again: Why?"

"That's what we need to find out."

"Maybe the fourth man can tell us," Harris said.

Fourth man?

Weezy shrugged. "If he's even alive, and if we can find him."

Harris grinned. "I think I've done just that."

Weezy straightened in her seat. "He's alive? Where?"

"L.A. Looks like I've got another trip ahead of me."

Jack said, "Anyone care to clue me in on what you're talking about?"

"Long story," Weezy said. "I'll tell you later."

"No offense to Jack," Harris said, "but don't you think we should keep this close?"

Weezy pushed herself from the seat and faced him. "He's saved my life twice in the past twelve hours. I think we can trust him."

"Okay, okay," he said, holding up his hands. "Just saying."

Jack could wait to hear. He already had too much unassimilated data drifting through his brain.

He pulled out his Tracfone. "I'm going to call Eddie."

Weezy frowned. "Why?"

"You need someplace to stay and—"

"She can stay here," Harris said, pointing to the couch against the far wall. "That folds out into a bed."

Jack looked at Weezy. "Your call."

She hesitated, then shrugged. "I might as well. I can work things out with Eddie during the day."

Jack wondered if she and Harris had ever "snuggled."

"Okay. Got a phone?"

She shook her head. "It's back at the house."

He handed her his.

"Take it. I've got others at home. I'll call you later. I've got something I want to show you."

"What?"

"It's a surprise."

If anyone could make sense out of the *Compendium of Srem,* it was Weezy.

4. Ernst Drexler paced his apartment's front room. He could not believe what he'd just heard.

"How does this happen? How does this *happen*?"

A few minutes ago the ringing of his phone had ripped him from sleep. The doorman apologized for waking him, but the visitor in the foyer insisted that this was an emergency. Szeto had entered a few minutes later. As soon as Ernst had seen his expression he'd known the news would be bad, but not *this* bad.

The man stood stiff and straight a few feet inside the door while Ernst ranged the room.

"She is some kind of ninja."

Ernst stopped and stared at him. "You're joking, right? Tell me you are joking."

"That is only explanation. These were three skilled men. They firebombed her house as directed. A perfect job. The house and everything in it is now ash. But all three are dead. Shot dead just like Max and Josef. Max's gun was missing. She must have taken it and used it against them. Max would not give up gun easily. She is ninja."

Had the Order bitten off more than it could chew? Five men killed while trying—unsuccessfully—to corral this one woman. What was she?

"She may be a cold-blooded killer, but she is *not* a ninja."

"She kills, then she vanish. If she kills our men, that means she was not in house when it burns. That means she is still out there."

"Then find her."

"We do not know where she is."

"But you know *who* she is."

"Just barely."

"But now you know where she lived. Learn more about her. Find out who she knows. See if she has family. Do I have to do everything myself?"

He had no time for this. The *Fhinntmanchca* trumped everything else. And what happened later today was crucial to its creation. He'd backed Thompson into a course of action that would leave Darryl with no place to turn, with no option other than the way out Ernst would offer.

5. Darryl was lying on his bed half asleep when he heard a knock. He rose and cocked a fist as he faced the door. If this was that asshole Hagaman . . .

"Yeah?"

The door opened and Hank stepped through. Darryl felt his jaw drop. Hank never came to his room. If he wanted to see Darryl, he always sent someone to fetch him.

"Hey, it's me. What's with the look?"

Darryl got a grip. "Wasn't expecting you. Thought you might be someone else."

"Yeah? Well, you might be wishing it was someone else real soon."

Darryl's gut writhed. "What do you mean?"

"We've got a problem."

"Like what?"

Hank walked past him to the window and looked out at the slowly fading day.

"Not 'what'—who. And that'd be you."

Aw, shit.

Suppressing a groan, Darryl sat heavily on the bed and jammed his hands between his knees.

"So you heard."

"Yeah. Fuck it all, Darryl. You're one of my main men. Why'd you have to go and—"

"I know how it happened," he said. "I've been racking my brain and I finally remembered."

He kept staring out the window. "Do I want to hear this?"

"Yeah. In fact, you gotta. It was a needle."

Hank turned from the window. "You're a junkie?"

"Naw. You know better'n that. It was back in Dearborn when I split from the old lady. I got this puny body, in case you haven't noticed."

"Even punier now."

"Yeah, well, I started going to this gym and—"

"Don't tell me—juice?"

Darryl nodded, thinking how stupid he'd been.

"Yeah. For a price this guy would shoot you up with some kinda steroid—guaranteed to jack you in no time. I looked at some of his customers and, man, were they ripped. I figured that was for me. That's the only time I had any needles since I was a kid. Had to be him. The sonovabitch must've been using the same needle over and over. That's where I got it."

"You idiot."

"Hey, I was single again. Nothing like a cut bod to bring on the babes, right? So I signed on."

"You'd've been better off with a dog. And where's this 'cut bod' you were supposed to get?"

Darryl shrugged. "I never liked working out, so I hardly ever got to the gym. And I stopped the shots after two or three. But that was enough, I guess." He pounded his fists on his thighs to keep from crying. "So fucking stupid!"

"Can't argue with that."

Darryl controlled himself and looked up at Hank. "So what's the trouble you talked about? I mean, I know my trouble, but—"

"The guys want you out of here."

A sudden rush of cold drove him to his feet. "What? They got no right! They can't—!"

"They've got no right, yeah—I make the call as to who gets to stay here. But they're all pretty worked up and worried about catching something and I've got no good excuse for why I should be letting someone with AIDS hang around."

"You can tell 'em all to just fuck off, can't you?"

Hank nodded. "Yeah, I can do that, but that's not the Kicker style, know what I'm saying?"

Yeah, Darryl knew. Hank was the headman—hell, he *invented* the Kickers—but he didn't want to look like the boss. Everyone treated him like he was, but he liked to pretend there was no boss.

"Well, then, tell 'em if they don't like it, *they* can move out."

He sighed. "Darryl, I need a reason why you should stay and they all should go. Got one?"

Darryl's mind raced. They couldn't kick him out. He couldn't let this happen.

"I'm like your number-one assistant, right? So you've

got to keep me here where you can reach me day or night. That works."

Hank shook his head and looked away again. "Afraid not. That ain't gonna fly."

"Sure it is. It makes perfect sense and . . ." A realization sucker punched him in the gut. "Hey, wait. It's you. *You're* the one who wants me out!"

"No, it's them. But I gotta say . . ."

"What?"

He looked at Darryl again. "Working with a guy with AIDS gives me the willies. How do I know I haven't caught it from you already?"

"That'd be impossible, Hank. I don't know much about it, but I know you need a needle or sex or something to catch it. It doesn't just come out the air. You gotta *work* to get it."

"Yeah, well, so you say—"

"That's what everybody says!"

"It's not what your fellow Kickers say. They're scared to have you around. In just a few hours you've become a major distraction. You're all anyone's talking about. And that's not good. We've got an evolution to run and nothing'll get done as long as you're here. So . . . you've gotta go, Darryl. I know it sounds cold, but I've got to put the Kickers first."

"But I *am* a Kicker."

"That's right. And you'll always be a Kicker. You just won't be living here."

Darryl fought back tears. His insides felt like they were tearing in two.

"But where'll I go? I can't go back to Michigan." He didn't know a soul who'd want to take him in except the police—for a ton of missed alimony and child-support payments. "And I don't know anyone to crash with here."

"Get an apartment. Get a hotel room."

"Ain't got no money, Hank. I've been working for you here for next to nothin'."

"I'd hardly call room and board in this city next to nothing."

"I should have five grand in my pocket for finding Dawn."

Hank looked at the ceiling. "Let's not get into that again. Yeah, you found Dawn, but is she here? No. She's with the creepy guy."

Yeah . . . the guy with the eyes.

"Maybe, but if he hadn't taken her, we'd still have her. Not my fault she was stolen away. I still think I got something coming."

Hank sighed. "Yeah, well, maybe you do. I'll dig you up some cash so you can—"

"I don't want money, Hank."

"You can't stay here, Darryl. I'm sorry, but you're too much of a distraction. You've gotta be out of here sometime tomorrow."

Tomorrow? Where was he gonna go? What was he gonna do? This was all he had, all he knew.

"But I can't—"

Hank jabbed a finger at him. "You can and you will. Don't make this any harder than it already is." His voice softened. "I . . ."

He looked like he really and truly hated what he was doing, and that made Darryl feel a little better, but not a whole hell of a lot. Not if he wasn't going to change his mind.

"Maybe I could—"

"You'll always be a Kicker, Darryl. Don't you ever think otherwise. But you just can't stay here."

As Hank started for the door, he half reached out to Darryl's shoulder but then dropped his hand.

He's even afraid to pat me on the back.

He hoped Hank didn't stop on his way out because Darryl didn't know how long he could hold back the tears that had begun slamming against the backs of his eyelids.

"Remember," Hank said as he closed the door behind him. "Gone tomorrow."

When the door clicked shut, Darryl sank back onto the bed, buried his face in his hands, and bawled like a goddamn baby.

6.

"You look tired," Gia said as she sliced Vicky's everything bagel. "Did you get any sleep last night?"

"Some."

Jack had grabbed a few hours of shut-eye, showered, and shown up at Gia's door with half a dozen bagels—including two everythings for Vicky.

He drained his mug of coffee and stepped to the counter for a refill. Gia's super-strong Colombian was working its wake-up magic.

"Ran into two blasts from my past yesterday—Eddie and Weezy Connell from good old Johnson, NJ."

Gia smiled her smile as she dropped the everything halves into the toaster slots. She was barefoot, wearing loose jeans and a tight pink sleeveless top. She had nice deltoids for someone who never worked out.

"Weezy? As in 'movin' on up' Weezy?" She grinned. "Does she live on the East Side in a deluxe apartment in the sky?"

"She was Weezy before *The Jeffersons*."

"How'd this happen?"

"Weezy's got trouble. Stuck her nose into places where, apparently, people don't want to see any unfamiliar noses, and now . . ."

The smile disappeared. "Is she in danger?"

As he reseated himself at the kitchen table, he glanced at the folded copy of the *Post* he'd picked up on his way over. The front page showed Weezy's house engulfed in flames under the headline BACKFIRE! A brief, hastily written article inside told of three dead, unidentified gunshot victims found in the backyard, and how they'd been linked to a van containing firebomb materials parked out front.

"Oh, yeah."

Odors of garlic and onion tinged the air as the bagel heated.

"Can't she go to the police?"

"It's complicated."

"It usually is by the time they call you. Do I want to know any of the details?"

"Probably not. It sounds pretty wacky, and all her reasoning may be way off base, but she's definitely stirred up a hornet's nest."

Gia pulled the bagel halves from the toaster and began buttering them with Jif Extra Crunchy. Jack shook his head. PB on an everything bagel . . . blech.

"Vicky!" she called. "Jack's here and he brought bagels!" She glanced at Jack. "Weezy and Eddie . . . were you close as kids?"

"Yeah. As close to them as anyone. For years Weezy and I were best buds."

"You've never mentioned them."

"Do I mention anyone from those days? To tell the truth, I'll bet I haven't given them a single thought in the last ten or fifteen years."

Pounding footsteps on the stairs, then Vicky charged in.

"Jack!"

"Hey, Vicks."

She threw her arms around his neck and kissed him on the cheek, then darted to the waiting bagel.

"Everything! Awesome!"

She dropped into her chair and tore into it.

"Human bites, Vicky," Gia said as she placed a glass of milk before her. "You're not a crocodile—human bites."

Jack leaned back and looked around as he sipped his coffee. Sun streamed through the open door from the small backyard as Gia wiped the bagel crumbs from the table and Vicky chowed down in lip-smacking joy.

Hard to believe that relentless forces were at work to take all this away, to make a moment like this impossible.

He couldn't allow that to happen, yet had no idea how to stop it.

But Weezy . . . maybe that unique brain of hers could help. Maybe if she added the contents of the *Compendium* to everything else in her head, she could come up with a solution, or at least point him toward one.

A long, long shot, but not trying was not an option.

7. "Nu?" Abe said as his surprisingly dexterous pudgy fingers examined Jack's Glock 19 with practiced expertise. "A cleaning it needs, but otherwise looks all right to me."

"It's seen dead people."

"Seen?"

"Okay. It made them dead."

"All by itself?"

"It had help."

"From you?"

Jack shrugged. "Yeah."

"How many dead people has it seen?"

"Five."

Abe rolled his eyes. "Oy. All at once? Such a thing would be in the papers. It's not."

"Two yesterday afternoon at Mount Sinai. Three more in Jackson Heights early this morning."

Abe's raised eyebrows caused furrows in his extended forehead. "Five in twelve hours?"

"Oh, and like you've never had a cranky day?"

"Cranky like you, I don't get. No one gets." He turned his free hand palm up and wiggled his fingers. "Spill. Details."

Jack gave him a capsule version of Weezy's troubles.

Abe shook his head. "With old friends like her, who needs enemies?"

"I hear that. But she's good people." He pointed to the Glock. "Anyway, that baby there can tie me to five corpses, so I need a replacement."

"All right. Lock the—"

"Done." He'd locked the front door on the way in. "Turned the OPEN sign too."

"Then let's go."

He led Jack down to the basement.

"Hey," Jack said, indicating the dead neon loops over the stairs. When lit they quoted a sign from *The Weapon Shops of Isher*. "What happened to the sign? It worked Monday."

"Dead. And considering the times, I'd be *meshugge* to have it repaired."

The Right to Buy Weapons Is the Right to Be Free . . . no, that would raise a host of warning flags in these political climes.

In the basement, Abe removed a box from a neatly stocked shelf and produced a new Glock 19. He swapped Jack's old loaded magazine for the empty new one, and handed it over. Jack racked the slide to chamber a round.

"Nu, I thought you liked—"

"An empty chamber? Yeah, but with the way things

are going these past few days, an extra millisecond could be the difference between . . . you know."

"You want I should set up a test fire?"

"Nah. I'll be fine. Hell, it's a Glock."

He'd owned at least a dozen over the years. Hadn't failed him yet.

8. Jack strolled east toward Central Park. The plan was to meet Weezy there around one. He'd considered Julio's but decided against it. Easier to spot a tail if they stayed out in the open. The *Compendium* rested in the backpack slung over his shoulder. If Weezy wanted, he'd lend it to her for as long as necessary. He couldn't imagine her turning him down.

He realized he had time for a brew, so he stopped into Julio's before heading for the park.

To his delight he found Glaeken—no, make that Mr. Veilleur—sitting at his table, a half-empty pint of Guinness before him. He looked eighty-something, maybe ninety, with blue eyes, white hair, wrinkled olive skin stretched over high cheekbones. Slightly stooped, but still a big man.

Jack held up two fingers as he passed the crowded bar—Julio spotted him and nodded. He knew what that meant.

"Mister V," Jack said, stopping beside him.

"I was hoping you'd stop by," the old guy said, remaining seated but extending a big, scarred hand. "I came looking for you yesterday, but when I peeked through the window I saw you were with an Oculus, so I moved on."

Yesterday? he thought as they shook hands. Was that all? So much had happened since then, it seemed like a week.

"Figured that. She sensed you and went rushing out."

He nodded. "She no doubt saw me, but she wasn't looking for an old man. She's had an Alarm, I presume?"

"Yeah. Something about a . . ." He concentrated on the pronunciation, determined to get it right. ". . . a *Fhinntmanchca*."

Veilleur frowned. "I haven't heard that word in thousands of years."

Julio brought Jack's Yuengling and pointed to the dwindling Guinness pint. Veilleur shook his head.

As Julio left, Jack took his seat and sipped his lager.

"Diana had no idea what it meant."

"No reason she should. It's a legend from the First Age . . . a sort of Unholy Grail sought after by the Adversary's forces back then."

"Grail?"

"Figuratively speaking. It was supposedly a superweapon, imbued with the Otherness, that could destroy any living thing it came in contact with."

"You mean like John Agar in *Hand of Death*?"

"I have no idea what you're talking about. What *I* am talking about is loosing something very destructive upon this world. But I've always believed it a myth, the equivalent of searching for the Philosopher's stone."

"Then why is it in Diana's Alarm?"

Veilleur leaned back and took a contemplative quaff of his stout.

"That's the disturbing part. An Alarm is often open to interpretation, but if she heard the word *Fhinntmanchca,* then we have to assume that it might not be a myth, that the Adversary has learned how to create such a thing—and perhaps already succeeded."

"What's the danger?"

"Tradition says it will start the Change. The word means 'Maker of the Way.' It would allow the Otherness in so it can change this plane into a place more hospitable—for its own."

Jack shook his head. "Then why do people work for it?"

"They think they'll be rewarded, and kept safe. Perhaps they will be, but I doubt it."

"What about Ra—the Adversary?"

"He's different. He's the One. If the Otherness wins and begins the Change, he'll adapt to a compatible form. But his fellow travelers may not be so lucky." He sighed. "This is not good. I'm meeting shortly with the Lady. Perhaps she'll know something. Do you wish to join us?"

"The Lady? Sure. Haven't seen her since just after the Staten Island mess."

For the past couple of years women of all ages and shapes and sizes and nationalities had been stepping in and out of his life. They all knew more about him than they had any right to, and each was unfailingly accompanied by a dog. He'd assumed there were many of them, but Veilleur had told him a while back there was only one. He'd avoided telling Jack who or what she was. Maybe if he could sit down with her she'd tell him.

Veilleur pulled a pen from his pocket and wrote on a napkin.

"Here's my address. Between Sixty-third and Sixty-fourth. Meet me there at one."

One? Hell, he had to meet Weezy—

An idea hit like a ten-gauge pumpkin ball.

"Can I bring a friend?"

Veilleur frowned. "I don't think that would be wise."

"She's already aware of the Secret History and she's got a brain like no one else's. I think she could be a big help."

"Why haven't you mentioned her before?"

"She was a childhood friend I haven't given a thought

to in years, and suddenly she's popped back into my life."

"Childhood friend . . ." he said, stroking his beard. "That wouldn't be Louise Connell, would it?"

Jack stared at him in shock. "How could you . . . ?"

"Yes, I believe Miss Connell will make an interesting addition." He drained his stout and rose. "Can she be there at one o'clock?"

"Yeah, but—"

"Excellent." He turned and strode for the door. "See you then."

9. Darryl's door swung open and someone said, "May we come in?"

He looked up from where he was sitting on his bed to see fucking Drexler standing there in his fucking white suit. He wanted to charge the son of a bitch, knock him down, beat the living shit out of him.

But Darryl wasn't feeling so hot, and Drexler had his cane, and Hank was standing behind him.

"You bastard," Darryl said. "You sent me to that doctor and he told everyone. Ain't that against the law?"

"It most certainly is. And if you can identify the member of his staff who abrogated your right to privacy, I believe you'll have excellent grounds for legal action."

"How am I supposed to do that?"

"I have no idea. And whatever happens won't raise your standing with your fellow Kickers here, nor will it alter the course of your disease. But I may have an option for you in the latter regard."

"What's that supposed to mean?"

"I repeat my initial request: May we come in?"

Darryl waved them in. "Yeah, sure, whatever."

Drexler stepped inside, followed by Hank who closed the door behind them.

"Darryl," Drexler said, "I believe your AIDS can be cured."

"That's what the medical grifters say, but you and I know it ain't so."

"I am not offering an alternative crackpot therapy. I believe I can offer the real thing."

Darryl stared at him. "You can cure AIDS? Yeah? Fuck you."

"I'm quite serious. But I don't mean that I can do it personally. I'm referring to the Orsa."

Darryl laughed—and had to admit it wasn't a nice sound.

"You're telling me that overgrown jelly bean in the basement can cure AIDS? You must take me for some sort of royal, world-class dumbass."

"Well, not the Orsa itself, but . . . remember the dark streak you saw inside it? It is an ancient, special compound. *That* holds the cure."

Darryl shifted his gaze from Drexler to Hank. "This true?"

Hank shrugged. "I know as much as you do. I just heard about this a few minutes ago."

Back to Drexler. "What's the catch?"

"No catch. Tradition has it—"

A phone started ringing. Drexler pulled his cell from his pocket and stared at it, frowning.

"Excuse me. I must take this."

He stepped out into the hall and lowered his voice, but Darryl could still hear him.

"Finally, some good news . . . Waste no time. I want you to see him immediately. Yes, you personally . . . I don't care about that. You go see him, take whoever you wish, do whatever necessary to learn what he knows, then end this . . . yes, that's just what I mean. I want this over and done with today. *Today,* is that clear? . . . Good."

Drexler returned, looking less distracted.

"Where was I? Oh, yes. Tradition has it that the compound within the Orsa holds the cure to all diseases."

"Riiiiiight."

Drexler's turn to shrug. "I can but quote tradition: 'A night spent upon the Orsa compound will heal all wounds, cure all ills.' "

Darryl snorted. "Yeah. Like they had AIDS back then."

" 'All ills' is fairly comprehensive, don't you think?"

"Maybe. But 'a night spent'? What's that about?"

"You must spread the compound upon the surface of where you lie"—he pointed to Darryl's bed—"and sleep upon it. Spread it on your sheet."

"What? That's crazy!"

"Hey, Darryl," Hank said. "What's the downside?"

"Sleeping on some kinda dirt? You do it!"

Hank's expression was grim. "I've already done it—when I was down and out. And I'm not the one who's going to be out on the street tomorrow."

Yeah, well, there was that. One thing he didn't get, though . . . He looked at Drexler. "Why are you doing this? You don't care about me. You're always trying to get me out of the room. Now you want to help? I don't get it."

"It is true I have tended to lose patience with you at times, but that doesn't mean I dislike you or wish you ill. Did I not arrange medical care for you as soon as I saw those suspicious lesions on your skin? I know you are valuable to Mister Thompson, and when I heard that he was being forced to evict you, I felt I had to act."

"He's offering you a chance, Darryl. This whole Orsa thing is so weird, it just might work."

Hank and Drexler stood before him, silent, waiting.

City sounds drifted in from the street below as Darryl tried to make up his mind.

Seemed crazy, but what if it worked? How could he refuse? And even if it didn't, he couldn't see much downside except . . .

Except that Drexler was offering it. Darryl knew he didn't give a shit about him. He remembered the look on his face yesterday morning when he'd seen those spots. His interest had seemed almost gleeful and . . . calculating.

Maybe it was nothing more than seeing Darryl as a guinea pig, a chance to try out the cure-all dust. If it worked, he'd have struck gold—a license to print money. And Darryl . . . Darryl would be cured.

"Okay," he said. "Let's do it. Bring it on. Bring me this stuff and I'll bed down with it."

"It's not quite so simple as that," Drexler said. "There's a condition . . ."

10.

"There?" Weezy said as they approached the canopied entrance to the apartment building on Central Park West. "He lives *there*?"

Jack checked the address on the napkin: *34 CPW.*

"That's what he gave me."

She stopped in her tracks. "I can't go in there like this. I mean, look at me."

She wore the same T-shirt and sweatpants as last night. No surprise. They were all she had left.

"You look fine."

She shook her head, looking around. "I've got to go buy something else. Of course, I've got no money."

Jack could front her whatever it cost, but that wasn't the point.

"You've got no time, either. He said one o'clock, and it's that now." He took her arm and pulled her forward. "He's not going to mind."

"You said you met him only a few months ago, and you never even knew where he lived until now, so how can you say he won't mind?"

Jack took a breath. He knew he'd have to be breaking the truth to her soon. Might as well be now.

"Because he's from the First Age."

She laughed. "So he's got no fashion sense, right? If that's supposed to make me feel better . . ." She looked at him, studying his expression. "Wait, you *are* kidding, right? You don't expect me to . . . ?"

"Not kidding."

"But the First Age was supposed to be twelve, fifteen thousand years ago."

"Uh-huh."

"So you're telling me we're going to visit an immortal."

"*Former* immortal. He started aging about the time World War Two started."

She stopped and stared at him. "You're serious, aren't you."

He pointed to the backpack slung over his right shoulder. "Completely. I even brought the *Compendium of Srem* along."

He watched her lips try to smile but they never quite made it.

"This isn't funny, Jack. You've always made fun of the Secret History, and that's okay. But this is . . . I don't know . . . mean."

He took her arm and guided her toward the door. "I'd never be mean to you, Weezy. You've got to believe that."

"Strangely enough, I do. But you're telling—"

"That the Secret History is real and I'm taking you to a guy who's lived it—the whole thing."

She said nothing as they stepped up to the liveried doorman.

"Mister Veilleur?"

He smiled and touched the brim of his cap. "Who shall I say is calling?"

"Jack and Louise."

He turned and held the door for them. "He's expecting you. Top floor."

"Which apartment?" Jack said.

The doorman smiled. "There's only one."

"Only one?" Weezy whispered as they approached the elevator. "He has the whole floor?"

"I imagine he's made a few good investments over the last few thousand years."

Once in the elevator and on their way up, Jack pulled the *Compendium* from the backpack. Its covers and spine were made of some sort of metal stamped with letters and symbols.

"Careful," he said as he handed it to her. "It's heavy."

She took it with both hands and stared at the cover. Jack remembered the first time he'd seen it, and knew what she was experiencing: The cover at first would seem decorated with two lines of meaningless squiggles, then they'd blur and morph into English. Two words. *Compendium* ran across the upper half in large serif letters; below it, half size, was *Srem.*

She gazed a moment then looked up at him with an awed expression.

"Then it's true . . . it's true what they said about the text."

Jack nodded. "Yeah. It changes into the reader's native language." He smiled. "And it's got capitalizitosis—big into uppercasing first letters. The Infernals and the One and the Adversary and the Ally . . . you'll see."

She opened it to a random page. "Ohmygod, Jack. Ohmygod! You weren't joking. This is it, really it!" Her eyes widened. "But then that must mean that Mister Veilleur is really . . ."

"From the First Age. Yeah."

He loved the look on her face, a desperate desire to believe battling a fear to commit to that belief, because here was proof of everything she had studied and pieced together and intuited since her teens.

The elevator doors slid open then and the man himself stood there smiling.

"Welcome," he said, extending his hand to her. "Louise Connell, I believe."

Weezy stood frozen, clutching the *Compendium* against her chest as she stared at him.

"Weez, you okay?" Jack said as the moment lengthened.

"Mister Foster?" She looked at Jack. "You didn't say he was Mister Foster!"

What the hell was she talking about?

And then he saw it. How had he missed it? He'd met this man once in his boyhood, but he'd been known then as the reclusive Old Man Foster who owned a piece of the Pinelands near Jack's hometown.

"Are you?" he said. "I had no idea."

Veilleur nodded, his blue eyes twinkling. "It's been decades, and I've aged since then."

Still clutching the *Compendium,* Weezy managed to shake hands with him.

"Come in, come in," he said. "I have someone else waiting to see you. It's going to be like old home week, I fear."

He was a big man, and his bulk had blocked their view of most of the rest of the apartment. But when he stepped aside they saw an elderly woman in a long black dress. She carried a cane and wore a black scarf around her neck. Beside her sat a three-legged dog.

Jack and Weezy spoke in unison.

"Mrs. Clevenger!"

Unlike Mr. Foster—Veilleur—she hadn't aged a day. She and her dog had been something of a fixture around their hometown of Johnson when they were kids. She'd kept pretty much to herself and had been rumored by some to be a witch. By the time they finished high school she'd moved away.

But of course she wasn't a witch, she was . . .

"The Lady!" Jack said. "That was you all along?"

She nodded.

I'm an idiot, he thought.

All these women with dogs traipsing in and out of his life and he never connected them with Mrs. Clevenger. Maybe he should have been less adamant about deserting his past and never looking back, because lately the past seemed to be inundating his present.

Weezy was staring at Mrs. C. "How can this be?" She turned to Jack. "You obviously know more about this than I do."

"Not as much as you think." He looked at the Lady. "I have a feeling today's the day you're going to bring me into the loop. Am I right?"

She nodded. "It is time, I think."

Way past time as far as Jack was concerned.

11. Weezy's mind whirled. Or maybe reeled was more like it.

They sat in the apartment's great room, its huge windows overlooking Central Park's Sheep Meadow. She didn't know much about décor, but knew this place was way out of date. Guys from *Interior Design* would fight over the chance to do an extreme makeover. But she kind of liked it the way it was, with its dark paneling and strange curios and odd mélange of mismatched paintings from all over and, perhaps, all time. A tray of sandwiches—homemade from the look of them—sat in the middle of a table set with crystal and china.

All very nice, except she was seated across from Mrs. Clevenger, a woman who had been elderly when Weezy was a kid, and should have passed on by now, but who looked not a day older than when she'd last seen her. Jack seemed to know her as someone else. He'd called her "the Lady."

And Mrs. Clevenger was seated next to the man she'd recognized as Old Man Foster, who *had* aged, but was going by the name of Veilleur. She wondered how Jack hadn't recognized him. Older, sure, but still a big man like Foster, and the blue eyes and high cheekbones were the same; even the beard was the same shape, though fully gray now.

Mr. Veilleur had announced at the beginning that he might have to excuse himself if his wife needed him. Apparently he'd given the help the afternoon off so they could have privacy.

When Weezy had asked if his wife would be joining them the old man said she was not having a good day.

She got the impression that Mrs. Veilleur didn't have many good days.

So . . . already surreal with Mrs. Clevenger and Mr. Foster—Veilleur—there, but then Jack had launched into this tale of a cosmic shadow war between two vast, unimaginable, unknowable cosmic forces. They had no names, just the labels humans had attributed to them: the Ally and the Otherness.

She'd stifled a yawn. The old tale of Good versus Evil vying for control of Earth or humanity—its oh-so-valuable souls or bodies, or whatever. The same tale that every human culture had invented and reinvented through the ages. She'd heard it all before.

Or thought she had until Jack explained that Earth's corner of reality was not the grand prize, just a piece—and not a particularly valuable one—on a vast cosmic chessboard . . . part of a contest between the two forces, with victory going to the one that could take and keep the most pieces. Commonly referred to as the Conflict, no one knew who was winning.

But these forces weren't so simple as Good and Evil. More like neutral and inimical. The Ally was an ally only in so far as humanity's purposes were in tune with its agenda, which it ruthlessly pursued. It would squash whatever got in its way with no more thought or concern than a human would give to swatting an annoying fly. As long as Earth's corner of reality stayed in the Ally's pocket, humanity could count on benign neglect.

The Otherness was another story. It was decidedly inimical because, in a sense, it devoured worlds, changing their realities, even their physics to an environment more to its liking. Almost vampiric in that it seemed to feed on the agonies it caused along the way. Humans shouldn't take this personally—it did this wherever it gained control.

"The Conflict," Jack said, "is what's been fueling the Secret History."

Weezy glanced at Mr. Veilleur and Mrs. Clevenger and found them nodding agreement.

She'd always suspected something like this, but to hear it from Jack, of all people . . .

She turned to him. "How do you know all this?" She pointed to the *Compendium*—how she hungered to dive into it—where it sat on a side table. "And how did you get hold of that?"

"Jack is one of the Heirs," Veilleur said.

"Heirs to what?"

"To the position I held for thousands of years—leading the Ally's forces against the Otherness."

"Jack?"

She almost laughed, but that was because she was thinking of the teenage Jack. Then she remembered how he'd killed five men over the course of a dozen hours and it didn't seem so ludicrous. The sweet, faithful Jack she'd snuggled up to in the bed—*what* had she been thinking?—had turned into a cold-eyed killer when threatened, and was now back to easygoing, affable Jack.

Two Jacks, polar opposites . . . how did they coexist?

She stared at him. "Really?"

"Really," Jack said, sounding none too happy about it. His expression made it clear that he wanted nothing to do with the job.

"It's a long, long story," Veilleur said. "Back in the First Age, when the Conflict was out in the open, the Ally's forces prevailed after a seemingly endless string of battles. As it retreated, the Otherness triggered a worldwide cataclysm that wiped out all civilization. Humanity had to start from scratch again. I was made immortal and put on guard, because the Otherness had not given up. It had its own immortal at its disposal, and we battled through the millennia. In the fifteenth century I finally trapped him and locked him away—for good, I thought. But on the eve of World War Two, the German army released him. I slew him before he could escape.

"At that moment, with its victory seemingly complete, the Ally released me to age. It retreated, turning its attention to hotter spots in the Conflict. But the Adversary was not finished. He was reincarnated in 1968. In response, Jack and a few others like him were conceived and prepared to take up the role of Defender should that become necessary. So far it hasn't. We hope to keep it that way."

She stared at him. "Jack . . . you're immortal?"

He shook his head. "Hardly. And not going to be if I have anything to say in the matter."

"How . . . how long has this been going on?"

The Lady said, "The Conflict began before the Earth was formed and will continue long after the Sun's furnace goes cold."

Weezy closed her eyes as she felt the facts and ideas and suspicions and suppositions that had filled her brain shift and expand and form new patterns. Because if all this was true—and she sensed it was—it explained so much.

And now, more than ever, she was certain that the nine/eleven attacks were part of the Secret History, which meant ultimately part of the Conflict.

But the *what* and *how* and *why* remained elusive.

"Okay," Jack said, "we know who I am, we know who Weezy is, and we know Mister Veilleur." He leveled his gaze at Mrs. Clevenger. "But who are you?" He held up a hand. "And please don't tell me you're my mother. I thought you were many, but was told you were only one. You're the Lady. I thought then that you might be Gaia or Mother Earth or something like that, but you said it wasn't that simple. So what's the truth? You've popped in and out of the entire course of my life. I think it's time I knew the truth."

She nodded. "So do I."

Jack leaned back and folded his arms. "You have the floor."

"Where to begin?" she said. "Be patient with me. I have never had to explain this before. In the past when you've asked, I've said I was your mother, but that's not even remotely true. I say that because I am female and because I am older than any living thing on this planet." She nodded toward Veilleur. "Even our friend here."

Weezy leaned forward, fascinated. Was Goethe's "eternal feminine" more than just a concept? Was she a real being?

"But I am not your mother in any sense. I have never called myself Gaia, though I have called myself Herta, but I am neither. I did not create you; you created me. I do not nurture you; you nurture me."

"Okay," Jack said. "That's who you aren't . . ."

"As to who I am, perhaps another name would help. Remember what I called myself in Florida?"

"Sure. Anya."

"Anya Mundy, to be exact."

"Anima mundi!" Weezy said. "Soul of the world!"

The Lady smiled at Weezy. "You always were a quick one."

Jack was shaking his head. "I was thinking of the guy who wrote *King of the Khyber Rifles*."

"Helps to know Latin," Weezy said.

He looked at her. "*Another* language?"

She shrugged.

The Lady said, " 'Soul of the world' is closer but not quite accurate. I am, for want of a better term, the embodiment of the sentience on this planet. I was born when the interactions of the self-aware creatures on the planet reached a certain critical mass. Like any infant, I had limited consciousness at first, but as Earth's sentient biomass expanded, so did my awareness. Eventually I appeared as a person—a child at first, then an adolescent, then fully grown."

"The noosphere," Weezy breathed, seeing it all come together. "Vernadsky and Teilhard were right?"

The Lady nodded. "Vernadsky originated the concept, but Teilhard was closer to the truth."

"You've lost me," Jack said.

Weezy spoke as the facts popped into her head. "Pierre Teilhard de Chardin was a Jesuit who theorized that the growth of human numbers and interactions would create a separate consciousness called the noosphere. Needless to say—but I'll say it anyway—this did not endear him to the Church."

"Are we talking cyberspace?"

"No," the Lady said. "There is nothing electronic, nothing 'cyber' about it."

"But where can it go from here?" Weezy said. "What's the next evolutionary step?"

"I don't know," she said slowly. "I sense other noospheres out there—other worlds, other realities with sentient populations—but I can't contact them. I am bound to my creators, to humanity. But perhaps the next step will be our noosphere achieving enough breadth and depth and strength to enable it to reach out and contact other noospheres."

Weezy had an epiphany. "And maybe that will lead to a community of interacting noospheres, which in turn will give rise to yet another level, an übersphere of collective noosphere consciousness."

Weezy felt herself trembling inside. This was wonderful.

Jack leaned forward. "Sounds like you're talking about God."

The wonder of it struck Weezy dumb for a few seconds. "Yes . . . maybe someday we'll create God."

They all sat in silence for a moment, then something occurred to her.

"They call you the Lady. Why? Do you always appear as a woman?"

She nodded. "Always. I don't know why. Strictly speaking, I should be considered an *it,* but I always appear as female. I can choose my appearance—any age, any race, any level of beauty or ugliness—but for some reason I can appear only as female. And I *must* appear, must be physically present in the world. I can be anywhere, but I must always be *somewhere.*"

Jack frowned. "You can't simply disappear, fade back into the noosphere?"

"No. The noosphere is everywhere, and I am its physical manifestation. As such, I must exist in the physical world."

Weezy feared she might explode with . . . what? Glee? Rapture? Triumph? Vindication? But she reined herself in. She believed every word that had been said at this table, but should she? Shouldn't she doubt? Shouldn't she do what she had always told everyone else: Ask the next question?

Is it real, is this the truth, or does it simply seem that way because I so *want* to believe?

She hesitated, then steeled herself to ask.

"Can you show me a different you?"

The Lady frowned. "Normally I would not even consider such a request, but for you . . . what would you prefer?"

"How about . . ."—something way different—"an Inuit woman?"

Mrs. Clevenger blurred, then sharpened to a shorter, darker-skinned woman with almond eyes and black hair braided into two long pigtails. She looked to be in her twenties and was snuggled in a fur-lined parka.

The dog barked and Weezy looked to see a large male husky standing on four legs and wagging its tail.

"Another question," Jack said. "You're always with a dog. Why a dog?"

She shrugged and spoke in a younger, softer voice. "He's my male counterpart. Just as something in the consciousness of the noosphere demands I appear as female—"

"The eternal feminine," Weezy said. It explained so much ancient mythology.

"Perhaps. But the noosphere demands that he appear

as a male dog. I don't know why. I am supposedly his mistress, but he doesn't always listen."

She picked up a knife from the table and held it before her, staring at the blade as she rotated it back and forth. Then she plunged it through the palm of her other hand.

Weezy let out a yelp of shock. "Ohmygod!"

The Lady smiled. "Not to worry. I do not eat or drink, and I cannot be hurt in the usual sense." She removed the knife and the skin immediately sealed itself. "But I *can* be hurt."

She rose and shed the parka, revealing small, dark-tipped breasts.

Weezy heard Jack say, "Yikes," but she could not take her eyes off the deep dimple in the Lady's abdomen to the right of the navel, wide enough to admit two finger-tips.

Then she turned and Weezy gasped as she saw her back. The skin was pocked with hundreds of punctate scars and crisscrossed with fine red lines connecting them. She noticed another dimple in the small of her back, similar to the one in front. For a second she thought she saw light flash within it, but that couldn't be.

She shook her head. *Couldn't be?* What did that mean anymore?

Neither Jack nor Veilleur seemed surprised, although Jack looked uncomfortable. He'd apparently seen it before.

"What . . . what happened?"

"Opus Omega," she said, then pointed to the *Compendium*. "You will read about it in there."

Again that instantaneous flash from the dimple. Weezy cocked her head and leaned a little to the right—and froze as she saw light from the window.

The dimple was a tunnel, a through-and-through passage.

Weezy didn't ask about that . . . wasn't sure she wanted to hear the answer.

"*All* about it?" she asked.

The Lady raised the parka back over her shoulders. It was closed when she turned to face her.

"Much of it. The *Compendium* is ancient and long out of date. Jack knows some of what is not in there. He can fill you in. Study it well, Weezy."

"And keep a special eye out for this," Veilleur said, speaking for the first time since they'd sat down.

He passed her a slip of paper on which he'd written a strange word: *Fhinntmanchca*.

"What is it?"

"A legend. See what, if anything, the *Compendium* has to say about it."

"I don't think she should be wasting her time on things that never were and never shall be," the Lady said.

Veilleur shrugged. "There's been an Alarm about it. We can't ignore it."

The Lady turned to Weezy. "Absorb all you can. Use your brain to help us thwart the Adversary."

The charge overwhelmed her. "Me? What can I do that you can't? What can I learn that you don't already know?"

"I have blind spots. Many things that involve the Ally and the Otherness are shielded from me."

"Like the *Fhinntmanchca,* perhaps?" Veilleur said, a smile peeking through his beard.

She sighed. "Perhaps. At times I can sense the Adversary's presence and know what he is doing—he is human, after all—but other times he seems to wink out of existence. He is active on a number of fronts now. Some are petty, involving simple vengeance, others are hidden from me. But he has a plan . . . he most certainly has a plan."

"To do what?"

"Open the gates to the Otherness and let it flood

through. And that will be the end of you and, as a consequence, the end of me. For once the Change occurs, the Ally will not want us back. By combining your knowledge of known history with the secrets of the First Age, you may find a way to impede the Adversary, or perhaps even stop him. He *is* fallible—he has made mistakes in the past—and therefore stoppable."

By me? Weezy thought. *Me?* I don't think so.

12.

"I have to go *in* there?" Darryl said, staring at the Orsa.

"Well, no." Drexler spoke from where he stood about ten feet away with Hank. "But you do have to reach in and remove the compound. 'He who would be healed must remove the compound from the Orsa.' Or so tradition says."

Darryl did not like that idea one bit. He didn't want any part of him inside that thing. But for a cure, he might go through with it.

"But the thing's alive. You said so yourself. And I'm reaching into its mouth and—"

"It doesn't *have* a mouth. It doesn't eat in the sense you're thinking. It draws sustenance from contact with the Opus Omega column buried beneath it. That column is planted at an intersection point in the Nexus Grid. That is why we dug up the concrete there, so the Orsa could have contact with the column and draw life from the Grid."

Darryl scratched his scraggly jaw, wondering what the hell Drexler had just said. Bunch of gobbledygook.

"I don't know, man . . ."

"See that groove encircling the very end there?"

He saw it. Maybe half an inch deep running around the conical end, maybe a foot in from the tip.

"Yeah?"

"That is a plug of sorts. You simply have to remove it, then reach inside for the compound. Place the compound in the bin by your feet as you remove it. Very simple."

Easy for you to say.

He stared at the thing. The light reflecting off its dull surface partially obscured the vein of brown dust within. He adjusted his angle to study it. He wondered how it had got in there. Then again, what did it matter? He had to get it out.

Okay. Here goes.

He slipped his fingers into the groove and felt the Orsa's surface ripple as he touched it. He stifled his own ripple—of revulsion—and kept his grip. Leaning back he began to pull and twist.

The plug moved surprisingly easily, almost as though the Orsa was helping to push it out. Darryl didn't know if he liked that idea. But maybe the Orsa wanted to be rid of it, like getting a splinter removed from its skin.

He thought of that old story about somebody removing a splinter from a lion's paw, and then the lion becoming his friend. Maybe that was how this worked. If he removed the plug, the Orsa would be his friend and cure him.

Finally it released with a slurping *pop!* He could have sworn he heard the Orsa sigh as the plug fell into his hands.

"Excellent," Drexler said. "Now, begin removing the compound."

Darryl stared at the pocket left by the plug. A ways beyond it lay the vein of dust. He reached in, immersing his arm to the shoulder.

"Hey, it's warm in here and kind of wet."

"Does it smell like fish?" Hank said.

"Not funny, Hank."

Thankfully it didn't smell like anything.

His questing fingers found the compound and he pulled out a handful. He stared at it. Brown and powdery, with little flecks of what looked like fine gravel.

Are you the stuff that's gonna make me better?

"Okay. I got some."

"You must remove it all."

He looked at the vein. It ran pretty far in.

"All? How am I gonna get to it?"

"By doing what is necessary."

"You can do it, Darryl," Hank said.

I don't need a cheerleader, Darryl thought. *I need someone to do this for me.*

But since no one was going to volunteer . . .

He dumped the compound into the bin and returned to his task. He stretched as far as he could, removed more, but the rest was beyond his reach.

He turned to Hank and Drexler. "I'll need a hoe or something to get the rest out."

"No-no!" Drexler said, waving his hands. "You might damage the inner membranes. That mustn't happen."

"Okay, then, how do I get to the rest?"

"Just crawl in and get it," Hank said. "Let's get this done with."

Darryl stared at the opening and didn't like that idea one bit. Something about this thing made him afraid. But he didn't see any way around it.

"Inside," Drexler said. "You must enter to retrieve the rest. And don't forget: You will be cured not only of AIDS, but of every illness hidden in your body. If you have a cancer, it will be gone; if you have hardened arteries, they will be cleared."

Well, that didn't sound so bad.

"All right. I'm going, I'm going."

He put one arm in, followed by the other. Then, taking

a deep breath, he ducked and slipped his head and shoulders inside.

Warm in here . . . much warmer than he'd figured. Light from the room filtered through. The sides of the cavity were softer than around the plug, and much, much softer than the Orsa's hide.

But forget about that—just grab as much of this junk as you can and get out.

Even better: Start grabbing the compound and pushing it behind him—the tight space made it hard but it was doable. That way he could scoop it up once he slid back out.

He cleared out the new area of the vein within reach. The dust seemed lumpier here.

Almost to the end. Just a little more and he'd be finished. As he inched farther in, he thought he felt the sides tremble. He froze, waiting to feel it again, wondering if he'd really felt it.

All remained still. Maybe he'd caused it himself. Maybe he'd just felt his own vibrations. More than ever now he wanted to get out of here ASAP.

The urgency pushed him forward again, stretching his fingers toward the final deposit. He grabbed a handful and felt some larger lumps. He pulled it closer and opened his hand. In the dim light the lumps had definite shapes. They looked familiar. Almost like—

Teeth! These were human teeth!

Just then the sides trembled again, but this time they tightened against him.

No!

He began a frantic struggle backward, pushing as hard as he could against the slick, rubbery surface, but his hands slipped and the space grew even smaller.

He screamed.

The walls began to weep a clear, sour fluid that pressed

against his face. He sealed his lips against it but it ran in through his nostrils. It soaked through his clothes and into his skin. And then the trembling in the walls organized into ripples running from his head, along his body, and down his legs. He felt the compound he'd pushed back beside his legs begin to slide away, following the ripples.

The walls tightened further, molding to him, sealing against him until he couldn't move a finger. He tried to scream again but the walls were so tight he couldn't draw a breath. He loosed a strangled groan that allowed the fluid to rush into his mouth. It ran down his throat, seeping through his tissues from within and without.

As his vision and consciousness dimmed he saw the hazy figures of Hank and Drexler through the encasing semitransparent walls. One figure struggling to move his way and the other holding him back.

Drexler! He knew all along! He set me up!

13.

"An awful lot to absorb," Jack said as he exited the Brooklyn Battery Tunnel and took the ramp to the southbound BQE.

He'd degaraged his own car for this trip, and the big black Crown Victoria moved easily into the flow. Traffic on the dreaded Brooklyn-Queens Expressway wasn't bad at the moment, but come 4 P.M. it would start to thicken into motorized sludge.

In a way he wished it were later. He knew a couple of good Russian restaurants out where they were headed. He could treat Weezy to some primo borscht. Wouldn't mind a little himself.

But she looked too dazed to eat. He felt sorry for her. What he'd learned in an incremental process over the past two years had been dumped on her in a matter of an hour.

She slumped in the passenger seat with the *Compendium*-laden backpack clutched against her chest like the handbag of an Omaha matron crossing Times Square.

"Yeah, a lot," she said after a bit. "I've been accused of having wild theories, but they're flat-out nothing compared to the reality you three just laid on me. Even though this doesn't contradict anything I've assumed or conjectured, it's going to take a while to sink in. I knew the truth behind the Secret History was big, but I never dreamed it was *this* big."

"Big as it gets."

"Who's this 'Adversary' Mister Veilleur was talking about?"

"He's the Otherness's point man."

"Does he have a name?"

"He does." *Rasalom.* "But we don't speak it."

"Why not?"

"Because he hears, and then he comes looking for whoever's taking his name in vain. So why don't we just call him 'R'?"

"Is he as scary as you're making him sound?"

"Ohhhhh, yeah," Jack said as memories flooded back. "I've seen him walk on water and float in the air, and he can paralyze you with a look."

"You're kidding, right?" Weezy looked at him. "No, I can see by your face you're not. He did it to you, didn't he."

He nodded. "Twice."

"So he had you in his power and he released you. That doesn't make sense, unless he doesn't know you're the Heir."

"Oh, he knows. The first time, he let me go because he said killing me then would spare me the pain that lay ahead in my life, and he didn't want to do that."

"Pain? Did he mean your father? I heard about that. What a terrible thing to happen to such a nice man."

"That was just the tip of the iceberg."

"It gets worse?"

"Much. Someday I'll tell you about it. The creep feeds on human death, pain, fear, misery, degradation. He had a feast with me."

"I wonder if he was here for nine/eleven?" she said. "He would have had a smorgasbord of fear, panic, grief, and misery. You could literally feel the panic in the air."

"Tell me about it. I live about four miles uptown from the Trade Center and—" A startling idea flashed to life. "Do you think he could have been behind the attacks?"

"You mean, could R be bin Aswad? I've never seen him. Does he resemble the man in the photos?"

"Hard to say, what with the graininess and the beard. But Sheikh did say he wanted maximum death and terror, which would be right in line with R's tastes."

"But that's what every terrorist wants. That's why they're called terrorists. And although I can't tell you exactly why, my gut tells me there was more than just a gourmet feast for R behind those attacks. But I still don't understand why, when R had you at his mercy, he didn't eliminate you."

"I doubt he'd admit it, but I think he's afraid to harm me."

"Why? You have some hidden powers you haven't told me about?"

He barked a laugh. "I wish!"

Traffic was light. They'd zoomed along the Gowanus and were now segueing onto the Belt Parkway. The monstrous, looming towers of the Verrazano Bridge ruled the landscape ahead.

"No," he said. "He's afraid of Veilleur."

"An old man?"

"Except R doesn't know he's an old man. He thinks he's still young and powerful and immortal, like himself. Back in the fifteenth century, Veilleur—R knows him by another name—tricked him and imprisoned him for centuries. I think he's wary of another trap. Since his reincarnation he's seen no sign of Veilleur, but he knows he's out there. Probably thinks he's waiting for a misstep, then he'll pounce. So he's keeping a low profile. Killing me would tip his hand . . . or maybe he thinks I'm out here as bait. Whatever, he seems to be leaving me alone."

Weezy sat silent a moment, then said, "I don't know how many years Mister Veilleur has left, but it can't be too many. I mean, he's *old,* Jack. What happens when he dies? Will R know?"

Jack found the prospect unsettling. That was the day he'd assume the Defender role.

"He might, he might not. Remember, he has no inkling that the Ally released Veilleur. In R's mind, Veilleur is immortal. So, if he stops sensing his presence, he has more reason to suspect that he's found a better way to conceal himself than that he's up and died."

"But what if he *does* sense his death? What happens then?"

"Then all hell breaks loose, because I'll be the point man and I haven't the faintest idea of how to stop him." He looked her in the eye. "You'd better get to reading, sister, and put that subconscious of yours into high gear. Find us something."

14.

"What the—?"

Hank ripped free of Drexler's restraining grip on his arm and rushed over to the end of the Orsa. Darryl's protruding lower legs had stopped kicking. He grabbed the ankles and pulled, but couldn't budge him.

He turned to Drexler who was ambling his way as if nothing had happened. "What . . . what . . . ?"

"Be calm, Mister Thompson. Be calm."

"But it's . . . it's *eating* him!"

He arched his brows. "Appearances can be deceiving."

Hank wanted to wipe that arrogant, self-satisfied look off his face. He balled a fist. In fact—

"Do not presume to try to injure me, Mister Thompson. You will mightily regret it."

Yeah, he probably would. Probably get the Kickers ejected from the Lodge. Hank needed this place. A perfect base of operations. He relaxed the fist.

"That's one of my men! Get him out!"

"That is beyond my power—quite beyond anyone's power."

Hank pushed past him and stared through the Orsa's translucent flank at the still form trapped within. Not a hint of movement, of breathing, of life. He looked like a swimmer frozen midstroke in a cloudy glacier.

Darryl . . . poor Darryl. Telling him he'd have to pack up and move out had been one of the hardest things he'd ever had to do. Darryl had his faults, but he'd been devoted to the Evolution, and devoted to Hank. Someone Hank could trust. Since his brother Jerry's death he didn't have too many people he could trust. Sure as hell not Drexler.

"He's dead!" Hank said, still staring. "You killed him!"

"Not dead, Mister Thompson. Your friend is still alive but has entered a special state."

"You promised to cure him."

"I never said *I* would cure him."

Hank turned to him. He wanted to break his bird-beak nose.

"Don't play word games with me."

"Very well, I did promise him a cure and I am delivering on that promise."

Hank pointed at Darryl's still form. "You call *that* a cure?"

"He's not cured yet. It's a process that takes some time, and has only just begun."

"He's fucking dead, Drexler. The thing smothered him."

"On the contrary, he's quite alive, just not in any way we're accustomed to seeing. The Orsa has taken over his bodily functions and put them in a suspended state while it works its—dare I say?—magic upon his diseased tissues."

"You said all he had to do was sleep with the compound or whatever."

Drexler pointed his cane at the streaks of brown dust around Darryl and inches beyond his outstretched hand. "He is."

Hank repressed an urge to strangle him. "Don't push me."

Drexler inclined his head. "I apologize if that sounded provocative. While I didn't entirely lie to him, I did bend the truth."

"Where'd you bend it—the part about him being cured?"

"No. He *will* be cured. I simply failed to mention what *kind* of sleep would be required and where it had to take place. You see, in order for the Orsa to cure him, he must sleep within it."

Hank couldn't believe he was standing here listening to this crap—and believing it. No way he would have bought a single word without having seen this . . . *thing* sitting in front of him. But the Orsa was real. And he'd seen it swallow Darryl.

"There's a curious aspect to the process: The afflicted one must enter the Orsa willingly."

Hank found himself nodding. Yeah, if that was true, he could see why a little verbal sleight of hand could be needed.

But a piece was missing . . .

"So, you did this all for Darryl's good. Considering how you can't stand him, that's very white of you."

He wondered if Drexler got the joke, seeing as that was the only color he ever wore.

Drexler shrugged and gave one of those European it-was-nothing pouts. "One does what one can for his fellow man."

"Yeah, right. You set him up."

Hank saw it now: Drexler had recognized the rash and sent Darryl to one of the Order's docs for confirmation. Once AIDS was confirmed, he made sure everyone in the Lodge knew Darryl had it, which eventually put Hank on the spot about letting him live among the others. Darryl wound up desperate and ready to do anything to keep from being kicked out—even crawling into the butt end of the Orsa.

Fast work.

Well, his business card identified him as an "Actuator" . . . a guy who made things happen, got things done. And he'd got this done. Saw an opportunity and seized it.

Had to admire a guy like that.

Had to watch out for him too.

"How long does this cure take?"

For the first time, Drexler looked unsure. "Not long."

" 'Not long'? What does that mean? An hour? Half a day? A day? What?"

"I don't know."

"You don't *know*? You know everything else, how come you don't know that?"

Drexler gave him a weak smile. "Because there has never been an Orsa before. There will never be another."

Hank stared at him in shock. "You mean this has never been done before?"

Drexler shook his head. "Never."

15.

The man who was more than a man, who was known as the One to members of the Septimus Order, and as Mr. Osala or "the Master" to members of this household, sat in his bedroom and waited.

Ever-faithful Gilda had informed him of yesterday's trespass, telling him she'd caught the girl opening one of his desk drawers. From the sound of it, he doubted she'd seen anything of importance. And even if she had, she wouldn't understand. He had instructed Gilda to leave the door ajar today. Knowing the girl as he did, he was sure she would find a second look impossible to resist.

He wondered what he should do with her. She was a burden. She complained constantly of her confinement here. He would have let her end her life that night but for the uniqueness of the child she carried, so deeply redolent of the Taint. Foolish, pathetic Jonah Stevens had thought he could use that child against him. It might have worked, but would have been a very long shot. For that reason alone he should eliminate the girl and her child.

However . . .

The day might come when he would have need of the child. If the *Fhinntmanchca* achieved his purpose, the point would be moot. In that case he could foresee no use for her or her offspring, except perhaps as a brief amusement. But should the *Fhinntmanchca* fail . . .

Better to hold the child in reserve, and make sure it and its reluctant incubator remained in good health. To that end—

The door to the outer room—his office—squeaked as it opened. He rose and waited until he heard one of his desk drawers slide, then stepped into the office. The girl had her hand in the drawer.

"Perhaps I can help you find what you are looking for."

Her startled reaction was almost comical. She stared in openmouthed shock as she flushed crimson.

"Mister Osala, I . . . I was just . . ."

"Just snooping?"

She took a breath, gathered herself, and faced him with a defiant expression.

"Yes, I suppose I was."

Well, well, well. Perhaps he'd underestimated her mettle.

"Is that how you repay my hospitality?"

"Hospitality? How about total imprisonment?"

He shook his head. "We will not have this conversation again."

"Okay, then. How about I'd like to know more about the guy who's got me locked up in his house?"

"I've told you—"

"Yeah, I know what you've told me, but how do I know it's true?"

She was trying his patience now.

"Because I say it is."

"Really? And what about this other ID in your drawer here? And the way you've been changing your looks. Who's the real you?"

She could never know that. Wouldn't be capable of understanding if she were told. As for that other identity and his change in appearance . . .

A man he thought he had destroyed was slowly rising from the ashes. His resilience was remarkable. He needed another crushing blow to complete his destruction. He had researched the man's circumstances and determined the perfect point of attack. He would insert himself into the hated one's life and obliterate it from within.

Of course, the success of the *Fhinntmanchca* would render his preparations a waste of time. But making plans to annihilate an enemy was almost as enjoyable as the act itself, so he proceeded anyway.

Just as he would proceed with assuring the safe birth of this Tainted child.

"The real me?" he said. "The real me is looking out for you and your baby. To that end, I have scheduled an appointment for you with an obstetrician later this week. He will examine you and—"

"Obstetrician? What for? I don't want to deliver it! I want it *out*!"

"That is not an option right now."

Her voice rose. "It's now or never! I'll be too far along!"

Reached out and brushed his fingertips across her forehead.

"Silence."

She quieted and stood there, staring at him.

"You vex me as you are," he told her. "So you will change. You want this child. You will do anything to assure its well-being. And you are happy here. You do not wish for anything beyond these walls. Now, return to your room for a nap."

She turned and walked from the room.

Perhaps he should have put an influence into her earlier—it would have prevented her little excursion back in May—but he had enjoyed the subtle, savory susurrance of her uncertainty and frustration, floating through the duplex like background music. And he'd been unsure of the effect on the new fetus. But the fetus was more mature now and . . .

And the *Fhinntmanchca,* the Maker of the Way, was imminent. If the fetus was damaged by the influence, what matter?

Only the *Fhinntmanchca* mattered.

16.

The bright orange, twenty-five-story wireframe mushroom of Coney Island's iconic Parachute Jump dominated the skyline as they approached Harris's apartment building.

"How does he rate a senior-citizen apartment? Probably subsidized too."

"His mother lived there. After she died he took it over. It's still in her name."

As they approached the building, Jack noticed two men sitting in a car with a good view of the entrance. Might be waiting for a friend . . . or waiting for Weezy. Were that the case, it meant they knew where Harris lived.

"Do you really need to see Harris again?"

She nodded. "I need that disk with the Sheikh video. I want to listen again and make sure I've got an accurate translation."

He pulled into the curb a hundred yards or so past the entrance.

"Wait here. I'll go get it."

"I'd better go with you," Weezy said, reaching for her door handle. "He might not—"

Jack gripped her arm. "I think someone's watching the place. Good chance they know what you look like now. Better if I go alone."

She looked worried. "But they've seen you too."

He didn't want to remind her that pretty much everyone who'd seen him with her was dead—except that self-styled Good Samaritan from the hospital. And Jack didn't believe for a nanosecond that Bob Garvey was his real name.

"Let me worry about that."

She stepped out of the car. "No, I'm coming."

"Weez—"

"We're wasting time." She pulled out her—or rather, Jack's—cell phone as she began walking toward the building. "I'll call him and let him know we're here."

Jack fell in beside her as she punched the buttons. He didn't like this, but short of locking her in the trunk . . .

After listening for a bit she thumbed the END button and looked at him.

"No answer. Maybe he's out."

This was looking worse and worse.

"Or maybe he can't answer. Go back to the car and—"

"No."

The finality in her tone told him arguing was futile. He looked back at his car. The Crown Vic had a roomy trunk . . .

Nah.

He checked under his T-shirt to make sure the Glock was nice and loose in its SOB holster, then adjusted his baseball cap as low as it would go over his forehead.

Outside the glass doors he kept his face turned away from the security camera as she pressed Harris's bell on the intercom. No answer. By luck, a stooped old lady in a babushka came out. He grabbed the door and held it for her, then they slipped inside.

No one about when they reached the eighth floor so they went straight to Harris's door. Jack positioned himself beside the doorframe with Weezy behind him—just in case a slug plowed through. The hallway walls were reinforced concrete, so no worry there.

He knocked. Again, no answer.

He tried the knob and froze when it turned.

Not good. Not good at all.

He rotated it back to neutral and lowered his voice to a whisper. "Is your pal the type to leave his door unlocked?"

"No way." Her hand shot to her mouth. "Ohmygod."

"Go back downstairs." When she shook her head, he pointed down the hall. "At least move away."

She backed up about ten paces.

Three possibilities here:

Harris went out but left his door unlocked . . . low probability—approaching zero.

Harris home but incapacitated or dead, and his attacker gone . . . possible.

Harris home, incapacitated or dead, and his attacker waiting inside to nab or kill Weezy when she walks through the unlocked door . . . also possible.

Best to play to the worst-case scenario.

Keeping far to the side of the doorframe, he turned the knob and pushed.

Instead of gunfire, a ball of flame exploded into the hallway, propelling the shattered remnants of the door ahead of it and knocking Jack to the floor. He quickly rolled to his feet and ducked away, checking to see if anything on him was burning. No, but the hair on his arms was singed.

Make that four possibilities: Harris home, incapacitated or dead, and the door rigged to explode.

Down the hall, a chalky-faced Weezy crouched and leaned against the wall. Her lips were moving but Jack couldn't hear over the whine in his ears. He didn't have to. He knew she'd be repeating "Ohmygod" over and over.

The fireball dissipated quickly but smoke and flame roiled from the doorway. He fought his way back against the heat and peeked inside. The entire apartment was ablaze. A man who looked a lot like Harris was duct-taped to a chair. The chair lay on its side. His eyes were open but seeing nothing. He showed no signs of life, and no way Jack could get to him through that inferno.

Vaguely he heard fire bells.

Time to go.

He found his cap, jammed it back onto his head, and ran for Weezy. Doors were opening up and down the hall.

"Fire!" he yelled. "Get out! Get out!"

He almost collided with a little old lady in a wheelchair as she rolled out into the hall ahead of him.

"Oh, dear God!" she cried, staring at the flaming doorway between her and the elevator. Her voice sounded faint and far away. "What do I do?"

As Jack stopped and looked around, Weezy reached him and clutched his arm. She looked ready to go into shock.

Options . . . push the old lady's wheelchair past Harris's apartment, but who knew if the elevators were working. A lot of them automatically shut down with a fire alarm.

She was thin and frail looking. Only one thing to do.

He turned Weezy and pushed her toward the EXIT sign. "Go!" Then back to the old woman. "Come on, lady," he said, lifting her out of the chair. He slipped one arm under her knees and the other around her back. "Looks like you're going for a ride." A thought hit. "You don't happen to have a dog, do you?"

"No, why?" Her words were faint.

"Just asking."

He got her into the stairwell where a mute, stricken Weezy held the door for them and they all started down.

"Wh-wh-what happened?" the lady said, clinging to him.

"Explosion of some kind."

She touched his cheek. "You're burned."

"Not surprised. I was in the hall when it happened. Knocked me off my feet."

And the truth shall set you free.

"What caused it?"

"No idea. Maybe some terrorist was making a bomb and it exploded."

A little disinformation couldn't hurt.

"Oh, dear God! A terrorist? In our building?"

"I hear they're everywhere. Then again, someone could have left the gas oven on, then lit a match."

"We're all electric."

"Terrorist, then."

They had the stairwell pretty much to themselves for a few flights until someone slammed onto a landing above and pounded down the steps. A sixtyish man, heavy but in good shape, lurched up behind them.

"Let me by, dammit!"

He shouldered Jack and his burden aside, and bumped Weezy against the wall as he raced ahead of them.

"Asshole," the woman said, then louder, "You always were an asshole, Frank!"

Jack's burst of anger dissipated as he laughed. "You tell him, lady."

Firemen were already on the first floor when they reached it.

He leaned close to Weezy. "Don't go out the front. Find a rear exit."

With a deer-in-the-headlights look, she nodded and moved away.

Jack kept his head down as he hurried past the firemen and out the front entrance. He saw an EMS wagon and an ambulance at the curb. He left the woman with them. She was profuse in her thanks and wanted to give him money, but all he wanted was out of here.

He looked around. The car with the two men was gone. A crowd of residents and people from the neighborhood had gathered to gawk at the smoke roiling from a blown-out section of windows on the eighth floor.

He joined the crowd for half a minute, then eased away, walking half backward, trying to look reluctant to leave.

He found Weezy waiting outside the car. He pressed the unlock button on the remote and they both got in.

"What happened?" she said, blinking back tears.

"Explosion."

"I *know* that. What about Kevin?"

Jack got the car rolling as he tried to think of a gentle way to put it. He came up empty, so he settled for simple and direct.

He shook his head and said, "Goner."

Weezy began to cry. The sound tore at him.

"What have I done? What have I started? This is all my fault. I brought him into this. If I'd just minded my own business—"

"I think the bomb was meant for you."

That stopped the sobs. She looked at him. "What?"

"I think Kevin was already dead." No need to mention that he appeared to have been tortured. "That bomb was set for the next person to come through the door."

"But how could they know it would be me?"

Jack pulled over to let another fire truck howl by.

"Maybe he told them."

"Kevin? He wouldn't do that!"

Looked like torture was going to rear its ugly head anyway.

"Maybe he was persuaded."

"Ohmygod! You think they tortured him?"

"Who can say? Maybe they knew he didn't have many friends and that if anyone came through that door it would be you."

"And it would have been if you hadn't—how did you know?"

"Didn't. Just took precautions."

She was staring at him. "Oh, Jack, look at you. Your skin . . . it's scorched."

He leaned right so he could see himself in the rearview. The left side of his face was reddened with a first-degree burn and the tips of the hairs in the left side of his beard were singed.

"I'm okay."

"That was good of you to carry that old woman out."

Well, he couldn't very well leave her up there to cook, especially since he'd been the one who'd triggered the explosion.

"Maybe I'll finally get that Boy Scout badge I've always wanted."

"Don't diminish it. That was very gallant."

The way she was looking at him made him uncomfortable.

"Gallant, hell. She made good cover for me."

True, but he hadn't realized that until he'd hit the first floor and saw the firemen.

Weezy folded her arms across her chest. "Right. You've become Mister Hard Guy."

He forced a smile. "And don't you forget it."

17.

"Do we have to do this here?" Hank said as Drexler set the glasses on the table.

He glanced uneasily at Darryl's still form stretched out inside the Orsa. It looked like some monstrously oversized transparent coffin, and made him feel like he was at a weird wake.

"Most certainly," Drexler said. "No place could be more appropriate."

At Drexler's request he'd moved a couple of chairs and a small folding table down from the basement—a little tight getting through that trapdoor—and set them up about a half dozen feet from the Orsa. Drexler arrived moments later carrying two odd-shaped wineglasses and a bottle of Poland Spring.

Hank pointed to the water. "That's your 'special drink'?"

"Don't be silly." Drexler alighted on one of the chairs. "Please turn off the lights."

"We're going to sit in the dark?"

"Not quite. I promise you illumination sufficient to our needs."

Shrugging, Hank walked over to the light switch by the stairwell and flipped the toggle. He expected to be plunged into darkness, but instead a faint blue light suffused the subcellar.

The Orsa was glowing.

He stared at it as he returned to Drexler at the table. It hadn't been glowing this morning when they first arrived. The light didn't seem to radiate from any point within, but from the very substance of the thing. The only reason had to be . . . Darryl, who now looked more than ever like a fly in an ice cube.

"Sit down," Drexler said.

He dropped onto the other chair and watched the man. His air of repressed excitement only compounded the weirdness factor.

"All right, I'm sitting. What next?"

Drexler pulled an envelope from his jacket pocket and removed a pair of sugar cubes and a strange slotted spoon. From another pocket he produced a silver flask.

This was getting interesting.

"Some hard stuff, ay?"

Drexler's lips twisted. "You have no idea."

He opened the water bottle and set it aside. Then he removed the cap from the flask and poured maybe three inches of clear green fluid into the globular base of each glass. He placed a sugar cube in the slotted spoon and held it over one of the glasses as he poured a thin stream of water over the cube. Hank watched fascinated as the green liquid turned a cloudy pale yellow.

"What the hell?"

"A hundred years ago we would have been at the tail end of the absinthe era in France."

"Absinthe. I've heard of that. Makes you crazy."

"Rubbish. Propaganda put forth by the winemakers who were afraid of the competition. In nineteen hundred the French consumed twenty-one million liters of absinthe. It was so popular that five o'clock became known as *'l'heure verte'*—the green hour."

He added another sugar cube to his spoon and moved it to the second glass, with the same effect.

"My father taught me the technique. He found absinthe most entertaining and was quite a connoisseur. Quite a man, actually."

"Was he in the Septimus Order too?"

He nodded. "My family has an unbroken string of membership back as far as anyone can remember."

"Was he an 'Actuator' too?"

Another nod. "He accomplished many great things for the Order. One might even say he helped change the course of history. Before he died he passed his vast store of arcana to me. He also passed me his cane and his private stock of absinthe. This is a custom blend from that collection."

Hank snorted and shook his head. "Hell, I barely knew my daddy. He only came by now and then. But I'm pretty damn sure he didn't drink anything like that."

Drexler had fixed up two glasses. He didn't really expect Hank to drink that stuff, did he? Obviously he did. He lifted one and held it out.

"*Bitte.*"

Bitter? Was he warning him about the taste?

He took the glass, saying, "It's not going to make me go crazy now, is it?"

He said it jokingly, but he was concerned. He'd stayed pretty straight and clean since this Kicker Evolution got rolling. Used to do weed regularly and a little crank now and then, an Oxy or two when he could get them, but he'd cleaned up once *Kick* found a big-time publisher that wanted to put him out in front of the public. He was the face of the Kicker Evolution now. He had a good deal going, the best deal imaginable, and he wasn't going to let anything screw it up by landing him in jail.

He was on a mission to change the world, to get everyone dissimilated, make everyone a Kicker.

Kickerworld.

Then what?

He had no idea. And that worried him at times.

"I've been drinking it since I was fifteen," Drexler said. "Do I seem crazy to you?"

"No."

Might have made him into one weird-ass dude, but Hank sensed he was not the least bit crazy.

"Then here."

Hank took the glass and checked out the cloudy yellow liquid. He swirled it but it didn't stick to the sides. He sniffed it. Not much of a smell.

"To the end of history," Drexler said, raising his glass. He clinked it against Hank's, then sipped. He tilted his head back and swallowed. "Ahhh. Wonderful."

Hank didn't drink—not just yet.

" 'End of history'? What's that supposed to mean?"

"A stolen phrase. I use it in my own sense. We are nearing the point when, as the Secret History of the World is revealed, we will see the end of history as you knew it—or thought you knew it. Then the reality to which the world has been blind through the millennia will be made manifest."

Hank stared at the liquid. One sip and already Drexler was talking crazy. How powerful was this stuff?

He took a sip and the burst of bitterness rocked his tongue. He looked for someplace to spit, didn't find one, so he swallowed. The back of his tongue tasted like sweet dirt. He'd never tasted sweet dirt, but if such a thing existed, that was how it would taste.

"That's like licorice mixed with—I don't know."

"That's the wormwood. This blend has extra. Come. Drink up. I wish to show you something."

Hank set the glass back on the table. "I'll pass."

"No-no. You must drink it. The wormwood will open your eyes to things that you cannot otherwise see."

"What is it—like LSD?"

"Not at all, not at all. It has a unique property I discovered quite by accident." He pointed toward the Orsa. "And it has something to do with our friend over there."

"Darryl?"

"No. The Orsa itself. You will see it as you have never seen it before, as only a privileged few have seen it. It is a . . . revelation, one I promise you will cherish because it concerns the future of you and your Kickers, and even your father's Plan."

Hank stiffened with surprise. "What do you know about that?"

"Everything."

"Can't you just tell me?"

He shook his head. "No. You must see. Drink up and you will see—literally." He took another sip from his glass. "Come, come."

Hank looked at the glass, then at the Orsa. Nothing else was making much sense right now. Might as well go with this and see what Drexler was talking about.

But he'd be damned if he was going to sip it.

He grabbed the glass and tossed down the contents in one bitter, convulsive swallow.

"Oh, my," Drexler said. "This is going to be quite entertaining."

18.

"How do you think they found him?" Weezy said as they tooled south on the turnpike.

Jack considered that as he drove.

Eddie wanted Weezy to stay with him and Jack thought it was a good idea. Weezy had argued against it, saying she didn't want to be out of the city. What if she needed to consult with Veilleur about something in the *Compendium*? Jack thought she'd be safer in Jersey, and she could hop a train in to Penn Station any time she wanted to. She'd finally given in.

So he'd shot the Verrazano, crossed Staten Island, then taken the Goethals Bridge to the New Jersey Turnpike. The plan was to meet Eddie at the service area near exit twelve.

"They could have known where he lived all along, or could have followed him home from the hospital yesterday."

Jack had thought he'd been a little too cocky about no one being able to tail him.

"Aren't you worried? Isn't it risky using your own car like this? I mean, what if someone took down your license plate numbers. They could trace you through the DMV."

Jack smiled. "I hope they try. Good luck if they do."

"Oh, I see," she said, nodding. "Fake tags."

"Well, yes and no. Ever hear of Vincent Donato?"

"Vinny Donuts? Sure. Who hasn't?"

"This is his car."

Her eyes widened. "You know Vinny Donuts? Well enough to borrow his car? Get out!"

"Okay, not his car itself, but exactly like it, right down to the plates and registration."

"Now why on Earth—?" She stopped and grinned. "Oh, I get it. Anyone who tries to track you down through the car—"

"—will wind up dealing with a notoriously ill-tempered mobster."

She clapped her hands. "I love it. It's so sneakily brilliant." She turned toward him and stared. "Just what are you, Jack? What do you do that makes it necessary to drive around in a clone of a Mafiosomobile?"

He shrugged, uncomfortable with the direction of the conversation. If it were anyone else, he'd give her the brush-off. But this was Weezy.

Besides, she'd seen him kill three men this morning. She already knew plenty.

"Remember my telling you about those stunts I used to pull as a kid—you know, Toliver's locker and Canelli's lawn? Well, I'm still at it, only I get paid for it."

"I'm not following."

"I hire out to fix things."

"Things? What sort of things?"

"Situations."

"And how do you fix them?"

"Depends. I do custom work."

"Please don't tell me you're a hit man."

He knew she was thinking about the recent gunplay. He forced a laugh.

"No. I've lost count of the number of times people have tried to hire me to kill someone, but no, I don't do that."

"But you have . . ." She seemed afraid of the word. "I've seen you."

"I do what's necessary, Weez—to protect myself, people I care about, or a customer."

"But you never hesitated, even for a second, and you didn't look the least bit shaken or upset afterward—not the slightest sign of remorse or regret."

"I've had regrets." He thought of Hideo back in May. "But those guys? How do I feel bad about stopping someone from killing us? No regret there." He smiled. "Is this where I start to sing 'My Way'?"

She didn't smile back. "I just can't help wonder what happened to the sweet boy from Johnson, New Jersey. The kid we all called Jackie when we were little."

He stared through the windshield.

"Shit happened, Weez. A whole load of shit happened."

"But—"

"Let's find a topic other than me. Like, how about them Mets? Some slump, huh?"

Weezy said nothing for a while and Jack concentrated on the road. He had the cruise control set at sixty-five and kept to one of the middle lanes. His New Jersey driver's license was the best money could buy, and was supposed to be able to pass muster against a DMV computer, but he'd rather not put it to the test. So he drove carefully, avoiding any moves that might draw attention.

Lack of an official identity made for safe driving. Everyone should try it.

Finally Weezy heaved a sigh and said, "Okay. New topic: I have a big favor to ask."

"Ask."

"Will you go to Los Angeles for me?"

Uh-oh.

"Why?"

"I need you to talk to someone out there."

"We have phones for that. Give me his number."

"He won't want to talk about this on the phone, maybe not even in person. I'm pretty sure I could convince him if we were face-to-face, but I need to study the *Compendium*. So I was wondering if you could go for me."

"Is it that important?"

"Very. Kevin and I . . ." Her voice choked off. "Poor Kevin."

After a moment she took a breath and continued. "Kevin and I have been looking for this man for a year now. Kevin finally tracked him down in L.A. We really need to talk to him."

"Why?"

"After nine/eleven—"

Jack fought an eye roll. He'd heard enough about that day lately to last a lifetime.

"Everything seems to keep coming back to that."

"Yes, it does. Odd, don't you think?"

"I think we should be more worried about R and what he might be up to."

"I've told you I have this feeling that somehow some way, they might be connected. And this man—his name's Ernest Goren—may be able to provide a missing link." She pointed to a sign announcing the presence of the Thomas A. Edison Service Area two miles ahead. "There's our stop."

The plan was to meet Eddie there. Weezy would transfer to his car and go home with him.

Jack nodded and kept to his lane. "I see it."

"Shouldn't you be getting over to the right?"

That was Jack's natural inclination too, but he resisted it.

"Let me do the driving, okay?"

"But—"

"Please? Tell me about this Goren."

"He was a member of one of the crews sent into the

bowels of the Trade Center to look for remains of victims. No one expected survivors. Their job was to bag up any human remains and bring them to the surface for identification."

"Nice."

"Somebody had to do it. He was with a crew of four and—Jack, you're going to miss the rest stop."

The entrance to the service area lay just ahead. At the last possible second, Jack jumped lanes and angled onto the ramp. He slowed after he was off the highway, watching in the rearview to see if anyone else made a similar move.

Nope.

"Never thought you'd turn out to be a backseat driver."

"I've been told I have control issues."

"Says who?"

"Most of my therapists through the years."

"Imagine that. Okay, back to Goren."

"Where was I?"

"He was down in the wreckage looking for body parts."

"Right. He was teamed with three others: Alfieri, Lukach, and Ratner. They'd worked together before. They all knew each other pretty well. They were deep down in the well of the Trade Center, along its eastern edge, when Lukach radioed back that they thought they heard voices down there. Well, that got everyone on the surface pretty excited."

"I don't remember hearing about that."

Abe had been obsessed with the attacks and in their aftermath had read his stack of daily newspapers even more closely than usual. He'd given Jack a distillation of every new development as it happened.

"Because moments later tragedy struck. A cave-in crushed Alfieri, Lukach, and Ratner."

"*That* I heard about."

Their funerals had been media events, with the tabloids screaming how al Qaeda had claimed three more American lives.

"What you most likely didn't hear about were reports from two workers elsewhere in the wreckage who said they thought they heard an explosion just about the time of the cave-in."

No, he hadn't—or at least Abe had never mentioned it.

He glanced at her. "Cover-up?"

She shrugged. "Maybe. Maybe just incompetence on the part of the investigators. They looked into it and supposedly found no evidence of an explosion."

"And found no source for the voices, I take it."

"Right. That was chalked up to an acoustic trick that allowed them to hear the voices of other workers elsewhere in the wreckage."

"And you don't buy that?"

Of course she wouldn't. Weezy always seemed to have an alternate explanation for everything that happened. But she surprised him.

"Again, I don't know. What I do know is that Ernest Goren survived the cave-in unscathed. Physically, at least."

"What do you mean?"

"He came out of the wreckage a mental basket case. He'd had a complete breakdown. When they asked him what happened down there, he just spewed word salad. His condition was chalked up to shock at seeing his friends get crushed."

"But you've got a better explanation."

Now the conspiracy.

"It's possible he was faking to cover up something, but I think it was real. I think he saw something down there that blew his circuits."

"That only happens in Lovecraft stories and B movies."

"He was fifty-two years old at the time with a wife, a

married daughter, and a grandson. His only known quirk was a belief in flying saucers, and not just the usual theories. He thought they came from inside the Earth. He was a member of SESOUP and—"

Jack shook his head. "Ah, yes. The Society for the Exposure of Secret Organizations and Unacknowledged Phenomena."

She leaned forward to look at him. "You know them?"

"Well. Too well, in fact. I attended their convention at the Clinton Hotel last year."

And it damn near killed me.

"You did? Are you into that stuff?"

"No. I was working—a missing-person problem."

"Then you might have met him. Because he was there too."

"I met a lot of people."

He remembered a guy showing him a photo of the North Pole taken from space, and pointing out a shadow he claimed was the opening where the saucers entered and exited the center of the Earth. That might have been him.

A question leaped to mind.

"How do you know so much about him?"

"Kevin got hold of the records of the police investigation after Goren's disappearance."

"Disappearance. Now we're getting somewhere."

He found a spot in an open area of the parking lot and watched the cars that entered after them. He'd seen no sign of a tail from Brooklyn but didn't want to take any chances.

"His doctors seemed convinced he'd had some sort of break with reality. They kept him for almost a week, medicated him, and sent him home. One day, not too long after, his house burned down. His wife died in the fire but no one could find a trace of him. He hasn't been seen since."

"He torched his house?"

"That's what the police think. And that's the way it looks. Torched his house, burning his wife alive. Then he emptied his bank account—"

Jack held up a hand. "*After* the fire?"

"First thing the next morning."

"That tells me he hadn't planned the fire, otherwise he'd have drawn it out first."

"Not if he wasn't in his right mind. Cleaned out his account and took off for parts unknown."

"But you found him in L.A."

"Kevin did. Goren keeps in touch with his daughter via e-mail. Kevin—"

"Whoa. Didn't you just say he burned her mother alive? Wouldn't she be just a little ticked?"

"You'd think so. Kevin uploaded a keystroke logger into her computer through her home Wi-Fi network."

Jack didn't know much about computers, but he could suss out what that did.

"So he could see whatever she typed?"

"Right. He used it to get Alice's e-mail username and password. After that he could log into her account from anywhere in the world and see what she was sending and receiving. She and her dad are pretty friendly. So either he managed to convince her it wasn't his fault—crazy, you know—or she was in on it for some reason. We don't know. How he smoothed it over is lost in the past. But Kevin tracked him to L.A. through some of the comments he made in the mails."

"And you want me to fly out there and talk to him."

"Please?"

Jack rubbed his eyes. "Brother."

"Don't tell me you're afraid to fly."

The flying didn't bother him—he'd done it only once. A cakewalk. He'd had bumpier bus rides. But getting through security was a hairy process for a guy who didn't exist.

Under normal circumstances, all he should need were his John Tyleski driver's license and credit card. That would be enough for ninety-nine percent of the zillion flights going in and out of airports every day.

But the what-ifs bothered him. He'd stayed alive and well and free by paying attention to the what-ifs.

Like what if there's an incident on a plane and airport security or Homeland Security starts backgrounding the passenger list?

John Tyleski has an excellent credit history—never once late paying his MasterCard bill—and an unblemished driving record. But his address is a mailbox. He doesn't seem to live anywhere, and he's never filed a tax form of any kind—ever. In fact, there's no record of his existence until a few years ago.

John Tyleski would become a person of interest—big time.

"No, flying's cool. I just . . ."

Just what? He had nothing else going on at the moment. Gia and Vicky would be fine without him for a few days. And if Weezy thought it was that important, he shouldn't blow her off. She'd been proven right too often to be dismissed.

He'd have to bite the bullet—and hope it didn't go off in his mouth.

"Okay. I'll go. How do I find him?"

"We don't have his home address—"

"Then how—?"

"—but we have a pretty good idea of where he works."

Eddie had said he'd be driving a black Toyota Camry. One was pulling into the lot now.

"There's Eddie," Jack said as he recognized the man behind the wheel.

He lowered his window and stuck his arm out. The Camry turned his way.

Weezy shifted in her seat to face him, her expression earnest. "Can you leave tomorrow?"

"Tomorrow? Is it that urgent?"

"His daughter's going out to visit him tomorrow—Continental flight 1159. Goren is going to meet her at LAX. I thought maybe you could get on the same plane. I mean, that's what I'd do if I were going."

Not a bad plan.

"Okay. I'll make a reservation when I get home. But I'll need more info."

"I'll meet you at the airport before your flight. Kevin e-mailed me all the details, including a photo of the daughter. I'll decrypt everything and go over it with you then."

"Sounds like a plan."

She leaned over and kissed him on the cheek. "Thanks, Jack."

She gave him a quick hug, then she was out of the car and bustling toward the Camry. When she was inside they both waved and took off.

Jack watched them go, keeping an eye out for anyone who might be following. He'd taken note of the cars that had pulled into the service area during the first five minutes after they'd arrived. He'd watched them do their business and pull away. None had stayed. No one pulled out and followed Eddie.

Jack sat and thought about L.A., and how he knew no one out there and even less about the place. But Abe would. Abe could set him up with some iron while he was out there.

And who knew? Maybe he'd be discovered and start a new career as a movie star.

Or not.

19.

"Mister Thompson," Drexler said, "I believe we have achieved the required state."

Hank looked at him from between his heavy lids. The only illumination was the faint ice-blue glow from the Orsa lying a half dozen feet away. They'd each downed three stiff absinthes—Hank chugging and Drexler sipping—and he was definitely feeling it. Drexler looked fine, however.

"Required for what?"

"To see what I wish you to see." He rose and motioned to Hank. "Come. We must be closer."

Hank wanted to stay put. He had a strange notion that Drexler was luring him close to the Orsa, and when he reached a certain point a glowing tentacle would whip out and snag him. He'd wind up trapped inside the thing like Darryl.

Drexler was standing by the Orsa, motioning to him with his cane. "Come. What are you waiting for?"

Well, he couldn't tell Drexler about the tentacle, and getting up and moving about might not be a bad thing.

He pushed himself out of his chair and stepped toward the Orsa. He noticed an odd, floaty feeling as he moved; not exactly light-headed; more like light-footed.

As Hank stopped at his side, Drexler made a flourish with his cane toward the Orsa.

"Observe."

At first Hank had no idea what he was supposed to see. And how was he supposed to look at anything else but Darryl? The poor guy's expression looked strained. His eyes were closed—thankfully—but his mouth was wide open, as if frozen in mid-scream.

"He looks dead."

"I assure you, he is not," Drexler said.

"He's not breathing."

"The Orsa is breathing for him. Now please disregard him and concentrate on the surface of the Orsa."

Hank ripped his gaze from Darryl and studied the Orsa's hide—could he call it a hide? What did—?

And then he spotted the little red and white dots scattered across the dimpled surface. They almost seemed to glow. He stepped closer. They *were* glowing, with a faint, pulsating light. And now that he was near he could make out hair-thin red lines arcing out from the red dots in an intricate, crisscrossing pattern. It looked like someone had played connect the dots with an ultra fine–tipped pen.

"When did these show up? They weren't here earlier."

"Tradition has it that the Nexus Grid appears when the Orsa wakes, but an observer requires what might be described as an altered state of consciousness to perceive them."

"You mean, drunk?"

"No. Alcohol alone will not do it. The special blend and balance of ingredients in what we've been drinking induces the necessary changes in perception."

Hank squinted at the dots and lines. He noticed now that the white dots outnumbered the red by a good deal.

"Okay. I'm altered. I see them. So what? What am I seeing?"

"Opus Omega . . . which was supposed to lead to the end of history."

"You mentioned that before. I still don't know what you mean."

Drexler glanced at him. "Your father told you about the Others, beings waiting outside and wanting to come in and remake the world."

Hank nodded. Daddy had talked about that a lot. And how those who helped open the door for them would be rewarded.

"Yeah. That was why he put together the Plan to make the baby—the Key to the Future. But now . . ."

"The baby is thriving inside his mother, who is being well taken care of."

Hank smiled. "Then the Plan is still a go."

"You must realize there are many plans, all geared toward achieving the same end."

"Bringing the Others in?"

"Technically, there are no 'Others,' only one. It has no name, but we call it the Otherness. And yes, that is the goal: Allow the Otherness mastery over our corner of reality."

"And when that happens, we'll be in the catbird seat, right?"

"Not 'we.' The catbird seat, as you call it, is reserved for the One, a man who has been the Otherness's instrument on Earth for . . . well, for longer than you would probably believe. We serve through him, and we shall receive our rewards through him."

"That's not the way my daddy explained it. He never mentioned anybody called the One."

"That is because your 'daddy' had an agenda of his own that ran contrary to the wishes of the One. He was going to use the child, your so-called Key to the Future, against the One. And that is why your 'daddy' is no longer among the living."

"This the guy we talked about earlier? The one who took Dawn and the baby? The one who says 'jump' and your High Council says 'how high?' "

Drexler nodded. "Precisely."

Hank could believe it. Something more than human about that guy—or maybe less than human. He'd admitted killing Daddy, and said how much he'd enjoyed watching his lingering death. Hank felt his insides twist in a mix of fear and anger.

"So it's best to be on his good side."

"The One will require loyal assistants after the Change. Those who have helped bring him to power will be rewarded."

Well, that made sense, but something else didn't.

"Why's he want Dawn's baby? If it was supposed to be used against him—"

"The One does nothing without a reason. Perhaps he sees a possibility where it might be of use to him. He knows all of the Secret History. It is futile to second-guess him. I advise you to expend your mental resources in more fruitful pursuits."

"Will do."

Drexler pointed to the Orsa with his black cane, bringing the tip to within an inch of a red dot.

"This and its other red brethren indicate nexus points. A veil of sorts separates our reality from the Otherness. There exist across the planet small areas where the veil is very thin. Under certain, fleeting conditions, some of the Otherness can leak through, but that is not our concern here. What I want you to notice is the network of lines running between the nexus points. Every nexus point is linked to the others by one of these fine lines of force."

"Okay. But what about the white ones? They're connected too."

"The white spots are placed wherever three or more lines intersect. Each white indicates the location of a buried pillar."

Hank stepped back for a broader look. There were hundreds, maybe a thousand white dots.

"You mean someone buried a pillar in every one of those spots? But that's . . . that must have taken—"

"A long, long time?" Drexler's lips curved. "Quite. Opus Omega has been under way for millennia. And it's almost completed. Only a few sites—indicated here by black dots—remain where a pillar must be buried."

"What happens then?"

"The veil will lift and the Otherness will flood through."

"But what if someone starts going around taking pillars out of the ground? Doesn't that undo something and set this Opus Omega back?"

"One would think so, but once the pillar is buried, the damage is done. If you went around the globe and dug up every single one, it would not change things."

"Damage? Damage to what?"

"Far too complicated to go into now. Suffice it to say that Opus Omega has slowed to a crawl."

Hank remembered their earlier conversation. "You mentioned the Dormentalists were in charge. If they're crapping out on you, and there's only a few more spots left to bury a pillar, why don't you let me get my Kickers behind this and—"

"I doubt your Kickers are disciplined enough, but it is not simply a matter of will or manpower." He waved at the latticework of lights and lines. "If you could superimpose this on a globe of the Earth, you would see that many of the remaining intersections are inaccessible."

Hank tried to imagine how this mess would look on a map but had no idea what went where.

"Inaccessible how?"

"Some of them are located on ocean bottoms, thousands of feet down. The planners, the original designers of Opus Omega, knew this. Perhaps they had the technology then to reach those depths—"

" 'Then'? When are we talking about?"

"It's not important. Suffice it to say they either had the ability or assumed when the time came that the technology would be available to reach those points. Alas, it is not."

"Of course it is. I've seen it on TV—"

"Yes, there are submersibles that can dive to sixty-five hundred meters—"

"What's that in miles?"

"About four. But it's quite another matter to transport a pillar to that depth, dig a hole in the ocean floor, and bury it—all without scrutiny. Quite impossible. Perhaps in the future, but not now."

"So, you have to wait. You say it's been going on for millennia."

"The One grows impatient, and he is not . . . pleasant when he is impatient."

I'll bet, Hank thought.

"I assume you have a contingency plan."

"We do. It's called the *Fhinntmanchca*."

"The Fint—?"

"The *Fhinntmanchca*."

"What the hell is that?"

"You are looking at it."

THURSDAY

1. They sat on the edge of an unused luggage carousel on the bottom floor of Newark Airport's terminal C, away from the new arrivals awaiting their bags. Weezy was wearing brand-new jeans and a yellow, short-sleeve top. Looked like she'd done some clothes shopping since Eddie had picked her up.

Jack had trained down from Penn Station; Weezy had driven Eddie's car.

"Here's what Goren's daughter looks like," she said, handing Jack a photo. "Her name's Alice—Alice Laverty—and it's a recent shot."

Jack saw a slim, plain-looking brunette in her thirties walking through what appeared to be a shopping mall.

"Where'd you get this?"

"Kevin took it. He loved the whole espionage thing, playing field agent, following people."

And being followed, Jack thought.

Weezy was silent, staring at the floor.

"How are you dealing . . . ?"

"With his death? I cried last night, and I cried this morning. But I'm slowly finding space for it, a place to tuck it away. The *Compendium* helps."

"You started?"

"As soon as I got to Eddie's. Jack, it's . . . it's like a

dream come true. No question the book's the real thing, an artifact from a forgotten age."

"The random, shifting page order is something else, huh?"

"When you told me about that, I couldn't imagine how that could be true, but you weren't kidding. Kind of confusing."

"Kind of? They should have called it the *Confusium*."

"I can't wait to get back to it. But in the meantime . . ." She handed him another photo. "Here's a not-so-recent shot of the man himself from the police report. It was taken about the turn of the millennium, so you can count on him looking older now."

Jack saw a grinning man with dark hair and graying temples wearing a T-shirt emblazoned with the outline of a typical gray alien and the words *They've Always Been Here!*

"Ernest Goren in happier days."

Weezy nodded. "Before he saw whatever he saw."

"And torched his home and killed his wife. You don't know that he saw anything."

"*Something* made him crazy."

"Maybe it was just his time."

"For what?"

"To break with reality. I mean, he believes in UFOs from the center of the Earth. How big a leap is it from there to Bonkersville where he believes his wife is an alien spy and he kills her?"

"Just because someone has ideas that don't conform to the mainstream's concept of reality doesn't mean they're psychotic. Look at me." She shook her head. "No, strike that. I'm not a good example."

"You're okay."

"I'm bipolar. Actually, I'm beyond bipolar. I'm *tri*polar."

"But you've been right all along."

"You mean my crazy ideas turned out to be not so crazy after all? How about that?"

"But you were into subtleties. You never believed in the Antichrist or space aliens manipulating events."

"But something *has* been manipulating us. I've always believed that—I just thought it was the work of secret societies like the Septimus Order. Now, thanks to you, I know it's so-so-*so* much bigger. And what about the Antichrist? Wouldn't R fall into that role? And then there are the believers in the New World Order conspiracy—are they so wrong? Isn't that what R and the Order are looking to create by opening the gates to the Otherness?"

She had a point. A good one. That brain of hers . . .

"Different interpretations of the same thing."

"Right. What if the End Times crowd and the UFO folks and the NWO believers, instead of being crazy or deranged or deluded, are blessed or cursed with some sort of sixth sense, some unique form of intuition that allows them to sense the manipulations?"

He remembered a conversation with a strange guy named Canfield at the SESOUP conference.

Jack said, "I have it on good authority that they're called 'sensitives.' Their nervous systems are more attuned to the Otherness than most. They sense the Otherness out there but they don't know what to make of it. Some go schiz because of the 'voices' they're hearing, and others see conspiracies everywhere or come up with elaborate theories."

Weezy nodded. "So they're like the blind men with the elephant. They get to touch only a small area of the beast, and each comes away with a different idea of what it is. In a way, they're all wrong, but not completely."

"Right. The New World Order, the gray aliens, the Bible, the Kabbalah, they're all attempts to explain what people sense going on."

"All different blind men reporting their interpretation of the elephant."

Jack shook his head. "Yeah, but what about us? Look at what we believe. It's far more out there than any of the others. What if *we're* crazy?"

"Then it's a shared delusion—and a doozy. Because it explains everything."

"The Grand Unification Theory."

"That's for physics, but I guess the term fits." She smiled. "Grand Unification . . . I like that."

"I can't take credit. Melanie Ehler, the former head of SESOUP, came up with it. But she never got a chance to prove it."

He wished he'd never heard of SESOUP. His involvement with the group led him into a situation that drew the attention of the Ally. It paid scant attention to this corner of reality—after all, Earth was already part of its collection—but it decided to begin turning him into a "spear."

He checked his watch. "I should get going. Half an hour till boarding and I still have to get through security."

Yeesh.

2. "Hey, that's cold," Dawn said.

The Asian technician, who'd introduced herself as Ayo, gave an apologetic smile as she smeared the gel across Dawn's slightly swollen belly. "Sorry. We try to keep it warm but it's hard with the air-conditioning set like it is."

"At least your hands are warm."

Someone had drawn blood and then the obstetrician, Dr. Landsman, had done the pelvic exam—the lubricant gel he'd used had been just as cold as this stuff, but it had been down *there* so it felt even colder. He'd said everything seemed fine, but the ultrasound would tell the real story.

Dawn lay on her back and hoped everything would be all right. She totally didn't know what she'd been thinking before when she'd wanted an abortion. This was her baby, her flesh and blood. She could feel it moving inside her. No way she could kill it. She just hoped it was all right—no birth defects or anything like that.

Ayo pointed to a monitor on a wheeled cart.

"After I start the scan, you'll be able to see the baby right there on the screen. You'll see its head, and its bones, and even its heart beating. And when we switch to three-D, you'll see its face."

"Will you be able to tell if it's a girl or a boy?"

Ayo shrugged. "Possibly, but no guarantee. All depends on the baby's position." She winked. "Some are more modest than others."

The door opened and Dr. Landsman came in with Mr. Osala. Dawn resisted an impulse to cover her belly. What was he doing here? Not like he was the father or anything—and not like she'd let the real father anywhere near her baby anyway.

"Is she all set?" the doctor said.

"Yes. I was just about to begin."

"I'll take it from here."

Ayo looked as if she'd been slapped. "But—"

"I said I'd take it, Ayo. Wait outside."

With a totally dumbfounded look, the technician nodded and left the room. Dawn didn't know what was going on here, but it sure seemed like someone was breaking with routine.

Dr. Landsman smiled down at her. "Now, Dawn, we're going to take a look at your baby. It won't hurt a bit. We use sound waves—"

"I know. Ayo explained it all. But I thought she was going to do it."

"Normally, she would, but you're a special patient and—"

Worry gnawed at her. "Why did you send her out of the room? Is something wrong?"

"Not at all, not at all. Just relax and this will be over in a few minutes."

He kept his eyes on the monitor as he began rubbing this gizmo that looked like an electric shaver over her belly. She watched the monitor too but couldn't make head or tail of the black-and-white image until Dr. Landsman pointed to a tiny black oval that seemed to be winking madly.

"See? There's the heart, pumping away."

Dawn stared at it, totally enthralled. Her baby's heart. How wonderful.

"It's okay, isn't it—the heart, I mean?"

"It's fine," he said with a smile. "Everything is—oh. Oh, my."

Dawn lifted her head. "What's wrong?"

"Nothing. Nothing at all." But he had this strange, avid light in his eyes.

He put down the gizmo and turned the monitor away from her, so that only he and Mr. Osala could see it.

The doctor said, "When Drexler told me what I'd be looking for, I couldn't—well, I didn't know what to believe. But he was right."

Dawn felt a surge of panic. "Believe what? What are you talking about?"

They ignored her as Mr. Osala leaned forward.

"Where? Show me."

Dr. Landsman pointed to the screen. "See that? That's one. And this here is the other."

"Other what?" Dawn cried.

Mr. Osala nodded. "I see. Very interesting."

" 'Interesting'? It's stunning! It's—"

"It is not to leave this room. You will not speak of this and you will delete all images now."

"But—"

"*Now.* I thank you for your efforts and your expertise. We will pay you periodic visits with the same protocol."

"What do you see?" Dawn screamed.

Dr. Landsman looked at her as if he'd forgotten she was in the room.

"Oh. It's . . . it's a boy."

A boy . . . her worries seemed to evaporate.

She was going to have a boy.

3. At the TSA checkpoint Jack waited in line until he reached an Arabic looking man with a bad toupee who matched the name on the boarding pass with that on the license, initialed the pass, and waved Jack through. He waited on line again and reached the scanning area where he doffed his work boots and belt, placed them in a bin, then deposited that and his carry-on bag on the conveyor belt. He breezed through the metal detector, retrieved his boots and belt, and that was it.

Simps. What had he been so worried about?

He looked back at the cadre of TSA workers, the armed guards, all the humming technology, and no one had a clue about the seven-inch composite dagger strapped to his left triceps.

He needed to get out more often.

He found Alice Laverty, looking better in person than in the photo, already seated at the gate when he arrived.

Good. She might have changed her plans, making this whole trip an exercise in futility.

Had she been involved in her mother's death? If not, what could her father have said to keep her from hating him?

He wandered back to the bookstore and browsed the shelves. He found copies of P. Frank Winslow's *Rakshasa!* and *Berzerk!* in all their exclamatory glory. He'd skimmed through those months ago and the way they paralleled episodes in his life still gave him the chills. He had no desire to revisit them, but he might want to revisit the author and find out what he'd been dreaming lately.

He found a Travis McGee novel he didn't remember reading—all those colors in the titles ran together after a while—and bought that.

The boarding announcement came and, after standing on line again, he found himself sitting two rows ahead of Alice Laverty. The doors closed, the plane taxied out and took off a mere ten minutes late.

Now *this* was the way to tail someone—no way he could lose her between here and L.A.

The hours dragged by. After almost six of them—during which he drank three cups of coffee, ate a tiny sandwich of cold mystery meat on a cold roll, and napped during an unwatchable romantic comedy—the head attendant announced that the plane was making its final approach into LAX.

Perfect timing, he thought as he finished the last page and closed the cover on the McGee novel. Good story, but though McGee's MO resembled Jack's somewhat, he seemed to run into a better class of people during the course of his jobs. And all of them so well spoken, at times verging on eloquent. In fact, they all talked like McGee.

He followed Alice off the plane and stayed a ways behind her as she hurried along the concourse. He lost sight of her for a few seconds but found her again on the far side of the security area in a tearful reunion embrace with an older man.

Ernest Goren had aged considerably since his photo—completely gray now, with a heavily lined face. Jack might not have recognized him without his daughter.

They looked close. Real close. Co-conspirators or . . . what?

As he passed, Jack noticed that even in the clinch Goren was watching the passersby with a wary, darting gaze. Still an alert fugitive. Why? After all these years, did he think the cops would be in active pursuit?

Or maybe cops weren't what he was afraid of.

Jack continued on to the baggage area. Alice'd been carrying only a shoulder bag, so he assumed she'd checked her luggage. He was right. She and her father showed up moments later.

Jack ignored them and joined the thickest cluster of waiting passengers, feigning avid interest as the chute began to vomit bags of all shapes and sizes onto the rattling carousel.

Out of the corner of his eye he watched Alice point to a large green bag. Goren lifted it free and wheeled it behind them as they headed for the exit.

Now the dicey part: following them home. Jack knew this was the weak link in his plan, where he'd lose them unless his timing was perfect. No problem if they took a cab. Easy to follow them then, but from what he understood about L.A., birthplace of the car culture, you needed a car to survive.

If he'd known someone out here he could trust, he might have arranged to be picked up, and he'd follow that way. But he knew no one. Abe had arranged a weapon for him, but couldn't do more than that on such short notice.

So no big surprise when Goren led his daughter into the parking area. Jack followed until he saw them get into a rattletrap Ford of uncertain vintage and mismatched front fenders. A second man sat behind the wheel. Goren put his daughter in the rear, then got in the front passenger seat. Jack memorized the license plate out of habit—couldn't imagine another car like that in the entire airport.

He hurried back and found a line for the taxis. Took ten teeth-grinding minutes to reach one. Too late to follow.

Damn. Tailing would have saved him a ton of legwork.

He turned away and crossed over to where the rental car vans were picking up and disgorging customers. He hopped on the first to come along.

4.

"Oh, shit!"

Hank had come down to the subcellar to check on Darryl. He hadn't turned on the lights, just followed the cold blue glow. The dots and lines he'd seen yesterday were gone. Or maybe not gone, simply invisible without the assistance of absinthe. If getting tanked on that stuff was what it took to see them, he'd skip a second look. He'd felt terrible this morning.

He stopped dead in his tracks when he saw that Darryl's legs were no longer sticking out. His feet, shoes and all, were now entirely within the thing.

He turned at a sound behind him and saw Drexler strolling in from the stairway.

"I came to check on our friend," he said, smiling as he approached, "but I see you've beaten me to it."

Hank pointed at the Orsa. He hated that his hand shook, but he couldn't help it. This was . . . he didn't know what it was, but it couldn't be good.

"Look at that! It's sucked him further inside."

Drexler stopped and stared. He looked surprised for an instant, then composed.

"Well, that makes sense, doesn't it. If the Orsa is going to cure his whole body, it must have access to his whole body. Don't be concerned. Just a normal part of the process."

"I thought you said this had never been done before."

"Yes, I did say that, but there are writings on the subject. Have no fear: Our friend is being cured."

As Hank turned away and resumed staring at the Orsa and the man trapped within, he wondered how much of that was bullshit.

"*Our* friend? Don't pretend you ever liked him. You made it pretty clear he got on your nerves."

Drexler stopped at Hank's side. "That is true, I suppose. But now I harbor only good feelings about him."

"Yeah? And what do you think Darryl's feeling?"

"I have no idea. Since he appears unconscious, I would assume he feels nothing."

Hank continued to stare at Darryl's still form. He hoped that was the case. He felt somehow responsible for the guy being in there. If he came out cured of AIDS, then good. He could be annoying at times, and had got himself infected in a really stupid way, but he didn't deserve AIDS.

He recalled a strange remark Drexler had made yesterday while they'd been staring at the dots and lines. He glanced at him.

"Yesterday you mentioned a word I'd never heard before—*fin*-something—in connection with Darryl. What were you talking about?"

Drexler looked suddenly uncomfortable. "Nothing. Forget I mentioned it."

That wouldn't be hard, since he barely remembered it, but Drexler's discomfort piqued his interest. He had a feeling the man never would have mentioned it if not for a snootful of absinthe.

"No can do. You said it about one of my Kickers, so I need to know what it means."

"It's nothing. Just an ancient word for the healing process our friend is going through."

"Bullshit. You said it was some sort of contingency plan."

Drexler looked even more uncomfortable. "I said nothing of the sort. I must have said the Order has contingency plans to aid the One, and you misinterpreted."

He was lying. Hank resisted the urge to take a poke at him, knock him down, dirty up his white suit, maybe work him over with his own fancy cane. Instead he replayed that scene from yesterday . . . they were standing closer to the Orsa, checking out the dots and lines . . . talking about Opus Omega . . . and Drexler had mentioned . . .

"*Fhinntmanchca,*" Hank said as it came back to him. "That was what you said."

Drexler looked pale now. "Excuse me. I've used up today's allotment of idle chatter."

He turned and strode away.

Fhinntmanchca, Hank thought. He needed to find out what that meant, but hadn't a clue as to where to look. He'd try to Google it, but he didn't even know how to spell it.

He stared at the Orsa. What did it mean? It had something to do with Darryl. But what?

He had an uncomfortable feeling he'd be finding out soon enough.

5. It called itself the Andaz West Hollywood now, but in the old days it had been the infamous Riot Hyatt.

Jack had programmed the hotel's address into his rental car's GPS, but when he pulled into the rear parking lot an hour later, he realized he hadn't needed it—except for the final hundred yards on Sunset Boulevard, he'd stayed on the same street, La Cienega, all the way from the airport.

The room was nothing much—a view of the traffic on Sunset, the House of Blues across the street, and the towers of downtown rising through the smog in the basin. But the hotel was special. He'd chosen the Riot Hyatt for its place in rock history, figuring as long as he had to make this trip, he might as well make it interesting.

Little Richard used to live here. Timmy O'Brien, one of Julio's regulars, had told him he'd been out here on a business trip during his heyday in advertising and had seen him getting into a limo in the parking lot. Timmy had had the presence of mind to call out, "Hey, how's it going, Mister Penniman?" which so pleased Little Richard he rewarded him with a pearly grin, a handshake, a pre-signed photo, and a couple of Seventh Day Adventist brochures. Timmy kept the photo, dumped the brochures.

The Hyatt gained the "riot" from all the rowdy rock bands that used to stay here when they passed through on tour. The Who and the Stones—those impetuous boys—threw TVs out windows. A member of Led Zep supposedly drove a motorcycle along one of the hallways.

Staying here had seemed like a cool idea last night when he'd been looking for a hotel, but now that he was here . . .

Meh.

So what? Big deal. Who cared?

He'd noticed that reaction more and more lately. Vicky and Gia aside, nothing outside the Conflict seemed to excite or interest him much. Maybe because he no longer felt that his life was his own, that he was being manipulated by forces beyond his control.

Wasn't that the way a paranoid schiz would think?

But he wasn't crazy, he wasn't imagining all this. He'd

seen and experienced things with no conventional rationale, understandable only as manifestations of the Conflict.

He wasn't a free, independent individual, he was a backup plan. He'd been in the crosshairs since his conception—yesterday's revelation of the Lady's presence in his hometown as Mrs. Clevenger clinched that.

So who cared about the antics of a bunch of drugged-up, self-indulgent cases of arrested development, whose major accomplishment was turning up the volume to eleven?

Jack stared out the window at the art deco façade of the Argyle Hotel across the street. Cool looking place. Should have booked there.

He shook his head. This wasn't like him. He used to enjoy life, used to put on his own personal film festivals built around a theme or an actor or director. When was the last time he'd done that?

On the subject of films, Kevin had gleaned from e-mails that Goren managed a film revival theater at night and worked at a hardware store during the day. The question was which revival house and which hardware store? The hardware made sense, given his construction background, but the revival house seemed out of left field. Unless he was a closet film buff.

What bothered Jack was that he had any job at all. If he was on the run and in hiding, the last thing he'd want to do was collect a check under his own Social Security number. He'd want another name, and that meant a new identity. Not easily come by in the post–9/11 world, but not impossible. You needed certain contacts, though . . . something a guy who'd spent the first half century of his life in construction was unlikely to have.

Unless he'd found someone who'd pay him off the books. Two someones: a hardware someone and a film revival someone. The film revival route seemed the way to go. Yes, this was L.A., but he figured that even here, hardware stores had to far outnumber film revival houses.

But where to start?

Well, this was a hotel and hotels hired guys to know stuff or be able to look up stuff.

The concierge was a short Hispanic guy who reminded Jack a little of Julio, but only a little. Julio was Puerto Rican, this guy had a lot of Olmec in the family woodpile. His name tag said HECTOR.

Right off the bat Hector knew of three revival theaters in greater L.A., and the computer spat out three more. Jack took the list and checked out the addresses. He had no idea where any of these places were, but his car's GPS would find them.

But not yet. Goren's e-mails had mentioned the theater as a night job. The sun was still high, leaving Jack hours to kill. And besides, he had to make a stop before looking for anybody. He showed Hector an address on Hollywood Boulevard.

"That's in the Hollywood and Highland Center," he said without having to look it up. "A big mall next to the Chinese."

"Chinatown?"

His smile was indulgent. "No, sir. Grauman's Chinese Theater."

"I'd like to see that."

"You can't miss it." He pointed and gave directions.

"How far?"

"A couple of miles."

Was that all? Hell, he'd walk it. And as a bonus he'd get to see Grauman's Chinese Theater.

Might as well be a tourist for the afternoon. Might never be back.

He remembered seeing Hollywood Boulevard on the revival list and took another look. Sure enough . . .

"Where's this Egyptian Theater?"

"Keep walking past the Highland Center," Hector said. "Cross Highland and you can't miss it. It's even older than the Chinese. The first Hollywood premiere was held at the Egyptian in 1922."

"Yeah? What film?"

"*Robin Hood* with Douglas Fairbanks."

Cool. Jack knew it well. He had a thing for silents. He'd be checking the place out even if it wasn't on the list.

He stepped out of the lobby onto Sunset and took a left. He passed some interesting looking eateries and watering holes interspersed among Starbucks and McDonald's. He came upon the Chateau Marmont, which did indeed look like a chateau. He strolled up the short, steep driveway. The lobby was small and elegant and the AC welcome after the heat of the street. He was tempted to ask if he could rent the bungalow where Belushi bought it but passed.

The environs became a little rundown as he continued east. Where was the glamour of Sunset Boulevard? Where was Erich von Stroheim driving Gloria Swanson's limo? Where was the Whiskey a Go-Go? Maybe he was headed in the wrong direction for that sort of thing. He found Hollywood Boulevard and soon stood before Grauman's Chinese Theater.

The famous red columns and huge circular forecourt were even more impressive than he'd expected. The place delivered on its reputation. He hung out for a while, checking out the footprints and handprints of the film industry's icons—from Jack Benny to John Woo, Cantinflas to Clint Eastwood. He grinned when he found Gene Autry's along with Champion's hoofprints.

For half an hour he took a vacation from reality and enjoyed himself. Then he moved on to the mall.

Abe's instructions had been to find the Mailbox Centre at this address.

No problem there, but he didn't go in right away. He hung out to see if anyone was watching the store. Overly cautious, maybe, but he had no schedule. Ten minutes of observation satisfied him.

He checked the combination Abe had given him: R10—L22—R13. He went to box 367, entered those numbers, and the door popped open. Inside he found a padded envelope. He slipped it out, closed the door, spun the combo dial, and headed back to the street.

A neat way to transfer merchandise: Abe's contact rents the mailbox; when he needs to make a delivery, he opens the door, adjusts the combination to a prearranged number, then sticks the package in with the junk mail already present. The buyer opens the box, removes his purchase, and takes off. Completely anonymous.

If Abe's contact was true to his word, the envelope should contain a Glock 27 loaded with .40-caliber Speer Gold Dot JHPs. The weight felt about right, but he'd have to wait before he knew for sure.

He continued east on Hollywood Boulevard, crossing Highland, until he came to a dramatic sandstone block façade. A side sign said "Egyptian" but "American Cinematheque" arched over the entrance in wrought iron. He strolled along the lines of stately palms, passing pharaoh heads and other Egyptian bric-a-brac. The sign over the inner entrance said "Grauman's Egyptian." Grauman again. Taste aside, you had to admit the guy had style.

Hokey as it was, Jack loved the place. Other than an exotic setting, what did ancient Egypt have to do with movies? But who cared? The place had a genuine *wow* factor. Back then they knew how to do these places up right. Better than the shoeboxes that passed for theaters today.

Gia's recurring comment came back to him: *You were born in the wrong generation. You don't like anything modern.*

Not quite. He hefted the package in his hand. He loved modern weaponry.

The Egyptian looked too legit to be paying off the books, but Jack had walked too far not to give it a shot. He asked to speak to the manager and soon found himself in the company of a slender man in his forties.

"Is Ernie working here tonight?"

Jack didn't expect Goren to be using his surname, but he might have kept his first.

The manager frowned. "Ernie? We have no Ernie working here."

"Older guy, sixtyish, gray hair. He's the night manager."

His head shake was emphatic. "No one like that working here, certainly not as night manager."

Well, it had been worth a try, and he'd eliminated a stop from his list.

He had a bad thought as he headed back to the street. This was Goren's daughter's first night in from the east. Wouldn't he want to spend it with her? Even if Jack found the right theater, he might not find Goren.

Swell.

6.

Back in his room, he opened the package and found exactly what he'd ordered. He checked the chamber—empty. He'd leave it that way for now. Checked the magazine—maxed at ten rounds. The Glock 27 was a pocket carry, smaller than his 19, with a smaller magazine. But he figured the extra stopping power of the .40-caliber hollowpoints would compensate should things come to that. He hoped not. He'd do whatever he could to keep this a safe, quiet, peaceful trip.

He slipped it into his right front pocket and stood before the mirror. Even with his loose-fitting jeans, the pistol left a bulge. He untucked his T-shirt. There. Hidden.

No Mae West wisecracks tonight.

He checked his watch: just after four. Not quite Miller time in L.A. but hours past it in New York.

But first, a couple of calls. After all, it was already seven back there and he didn't know when he'd have another chance tonight.

He checked in with Gia and gave her a rundown of all the pulse-pounding excitement so far. Then he called Weezy, and sensed the dismay in her tone when he told her about the problem at the airport.

"You lost them?"

"We knew all along that was a good possibility. I'm going to start making the rounds of the revival theaters in a little while. Meantime, how are things going with the *Compendium*?"

"Jack, it's just incredible." He could hear her spirits lifting. *"Literally incredible. There's so much here, and it's all so . . . so . . ."*

"Incredible?"

"Yes! I'm having a hard time believing what I'm reading, and an even harder time wrapping my mind around it."

"How are you managing with the changing pages?"

"It doesn't seem to matter. I can somehow remember the pages I've read and my brain puts them in sequence no matter what order I see them."

Remembering his months of frustration trying to make sense of the book, he said, "I hate you."

"No, you don't."

"Okay, I seethe with envy. Any helpful flashes of insight yet?"

"Not yet. Maybe never."

His stomach dropped. "Don't say that."

"Jack, there's so much.*"*

"Keep at it. Got to be something."

He rang off and headed for the elevators. He figured the House of Blues ought to be as good a place as any to grab a couple of brews and a decent steak.

7. "What do you wish me to do?" Kris Szeto said.

Ernst Drexler watched the man fidget and drum his fingers on the table between them.

"I want you to complete your assignment."

Szeto glanced away, as if afraid to speak his mind.

"Go ahead," Ernst said. "Spit it out. I want to hear your thoughts. I want an honest assessment. Don't worry about telling me what I don't want to hear. I've already had a bellyful of that: You saw her go in, you saw the explosion, you didn't see her come out so you thought she was dead and you left. But there's no report of her body in the wreckage. Yes, *quite* a bellyful."

"Very well. I wish to say that perhaps assignment *has* been completed."

"Oh, really?" Ernst felt a spike of anger but suppressed it. "Five of our enforcers dead and their target still at large . . . how can you possibly spin that into even a subatomic particle of success? Even string theory won't help you there."

Szeto shrugged. "The purpose was to get her off line. That is exactly where she is now. She has no house and her computer is slag. She is on run and too terrified to go back online."

"*Terrified?* Of what? Us? No one we send against her comes back. We try to blow her up and she survives. We should be terrified of *her*."

"Is not her. Is that Jack fellow Harris tell us about. Woman did not steal gun from Max. It was this Jack."

"An assumption on your part. You told me Harris said he was just an old friend."

"An old friend with gun." Szeto straightened in his chair. "Whatever the case, the end was to neutralize her. I believe such end has been achieved."

"The end was to *permanently* remove this thorn from our side. You cannot guarantee that she'll stay neutralized. She has proven herself resourceful and dangerous. I sense a core of tenacity within that woman. I have no doubt she will be back. Do you?"

"We have not stopped looking for her. I will be circulating photo to our brothers in the Order and—"

"Where did you get a photo?"

"Hospital took one when she was Jane Doe. They were going to give to police departments."

Ernst nodded approval. Szeto was resourceful. And to give him his due, he had planned his moves well. His one mistake had been assuming that his men would be the only ones equipped for deadly force. He had erred in that assumption. Ernst was sure he would not err so again.

"A good idea. That will give us extra eyes. I'll have McCabe contact the Dormentalists. As a measure of our new détente, we'll have them disseminate her picture as well."

"And the Kickers?"

Ernst nodded. "Oh, yes. The Kickers most certainly. They're everywhere. But we will need to offer them a reward as an incentive. They're devoted to Thompson but cash will ensure more active participation on their part."

"Our people have located her credit accounts. If Louise Myers uses her MasterCard or AmEx, we will know it."

"And after you locate her, what then?"

"We take her and whoever is with her. Then we begin erasing all trace of them from planet."

Once again Ernst nodded approval.

The Order had nurtured the various 9/11 conspiracy theories, sometimes going so far as to plant false evidence or start blogs and Web sites of its own to direct suspicions or start theories of its own creation, the more outrageous, the better. The doubters were looking for the truth and the Order wanted to keep them looking in every direction but the right one, to deflect blame and suspicion from itself. Everything had been working perfectly until this "Secret Historian" had begun asking the wrong questions. Even her username had set off alarms. She obviously didn't know the truth, but she was pointing in dangerous directions. She had to be stopped.

Or did she?

Ernst was hoping the *Fhinntmanchca* would make her irrelevant. But it was a nebulous hope. He didn't know if they could succeed in creating one. He had followed all the ancient lore to the letter, but he was treading terra incognita.

So far the lore had been on the mark. The Orsa had come to life, and then it had awakened. And then it had swallowed Darryl.

But could the *Fhinntmanchca*—if they succeeded in creating it—accomplish what the One wanted? If so, then chasing down this woman was an exercise in futility. She would not matter. But no one knew how long it would take to create the *Fhinntmanchca*. And once created, no one, not even the One, could guarantee its success.

And so the search for Louise Myers had to be pressed. She had to be stopped from further interfering in matters she should leave alone—matters everyone should leave alone.

8. Weezy's eyes burned. She closed them as she leaned back to rub her throbbing temples. After leaving Jack at the airport she'd returned here and had been poring over the text ever since. Usually she could read till all hours with no problem, but this *Compendium* . . .

Maybe it was the book's autotranslating feature. She couldn't imagine how it worked, but perhaps the process of changing all the print to the reader's native language had an effect on the eyes and brain. That, plus the density of new information on each page . . . Jack said he'd been told that the author was a woman named Srem . . . this must have been her life's work.

Whatever, Weezy needed a break. The fraction of the text she'd absorbed was a mind-numbing jumble of facts that read like fancies . . .

A group of devices called the Seven Infernals . . . she'd come across two of them so far and they were wonderful and terrible in what they could do. Where in the text she'd find the other five—or *if* she'd find the other five—she had no idea.

A word called *The Answer*—Jack had been right about Srem's love of capitals—would not translate, but instead remained an indecipherable tangle of squiggles that she suspected might not make sense even in the Old Tongue. Supposedly when uttered it gave the best answer to whatever question was asked. She had no idea how that could be.

And repeated references to "the Seven." But the Seven what? Sometimes it sounded like a group, sometimes a single entity. Srem tossed off the references as if everyone should know. And most likely everyone did know about the Seven back in those days, but Weezy hadn't a clue.

And what was it with the number seven? It kept popping

up everywhere. Either Srem had a fetish for it or was simply reflecting the times. Seemed like seven was on everyone's mind back in the First Age.

But so far, not a single mention of *Fhinntmanchca.*

"You look beat," Eddie said as he walked into the spare bedroom she'd commandeered. "Time to call it a night." He carried a glass of water and a small plastic bottle. She'd complained of a headache and he'd gone to find her something for it. "Hold out your hand."

He shook a couple of Advil into her palm.

"Two more," she said.

"You're only supposed to take two."

"This is an eight-hundred-milligram headache."

He shook out two more and handed her the glass of water. She washed them down and finished the rest of the water.

"You're a good brother, Eddie. The best. Thanks for putting me up and putting up with me."

He smiled. "That's what family is for."

Although they qualified as "Irish twins"—barely a year separating their births—they'd never been close growing up. Maybe because they were so opposite. She sometimes wondered if Eddie's childhood apathy and couch potato lifestyle had been a reaction to her restless energy and intellectual curiosity. When it came to a choice between schoolwork and Atari, the games always won out. Her straight A's hadn't helped matters, she guessed, especially when he was bringing in B's and C's.

She supposed her emotional lability put an extra burden on their relationship—on the whole family. When her mood swings finally backed her folks into consulting a child psychiatrist, Eddie had been anything but sympathetic. She became "my crazy sister" until their folks issued a gag order: No one in town was to know about her visits to Dr. Hamilton.

Their strongest connection had been Jack, who had the smarts to keep up with her, the patience to go along with her, and who loved video games almost as much as Eddie. They were often three musketeers, but more often than not it was just Jack and Weezy.

But Eddie had changed during college. He got his act together—physically and academically—and was now successful and financially comfortable.

But was he happy? She wondered about that. He didn't seem to have anyone in his life. He had this big, three-story townhouse condo all to himself. She didn't care if he was straight or gay, he should have someone. She remembered her years with Steve as some of the best of her life. Bad enough he'd left her, but the *way* he'd left her . . .

His smile faded. "I won't pretend to understand what you're into, Weez, but I wish to God you'd drop it."

She looked up at him. "I wish I could. I wish I could simply up and walk away, but I can't."

"Your friend Kevin is dead—murdered."

Weezy watched him step to the nearest window and peer out at the twilight.

Was he worried he'd be next? Had she put him in jeopardy?

"Maybe I should find a hotel—"

He whirled toward her. "No way. You're safe here and so you're going to stay here. It's just that . . ." He looked away, then back at her. "Six men dead since Tuesday, five killed by Jack, you say." He shook his head. "Even as I'm saying those words, I can't believe them. Jack . . . of all people . . . you're sure—?"

"Absolutely."

"What happened to him? How'd he become a killer?"

Weezy tensed. "Don't call him that. He didn't want to. It was them or us, so he did what he had to."

"But why was he carrying a gun in the first place?"

"I'm glad he was. I have no doubt I'd have ended up like Kevin if he hadn't been."

"But we're talking about *Jack,* the guy who used to ride his BMX over to our house to play *Asteroids,* who used to hang out in your room and complain about your music."

Weezy warmed at the memory of those days. Lost innocence . . .

"Yeah."

"Which, by the way, was truly awful."

She put on a shocked face. "Bauhaus and the Cure?"

"Awful. Give me Def Leppard any day." He waved a hand. "But anyway, this is the guy who picked up cash cutting lawns and working at USED. God knows how he earns his living now. What changed him?"

"I'll bet it was his mother's murder."

Eddie stared at her. "Murder? No one was out to get her. She just happened to be in the wrong place at the worst time."

No one was out to get her . . .

Weezy wondered.

She hadn't told Eddie about the meeting at Mr. Veilleur's, but the revelation of the Lady, and her appearing there as Mrs. Clevenger, made Weezy suspect that Jack's mother's presence in the wrong place at the worst time might not have been accidental.

"Still . . . she died horribly."

Eddie made a face. "And what? He became Batman?"

She had to smile. "I'm picturing Jack in tights and a cape . . ."

Not bad.

"You know what I mean."

"Batman fights crime. I can't see Jack into that. In fact, I'm pretty sure some of his best friends are on the wrong side of the law. But Jack's not the issue now." She turned and tapped the *Compendium.* "This is."

His tone oozed doubt: "Ah, the magic book that anyone can read, no matter what language they speak."

She'd given him only the vaguest description of the book's origin without mentioning the First Age. Didn't want to open *that* can of worms. She'd told him it might contain information on the 9/11 attacks.

"Yeah. But so far, no good. I'm looking for information on something called 'Opus Omega.' It's—"

"That's Latin. If your book translates itself into English—and I don't believe for a moment that it does—why do you expect to find Latin words?"

Good question, one that hadn't occurred to Weezy. But she'd found "Opus Omega" mentioned in passing in the *Compendium* a number of times already, so how . . . ?

"Half Latin, half Greek, actually. Maybe because it's been in and out—mostly out—of circulation since ancient times, and the scholars who wrote about it most likely used the languages of most Western scholars since before the Common Era. Maybe some of those phrases have become the preferred terms for certain references in the book. So that's how the book translates them."

"You really believe that?"

She shrugged. "Works for me."

He moved up beside her. "Mind if I take a look?"

"Be my guest."

She rolled her chair back and watched as he flipped through the pages. Abruptly he stopped and stared, slack-jawed.

"Th-that illustration," he said, pointing. "It's moving!"

Weezy rose and moved in beside him. Sure enough, a drawing of a globe that looked like the Earth spun in empty space. It had a 3-D look to it. The outlines of the continents confirmed that it was indeed Earth, but its surface was peppered by dots and crisscrossed by lines. It reminded her of an airline flight map.

And then she realized she'd seen that pattern before: on the Lady's back.

She leaned closer, trying to see where the dots fell and the lines crossed but the globe was spinning too fast. She put her hand on it to try to stop it but felt only a flat page without the slightest sense of movement.

"Look at the header," Eddie said.

She did. *Opus Omega* sat above the animation.

But that was the only text. She turned the page and found the reverse side blank. The facing page began in mid-sentence about something unrelated.

Eddie put his hand over hers and turned the page back to the animation.

"How is this possible?" he said in a hushed voice.

"I don't know, Eddie, but there it is. And it refers to Opus Omega—in Latin and Greek. Part of what I'm looking for."

But a spinning globe was useless. She needed the equivalent of a Mercator projection map. Did they have such a thing in Srem's time?

Eddie continued to stare at the animation. When he spoke he sounded like a motorboat.

"But-but-but how do they do that?" He looked at her. "It really is magical, isn't it."

She nodded.

He said, "But if it's as old as you say, how could they know the Earth was round? And how could they know—I mean, the continents on that globe are accurate. How can that be?"

"Because it's very old, Eddie. It's from a time when we knew, from the time before we lost all that knowledge."

Eddie was nodding. He was becoming a believer.

9. Jack stood outside the Vintage Theatre on Melrose and hoped this was it. He didn't know where to turn if it wasn't.

He'd been to The Silent Movie Theatre on Fairfax and three others around town, finally ending up at the Aero in Santa Monica. None of the theaters could hold a candle to the Egyptian. The Aero had a few deco touches but seemed like a typical neighborhood theater. And like the others, its night manager was young and knew of no gray-haired fellow employee in his sixties.

He did however know of one other theater playing vintage films—a three-hundred-seater on Melrose called—of all things—the Vintage. But he wasn't sure it was still operating.

Jack had found Melrose and followed it until he spotted the lit-up Vintage marquee in a seedy area of down-market shops and specialty boutiques. At least it was open.

A sign announced GARY COOPER WEEK! and tonight they were offering a double bill of *Beau Geste* and *High Noon.*

The closer he got, the more it looked like the sort of place that might not be opposed to paying off the books. Cracks laced the heavily smudged glass of the empty ticket booth. He had to rap on the glass three times before a pierced-up teenage girl with black hair and white makeup appeared and sold him a ticket. She tore it in half and told him he could go in.

Inside, the industrial carpeting was worn and the art deco moldings needed refurbishing. To look like he was here to watch a movie, he bought a large popcorn. Soft and chewy—stale. Probably left over from last night, or even the night before.

He asked the gothoid teenage boy behind the counter—

were he and the ticket girl a couple?—if he could speak to the manager.

The kid turned and called, "Ernie! Someone to see you!"

Ernie—yes. A good start.

A few seconds later Ernest Goren stepped into the doorway. He'd kept his first name, but probably had changed the second. His eyes narrowed as he frowned at Jack.

"Can I help you?"

Jack walked over and extended his hand. "John Tyleski."

Goren gave a quick shake but didn't offer his name.

Knowing his interest in UFOs, Jack had his next line all set.

"I was wondering if you have any plans to show *Earth vs. the Flying Saucers*. You know . . ." He cupped his hands around his mouth and lowered his voice, imitating the alien announcer. "'*People of Earth*' . . ."

Goren's mouth twisted. "That's not bad. But you missed it by three weeks."

"Really? Damn! I've wanted to see that on a big screen for ages."

"We ran a UFO festival—double features every night Monday through Thursday."

Okay, the ice was broken. Now to get on his good side, gain a little trust. Jack didn't have to feign interest.

"You're killing me. What did you show?"

Goren ducked back into his office. Jack stepped up to the doorway but didn't enter. A tiny space. He was surprised to see Alice Laverty sitting in a chair opposite the desk.

"Hello," he said.

Jack looked for a sign of recognition—after all they'd been on the same plane for almost six hours—but she simply nodded and gave him a polite smile. Well, why should she remember him? Except for one trip to the restroom, he'd stayed in his seat the whole time.

Looked like Goren hadn't been able to arrange coverage for tonight, but that hadn't stopped him from spending time with his daughter. Good for him.

Goren pulled a couple of sheets from his desktop and handed one to Jack.

"Take a look."

Vintage Theatre UFO Festival

MONDAY
Earth vs. the Flying Saucers
Devil Girl from Mars

TUESDAY
Close Encounters
Plan 9 from Outer Space

WEDNESDAY
This Island Earth
Invasion of the Saucer Men

THURSDAY
The Thing from Another World
Invaders from Mars

"Cool," Jack said. "Except for Thursday, you've paired a goody with a turkey."

"One man's turkey is another man's steak." He handed Jack another sheet. "If you'd have liked that, you'll love next week's festival—five days."

Vintage Theatre INVASION Festival

SUNDAY
Robot Monster
Killers from Space

MONDAY
Invasion of the Body Snatchers
It Conquered the World

TUESDAY
Night of the Blood Beast
The Brain from Planet Arous

WEDNESDAY
I Married a Monster from Outer Space
Teenagers from Outer Space

THURSDAY
Invisible Invaders
The Cape Canaveral Monsters

"Wow. I'm so there. And in chronological order too."

Goren was staring at him. "You seem to know your stuff."

"Who picks these?"

"I do."

Jack folded his hands in supplication. "Can I be you when I grow up?"

"I don't think this theater will last till then. But let's see if you can figure this: These ten films have something else in common besides invasion from space. Know what it is?"

Jack hadn't a clue, but he needed to keep impressing Goren.

"Well, you've got a couple of Agars and a couple of Cormans . . ."

"Good, very good, but that's not it. They were all filmed in part in and around the Bronson Caves."

"I've heard of them. They're nearby, aren't they?"

"About five miles as the crow flies."

"Ever been there?"

He smiled. "Lots of times."

"Could you show me sometime?"

The smile faded and shutters seemed to drop behind his eyes. "I don't think so. I have a day job."

"We can do it on your day off. I'm willing to pay for your time."

He took a step back into the office. "No, I don't think so."

"A hundred bucks for what—a couple of hours."

Goren shook his head.

"Then give me a pen."

Goren complied with obvious reluctance. On the back of the UFO festival list Jack wrote "John Tyleski—Bronson Caves" and his Tracfone number.

"You change your mind, call me, okay?"

"You're missing the movie," Goren said and closed the door.

Jack knew the guy had to be wary, but he'd come on like a total film geek, and wanting a Bronson tour was in character. What had he done, what had he said to shut the guy down?

10. Jack sat through the end of *High Noon* and revisited Fort Zinderneuf and the Geste brothers in *Beau Geste*. He was too restless to enjoy them, but felt he had to stay. Any suspicions Goren had about him would be confirmed if he'd walked out after their conversation. So he hung on.

But he sat in a back row where he could get up every so often and squint through the crack between the doors for a peek at the manager's office. Goren had opened the door again and Jack could see a bit of the desk. He was banking on him not trusting the teenagers to close up and staying to do that himself.

As the closing credits began to roll after *Beau Geste*'s bittersweet final scene, Jack took his time exiting with the thirty or so other patrons. As he passed the manager's office he tapped on the door and stuck his head in. Both Goren and his daughter jumped at the sight of him.

Why were they so spooked?

"Great to see those on a big screen," he said. "Change your mind about the Bronson tour?"

Goren swallowed as he shook his head. "No." His voice sounded hoarse and tight.

Jack could only describe Alice's expression as a frightened glare.

"Well, you have my number if you do. And I'll up the price to two hundred bucks."

Baffled by their frightened reaction, he gave a friendly wave and headed out, wondering where he'd gone wrong. Had Alice remembered him from the flight, or were they wary of any stranger who seemed overly friendly? Jack didn't think he'd been overly anything but geeky. Had he let too much of his inner movie geek shine through?

Well, since Godot would probably call before Goren, Jack would have to follow them home. But first to check for possible escape routes.

On his way in he'd spotted an alley along the building's left flank. He checked that out now and was relieved to find it blind. Exit doors, litter, a Dumpster, a beat-up motorcycle chained to a standpipe, and high walls all around.

Two ways out—the front or the alley—both onto Melrose. Excellent.

He slipped behind the wheel of his car down the street to watch and wait. He got his first inkling that things might go sour when the two teens left the theater and walked away. He'd assumed one of them owned the motorcycle.

Then the entrance went dark, followed quickly by the marquee. A few minutes later the motorcycle with two helmeted riders—the passenger obviously female—roared out of the alley headed east on Melrose. Jack hung a U and followed.

For a guy living off the books and trying to limit expenses, a motorcycle made a lot of sense. Even more sense if the legendary L.A. traffic jams lived up to their hype. The junker at the airport probably belonged to the driver. No room for luggage on a bike. Must have dragooned a friend into picking up his daughter.

He followed them along Melrose for a few miles, then onto the 101 South ramp. Jack didn't get much farther than the ramp. Traffic was stopped. Umpteen lanes going nowhere.

Welcome to L.A.

But worse, the motorcycle was unaffected. It kept moving, leaving him behind as it wove between the stagnant lanes. Jack sat and watched helplessly as it disappeared from view.

He banged on the steering wheel a few times—just to make himself feel better—then began planning how to rent a motorcycle for tomorrow night.

11.

Jack's Tracfone rang at 11:10 as he was surfing his movie choices on the pay-per-view channel.

"Hello?" said a voice he thought he recognized. *"Is this John Tyleski?"*

"Speaking."

"This is Ernie, the manager from the Vintage Theatre. You still up for that Bronson tour?"

"Sure am."

"The two-hundred offer still good?"

"Waiting right here in my pocket."

"Then how does seven o'clock tomorrow morning sound?"

"Kind of early."

"Sunrise is at six. You won't miss anything. Told you I had to work. This way I get in just a little late. For two hundred, I can afford to miss an hour or two. I'll meet you up there. Need directions?"

"Can't you pick me up?"

"Nah. I'll be biking it."

"I'll pick you up then."

"No-no," he said quickly. *"That won't work. It's easy to get to. I'll give you directions."*

Jack used the room's pen and pad to write them down, then hung up.

He stood at the window and watched the thinning pedestrian parade below, then stared at the smog-smudged lights of the downtown buildings in the basin. This situation stank like the air down there looked.

Earlier tonight Goren had looked at him like he was Sergeant Markoff, or maybe Frank Miller. Now he was up for guiding Jack on a tour.

Why the change of heart? Two hundred bucks? Maybe. But Jack had his doubts.

He'd have to be careful.

FRIDAY

1. Despite hitting the rack around midnight, Jack found himself wide awake at 3:30 A.M. This time-zone change wasn't working for him. His internal clock thought it was 6:30.

He killed time showering and wandering the West Hollywood streets in a fruitless search for caffeine. The Andaz's coffee shop was closed until seven and the Starbucks down the street didn't open till six. This was not what he'd expected in a major city. Unlike New York, Los Angeles slept.

Finally he broke down and asked the Andaz's night man where he could get coffee. The guy pointed him across the street to the Sunset Plaza Hotel where the coffee shop stayed open twenty-four hours.

Maybe he should have stayed there.

The coffee wasn't the greatest but it was coffee. He killed half an hour reading *USA Today* cover to cover and was first on line at the Starbucks when it opened its doors as the sun rose. He found things about the chain annoying—like calling their largest serving "venti" instead of just plain old "large"—but they served consistently good coffee. After a large of their "robust" coffee of the day, he felt his serum caffeine concentration reach an acceptable level.

Back at the room he pulled the Glock from under the mattress, chambered a round, and slipped it into his right front pocket.

2.

The directions led him back to Hollywood Boulevard and then uphill from there along Canyon Drive through a residential district. The houses abruptly vanished as he passed between two stone columns. A sign announced Griffith Park.

The park road—Jack recognized it from dozens of films—snaked into the hills through acres of mostly scrub brush that looked sere and seared, past a picnic area and a caged kiddie playground. It ended at a small parking lot with an odd sign: CAMP HOLLYWOOD LAND, whatever that meant. His was the only car about. He got out and checked his reflection in the window glass: His T-shirt hung long and loose, leaving no hint of the pistol in his pocket.

He heard an engine roar down the road and soon a motorcycle cruised into the lot. Goren was the only rider this time. Jack watched him as he secured his bike. He wore a tight T, tucked in. It showed off his muscles but also left no place to hide a weapon. Jack saw the square of his wallet in the back pocket of his jeans, but no other bulges where there shouldn't be. He wore sneakers—no place to hide a weapon there. Jack allowed himself to relax . . . but just a little.

Goren stepped up to him but didn't offer to shake hands.

"I'll need to get paid in advance."

"Sure thing." Jack pulled out his wallet and extracted a pair of hundreds. "Here you go."

Goren stuffed them into a pocket and said, "We walk from here."

Jack gestured to the empty parking lot. "Why so deserted?"

"It's an unstaffed park, but tourists will be straggling

in soon. Too bad a film isn't in production. Then the joint would be jumping."

Not too bad for Jack. He didn't know what it would take to get Goren to open up about what happened down there in the bowels of Ground Zero.

He followed him across a small concrete bridge where they skirted a red-striped car gate and stepped onto an uphill dirt path. Jack noticed fresh tire tracks.

"Somebody's been driving along here."

"Looks like it, but you need a permit. I don't want to get hassled."

And Jack knew why. But then, he didn't want to be hassled for pretty much the same reason.

Goren waved ahead along the incline. "*Earth vs. the Spider* had a few scenes right along here." He pointed left to a break in the rocks. "Recognize that?"

Jack stared a moment, then saw Kevin McCarthy, in full-blown panic mode, scramble into view and run toward him.

"*Invasion of the Body Snatchers*."

Goren gave him an appraising look. "You do know your stuff."

"Why do you sound so surprised?"

He looked puzzled. "Do I?"

A couple of bends in the road, then over a low rise where Goren stopped and gestured.

"We're here."

It all looked smaller than he'd expected, but he immediately recognized the dark maw in the rocks he'd seen so many times on reruns.

"The Bat Cave!"

"Except it's not a cave. Take a look."

Jack stepped closer and saw daylight on the other side.

"A tunnel."

"Yep. The Bronson Caves are really a tunnel. It was

dug through for Douglas Fairbanks's *Robin Hood*. It's got three exits into the quarry on the other side. Let's see if you can recognize the one where Ro-Man set up his bubble machine."

Robot Monster . . . one of the worst, cheapest-looking, most laughable sci-fi films ever made, yet Jack felt a tingle of anticipation as they entered the cave-tunnel. Dark inside, almost black, maybe fifteen feet wide, and no more than a dozen feet high. He felt as if he'd stepped into *The Brain from Planet Arous* or *Attack of the Crab Monsters*.

Okay, rein in the geek. That's not why we're here.

But that didn't mean he couldn't soak up some of this film history. He couldn't help it, he was psyched.

The shaft ran straight through the mini-mountain, maybe a hundred fifty feet from end to end. As they walked, Jack kept Goren on his left and stayed half a pace behind, keeping an eye on him.

About three quarters of the way through, side shafts to the left and right came into view. The openings were too small to walk through upright so he and Goren continued along the main shaft into the quarry beyond. As they stepped out into the light, Goren pointed to the left.

"Take a look."

As Jack turned, Goren grabbed his right wrist in an iron grip. Before Jack could react he heard a woman's voice behind him.

"Don't move or I'll shoot you dead."

Jack half turned to see Alice pointing a small, nickel-plated semi-auto his way. Looked like a .38. She'd been hiding behind an outcrop along the edge of the mouth. He noticed her hand shaking, but also saw murder in her eyes.

Jerk. He'd known Goren was suspicious of him, but never dreamed he'd involve his daughter like this. The co-conspirator theory was looking better and better.

Best course: Play dumb.

"What's this? You're mugging me? I don't have much left after that two hundred I gave—"

"Drop it," Goren said, tightening his grip. Jack could have broken it, but not a good idea with a pistol pointed at him. "We know you followed Alice from Newark."

They did?

"What makes you think that?"

"You looked familiar last night," he said, "but I couldn't place you. Then I remembered seeing you at the airport. You passed within ten feet of us. When I asked Alice if you'd been on her plane, she remembered you."

Well, damn. He tried so hard to be easy to forget. But with a hyperaware fugitive, expecting trouble from all quarters, the rules changed.

Time for a change of tactics.

He heaved a sigh of resignation. "Okay. You got me. But you don't need the hardware. I'm not a cop."

"I never thought you were."

"Then who—?"

"You killed my mother!"

The words came at screech pitch, forced through Alice's clenched teeth. She looked bug-eyed scary, ready to pull that trigger, like she knew of nothing else in the world she wanted to do more.

And at this range, she couldn't miss.

So much for the theory that she was in on her mother's death. But if she didn't blame her father for it, then who—?

Later for that. Had to keep her calm.

"*I* killed your mother?" He pointed to Goren. "*He* killed your mother."

"He did *not*!"

"That's what everybody thinks."

"But you know better!"

Who did she think he was?

"Look, I'm not here about any of that. I simply want to ask your father some questions."

"Bullshit!" That screech again. She inched the pistol forward. "She was burned alive and now you're here to finish the job!"

The new angle on the pistol allowed Jack a look at its safety . . . she had it in the *on* position.

Sweet.

"Easy, Alice, easy," Goren said. He faced Jack. "We don't want to hurt you—"

"*I* do!"

He ignored his daughter and spoke in a rush. "Look, we could kill you here and now and get away with it, but I'm sure you've reported back already, and they'll only send someone else. All I want is to live in peace. You can go back and tell them I won't say anything. I haven't breathed a word in all these years and I'm not about to change now. I've proven I can keep silent. Please, there must be a way we can work this out."

"Don't beg, Dad."

Baffled, Jack said, "Who do you people think I am?"

A hint of uncertainty crept into Goren's tone. "You . . . or someone connected to you . . . you tried to kill me and my wife."

That could simply be the story he concocted to square himself with his daughter. But he seemed to believe it himself.

Jack looked around. "Did they ever film *The Twilight Zone* here? Because I feel like I just stepped into it." He faced Goren. "I'm not who you think I am. Let go of my arm. She's got the drop on me. Let's discuss this like civilized people."

"Civilized?" she screeched.

Goren hesitated, then released him.

"Dad, no!"

Jack had had enough. He took a quick step toward Alice, saw her finger pull against the trigger, but it wouldn't move. He snatched the pistol away and pushed her into her father.

"You forgot the safety."

He made a show of flicking the lever as he trained it on them.

Goren pushed her behind him. His mouth worked but no words would come. If this were one of the movies they tended to film here, he'd be saying, *It's me you want! Kill me if you must, but let my daughter go!*

Or something like that.

Jack popped the magazine from the grip, ejected the chambered shell, then tossed the pistol to Goren. He caught it and gave Jack a baffled look.

"I don't . . ."

"Like I said: I have no idea who you think I am, but I had nothing to do with anything that happened to you in the past. I heard your name for the first time yesterday. I just want to ask you some questions."

"Oh, God!" Alice said through the fingers pressed against her mouth. "If the safety had been off, I could have killed you."

Jack smiled. "Trust me, lady. If the safety had been off, I wouldn't have made that move."

"How did you know to follow Alice?"

He looked at her. "If you've got something to hide on your computer, Wi-Fi is not a good choice. An investigator tapped into your e-mails."

"Investigator?" Goren said. "Who's investigating Alice?"

"Someone unconnected to whatever you saw down there or what happened after. Someone with questions about nine/eleven. I'm here to find the answer to one of them."

"Are you with the government?"

"Not likely. But let me get this straight: You didn't torch your house and you've been on the run from somebody other than the police?"

He nodded. "Don't ask me who because I don't know."

If Goren was telling the truth—and Jack believed he was—then Weezy was right: Something more than Islamic fanaticism hid behind the fall of the Towers.

Conspiracies everywhere.

"Maybe I can find out—if you tell me what you saw. Nothing you say will be recorded anywhere. Only one other person besides myself will know, and we won't be talking."

"But what value—?"

"It may furnish a missing piece to the puzzle, it may be useless. The fact that someone tried to kill you tells me it's important. So what do you say?"

Goren hesitated.

"You never know," Jack added. "We might bring down whoever torched your place. Give you a chance to get right with the law."

Though Jack doubted very much that would happen, it wasn't impossible.

Goren finally nodded. "All right. Maybe somebody should know. But I gotta warn you: Some of what I'm going to say will be hard to swallow. You may think I'm crazy."

"Don't count on it."

He turned to his daughter. "Wait for me down at the parking lot, Alice."

"I want to hear this too."

He shook his head. "It's better if you don't. I wasn't supposed to see what I saw, and someone tried to kill me because I did. You're safer not knowing. Go. Wait by the cycle."

She hesitated, then started to walk off. Jack didn't like

the thought of her hanging out alone down there. He pulled out his keys.

"Here." He tossed them to her. "Sit in my car."

She made a two-handed catch and stared at him with a confused expression. He understood. She'd tried to shoot him a moment ago, now he was offering his car.

"Yeah," he said. "Ain't life screwy?"

She entered the tunnel with a couple of backward glances. When she was out of sight, Goren pointed to the far side of the quarry.

"Let's talk over there."

They found a couple of neighboring boulders and seated themselves. High on a hillside far off to his right, he could see the famous Hollywood sign. And directly before him, a familiar cave mouth.

"Ro-Man's spot! And the place where the Blood Beast hid!"

"Yes-yes." Goren looked annoyed. "Christ, I thought you wanted to know what happened in the wreckage."

"I do. It's just—"

"Well then, let's get to it. I want this over and done with so I can get back to Alice."

Jack sighed. So much film history . . . he'd have to let it go for now.

"Okay. I know the basics. You were part of a team of four—"

"Right. Alfieri, Lukach, and Ratner. Good guys, all of them."

"And I know that Lukach called up and said you heard voices. 'Experts' later wrote that off as some acoustical trick, but I've got a feeling you're going to tell me different."

His expression was grim as he nodded. "Oh, yeah. Ohhhhh, yeah."

3. "There!" Lukach said, his voice muffled by the half-face respirator. "I heard it again. Listen."

Ernie tried but couldn't hear much past the roaring in his ears.

What was wrong with him today? This was his fourth trip into the foundation of WTC-4 and he'd been fine the first three. But today . . .

Sweat oozed from every pore, soaking his hair under the hard hat, darkening his shirt, fogging his goggles. His heart pounded like a wild animal against the cage of his chest. He felt shaky inside and out, and didn't seem to be able to draw a full breath. He fought the urge to pull off the respirator mask. The dust down here could be toxic.

Something else was toxic as well . . . something he couldn't identify, couldn't smell or touch, but he could sense it. It hadn't been here yesterday, but sweet Jesus, it was here now.

Or maybe it was because they'd never been this deep—seventy feet below street level now. Like the towers, WTC-4, the nine-story building that had squatted next to the south tower, had six underground levels. No one had wanted to trust the weight of the Trade Center to the sediment and landfill at the site, so they'd excavated down to bedrock for the foundation. That's where Ernie and the crew were now—level one, the very bottom.

He'd never had a panic attack, but he sure as hell felt panicky now.

Why?

It had started as soon as they'd reached this new search area. A little jittery at first, then building and building until . . .

"It's coming from over there," Lukach said, pointing to a pile of rubble. "And—damn! Turn off your lights."

Alfieri and Ratner doused theirs along with Lukach, but Ernie left his on. He did *not* want to be in the dark down here. Not today.

"Hey, Goren," Lukach said. "You deaf? Put it out."

Ernie couldn't tell them that, at age fifty-one, he was suddenly afraid of the dark, so he took a breath, held it, and hit the off switch.

Lukach's voice floated out of the blackness. "See? See what I'm talking about? There's light on the other side of that mound."

Light? Any light would be welcome. Ernie squinted through his fogged goggles and saw it. Faint as could be, a dim, barely visible glow lit the upper edge of that pile.

"Got to be another team," Ratner said.

"Yeah? Last I looked, that's east of us, and we're just about as far east as you can go in the foundation."

"Then who's there?" Alfieri said.

Lukach turned on his light. "Good question. Especially since there ain't supposed to be any 'there' over there. Let's go take a look."

No-no-no, Ernie thought. Let's not. Let's not go near there. Let's turn around and get back up to clean, pure sunshine.

But he couldn't say that, because he couldn't tell them *why* they shouldn't go there. He didn't know.

"Maybe we should wait for backup," he said, holding back as the others moved ahead.

" 'Backup'?" Lukach said without turning. "You've got to be kidding."

Ernie forced himself to follow, but trailed a good dozen feet behind. When they reached the pile of crushed masonry and began to climb, he hung back, watching, waiting, trembling. He saw Lukach reach the top first and motion the others to join him. Ernie saw them pointing, heard them babbling but couldn't understand what they were saying.

Finally Ratner turned and waved him up.

"C'mon, Ernie. Y'gotta see this. It's some sort of tunnel."

Tunnel? Tunnel to where? The way he was feeling, it had to be a straight shot to Hell.

Steeling himself, he made the climb. When he reached the top he saw what had excited them. Below, on the far side of the mound, near the floor, part of the foundation wall had fallen away, revealing an irregular opening, maybe half a dozen feet across. Light flickered from within.

The fires of Hell. No, not Hell . . . something worse.

What was he thinking? Where were these ideas coming from?

He tried to shake them off but couldn't . . . right now he wanted nothing more than to turn and run. But he was part of the team. He couldn't leave these guys.

"Let's go," Lukach said.

"No-no-no!" Ernie said. "We should get backup!"

"Fuck backup. I'm going down."

With Ratner and Alfieri on his heels, Lukach quickly descended the far side of the pile and picked his way to the opening. When he reached it, he stopped and stared, then stepped through, shouting, "Hey!"

Ratner and Alfieri followed.

Raised voices echoed from the opening, one of them unfamiliar. Had they found someone?

Fighting the fear, he eased down the pile and crept to the opening. Every step was an effort. He felt as if he were struggling against a hurricane-force wind roaring through that opening. When he reached it he dropped to his knees and peeked around the corner.

4. "Next thing I saw was the ceiling of a hospital room."

Oh, hell, Jack thought.

"That's it?"

"That was it then. The doctors told me I'd been spewing word salad—that's what they called it—for days. Now I could talk and make sense but I couldn't answer their questions about what happened down there. I had a hole in my memory running from the instant I leaned in to take a look to that moment in the hospital.

"When they told me that the guys were dead, crushed in a cave-in, I cried. Later I figured that's what I'd been afraid of. I sometimes get premonitions—little things, you know, like someone coming for a visit—and maybe what I was feeling was one of those, but scary because it involved death."

"What did they think it was—shock-induced amnesia?"

He nodded. "Something like that. They said I was in what they called 'a fugue state' when they found me."

Pissed, Jack rose from the uncomfortable boulder and brushed off the seat of his jeans as he paced about. This was looking like a major waste of time.

"Well, if you can't remember, that brings up the question of why someone would try to off a guy who had amnesia."

"Because my memories of that morning returned."

Jack stopped and looked at him. "Why the hell didn't you say so?"

"I'm saying so now. They sent me home on three head drugs that made me feel like crap, but I hung with them, hoping I'd get my memory back. I lived in East Meadow then. That's a town on—"

"Long Island. I know. Go on."

"Well, this detective from the city named Volkman kept coming around, asking me questions I couldn't answer. He told me some people were saying an explosion had caused the cave-in that killed my buds and did I know anything about that, or had I seen any explosives, and so on."

Something wrong there.

"He traveled all the way from Manhattan to chat with you?"

"Yeah. Lots of times." Goren shrugged. "Maybe he had nothing better to do, maybe he was trying to make a name for himself. Whatever, I couldn't help him. Until . . ."

"Your memory came back."

"Right. Happened in a flash. Suddenly I found myself reliving the whole thing. I was back at Ground Zero, in WTC-four's foundation, peeking around the edge of the hole. I was barely aware of Lukach, Ratner, and Alfieri standing about twenty feet away, talking to half a dozen workers wearing dark coveralls and respirators. I couldn't pay any attention to them because my eyes became glued on this . . . thing."

"What kind of thing?"

"I don't know. It was big, maybe a dozen or more feet long and, say, half that wide."

"Cylindrical?"

"Could have been. Hard to tell under that tarp."

Jack had once seen an Opus Omega pillar with those dimensions . . . a concrete column . . . and it had contained the body of a woman he knew.

"Was it upright, like a column?"

"No. It was on its side on a dolly attached to a backhoe."

"A backhoe? How'd they get one down there?"

"Through a tunnel. And I don't mean a hole shoveled through the dirt. This was big and wide with an arched ceiling all done up in brickwork."

"A subway tunnel?"

Goren nodded. "The only thing it could be."

"Well, the E train had a World Trade Center stop."

"But that was under building five."

"The PATH then?"

"The PATH comes under the Hudson from the west. This tunnel was heading east."

Jack shook his head. He knew the subway system backward and forward.

"There's no other line down there."

"Right. And I didn't see any rails in that tunnel, just a dirt floor."

"Then . . . ?"

"I've done a lot of research since then. A number of subway lines were started down that end of the city and never completed. I think that was a branch of one of them, but I've never been able to find a record of it."

"That doesn't surprise me," Jack said, thinking of the disappearing Aswad.

"But none of that mattered at the time. I don't remember wondering about the tunnel, or the backhoe or much of anything else. All I could see was that . . . thing. My eyes were glued to it, I couldn't look away . . . I felt this roaring in my ears, this buzzing in my head . . . my vision was fading in and out . . . I felt like all the energy was being sucked out of me." He looked at Jack with a tortured expression. "I was sure, I mean I just knew I was dying."

"But you were wrong."

There I go, he thought. Master of the obvious.

"Yeah, but I didn't know that then. I realize now that I was just passing out. But as everything was going black, I heard shouting. I looked over to where I'd seen my guys and saw them being clubbed to the ground with pry bars and such. That was the last thing I saw. After that I was out."

Jack wanted to know what happened next but didn't bother asking. Goren couldn't remember things he hadn't seen. He resumed his pacing.

Bizarre . . . bizarre . . . bizarre . . .

"That thing under the tarp," Goren said after a while. "It was an alien artifact, wasn't it."

Jack looked at him. Goren was obviously a sensitive, and if his frame of reference was UFOs, it would be natural for him to think that. Jack knew the truth and had no doubt Goren had seen an Opus Omega column. But he didn't have time to get into that. And besides, the guy wouldn't believe him anyway.

So he played dumb.

"What makes you think I know?"

"Just a suspicion."

"What makes you think aliens were involved?"

"The way it affected me. The other guys didn't notice a thing, but me . . . I sensed it right away. It was causing my panic attack."

Jack continued his impression of a psychiatrist. "Why do you think that was?"

He looked away. "I've always suspected that I was abducted by aliens when I was a kid. I'm sure of it now."

"Oookaaay."

Goren's head snapped around, his expression angry. "Go ahead. I'm used to it. But I was out camping with my folks when I was six. They woke up and I was gone. They found me a mile away, naked, turning circles till I threw up and passed out."

Using Occam's razor, Jack could come up with a half dozen explanations off the top of his head, none of them involving space aliens.

"Do you remember the aliens?"

"Of course not. You never do. Or at least you're not supposed to. But they either implanted something in me or added some of their own DNA to my system. Whatever the case, something inside me, something they inserted in me, responded to whatever was under that tarp."

Jack knew it had been the Otherness he'd responded to, not aliens. But he wasn't about to open that can of worms.

"Can you remember anything else?"

Goren shook his head.

"Think," Jack said. "Picture the scene. You've got your three friends, you've got half a dozen bad guys, you've got the . . . the artifact under the tarp . . . what else?"

Goren squeezed his eyes shut. After a moment, he said, "As I picture the artifact, I can see someone standing in the background. They'd strung lights along one wall of the tunnel and he was as far back as anyone could be and still be visible."

"What was he doing?"

"Just watching, I think. I remember him because he looked like he didn't belong."

"Why not?"

"He wasn't dressed like the others. They were in dark clothing, he was in a much lighter color. The light wasn't good, but he seemed to be in white."

Probably one of the Dormentalist bigwigs, possibly even Luther Brady himself overseeing the operation.

"Anything else?"

Another moment of deep concentration, then, "The guys were standing around a hole in the bedrock. It was five or six feet across. They must have pulled the artifact out of that."

No, Jack thought. They'd come to bury a pillar. Opus Omega was all about inserting them in specific locations.

Goren shot to his feet. "Oh, Jesus! Do you think . . . ?

I've heard talk about the government being involved in the Trade Center attack, but could they possibly have done it just so they could dig up an alien artifact?"

The idea stunned Jack. Not because he believed Goren had seen government operatives digging up something. More likely he'd seen a group of Dormentalists preparing to bury another of their damned Opus Omega columns.

"Sweet Jesus," Goren was saying in a hushed, awed tone. "All these years I've been thinking what monsters they were to collapse the tunnel on those guys. Now . . . I mean, the truth is so much worse. They brought down the towers and killed *thousands* just so they could get to that artifact. I'd heard Majestic-twelve was ruthless, but I never dreamed . . ."

Majestic-12 . . . the UFO crowd's name for the government's secret, alien investigation unit. But Jack knew who was in charge of Opus Omega—the Dormentalist Church.

Could it be? Could the Dormentalists have been behind 9/11?

Jack hated to think so, but he'd seen what they were capable of, so it was possible. With their international membership, they had global reach. But could they have infiltrated al Qaeda? Could Wahid bin Aswad, Weezy's Man Who Wasn't There, be a Dormentalist?

Goren said, "That would mean my own government killed Marilyn!"

Where'd that come from?

"Monroe?"

"What? No, my wife."

"Tell me how that happened."

"Marilyn had gone to bed—she was a secretary at the high school and had to get up in the morning. Me, I couldn't sleep so I went out for a walk. I got a coffee at the 7-Eleven and as I was on the way home it hit me like a ton of bricks. I mean, suddenly it was all back, everything I'd seen. I ran home and called Detective Volkman."

"The cop from Manhattan?"

"Yes. He'd given me his cell number and said to call him any time day or night if I ever remembered anything. I didn't know what else to do, so I called him."

Jack winced and shook his head. "Big mistake."

"I know that now, but I had no one else to turn to, and I had to tell somebody. I told him I'd got my memory back. He said to write it all down in case I forgot again and he'd be right over to take a statement. Ten minutes later four men busted in and knocked me down. They held a funny-smelling cloth over my face and that was it—I was gone."

Jack nodded. "And then they torched the place. You'd be found burnt to a crisp with no sign of injury or foul play."

"I guess so, but I woke up with the house burning around me. Maybe the drugs I was on interfered with whatever they doped me with, I don't know. I got up and ran to the bedroom but it was like a furnace and I could see Marilyn in the bed, burnt." He blinked, swallowed. "She never had a chance."

"So you ran."

He looked at Jack. "What else could I do? I—"

"No criticism. You did the smart thing."

"As far as I could see, it was the only thing. I realized then that Volkman was a fake and that someone—a *bunch* of someones—didn't want me talking about what I'd seen at Ground Zero. If I showed my face, they'd only come after me again. I figured it would take a while to put out the fire and sift though all the ashes. Everyone would assume I was dead until they couldn't find my body. So I hid until my bank opened. I withdrew all I could in cash and hopped a Greyhound."

"Why L.A.?"

"It was as far as I could get from that thing at Ground Zero without buying a plane ticket. Plus I figured it would be easy to get lost in a big city like this. And it was . . . until you came along."

"Tell your daughter to ditch her Wi-Fi or I might not be the last. How'd you convince her you had nothing to do with it?"

"She knows me, she believed me. She knew I could never hurt her mother."

Jack couldn't think of anything else to ask him.

"Well, I guess that's it then. Let's get back up to the parking area. You've got to get to work and I've got to get back and make my report."

He figured that sounded pretty official.

"Who do you work for?" Goren said. "I've got to know."

Jack shook his head. "You don't want to know. If I told you, I'd have to kill you."

Goren blanched and backed up a step.

"Only kidding."

5. Ernst jumped as Hank Thompson slammed open the door and stormed into his office.

"Have you been downstairs yet?" he said through clenched teeth.

"You mean the subcellar? No. I just got here and—"

"Then you'd better get down there. Something's happening."

Of course something was happening. Hank's little friend Darryl was undergoing a transformation. Ernst was curious to see what development had put Thompson into such a dither, but could not allow himself to appear too concerned or too curious. Must appear to be on top of the situation at all times.

"I have some calls to make, then—"

"*Now!*"

Well, well. Feeling assertive today, aren't we?

He had a few decades on Thompson, but had no doubt he could subdue him if necessary. The man had gone soft since achieving bestsellerdom. But that hadn't lessened the powder keg of violence within him, and Ernst saw no point in lighting a match. Causing a scene would be counterproductive at this point.

"Very well, since it appears to be of great importance to you, lead the way."

As Thompson turned and stomped from the room, Ernst rose and followed, grabbing his cane on the way out the door. It had belonged to his father and he treasured it. And one never knew when one might need something with a heavy silver head . . .

When they arrived in the subcellar, the lights were already on. Thompson strode to the Orsa and stood beside it, pointing.

"Look!" he said, a tremor in his voice. "Look what it's doing to him!"

Ernst stepped up beside him, but not too close, and stared.

He could understand why Thompson was so upset. Yesterday he'd discovered Darryl fully encased, feet and all, within the Orsa. How the Orsa had accomplished that, Ernst had had no idea. But now he had an inkling.

Darryl seemed to be in the grip of some sort of slow peristalsis. Yesterday the soles of his shoes had been just inside the end of the Orsa; now they lay perhaps eighteen inches from the end.

But something different . . .

Ernst stepped forward and suppressed a gasp when he saw what it was.

"Yeah, look at him," Thompson said. "His fucking skin's melting off. He's not being cured, he's being . . . digested!"

Ernst looked at the hands, the face, the scalp . . . all the exposed flesh seemed to be melting away, baring the muscle and fat and connective tissues beneath. The eyelids were gone, exposing the orbs. But oddly, the lanky hair remained.

No . . . it couldn't be . . . this wasn't supposed to . . .

He stepped closer for a better look. When he saw what was really happening, his knees softened with relief. He leaned on his cane and motioned Thompson forward.

"Not at all, Mister Thompson. Take a closer look." He pointed to Darryl's outstretched hand where the tendons were plainly visible. Oddly enough, the dirty fingernails appeared unaffected. "The skin is still there, it has simply become translucent."

Thompson stared a moment, then seemed to sag as if tension were leaking out of him.

"Okay, yeah, I see it now." He shook his head. "I walked in this morning and took one look and . . . man, it looked like he was dissolving. I just about lost it."

"I understand," Ernst said.

But he didn't. The lore of the Septimus Order mentioned nothing of such a change in the skin. But then, the lore was incomplete—bits and pieces gathered over the millennia from ancient manuscripts like the *Compendium of Srem* and other forbidden tomes. If anyone besides the One had ever known the true nature of the *Fhinntmanchca,* that knowledge was lost. Perhaps no one else had ever known.

"But is this supposed to happen?"

"Yes, of course," Ernst said quickly.

"You should have given me some warning."

Ernst gave a sage nod. "Yes, I suppose that is true."

"But why's it doing that to him?"

"Well, it stands to reason," he said, fabricating on the fly, "that if the Orsa is going to purge Darryl's body of all disease, it must penetrate his cells. The transparency is simply part of the cleansing process."

"Yeah? Makes sense I guess. I mean, as much as any of this makes sense."

Ernst repressed a satisfied smile. A brilliant ad lib, if he said so himself.

Thompson shook his head. "It's just that he looks so weird and dead with that bug-eyed stare."

"But he's obviously not dead." Ernst pointed to Darryl's wrist where his throbbing radial artery was clearly visible. "See? He's got a pulse."

"I guess that's good."

Good? Ernst thought. It's *wonderful*.

6. Weezy shook her head. "It doesn't make sense."

Jack leaned back and rubbed his burning eyes. He'd taken the first flight he could out of LAX. It had brought him in late—five hours or so in the air but more than eight hours on the clock.

Eddie had offered him a Heineken, which Jack had gratefully accepted. Then, saying it had been a long day, he'd hit the hay.

Jack envied him. He felt unaccountably tired. He hadn't done much of anything today but talk to Goren and Weezy and sit in a flying sardine can. Couldn't be the time change because he hadn't been out west long enough. Maybe it was the plane. Maybe the proximity to all those people had sucked the juice out of him.

He'd related his conversation with Goren as near to verbatim as he could, and Weezy had drunk in every word. She'd been perplexed and dubious about Jack's conjecture that the Towers had been brought down so an Opus Omega pillar could be buried where they'd stood.

"If you knew Dormentalism like I know Dormentalism," he said, "you'd think it made perfect sense. Someone has to die in each of those pillars before they bury it. Who knows how many victims Opus Omega claimed before nine/eleven? A few thousand more wouldn't make any difference."

"But they had forever before the Towers went up to bury that pillar. Don't forget, Opus Omega was started millennia ago."

"But Dormentalism wasn't. And it didn't get involved in Opus Omega until Luther Brady took over. And in 2001, Brady was in full command, with a cadre of fanatics willing to do his bidding."

Weezy nodded. "That's a point. The Septimus Order had been handling it alone before that. But my question is, why didn't they bury the pillar before the Trade Center went up?"

"Maybe they tried and couldn't get to the spot. Or couldn't get to it in time."

Weezy bolted up stiff and straight in her chair.

He looked at her. "What?"

"What you said—couldn't get to it in time."

She bounded up and headed for another room.

Jack followed. "So?"

She stopped and faced him. "So, a lot of people didn't want the Trade Center. A number of groups and committees were formed to stop it. They almost succeeded. I had stacks of old papers with articles about it back at the house."

"I saw them—even the old *Journal-Trib*."

She sighed. "Yeah. Gone, but not forgotten. I scanned a bunch of the articles over the years."

"But aren't they lost?"

She gave him an annoyed look. "You're kidding, right? I always back up—the magnetic, optical, and online."

"Online?"

"Of course. That way I can access it from anywhere."

"But so can everybody else."

"Not unless they know the password, and in my case, not unless they know the decryption key. I'll download the stuff and we'll go over it together."

Be still, my heart.

As she headed for the room where he assumed she kept the computer, he said, "Great. I'm going to help myself to another Heinie. You want one?"

She shook her head. "Started myself on a low-carb diet. But I'll take a diet anything."

"You got it."

With a fresh brew and a Diet Pepsi in hand, he found her hunched over a keyboard in a small extra room. Jack noticed the *Compendium* sitting next to the monitor. What looked like newspaper clippings were flipping across the screen. He pulled up a chair and tried to make sense of them, but they were moving too fast.

"Slow down. I haven't seen these."

"Neither have I," she said, but slowed her progress.

Even then Jack had to struggle to keep up. How she could absorb anything at that speed was beyond him.

"Here," she said, stopping the parade. "A familiar name."

Jack stared at the screen. "Where?"

She moved the mouse pointer to the caption under a photo of a group of stern-looking men. Jack squinted to read the fine print.

"'The Committee to Save the Hudson Terminal,'" he said, then scanned the names until he got to—"Holy shit!"

Among the committee members shown, the third man from the left was named Ernst Drexler.

Jack searched the photo and zeroed in on that third man. He wore a dark suit and a fedora. He appeared to be in his sixties and had a sharp-featured face that looked vaguely familiar.

"It's not him . . . but it's an awful lot like him."

After a series of deaths at the Septimus Order's Lodge in Jack's hometown when he was a teen, a man named Ernst Drexler had arrived and stayed for a few months to get the local chapter back on track—"reorganize" was how he'd put it. Both Jack and Weezy had had contact with him back then.

"It can't be him. How old do you think he was when we knew him?"

Jack shrugged. "Mid-thirties, I'd guess, if that. Certainly no older."

"I agree. Now, that was back in eighty-three. This photo was taken in sixty-five. So, unless he was growing younger, this is probably his father."

Ernst Drexler II flashed through Jack's head.

"Not probably. Remember I showed you the card he gave me?"

She nodded. "'Ernst Drexler Two.'"

"Which means his father had the same name."

"I remember it said he was an 'Actuator,' whatever that is."

"I got the impression he was some sort of troubleshooter for the Order. But what was his father doing with this committee? And what's the Hudson Terminal?"

"The long-gone and forgotten terminus of the long-gone and forgotten Hudson and Manhattan Railroad, which was bought out by the Port Authority in the early sixties. It sat under the site where the PA eventually built the World Trade Center."

Pieces were falling together.

"That subway tunnel Goren saw . . . it could have been left over from that railroad."

"Except he said it was running in from the east. The Hudson and Manhattan lines came in from the west under the river. More than likely what he saw was an aborted or abandoned link to the Hudson Terminal."

Jack pulled up a chair and sat next to her.

"All right . . . we've got the father of the Septimus Order's 'Actuator' trying to stop the PA from digging up the terminal that sat near the spot where Opus Omega needed to plant a pillar. If Ernst Two is in the Order, I think it's safe to assume that his father was too."

Weezy nodded. "And maybe an 'Actuator' as well." She turned back to the computer. "Let's see if he appears anywhere else."

She began running the scans across her screen. Jack didn't protest this time. No point in slowing her down.

"Here he is again," she said after a while. "Another 'save' committee."

Jack saw the same man pictured with a group of five. In this photo he carried a black cane that Jack recognized. No doubt now about lineage—his son carried one just like it, maybe even the same.

" 'The Save Radio Row Committee.' What's Radio Row?"

"A cluster of stores that sold radio, hi-fi, and stereo equipment. Want to guess where they were located?"

"Right over the Hudson Terminal?"

She nodded. "Right. They were knocked down to dig the Trade Center's foundation. I'll bet if we keep looking we'll find him on the committee to save some of the historic buildings in the thirteen square blocks that were razed along with Radio Row."

Jack leaned back. "So . . . according to Veilleur, the

Order was originally charged with completing Opus Omega. Since the Dormentalist Church didn't exist in sixty-five, Ernst the First was sent in to keep the PA from interfering with their pillar placement."

"But he failed. The PA broke ground on the project in sixty-six." She swiveled to face Jack. "You can see why they were concerned. The plan was to dig down to bedrock, some seventy feet below. A *huge* hole. They removed a million cubic yards and dumped it in the Hudson. It pushed the river far enough back to create Battery Park City."

Jack gave a low whistle. All this was news to him. He hadn't moved to the city till the nineties, long after all this had happened.

"A thirteen-square-block hole, seventy feet down. A lot of dirt—and a lot of new real estate."

Weezy smiled. "Can you imagine how frantic the Order must have been? They'd probably planned to buy one of the buildings in those blocks, one right over the spot where they planned to bury the pillar. But if the Trade Center was built, they'd be locked out."

"But they got their way in the end, didn't they."

Weezy's smile disappeared. "All that destruction, all that loss of life, just to bury one of their obscene pillars. It seems too . . . too evil, even for them."

"But they're working for the Otherness, which, I'll bet, has another definition of evil."

"But—"

"Too evil for the Order but not too evil for a bunch of crazy Arabs?"

" 'Those who can make you believe absurdities can make you commit atrocities.' "

"Hey, I like that."

"Not mine—thank Voltaire. But history's proven that a religion can justify pretty much anything in the name of its god."

"Well, think of the Otherness as the Order's god. And since Opus Omega is crucial to bringing their god into this world, they consider themselves to be doing the lord's work."

She shook her head. "Al Qaeda was committing a terrorist act. Attacking the Towers was an end as much as a means. Their lord's work or not, I think the Order could have found another way to bury their pillar. During the excavation phase, or during the very early pouring of the foundation, they could have found a way to sneak in and get their job done."

"A thirteen-foot concrete pillar weighing tons?" Jack shrugged. "Maybe they could have, maybe they tried. Whatever, they didn't succeed, so they had to find another way. Ernest Goren and his fellow workers had the misfortune of catching them in the act."

Weezy kept shaking her head. "I don't know."

"One way to know is to learn all there is to know about Opus Omega." He pointed to the *Compendium* lying on the desk. "How's it going? Able to make sense out of those pages?"

She shrugged. "Some. The picture is piecing together, but it's slow going."

"Well, then, the other option is to identify bin Aswad. If we can connect him to the Order . . ." An idea struck like a punch, propelling him from his chair. "Drexler! Could Drexler—our Drexler—be bin Aswad?"

Weezy shook her head. "No. The nose is different. Plus he had blue eyes and bin Aswad's are dark."

"Ever hear of tinted contacts?"

She was still shaking her head. "From what we see above the beard, I say no. As for the rest of his face, who knows?"

"Is there a computer program that'll remove a beard?"

She shrugged. "I don't know. Computers were Kevin's department."

Jack thought of Russell Tuit.

"I know a guy who did time for hacking."

Weezy smiled. "You know a criminal? What a surprise."

"Some of my best friends . . . well, anyway, he's a guru of sorts. Why don't you print me out—"

"Printing's no good. They'll lose resolution, especially using Eddie's inkjet, and your guy will sacrifice even more scanning them back in. I'll crop and copy any photos I have onto a disk so he can put them directly into whatever software he finds."

"Do it. And then I'm out of here. We both need some sleep."

SATURDAY

I. After some obligatory small talk, Russ said, "So, what brings you to my humble abode?"

Humble it was, a tiny one-bedroom over a Tex-Mex restaurant on Second Avenue in the East Nineties. The place tended to smell better when the kitchen below was going full blast, but they didn't do breakfast. Russell Tuit—he pronounced it like bird talk—didn't have a pocket protector or taped horn-rimmed glasses, but had the mouse-potato pallor and flabby look of someone whose fingers did all the walking. A certifiable geek; and it seemed a while since he'd had a shower.

Jack pulled out Weezy's disk. "Wondering if you might take a look at this."

Russ took the disk and headed for his computer in the corner of the sparsely furnished front room. *Barely* furnished was more like it, and what he had looked fourth hand.

Following him, Jack said, "You still stealing Internet?"

A federal judge had banned Russ from all online activities for twenty-five years. His crime: hacking into a bank and siphoning a fraction of a cent off each transaction. He'd accumulated a seven-figure haul before he was caught.

"It's not stealing, it's sharing. It's my compensation."

Russ had helped the guy in the neighboring apartment

install a Wi-Fi system. He'd made sure to place the access point on the wall they shared.

He thought of Alice Laverty.

"Just met a lady whose life was complicated by someone hacking into her Wi-Fi system."

He slid the disk into a slot in his computer. "Unsecured, right?"

"I suppose so."

"Hardly anyone secures their home network. But no worry here. I insisted that Bill create a password-protected gateway and firewall—for his protection, of course."

"And yours too, maybe?"

"Of course."

"And you know the password?"

"Of course."

"What if he changes it?"

"He already has—twice."

"So . . . aren't you locked out?"

He gave Jack a sheepish look over his shoulder. "I installed a keystroke logger when I set up his Wi-Fi."

Again? Jack wondered how many computers were bugged with those things.

"Swell."

"Hey, I don't abuse it, man. I respect his privacy. It just sends me a signal whenever he opens the password manager. That's the only time I peek."

Russ hit a few keys and an array of pictures of bin Aswad's face popped onto the screen. He stared at them a moment, scratching his red hair, then swiveled his chair and faced Jack.

"Who's this—a terrorist?"

The question jolted Jack. Then he realized that any bearded, turbanned Islamic could look like a terrorist.

"Uh-huh. I've joined the CIA."

Russ laughed. "That'll be the day. No, seriously."

"Just a guy I need to find, except there's a good chance he doesn't have a beard anymore. Any way you can use some computer magic to remove those whiskers?"

"Remove?" He shook his head. "Not that I know of—at least not that I've heard of."

"I was counting on you having heard of everything."

"Well, there's facial-recognition software, but that's used for comparison—you know, does this face match that one? This is something different."

"Come on. They've got these police identi-kit programs that can put a beard on a face; there's got to be some program that'll take it off."

"It's not that simple. If you have the underlying facial structure, it's nothing to add some facial hair to see what he looks like with a beard. But beards, especially these long, raggedy Muslim types, they hide the underlying facial structure—lots of times they hide the *lips,* f'Christ sake."

Jack pointed to the screen. "Look, you've got multiple angles here, and you can see his lips. Do *something.*"

"I'll try, man. That's all I can say. I'll check around, see if someone's come up with an algorithm that'll work. Can't promise anything, though."

"Can't you write one yourself?"

He laughed as he shook his head. "Oh, man, that's way above me." He cleared his throat. "I'll need something for my time, even if I come up empty."

Jack was okay with that. Time was life.

He wondered how much of either anyone had left.

2.

Finally! Weezy thought as she turned the page and saw the words "Opus Omega."

The Final Task . . . what she'd found so far gave the impression they thought they'd have it finished before too long. But thousands of years had passed and it still wasn't completed. Sort of like the very early Christians who thought the Second Coming was just around the corner. Opus Omega's age was multiples of Christianity's.

The title read "BEGINNING THE END" and described the dimensions of the pillars, the symbols that had to be engraved on the sides, the size of the opening in the end, and how a living person—the "Sacrifice"—had to be sealed within. She knew all of this from Jack.

Come on, come on, come *on,* she thought. Tell me something I *don't* know.

Then it began to describe the age of the Sacrifice, how he or she couldn't be too young or too old, but should be in the prime of life. Weezy guessed that was to dodge the possibility of some sick old crone volunteering herself . . . or a family ridding itself of a deformed or severely crippled child. The pillar demanded a healthy male or female.

In other words: with everything to lose.

The message was sick enough, but the dry, matter-of-fact delivery made it worse. Like reciting the rules of baseball.

The batter shall take his position in the batter's box promptly when it is his time at bat . . .

It described the pattern of column placement—lines of force supposedly ran between all the nexus points, from each one to every other one. A pillar had to be placed wherever three of those lines crossed.

The pillar had to be inserted vertically but did not have to remain in the ground to have its effect. Mere insertion was sufficient to accomplish the purpose—like injecting a toxin.

What purpose? Do damage? To whom or what? The Lady?

But as with so many things within its pages, the *Com-*

pendium assumed the reader already knew. Then it moved to the order in which the pillars had to be placed.

Weezy straightened in her chair. Here was something new. She'd gathered from Jack and Mr. Veilleur that the pillars were being buried in no particular order.

But as she read on she realized that only the first pillar's placement mattered. The Final Task had a set starting point. The first pillar had to be inserted at a very specific location called the Null Site. All others could follow in random order, but the first must occupy the Null Site.

Of course, nothing was said of what made the Null Site so special, or why Opus Omega had to start there.

She turned the page and found herself in the middle of a paragraph on some unrelated subject.

She clenched her teeth. Just when she was making progress. So frustrating.

She turned back. Both the pillar and its insertion point shared the same name, a Latin word she knew. It meant "beginning."

Orsa.

3. Time on his hands.

Gia had taken Vicky to her weekly art lesson down in the West Village. Too early for Julio's. Didn't want to interrupt Weezy's study of the *Compendium.* Too soon to hear from Russ. He could go hang with Abe or . . .

The photos of the senior Drexler had parked the Septimus Order in Jack's mind and it wouldn't budge. Maybe he could get it to move on if he wandered down to the Lodge and checked what the Kickers were doing. Their presence at a Septimus Lodge meant intimate involvement with the Order. But why? Why was the Order interested in them? Unless it was thinking of involving the Kickers in Opus Omega to speed its conclusion.

Might be a good idea to put in an appearance anyway. He tried to show his face once or twice a week. Hadn't been there since Monday, so maybe he was due.

So he donned his down-market Kicker clothes, put on the sunglasses and the Mets cap, then hopped a C train downtown. After a couple of switches he emerged from underground and strolled the rest of the way to the Lodge, weaving through the Saturday shoppers like a man with nothing better to do.

When he reached the Lodge he hung around outside, making his cigarettes available. Kewan sidled up and took one. Borrowed Jack's lighter too.

"So when do we kick some more Dormentalist butt?" he asked as Kewan lit up.

His dark, pocked cheeks puffed as he blew smoke. "Johnny, ain't you heard? We supposed to leave 'em be."

"What?" This was news.

"Yeah. Word come down Monday after we got back. We all best friends now. How come you don't know that? Where you been?"

"Oh, I, um, got a little job doing landscaping in Queens."

He'd done that when he'd first come to the city so figured it was as good a cover as anything.

"He pay cash?"

Jack nodded. "Every day before we split."

"Can he use another body?"

Jack shook his head. "Don't know, but I'll ask."

"You do that. 'Cause I'm tired of being busted all the time. And I'm gettin tired of hangin out here."

"I hear you, man. I—whoa, check this." A black Bentley was pulling up to the curb. "What do we have here?"

"That Lodge guy again."

"Lodge guy?"

"One of the peeps that own the place."

"Oh, someone from the Septimus Order."

"Yeah, them. I seen him before. Used to stop in every few weeks or so, but he's been in every day this week."

"Really."

"Yeah, but you wouldn't know that, seein as how you been out makin money an all."

A guy from the Order making frequent visits. Had to be Hank Thompson—who else would he care to see? Jack could understand sporadic visits just to make sure the Lodge was being well treated. But every day?

Add that to the sudden cessation of hostilities against the Dormentalists and something was up.

Jack turned back to the Bentley in time to see a door open and a man in a white suit glide from the rear. He carried a black cane that Jack knew was wrapped in rhinoceros hide.

"Holy . . ."

"What? Whassup?"

For a single, frozen heartbeat he was fourteen again. He knew this man . . . Mr. Drexler.

No, make that Ernst Drexler II.

He hadn't changed much. He looked older—wrinkles at the corners of the eyes, maybe a touch of gray around the temples—but the rest of his hair was still black and slicked back, his blue eyes just as piercing as in 1983.

Afraid he'd be recognized, Jack felt an urge to turn away, but fought it. That would only draw attention. And besides—no way Drexler could recognize him. More than a quarter century had passed. Jack wasn't a kid anymore, and had a beard. But Drexler . . . still wearing that damn white suit and carrying that same cane.

So Jack watched him stride across the sidewalk and ascend the stone steps without a nod or even a sideways glance to acknowledge that anyone else was about.

Same old Drexler. He remembered some of the elitist crap he'd poured into his ear when he was a kid, little knowing it was running out the other side.

First Eddie, then Weezy, now Ernst Drexler. Jack's past was taking over his present.

Drexler was a honcho in the Order, and the Order was pulling strings in the Dormentalist Church, and the Dormentalists were heavy into Opus Omega. Could Drexler's presence have anything to do with—?

"Shit!"

Goren's words flashed back to him.

I can see someone standing in the background . . . as far back as anyone could be and still be visible . . . wasn't dressed like the others . . . in a much lighter color . . . seemed to be in white.

"Wussup, John Boy? You look like you just seen a ghost."

"What? Oh, just some stomach cramps. I gotta go inside."

Kewan grinned. "Oh, yeah. Don't wanna be messin your Depends."

Jack hurried up the steps and inside. As always, he was struck by the huge version of the Order's sigil embossed on the rear wall of the high-ceilinged foyer.

He arrived in time to see Drexler approach the sigil, then hang a right into the hallway. He followed a ways and saw him step into the third doorway down on the right. Jack entered the hall and passed just as Drexler closed the door behind him. He kept going and was about to enter the bathroom when a Kicker stepped out.

His name was Ansari and he acted as security of sorts. Jack had seen him a few times. He'd started out a regular guy but lately he'd developed a strutting, aggressive mien.

"Where you going?" he said, voice thick with challenge as he blocked the doorway.

"Where you just came from."

"This ain't public."

"Well, I ain't public," Jack said with plenty of 'tude as he flashed his faux Kicker tattoo.

Ansari stepped aside.

Jack went into a stall and leaned against the door, wondering what to do. He'd had no plan other than showing his face to keep it familiar and finding out what the Kicker hoi polloi were up to. Sure as hell hadn't expected to see Ernst Drexler here.

After a few minutes he flushed the toilet and was pushing on the door to the hallway when he heard voices. He eased the door open half an inch for a peek and saw Hank Thompson standing outside Drexler's door.

"He's moved," Thompson said. His voice sounded strange . . . strained.

"How far?"

Jack assumed the accented voice was Drexler's. A long, long time since he'd heard it, and the accent was lighter, but it had to be him.

"Past the halfway mark. And he's changed some more. Lots more."

"Interesting. Let's go."

A few seconds later, Drexler, cane in hand, stepped into the hallway and closed the door behind him. The pair walked off.

Well, that was an enlightening conversation. Who were they talking about?

As they walked away, Jack slipped from the bathroom and followed. They crossed the rear of the foyer and headed down a stairway that Jack knew led to the basement.

He did a quick scan as he entered the foyer. Ansari was talking to someone, looking the other way, so Jack scooted past behind him and took the steps down. The doorway at the bottom was closed. He hesitated, baffled as to what he might find on the other side.

Past the halfway mark . . .

So? Some guy halfway through a PowerPoint presentation? A brunch with the eggs Benedict half gone?

Yeah right.

He pressed his ear against the door and heard nothing. He decided to risk an entry by pretending to be looking for someone. Not Thompson. Someone just a little bit down the food chain.

Knocking as he turned the knob, he said, "Darryl?"

The room was empty except for a couple of folding tables and maybe a dozen chairs. He looked around and spotted another door. When he reached it he listened. More silence. He shrugged and decided to try the same approach as before.

"Dar—?"

The knob wouldn't turn. Locked. Jack checked the jamb and saw a quarter inch of exposed latch bolt. He fished out the notched credit card he kept in his wallet and stared at it a moment, thinking risky thoughts. One thing to barge into a room pretending to be clueless. Quite another to pop the latch beforehand.

He decided to knock first.

"Hey, anybody in there?"

After two tries and no answer, he worked the corner of the card into the space. He hooked it into the receptacle in the striker plate and twisted, pushing back the spring latch. The door popped open.

"Darryl?" he said as he palmed the card and stepped inside.

A smaller room, and empty as expected. But a closet door stood open, and in the floor of that closet, an open trapdoor.

Jack peeked over the edge and saw a circular stairway leading down. He listened and thought he heard voices but they were too faint to understand.

The idea of sneaking down rose but he tossed it. The wrought iron on the circular stair left nowhere to hide. Better to get out of here unseen while he could.

Locking the door behind him, he returned to the main basement room and was almost to the exit when Ansari appeared.

"You again. What're you doin down here?"

"Looking for Darryl."

He sneered. "Darryl ain't here. He's gone."

"When's he due back?"

"He ain't, leastways not if any of us got something to say about it."

Here was something unexpected.

"Hey, I ain't been around since that Dormie thing on Monday"—nice to be able to mention that—"so I got no idea what you're talking about."

"You ain't heard? For a minute there I thought you might be one of his butt buddies."

"What the—?"

"Guy's queer. Got the virus—AIDS. He's outta here. The boss gave him the boot Wednesday. Ain't seen him since." His eyes narrowed. "What you want with him?"

"Just checking in."

Ansari shoved Jack. He probably thought it was a surprise move, but Jack had seen him tense for it. He let it happen and bounced off the wall behind him.

"You *are* one of his butt buddies, ain't you!"

So what if I am? Jack felt like saying, but held back. He also held back from putting Ansari face-first on the floor—despite his presenting about half a dozen openings—because he didn't want an enemy in this place. Well, not another in addition to Thompson, who'd probably try to kill him if he recognized him.

"Hey-hey!" he said, raising open-palm hands and backing away with a cowed expression. "Dude, I just seen him around a lot, is all. Everyone knows Darryl."

"Yeah, well, not any more they don't. Better forget about him. Now get your ass upstairs where it belongs."

"You got it," Jack said and ducked out the door. "You got it."

He hurried up the steps to the foyer, no doubt leaving Ansari feeling pretty tough. Good. If Jack had to go up against him in the future, the guy would be overconfident. Nobody fell harder and faster than an overconfident bully.

The news about Darryl answered a few questions, especially why he'd been looking under the weather lately. Poor guy. Not a bad sort for a Kicker, and Jack had got the impression he was smarter than he looked. He'd wondered what he was doing at Mount Sinai Tuesday. Now he knew.

But bigger questions had replaced it.

Most immediately: What was Ernst Drexler doing here every day this week? The answer lay at the bottom of those winding steps. Some sort of lower level down there. Good bet it wasn't a wine cellar.

But more important: Was Drexler the man Goren had seen at Ground Zero? If so, it left little doubt that the Order had had something to do with the 9/11 attacks.

Jack balled his fists as he walked past the Order's sigil. His teenage impression of Drexler had been that he was strange and potentially dangerous. He'd never imagined him a monster.

4.

"Look at him, will you." Hank felt his gut clench as he leaned close to the Orsa and stared at Darryl. "I don't believe it."

When his daddy had visited him during his growing years, he'd filled his head with tales of Other Gods wanting to come in from the outside, and how he was part of a special bloodline, and how his daddy could see things with his ruined left eye that people with two good eyes had no clue about.

Hank had listened and he'd believed all that weird shit because his daddy so obviously believed it. But all those years they'd been words, just words. He'd never *seen* anything to back them up.

Until now.

Darryl was barely visible.

"It's like he isn't there."

"But he is," Drexler said beside him. "He is very much there."

Yesterday it had been just his skin. Today it was his whole body, through and through.

From a distance he looked like a shirt, jeans, a pair of shoes, and a clump of hair suspended in a block of Lucite—something some asshole in a museum would call "art." But when you got closer you could start to make out details.

Yesterday just his skin had gone transparent. Now Hank could see right through him. He wasn't invisible. Still a faint outline of the scalp—easier because the hair was the same as ever—around an even fainter outline of the skull beneath, and a vague tracing of the irregular contours on the surface of the brain within.

"I think we might be nearing the end of the process."

" 'Might be'? You're supposed to know."

"Well, none of this is on a strict timetable. It matters

how sick he was. Maybe he had more illnesses than we knew, or even he knew. The Orsa is going to cure everything wrong with him."

Seemed to Hank like Drexler was trying to sound more certain of this than he really was.

"Yeah, well, he keeps sliding, though. He's past the halfway point now. Will it spit him out when he's cured?"

"Yes."

Hank wheeled on him. "You don't have a fucking clue, do you?"

"Of course I have. It's all been written down over the centuries, the millennia."

"But you said it's never been done before."

Drexler gave him a stony look. "He *will* be cured when he emerges from the Orsa."

"Yeah? But what else will he be? The invisible man? I think he might rather be dead."

"Then that will be his choice, won't it."

Again that urge to strangle Drexler. The guy must have sensed it because Hank noticed his knuckles whiten as he tightened his grip on the cane.

He forced himself to turn away.

"When do you think this will be over?"

"At the rate he's moving, tomorrow or the next day."

He stared at Darryl. You poor bastard. You went in a human being. What'll you be when you come out?

A *Fhinntmanchca*?

What the hell was a *Fhinntmanchca*?

5.

"You're serious about this?" Eddie said as he positioned her on the treadmill.

Weezy nodded. "Deadly serious."

She'd made up her mind to get in shape—lose weight,

gain tone. The first inkling had come as she'd watched Eddie eat high-protein, low-carb meals. It had solidified today when he'd told her he was going down to the basement to work out. She'd followed him downstairs and found a treadmill and one of those Bowflex mini gyms she'd seen on TV.

She needed to do this. She'd let herself go too long. Time to take control. As much as she itched to push further through the *Compendium,* this was important too. She could spare thirty minutes for herself.

"Okay," he said once her feet were positioned to either side of the belt. "We'll start off slow and easy. As you get in better condition and more comfortable on the machine, we'll begin upping the speed and the incline."

"What about that?" she said with a nod toward the mini gym. "I could use some weight training too, I imagine. My muscles must be like Jell-O."

"Weight training is very important. Do fifteen minutes low and slow here, and then I'll walk you through a few exercises over there."

He turned a knob and the belt began moving. Gripping the hand bars, Weezy stepped on and began walking.

"Too slow. Speed her up. This is like I'm eighty years old. I need to work up a sweat if I'm going to lose weight."

He gave her a puzzled look. "Why this sudden interest in getting in shape? I've been after you for years."

She shrugged. "Guess I'm finally listening."

A sly smile. "This wouldn't have anything to do with Jack, would it."

She felt herself redden. "Don't be ridiculous. I'm not getting any younger and I've let myself go long enough. Nothing more."

His smile held. "If you say so."

"I do say so."

Was it Jack? She found herself thinking about him a lot—mostly cringing at the memory of coming on to him the other night. What had she been thinking? Obviously she *hadn't* been thinking. And that wasn't like her.

"Hello?" Eddie said, waving a hand before her face. "Earth to Weezy."

She shook herself. "Sorry."

"Increase the speed by turning the knob clockwise, but do it slowly."

She nodded. "Got it."

As Eddie stepped over to the mini gym and began setting the resistance bars, Weezy notched the belt speed up to somewhere near a brisk walk. Once she was comfortable, she glanced over at her brother. As a kid she'd always thought of him as a fat, lazy dork, but he'd changed. He'd shaped up physically and mentally. He had his life in hand and had made something of himself.

What had *she* done?

Well, she'd had a good marriage—at least she'd thought so, until Steve brought it to a screeching halt. But beyond that, what? Last week she might have answered, *Nothing* . . . that she'd spent her life chasing phantoms. But in the past few days she'd been given proof that they weren't phantoms.

Vindication. She hadn't wasted her time. But since Steve's death she'd been living from only the neck up and letting the rest go to seed. Time to change that, get back to her old self.

Things were moving so fast. Jack's call a little while ago about Mr. Drexler with the Kickers, and the possibility that he'd been the man in white Goren had seen at Ground Zero . . . it all had a crazy, surreal logic to it. If she could learn more, maybe the crazy and surreal would go away, leaving only the logic.

But she needed a break from that book. She was getting logy and sluggish from complete lack of physical activity. This was exactly what she needed to keep her sharp.

Maybe she could bounce some ideas off Eddie as they worked out. She saw him seated on the bench, back to her, stretching his arms this way and that. Then he pulled off his T-shirt.

When Weezy saw his back her knees locked and she stumbled. She fell, landing on the belt and rolling off the treadmill onto the basement floor.

Eddie was at her side in seconds.

"Jesus, Weez! Are you all right?"

She nodded, unable to speak—not because of the considerable pain, but because of what she'd seen on his back.

Finally she found her voice.

"I'm fine," she managed, struggling to her feet.

But she wasn't fine, not fine at all, anything but.

"Maybe you should stay down," he said, "until we're sure nothing's broken."

"Nothing's broken."

Except maybe my heart.

"You're sure?"

"Yeah. Sure. I'm gonna go upstairs and get an ice pack."

"Let me get my shirt and I'll help you."

He turned away and she saw his back again and felt her gorge rise.

"No-no," she said, moving toward the stairs as quickly as she could while hiding the pain that screamed through her twisted hip. "You stay here. I'll just put some ice on it and I'll be fine. Just fine."

"You're sure?"

She didn't—couldn't look at him.

"Positive."

Once upstairs she yanked a plastic trash bag from a box and limped to her bedroom. She threw all the clothes she'd just bought into the bag, then grabbed the *Compendium,* scooped up Eddie's car keys, and headed out the door. All the while the silver dollar–size scar—the *brand* on his back—kept flashing across her vision.

6. Jack found her just where her frantic call had said she'd be—hiding in the rear of the Book Corner in Penn Station. Her eyes were red, her face blotchy. Looked like she'd been crying.

"Thank God!" she said when she saw him. She fell against him, clutching and clinging like a drowning sailor.

"What's wrong? What's happened?"

Her call had been mostly incoherent, something like, *Come get me, please come get me, I'm at Penn Station, please, please, please!*

He'd rushed downtown.

"It's Eddie," she gasped and began to sob.

Aw, shit. Had something happened? Had they found him?

"He's not hurt, is he?"

"I almost wish he were. This is worse. Eddie belongs to the Order!"

Jack stood stunned, cold—no, frozen, barely able to breathe. Eddie a member of the Ancient Fraternal Septimus Order . . .

"No way. It can't—"

"It's true! I saw the brand on his back! Just like we saw

on Mister Sumter's when we were kids, remember? Well, Eddie's got one too! He's a member!"

"Don't you think he would have said something?"

She shook her head. "First off, we're not all that close. He's helped me out with certain professional matters, and making me hard to find, but we don't sit down for regular heart-to-hearts. Besides, you know as well as I how secretive the Order is."

"Not so secretive that he didn't keep his shirt on."

"I don't think it even occurred to him. I think he must always work out shirtless and he took it off without thinking."

"How did he explain it?"

"He didn't. I didn't give him a chance. I panicked and ran. Parked his car at Newark Airport, then called him and left a message where it was. I withdrew as much as I could from an ATM and took a train here." She gripped the front of Jack's shirt. "Do you think he's been keeping tabs on me for the Order?"

Jack considered that, then shook his head.

"No. Whoever's been out to get you lately didn't know who you were or where you lived. If it *is* the Order after you—and I'm pretty damn sure it is—I doubt very much they have any inkling that Eddie's your brother. You're a Myers, he's a Connell. And does he know you suspect the Order?"

She shook her head. "It's never come up. He doesn't seem to want to talk about anything related to what we're after—doesn't seem to want to know about it. It's all too strange for him. But Jack, I can't go back there. I can't live with a member of the Order, even if he's my brother. Not after what we know and what we suspect."

"Eddie wouldn't hurt a fly."

"But what if they connect me to him?"

Maybe she had a point.

"All right, I'll rent you a hotel—"

"No hotel—please! I won't feel safe there. The two of us are up to our necks in this and we need to work on it together if we're to find any answers." She looked up at him, eyes pleading. "Let me stay with you. Please? I know that's probably like asking you to jab a sharp stick in your eye, but you'll hardly know I'm there. I won't be in the way. I'll sleep on the floor. I'll—"

He held up his hands. "Whoa. Stop. Enough. Sheesh."

Jabbing a sharp stick in his eye . . . yeah, that pretty much nailed it.

"I don't do roommates, Weez."

Well, except maybe for Gia, but only Gia, and she'd never stayed more than one night, so that didn't count.

"But I need to feel safe, Jack. I can't go full focus if I'm always looking over my shoulder. You make me feel safe. Please? If not for anything else, for old times' sake, then?"

Jack hated to hear her beg, but it was "old times' sake" that was holding him back. He didn't want to find her in his bed again.

She must have read his mind. "Hey, if you're worried about a replay of the other night, that was just momentary insanity. You made it clear you're in a relationship, and even if you weren't—never happen again." She sighed and looked up at him with big, dark, frightened eyes. "But I need to feel safe again, Jack. I really do."

His turn to sigh. "Okay. But just for a while. Until we get this thing straightened out."

She hugged him. "Thank-you-thank-you-thank-you!"

He hoped this wasn't a mistake.

And somehow he'd have to find a way to break it to Gia that another woman was moving in with him.

7. Weezy turned from Jack's front room window where she'd been staring down at the street three floors below. He'd assured her they hadn't been followed from Penn Station but she worried.

Now she stared at the front room itself—again. Not a good place for a claustrophobe. She couldn't get over how cluttered it was with . . . *stuff.* The furniture was fine old golden oak Victorian, but most people would consider everything else junk. A Shmoo clock? A Daddy Warbucks lamp? Membership certificates of organizations led by long defunct and mostly forgotten pulp-fiction heroes?

But then, even as a kid, Jack had always seemed to be just a little bit off the beat, just a little out of step. Not an Asperger's sort of thing, more like the title of the Stan Getz song, "Desifinado": out of tune. Most people never noticed back then. On the surface he'd been a normal, BMX-riding, Atari-playing kid. But Weezy had noticed, because she'd been out of tune too, even more so. That was why they'd been such fast friends. Working at old Mr. Rosen's junk shop had only exacerbated Jack's retro tendencies, introducing him to a gallimaufry of artifacts from other eras, ones he'd found more interesting, more simpatico than his own.

The room was Jack, Jack was the room. Off-kilter, out of step, a fortress of solitude from the goings-on outside. She felt safe here. The quadruple bolt system on his door—top, bottom, and both sides—didn't hurt, but Jack himself was the main reason. A massive firewall.

She certainly needed one. Because out there her brother had joined the Septimus Order.

The phone Jack had given her the other day began to ring. Again. She ignored it.

Jack picked it up and looked at its screen.

"Eddie again."

"Don't answer."

Jack hit the talk button and thrust it into her hand.

"He's probably worried sick. You need to talk to him at least once."

Weezy hesitated, then reluctantly put the phone to her ear.

"Hello?"

"Weezy, thank God! Where are you? What happened? I came upstairs and you were—"

"You belong to the Order, Eddie. Why?"

"What?"

"Why did you join the Order?"

"Because they asked me."

"Why didn't you tell me?"

"Because I know you think there's something sinister about them, but they're just like any fraternal order. No different from the Masons or the Elks."

"You really believe that?"

"Of course I do—"

"They branded you, Eddie!"

"Just a ritual. They numbed it up beforehand. And really, Weez, the contacts, the networking I've had access to, it's been great for business."

"Good-bye, Eddie. I'm alive and well and that's all I'm telling you."

She cut the call.

"Eddie, of all people," she said. "He was always scared of the Lodge. Remember the Lodge?"

Jack nodded from where he sat and sipped a beer. He'd offered her one but she'd accepted a bottle of seltzer instead.

"How can I forget. I used to cut its grass."

She could picture the two-story stucco cube sitting on

the rise on the Old Town side of Quaker Lake. On the surface, Johnson, New Jersey, seemed the last place the Ancient Fraternal Septimus Order would set one of its Lodges. But when you learned how old the town really was, and how closely the Order was associated with the Pine Barrens, it made perfect sense.

People in town used to refer to the Septimus Order as "the Lodge" back then—still did, most likely—because to them that building by the lake was all they knew of the Order. They'd had no idea how ancient it was and how long its reach.

"I just can't imagine Eddie joining."

"You don't join the Order," Jack said, rising and heading for his tiny kitchen. "The Order joins you. You have to be asked."

"Why would they ask Eddie? And why would he join?"

"Maybe he was flattered," he called from the kitchen.

"He said it was good for business, for networking."

"Well, all sorts of influential people belong, although I can't see them all knowing about Opus Omega, and especially not nine/eleven."

"I know Eddie has no idea about Opus Omega."

He stepped back into the room with another beer. "How?"

"Because he saw a page in the *Compendium* with the words big as day and he didn't react. He was more interested in the animation beneath it."

Jack shook his head. "I've seen those animations. Amazing. But anyway, I'm sure the Order has lots of levels of membership with the folks on the bottom like Eddie knowing nothing about the doings of the guys on top." His smile was grim. "Pretty much like the whole world."

"But in the Order's case, top would be the High Council of the Seven. As for levels of membership, I'll bet there's seven. They're really into sevens."

Jack nodded. "I think the Otherness itself is into sevens—I mean, the way the number keeps popping up."

"Well, it's prime, and it's versatile, and it's manageable."

She jumped at the sound of the door buzzer.

Jack frowned as he reached behind him. A pistol appeared as he stepped to the intercom and pressed a button.

"Yeah?"

"It's us," said a woman's voice. And in the background a little-girl voice said, *"Surprise!"*

Jack did look surprised for an instant, then he smiled and pressed the door-release button.

"Come on up!"

He opened the closet near the front door and placed the pistol on a high shelf. Before the door closed again she thought she spotted something that looked like a dai katana leaning up there as well.

He turned to her. "Company."

"I gathered that. Is it who I think it is?"

He nodded. "My ladies."

My ladies . . . he said it as if they were royalty. From the look in his eyes they were . . .

Weezy looked down at herself. Jack's woman—his *lady*—would be here in seconds and she was still dressed in the sweats she'd put on for her aborted workout. No time to change. This was awful.

"Why didn't you tell me?"

"I didn't know," he said as he turned the central knob that withdrew the four bolts on the door and pulled it open.

Seconds later a grinning nine- or ten-year-old girl in shorts and a T-shirt bounded out of the stairwell and leaped into his arms.

"Jack!"

"Hey, Vicks!"

As they hugged, a slim woman with blue eyes and short blond hair stepped through the door and planted a light kiss on Jack's lips. She wore a white tank top and a short black skirt.

Oh, God, she's beautiful.

Jack said, "Gia, Weezy. Weezy, Gia."

The woman's eyes locked with Weezy's for an instant, then she smiled and stepped forward, extending her hand.

"Hi. Nice to meet you. Jack's told me so much about you."

Not too much, I hope, she thought. Like making a fool out of myself the other night.

"Good things, I hope. He's told me about you too."

Close up, she wasn't really *beautiful*—that had been the initial gestalt impression—but she was very, very good looking. Next to her Weezy felt like a total frump.

"And this is Vicky," Jack said, easing the child to the floor.

The child had her mother's blue eyes but someone else's dark hair. She wore it back in a single braid.

"Pleased to meet you."

Good manners.

As they shook hands, Weezy said, "My mother named me Louise, but you can call me Weezy."

She giggled. "Like Lil Wayne?"

People usually referenced Louise from *The Jeffersons,* but . . . "Lil Wayne?"

"Rapper," Jack said. "That's his nickname."

She looked at him. "You like rap?"

"Some. Mostly no. But now and then I get stuck spending time with folks who do." To Gia, he said, "What's the occasion?"

"Well, I heard Weezy was here so I figured we'd stop over and get acquainted."

So that was it. Jack had been on the phone while she'd

unpacked the few things she'd brought. He must have told her about his houseguest and she'd come for a first-hand look. Weezy could understand that. Completely.

And now that you've seen me, you know you—especially you—have nothing to worry about.

"Are you hungry?" Vicky said to Weezy.

She was starved but determined to hold back.

"Well, um—"

"I am. Wanna eat?"

"She's a stomach with feet," Gia said. She hefted the pair of plastic grocery bags dangling from her left hand. "And since Jack never has anything to eat—"

"Just stocked in a brand-new, giant-economy-size box of Lucky Charms," he said.

Vicky pumped her fist. "Yes!"

Gia said, "Ohhhh, no."

Weezy could have told her about a study years ago that fed rats a diet of only breakfast cereal and how the ones on Lucky Charms did the best, but decided against it.

As Jack relieved Gia of the bags, she said, "There's wine, crackers, and a couple of cheeses in there."

"Come on in here and help me unpack," Jack said to Vicky, "and we'll check the fridge."

"Okay!"

Weezy watched her run after him.

"I know he's going to give her Lucky Charms in there," Gia said softly, smiling, her eyes on the kitchen door. "I have to take a public stand against it to keep it verboten at home, but it's Jack's thing to sneak her whatever she wants. That's why she loves coming here."

"How long since she's seen him?"

"A couple of days."

"Really? I thought from the way she greeted him—"

"Day, week, month, she's always that way with Jack."

Weezy felt a lump of envy in her throat. Jack had a family . . .

Raising her voice, Gia turned back to Weezy. "Anyway, as far as edibles go—"

"I've got fairly recent leftover General Tso's chicken," Jack announced from the kitchen. "Hey, what's this stuff? Quinoa?"

"It's pronounced *keen*-wah," she called back.

"Well, it's spelled 'quinn-oh-ah,' and you know I don't eat things I can't pronounce."

"As I was saying," she continued to Weezy, barely missing a beat, "as far as eating goes, it's BYO to Jack's, unless you consider beer a food group."

"Hops and malt," he called. "Malt is a grain, and hops are a vegetable, which makes beer a two-fer."

They'd obviously had this conversation before—many times. They were enviably comfortable with each other. She and Steve had shared something like that. They'd been close, but apparently not close enough to keep him from calling it quits on life.

These two had something more, something else running beneath the surface. She sensed a shared hurt, a shared trial, a fire that had scarred them but also fused them in the process. Weezy could almost see the voltaic arc of love flashing between them.

And could almost feel her heart break.

8.

"Well?" Jack said. "What do you think?"

He was walking Gia toward Columbus Avenue for a cab, his arm around her shoulder, her arm around his waist. Vicky ambled ahead, gyrating to whatever was playing on her iPod.

He'd thought it had gone well. It could have been a bonfire of the ovaries, but they'd got along.

Gia looked up at him, a faint smile playing about her lips. "I think she's in love with you."

The idea stunned him. Weezy? In love with him? Sure, she'd hopped into bed with him, but that had seemed more like a desperate kind of need than . . . love.

"No way. We've known each other for ages and haven't seen each other since the eighties. She can't be."

"She might not know it herself, or be in denial. Maybe it's just infatuation, but something's there."

"Swell. What do you think I should do?"

"Tell me again why she has to stay with you?"

"Long story."

"Vicky took to her. I could put her up—"

"No."

She paused, then, "You said that way too fast."

He thought about what had happened to her house, to Harris, to Harris's place. Lots of collateral damage around Weezy these days.

"Did I?"

"How much trouble is she in?"

"A bunch."

"Do I want to know details?"

"Probably not. It's complicated. She's gotten herself into a situation. It's better for you and Vicks not to be connected to her."

"And a hotel or motel won't do?"

"She needs to feel safe while she tries to make sense of the *Compendium*. It's a temporary thing."

Gia sighed and leaned against him as they walked. "Why isn't anything ever simple anymore?"

"Because you're involved with me, and I'm involved

with . . . well, you know. Let's face it: Life would be so much simpler and better for you if we'd never met."

But awful for me.

He felt her stiffen. "Simpler maybe, but don't you say 'better.' Don't you ever say 'better.' "

"You wouldn't have lost Emma."

"Emma wouldn't have existed without you."

"Exactly."

"Let's not go there, Jack."

"Okay."

Gladly not. He still hadn't found a way to tell her that Emma had died, and she and Vicky had almost died, because Emma was his bloodline . . . a branch marring the symmetry and aerodynamics of a spear.

They reached Columbus just as a cab was disgorging a trio of sweet young things eager for the Upper West Side's Saturday night bar scene. Jack grabbed the door and scooted Vicky into the back. He took Gia in his arms and she pressed against him.

"So . . . should I lock my bedroom door?"

She smiled. "I'll leave that up to you, but you never know . . . it might avoid an awkward moment."

"Think so?"

She shrugged. "I don't know. I do know I like her. She's got a sweetness about her. I don't think she has a mean bone in her body. But her mind . . . she doesn't flaunt it—in fact, I think she tries to hide it—but she reeks of intelligence. I think she's scary smart."

"She is. That's why we need her to decipher the *Compendium*."

"But as for her feelings for you . . . I feel kind of sorry for her if she does love you."

"Why?"

"Because she's so shit out of luck."

Jack barked a laugh. "You said the *s* word! I thought four-letter words were unnecessary."

She nodded. "A refuge for the inane, the insipid, and the inarticulate."

"But—"

"But sometimes they say it all."

He laughed again. "You're that sure of me?"

"As sure as you are of me."

"Well, then, that's a lock."

They kissed, long and hard. Then he guided her into the cab, closed the door, and watched his two ladies roar off toward the East Side.

9. "Jack, ohmygod! Jack!" Weezy cried, running up to him as he stepped through the door. "I found it!"

"What?"

"In the *Compendium*—the Orsa, the Null Site, even the *Fhinntmanchca*! It's all there! And it's . . . awful."

"Let me see."

"Oh, I hope that page is still there," she said, leading him to the round oak table where the book lay. "Please-please-please . . . yes!"

She slammed her hands down on the exposed pages as if trying to keep them from blowing away. It looked like a two-page spread of the Opus Omega cross-hatching.

Jack craned his neck. "What—?"

"In a minute. Let me tell you what I've been able to piece together. I had a fair amount of the picture when I walked in here today but I was missing vital parts. After you and Gia left, I pulled this out for a little more study. Remember I told you that the first pillar had to be placed in a specific spot called the Null Site?"

"Right, but you didn't know where or why."

"Well, I found out why almost as soon as I opened the *Compendium*: It's the spot that's crossed by the most so-called lines of force running between the nexus points. No locus is intersected by all—that's impossible—but the one with the most is designated the Null Site, and that's where Opus Omega was started."

"And where was that?"

"It didn't say."

"Swell. Then what's all the excitement?"

She turned back to the *Compendium* where her hands still pressed against the pages.

"I found this map. You see, one of the problems with trying to understand Opus Omega has been the lack of orientation. You're shown these diagrams with all the nexus points and all the lines of force between them and all the intersections that have pillars and those that still need them, but I've yet to see one superimposed on a Mercator-type map of the world—until now."

She slid her hands to the sides, revealing a two-page spread of the continents overlaid with the Opus Omega grid. He saw the red lines of force connecting the red splotches of the nexus points, and the white dots at the intersections where the pillars had been set.

"Nice. Where's the Null Site?"

"Take a look and tell me where you think," she said. "I want to see if we come up with the same spot."

Jack leaned over the book and studied the network of lines. He found thick intersections in all the continents, but the thickest seemed . . .

"Here," he said, pointing to an area in the northeastern United States. "This looks the busiest."

"That's what I thought too. Touch it."

"What do you mean?"

"Touch the spot."

Jack did, and jerked his hand back as the image expanded, bringing the area to the center. The northeastern and mid-Atlantic U.S. now dominated the two-page spread.

"Touch it again," she said.

He did, and it expanded further, bringing the Tri-State area front and center.

He smiled. "Ancient interactivity."

At another, earlier point in his life he might have been awed, but the events of the past couple of years had depleted his awe reservoir.

He touched it again and the lower half of Manhattan Island filled the spread. But . . .

"It looks different."

"That's because the map shows the island as it was thousands of years ago. We've changed its shape since the Dutch first settled here in the sixteen hundreds."

"You mentioned Battery Park City."

"Right. And that was just back in the sixties. Three hundred years of filling this and excavating that preceded it. One more zoom-in ought to do it."

Jack touched the busy intersection of lines and the image enlarged once more. He saw a symbol at the center of the intersection.

Ø

"Zero?"

"That's the mathematical symbol for an empty set, also known as a null set."

"The Null Site?"

"I don't see what else it can be. Notice where it rests."

Even with the vaguely distorted shape of the island, the location was disturbingly obvious.

"The World Trade Center."

"Right. Ground Zero."

Jack shook his head. "But that doesn't make sense. You said that for Opus Omega to work, the first pillar—"

"The Orsa pillar."

"Whatever—it had to go there."

"It did."

"Then what . . . ?" Jack didn't get it. And then with a high-voltage shock, he did. "Goren and his crew caught them *removing* the pillar."

Weezy was nodding. "Exactly."

"They killed thousands of people just so they could dig up an old hunk of stone?"

"It wasn't stone anymore."

Jack stared at her a moment, trying to make sense of that. "You'd better explain that."

"Long story."

"We've got time. But I need a beer. Want one?"

She gave her head half a shake, then stopped. "Got anything stronger?"

"Some single malt."

"That'll do."

On his way to the kitchen Jack decided he'd join her.

10.

"Apparently the Orsa is unique among its fellow pillars in a number of ways," Weezy said.

They sat facing each other across the round oak table, the *Compendium* and a bottle of Old Pulteney between them. Each held a small glass containing a couple of fingers of the Scotch. Jack felt like tossing his back but forced himself to sip.

"Tell me the not-stone-anymore part."

"I'll get to that. Let me lay the groundwork first. I've put in a lot of hours on this and I'm still kind of sorting it all out."

Jack leaned back. "I'm listening."

"First off, the Orsa must be buried in bedrock—just sticking it in the dirt is okay for all the others, but it won't do for the Orsa. So whoever figured out the Opus Omega was very lucky that all those lines of force intersected near the lower end of Manhattan rather than in Soho or the Village."

"Why?"

"Because the Manhattan schist is two hundred fifty feet down there." She held up a hand. "I know you're going to ask, so I'll tell you: Schist is a kind of rock that forms the foundation of Manhattan."

Jack said, "No schist!" and waited.

She closed her eyes. "I knew, I just *knew* you'd say that."

"Sorry. Couldn't help it. You bring out the adolescent in me."

She looked at him again, almost defiant. "The *schist* is near the surface in Midtown, starts dipping in the thirties, bottoms out in the Village, and rises again way downtown. That's why you don't see any skyscrapers in the Village and never will: The schist is too deep." She folded her arms and looked at him. "Go ahead."

"Go ahead what?"

"Make a comment about 'deep schist.' "

"I'm insulted!"

"You know you want to. You know you're dying to."

Jeez, she knew him.

"Just continue."

"All right. They seemed to think—or maybe they knew somehow—that being sunk in the bedrock at the intersection of all those lines of force would work an astonishing change on the pillar."

"Like?"

"Like transmuting it from nonorganic to organic."

Jack stared at her. "How is that poss—? Never mind."

"Possible" had lost its boundaries.

"Let's assume they were right," she said, "and that somehow the minerals of its stone were converted to carbon compounds. But the story doesn't stop there. Not only is it then composed of organic compounds, but as the millennia pass, it starts to *live*."

"Come on now."

"Oh, it gets better. Not only will it begin to live, but get this—at a certain point the *Compendium* says it will *awaken*."

Jack's mouth went dry. "Diana's Alarm."

"Right. It all fits."

"Some of it, yes. But not all. If that was the Orsa under that tarp Goren saw, why wait till 2001 to dig it up? Why not go after it when the city was excavating for the Trade Center?"

"I can't know for sure," Weezy said, "but I'll bet they had to wait until it was alive before they could dig it up. That was why they tried to block the project—not because it prevented them from burying another pillar, but because it would interfere with their digging up the Orsa."

"So when the time came, they destroyed the World Trade Center to get to it."

As she nodded, Jack shot the rest of his Scotch and poured himself some more. Weezy was still nursing hers.

He said, "But the thing was buried in the bedrock beneath six stories of basement under the Trade Center foundation. How did they know it had become alive?"

"Maybe they have sensitives who could feel it. Someone like Goren. He's obviously a sensitive. Look what being in the foundation with the Orsa did to him—gave him a panic attack."

"When do you think it came alive?"

"My guess is sometime in the nineties. That's when they began to look around for a way to get to it."

"No matter what the cost."

"Right. The 1993 bombing of the North Tower may have been their inspiration. Those fools thought they could topple one tower into the other and bring down both. That wasn't about to happen, but it may have planted the seed as to whom to contact and facilitate and manipulate into another sort of attack."

Jack leaned back, letting it sink in. The number of lives lost in the towers was minuscule compared to the mass exterminations of Stalin and Hitler and Pol Pot, but still . . . just to dig up a pillar? Even al Qaeda had a more comprehensible—he might even go so far as to say explicable—motive than retrieving a buried pillar, even if it was "alive."

"Why?"

Weezy finished her Scotch and leaned forward. "Because once the Orsa is alive, it's only a short while before it awakens."

"It was *years* between the attack and Diana's Alarm."

"The blink of an eye to something that's been gestating for millennia."

"But what's so important about it that they had to dig it up?"

"Because, according to the *Compendium,* once awakened, the Orsa can create the *Fhinntmanchca*."

"That word again. What is it?"

"I don't know." Weezy began pounding a fist on the table. "I don't know and it's driving me crazy! I keep coming across the word but never an explanation of what it does or what the Opus Omega people hope or think it's going to do."

"But considering what they went through to get their hands on it, it's got to be big."

Weezy nodded, her expression grim. "Very big."

11. Ernst studied Darryl within the Orsa. His outstretched fingers were only a half dozen inches or so from the end. Sometime since Ernst's last visit, the fellow's flesh had lost its translucency and returned to normal. He now looked just as he had when he'd entered the Orsa.

Had the process failed?

Ernst banished the thought. After all they'd gone through—the time, the effort, the risks, the manipulations—failure was inconceivable.

And yet . . . the thought persisted.

The transformation had to have taken place. No, more than a transformation—a *transubstantiation.*

Transubstantiation . . . the changing of substance without changing perceivable physical attributes. The Catholic Church believed in transubstantiation. It proclaimed that when one of its priests offered up the consecrated bread and wine at mass, they maintained their outward appearances but literally became the body and blood of Jesus Christ. The bread became holy flesh, the wine became holy blood from the son of the Christian god. Many Protestant sects, on the other hand, considered the bread and wine of the ceremony merely symbolic.

What had happened to Darryl was not symbolic. He maintained the physical aspect of a typical human being, but his substance had been changed—transubstantiated—into something totally Other. He had entered the Orsa a human, but he would emerge as something else.

The *Fhinntmanchca.*

Or so Ernst hoped.

Darryl . . . simple, insignificant, trivial Darryl would be the *Fhinntmanchca* . . . the Maker of the Way. What did that mean? What was he expected to accomplish? Only the One seemed to know the nature of the *Fhinntmanchca,* but even he didn't seem too sure if it would or could accomplish its purpose.

Maybe tomorrow Ernst would know. Maybe tomorrow the world would know.

SUNDAY

I. *Drifting in the harbor a thousand feet off the Battery, Ernst watched the towers burn in silence.*

Nearly ten o'clock. Almost an hour since the Arabs had completed their mission here. They'd also wanted to crash planes into the Pentagon and the White House. Fine. Go ahead. Knock yourselves out, as Americans liked to say, as long as you hit the towers—especially WTC-2, the South Tower.

And they had. Indeed they had.

He watched the boiling black smoke and tried to imagine what it was like in and around those towers.

The One knew. He was there somewhere in the thick of it, perhaps pretending to be an emergency worker. Wherever he was, he was soaking up the pain, panic, terror, fear, grief, anguish, and dismay, feasting on it.

His instructions were to let the initial shock pass, lull them into thinking the worst was over, then proceed to step two, the real reason for this endeavor. Ernst knew that none of this delaying had anything to do with the ultimate purpose. It was all about the One's hunger and how he would gorge on the emotional fallout of the attacks. And who was Ernst to question the One?

He looked down at the little gray box in his hand—the one marked with an S for the South Tower. WTC-2 was the important one, although not the ultimate target.

All this was happening because of what was buried under WTC-4, the nine-story building directly to the east of the South Tower.

He studied the scene. The South Tower, closer to him, had been hit second. The Arabs were supposed to hit it first, but you couldn't trust those lunatics. So full of hate. Allah this and Allah that, and all worked up about martyrdom while attacking the Great Satan. So many things could have gone wrong but they somehow managed to pull it off, though not without some deviation from the plan.

So the South Tower had been struck second. That was the bad news. The good news was that the impact was lower than on the North Tower—fifteen floors lower, according to the radio. That meant significantly more weight above the structural damage. Which in turn made it plausible that the South Tower would collapse first.

He extended an aerial from the S box, then slid up a little safety cover on its front panel, revealing a black button. He took a breath and pressed it, then watched and waited. If all went as planned, a sequence of explosive charges would begin detonating. The Order's operatives, posing as building inspectors, structural engineers, and elevator repairmen, had spent the last year and a half setting them in precise locations in the floor joists and perimeter columns. Now . . . the proof of the pudding.

Suddenly orange flame and a cloud of gray smoke belched from the wound in the building's flank. The smoke rose quickly, appearing to engulf the floors above it, then spread down toward the ground. Ernst couldn't be sure what was happening. Had the charges failed in their task, leaving the Tower merely sheathed in smoke, or had they succeeded in what had been planned all along?

And then a deep rumble broke the silence and he knew before he saw—or rather didn't see. The Tower was gone.

WTC-2 had collapsed, leaving a column of smoke in its place. The charges had worked—perhaps too well. It had looked like what it was—a controlled demolition. That would start tongues a-wagging. He wondered who would be blamed. As long as it wasn't the Septimus Order, who cared?

What really mattered was what had happened to WTC-4. He wouldn't know for a while. The fall of the Tower had been designed to damage the smaller building beyond repair without completely burying it in debris. They had to avoid severe damage to the eastern edge of the Trade Center's foundation. The Order had men ready to move in and break through the slurry wall and foundation floor to get to the Orsa.

Ernst watched the secondary cloud rising from the building's impact with the ground. The builders had only themselves to blame. His father had marshaled highly placed politicians and businessmen who belonged to the Order to dissuade the Port Authority from building the World Trade Center, but no one would listen.

The Order had tried a less destructive course, but found it impossible to break through the WTC foundation and retrieve the Orsa without the world knowing. Certainly not after those Islamic idiots tried that car-bomb attack on the North Tower in ninety-three.

So more drastic measures came into play. It took years of effort and millions of dollars to put everything in place for this moment. And yet, if the PA had simply left well enough alone back in the sixties, none of this would have been necessary.

Ernst put away the S detonator but left the N box in his pocket until he received a call. The One would feed on the fresh panic from the collapse, then let Ernst know when he wanted the North Tower to fall.

No real need to bring down the North Tower. In fact, if its demolition went wrong and it fell the wrong way, it could do more damage—too much damage—to WTC-4 and jeopardize the ultimate purpose of the whole endeavor.

But the One wanted both towers down, and no one—certainly not Ernst—argued with the One.

⟐

Ernst awoke stiff and sore on the couch in his office. He had decided to spend the night in the Lodge, to stay close to the Orsa, just in case . . .

He threw off the borrowed sheet and sat up in the warm humid darkness. The Lodge wasn't air-conditioned because, as a rule, it didn't need it. The thick stone walls tended to hold out the summer heat, but not tonight. He'd stripped to his underwear but that had helped only a little.

He thought about the dream. He'd lately found himself reliving that day. No surprise why. All the effort, and all the death and destruction that went into making it happen, were coming to fruition. The deaths didn't bother him. The dead were the lucky ones, actually—spared what was to come when the Otherness gained ascendance. A living hell for those who had not aided that ascendance. Should it happen in his lifetime—and all signs said that it would—Ernst would be rewarded. The One would rule, but Ernst and the other high-ups in the Order would be compensated not only with immunity from the terrors of the transformed Earth but with a level of power over its inhabitants. And like the One, they'd feed on the global misery.

Ernst often wondered what that would be like. He wasn't sure he'd even like it, but he was certain it would be preferable to being fed upon.

He sat up and rolled his shoulders. Yes, they ached, but not that much. Why was he awake? The dream? Or something else?

2.

Mother.

The word awoke him and he began to cough, deep retching spasms that raised a thin, sticky, salty fluid.

I'm wet, he thought after he stopped coughing.

More than just wet. Soaked.

Where was he? Everything was black. Not the slightest trace of light. He felt panic begin to nibble at him.

Was he blind?

Mother.

The word calmed him. He felt around him. He lay on a hard floor, concrete or stone, in a puddle of some sort of thin, sticky goo. He tried to push himself up but his arms felt like rubber. Too weak.

And then he realized that not only did he not know where he was, he didn't know *who* he was. He had a name, he had to have a name, everybody had a name.

Panic threatened again.

Mother.

Again the word calmed him. He relaxed, closed his eyes, and the name came to him.

Darryl. That was his name. Darryl. But who was Darryl?

If he could see himself, maybe he'd know. And when he knew, maybe he could remember who his mother was, and then he could go and find her, because he needed to find his mother.

Light . . . he needed light.

He tried to speak but that caused another coughing fit. When it passed he found his voice.

"Give me some light!"

3. "Oh, hell!"

The phone—one of his Tracfones.

Jack rolled out of bed, searching in the dark by following the ring. Nobody called him at this hour unless it was an emergency and the only ones who'd call him in an emergency were Gia, Abe, and Julio.

He found it, fumbled to press the ON button, and jammed it against his ear.

"Gia?"

"No," said a vaguely familiar female voice. *"It's Diana."*

A flood of relief and confusion—relief that it wasn't Gia, confusion because . . .

"Diana?"

"The Oculus."

"Oh, right. Sorry. Still not completely awake." He remembered now—he'd given her his number. "What's wrong?"

"The Fhinntmanchca *. . . it's here."* Her voice was shaking.

"You just saw this in an Alarm, I take it."

"Yes. It was born tonight, just minutes ago."

"Born? Where is it?"

"I don't know exactly . . . but I do know it's not far from you."

"How far?"

"Somewhere in Manhattan. In a dark place."

Swell. That narrowed it down. He glanced at the glowing hands of his Felix the Cat clock. Lots of dark places in Manhattan at ten after three in the morning.

"What's this thing look like?"

"I don't know." She was starting to sound panicky. *"I couldn't see it. It was just a blur. In the last Alarm, it was*

only flickering blackness, a word, now it's real and it's here and it's . . . it's evil."

Evil . . . Jack used to think good and evil were man-made, that the universe was indifferent and good or evil solely the products of human action. No more. As far as he could see, humans were still the only source of good. But evil . . . evil could be human and beyond human.

He knew when Diana called the *Fhinntmanchca* evil, she meant it came from out there . . . from the Otherness.

"Okay. Stay cool and think. Give me something to go on."

"All I saw was its egg and . . . and this weird star."

"Like Polaris, or a constellation?"

"No, it was a symbol, like the Jewish Star, the Star of David, only it had an extra point."

A seven-pointed star . . . that could mean only one thing . . .

"The Order."

"What order?"

"The Septimus Order. You must know—"

But obviously she didn't. Yeah, he'd expect an Oculus to know, but she wasn't a typical Oculus. She'd been thrust into the job half a year ago at age thirteen, with no warning and minimal preparation. One day a normal-looking teen, the next she's got big, black, bug eyes and she's become an antenna for warnings from out there.

"I don't know, Jack. What's it mean?"

"Davis can explain it. Tell him it may seem like the Order has been quiet, but it hasn't. It's been very, very busy."

"But what about the Fhinntmanchca*? How will you find it?"*

"You've just given me a good idea where—a place that makes perfect sense."

"But I mean, you don't even know what it looks like."

"Got a feeling I'll know it when I see it."

I think. I hope.

"Jack, you've got to find it and stop it. If you and the Defender work together . . ."

Right. Me and the Defender . . . she still thought him hale and hearty and powerful. What would she think if she knew he was an arthritic old man?

"It's just me at the moment, Diana."

"Then you've got to stop it. It's going to do something awful."

"Like what?"

"I don't know, but it's going to be terrible . . . horrible . . . the end of everything." Words seemed to fail her after that.

The end of everything . . . bringing in the Otherness would certainly mean the end of everything.

"Relax. I'm on it."

Did that sound reassuring? Not to him.

"Be careful, Jack. It's dangerous. It's deadly."

"Deadly how?"

"I don't know. I just know that it is."

Swell.

4. Finding sleep impossible, Ernst decided to give up and start the day. A momentous day. The first day in all time that the *Fhinntmanchca* would walk the Earth.

At least that was what he hoped.

He had followed all the ancient teachings, all the lore. It was up to the Orsa now to complete the process.

But if it failed, what would the One say? More important, what would the displeased One *do*?

His hands shook as he began dressing, making a chore out of fastening his buttons. His suit was wrinkled, but that couldn't be helped. He needed a shower and a shave, but certainly wasn't going to share the facilities used by the residents. Besides, the company around here would never notice.

Leaving his cane behind, he stepped out into the hall—and to his shock discovered he was not alone.

At least a dozen Kickers were awake and wandering around. The one called Ansari, bleary-eyed and unshaven, stopped and stared at him.

"You spend the night in your office? What? Your old lady kick you out?"

What an absurd thought. He'd been married for a while—mostly to sire a son—but had learned he was sterile. No point in being married then.

He noticed that the malice in the man's smile seemed perfunctory, as if he had something troubling weighing on his mind. He glanced around and saw the same look in the other Kickers' eyes.

He turned to Ansari. "What are you doing up? Why aren't you sleeping?"

The uneasy look deepened as he shrugged. "No reason. Just awake."

"Aw, bullshit," said a passing Kicker. "He had nightmares just like the rest of us."

"Shove it, Hagaman."

Hagaman looked at Ernst. "Check out that face. He had bad dreams too, but Mister Tough Guy ain't gonna admit it."

"What kind of dreams?"

Hagaman looked uneasy. "Don't know. Don't remember much, just that it was bad. Woke me up, and I got up because I didn't want to go back to sleep again."

Could the impending arrival of the *Fhinntmanchca* be behind the dreams? If so, why hadn't he had any?

"Pussy," Ansari said, and walked away.

Hagaman appeared about to go after him, but stopped when he looked over Ernst's shoulder.

"Hey, it's the boss. And he don't look so hot neither."

Ernst had to agree. Hank Thompson looked haggard and haunted.

"Something's changed," Thompson said. "Feel it?"

"No." But he did feel a charge of excitement from what that might mean. "But everyone else seems to."

Thompson looked at him. "Do you think . . . ?"

"Let's find out, shall we?"

They headed down to the basement where they found a number of Kickers lounging around the coffeepot. It smelled wonderful, and a few moments ago Ernst would have craved a cup. But the thought of what they might find on the level below had energized him to the point where caffeine would be superfluous.

Thompson turned to him and spoke in a low voice. "Want me to kick them upstairs?"

Ernst's first instinct was to have him do just that, but he shook his head instead. No use in piquing the curiosity of the rabble.

"That will only draw attention. Proceed as casually as you can."

"You want to see casual? I'll show you casual."

He filled a Styrofoam cup with coffee and then strolled through the basement's main room. Ernst followed, watching him nod to his followers and slap one or two on the back. They looked up to him. He'd shown them the Kicker Man symbol and awakened them to a brotherhood they hadn't known they shared. He was "the boss."

He unlocked the door to the side room. They entered and locked it behind them. Ernst took the lead then, descending to the subcellar. Light from above lit the stairway, but the space below lay in Stygian darkness. Reaching the floor, Ernst felt along the wall, found the light switch, but hesitated. What would he see when the lights went on?

He flipped the switch and the first thing he saw was the Orsa.

"No! Oh, no!" he said, gasping as he hurried forward. "What has happened?"

"What the fuck?" said Thompson behind him.

The Orsa had changed. It looked . . . deflated. Its sides were sunken, caved in; its ends sagged. Its translucence had faded to a dull gray. When he reached it he touched it, and jerked his hand back.

It felt . . . dead. Or if not dead, moribund.

"Hey, where's Darryl?" Thompson was saying. "Where the fuck is Darryl?"

Panic gripped Ernst. Was Darryl still inside? All was lost if he was. All the years of planning, the expense, the risks . . . all for nothing.

"Mother?" said a weak voice from somewhere beyond the far end of the Orsa.

Ernst's heart leaped as he and Thompson hurried around to find Darryl kneeling in a pool of clear fluid.

He looked . . . different.

He still looked like Darryl, but a sick Darryl. His face was white, his eyes sunken into dark recesses; his once shaggy hair was plastered to his scalp and forehead, and his beard looked more scraggly than ever. His blue work shirt and worn jeans were wet and stained and seemed to have shrunken on his frame.

And then, just for an instant he shimmered—like a heat mirage.

"Darryl, you made it!" Thompson said as he placed his coffee cup on the dying, desiccated Orsa. Apparently he'd missed the shimmer. He stepped in front of Ernst and approached the man.

Ernst grabbed his arm. "Don't get too close."

"Yeah?" Thompson snatched his arm away. "Why the hell not?"

"Look at him. Look closely."

"I don't need to look any closer than I'm looking. He looks like a fucking zombie. What—?"

Darryl shimmered again.

Thompson backed up a quick step. "Oh, shit!"

Ernst realized that Darryl himself wasn't shimmering, but rather the air around him. Looking closely, Ernst could make out an inch-thick layer of roiling air, outlining him like an aura. It didn't glow, but seemed rather to writhe as if in agony from contact with him.

"It must be part of the change."

Thompson looked at him. "Change? What change? He was supposed to be healed."

"Well, healing involves change, of course. Changing from a diseased state to a—"

"Mother?" Darryl said, looking up at Hank.

"Hey, Darryl. It's me . . . Hank."

Darryl gave him a blank stare. "Want mother. Thirsty."

"Okay." Thompson grabbed his coffee from atop the Orsa. "Try some of this."

Ernst gripped his arm again. "Be careful."

Not that he cared about Thompson per se, but as leader of the Kickers, he was the key to a pool of manpower that might prove useful in the future—perhaps the very near future.

Thompson snarled at him. "Why? What have you done to him? You call this *cured*? Look at him."

"Just . . . be careful." He pointed to the floor in front of Darryl. "Why not simply place it there? If he wants it, he can take it."

Thompson hesitated, then bent and placed the cup a foot or so in front of him, just outside the puddle. Darryl's hand trembled violently as he reached for the cup. When his fingers reached it—

—the cup exploded, splattering coffee and shards of Styrofoam in every direction.

"Shit!" Thompson cried, ducking away and almost knocking Ernst over.

Ernst stumbled back, brushing coffee from his white suit. Too late. It was stained. Normally he would be infuriated, but not now. Not at all. This was wonderful.

He didn't know whether to laugh or to cry. He'd succeeded. Darryl was now the *Fhinntmanchca.*

He glanced at the Orsa. Good thing, too. If it wasn't dead, it was near dead. They would have no second chance.

Looking more confused than ever, Darryl said, "Thirsty."

"Then you must drink," said a fourth voice.

Ernst recognized it immediately. He turned and found himself face-to-face with the One.

5. The knocking startled Jack. No one was supposed to be knocking on his door.

Weezy raised her head and gave him a questioning look from where she was sipping coffee and studying the *Compendium.* Morning light filled the windows. The air was redolent of microwaving Taylor Ham and cheese.

He stepped to the closet beside the door and pulled the Glock from the top shelf by the katana.

Weezy's voice held a note of exasperation. "Is that necessary every single time you answer the door?"

"Don't know," he told her in his most patient tone. "Can't know till I see who's at the door—*then* I'll know if it's necessary."

Whoever had knocked was either a neighbor or someone

who had got past the entrance without buzzing up. He put his eye to the peephole and blinked when he saw a familiar old woman dressed all in black.

"Not necessary," he told Weezy as he opened the door and allowed Mrs. Clevenger to enter. Her three-legged dog followed.

"Knowing you," the Lady said, "I thought you would have fewer questions if I looked this way."

"You thought right," he said as he replaced the Glock on the closet shelf.

"Your ivy is dying of thirst," she said as she passed the Shmoo planter.

Jack was sure she hadn't even glanced that way.

"Good morning," Weezy said, rising.

"Not so good." The Lady's expression was grim. "Something is wrong. Something that doesn't belong in this world has entered it."

Jack and Weezy looked at each other and spoke simultaneously.

"The *Fhinntmanchca*."

The Lady frowned. "You think so?"

Weezy stared. "You don't know? But you're attuned to—"

"I'm a product of this sphere and, yes, I am attuned to it. But as I told you, certain doings involving the Otherness are hidden from me."

"I had a call from the Oculus. She had another Alarm about it. She says the *Fhinntmanchca* is here, in the city."

"But for what purpose?"

"No one knows," Weezy said. "I've been hunting through the *Compendium* for days now, but—"

The Lady waved a hand. "Don't expect to see it in black and white. It is something you will have to piece together yourself, for not even Srem knew the purpose of the *Fhinntmanchca*. No one but the Seven ever knew."

"The Seven," Weezy said. "The *Compendium* mentions them time and again."

The Lady nodded as she seated herself in the big wingback chair. The dog settled on the floor next to her. The Shmoo planter sat near her elbow.

"Water this now. It suffers."

Jack raised his hands in surrender. "Okay, okay."

As he headed for the kitchen, she said, "The seven mages who championed the Otherness in the First Age. A huge cult grew up around them. They controlled the q'qr hordes. They almost succeeded in bringing this sphere under the domination of the Otherness. The *Fhinntmanchca* was part of that plan, but none of it ever came to fruition, and by time the First Age came to an end, only one of the Seven remained alive."

"Let me guess who survived," Jack called from the kitchen as he filled his coffee cup with water. He fought an urge to imitate the Church Lady. "Could his name begin with R?"

"Yes, the Adversary. Unwilling to share power when the Otherness became ascendant, he killed off his six fellow mages one by one until only he remained."

"And so the Seven became the One," Weezy said.

"Yes. But the Otherness was defeated, and then came the cataclysm and the end of the First Age, and all of his intrigue and murderous plotting proved for naught."

Jack returned to the front room and poured some water into the planter.

"Until now," Weezy said.

"What do you mean?" The Lady caressed the ivy and its leaves immediately plumped up and deepened in color.

"It seems that somehow, some way via Opus Omega, he has succeeded in creating or summoning the *Fhinntmanchca*."

The Lady stiffened and stared at her. "Via Opus Omega? What do you mean?"

Weezy explained her theory about using the Orsa to create the *Fhinntmanchca*.

The Lady looked concerned. "So if you are right about the *Fhinntmanchca* being a by-product of Opus Omega, that means the *Fhinntmanchca* will be used against me."

"Why is that?"

"Very simple: The purpose of Opus Omega is to destroy me."

6. The scary guy . . . the guy with the forever eyes . . . the guy Drexler called "the One." Physically he wasn't the least bit imposing, even less so than the first time they'd met. Now he seemed almost . . . delicate. But he had an air of authority about him, of hidden power that warned away. Hank had hoped never to see him again, but here he was. And where had he come from? Maybe he'd already been here, standing in the shadows. But how had he got in?

Hank wasn't about to ask.

Drexler gave a little bow—Hank half expected him to click his heels—and gestured toward Darryl.

"The *Fhinntmanchca*."

That word again . . . and they were both looking at Darryl. Was that what this was all about? He'd entered the Orsa as Darryl and emerged as this poor, confused son of a bitch. Hank had a feeling a *Fhinntmanchca* was more than a poor, confused son of a bitch.

"So I see," the One said to Drexler. "You've done well, Ernst. Very well. I am pleased."

Drexler seemed to swell inside his stained white suit. He gave another little bow.

"We exist to serve."

We? Hank thought. Does that mean me too? Like hell. But he wasn't about to say that.

The One stepped forward and Darryl said, "Mother?"

"No." He looked down at him. "I am not your mother. You thirst? Then you must drink."

He pointed to the near end of the sagging Orsa, to where clear liquid trickled from a half-inch pore at its center. Darryl looked at the trickle, then back to the One.

"For me?"

The One nodded. "For you."

Hank recoiled as Darryl shuffled over on his knees and began to lap the fluid, swallowing greedily.

"Hey, Darryl, man, get off your knees. You're a Kicker and—"

Without looking at him, the One raised a hand and Hank stopped. He didn't want to, but his words dried up.

Drexler said, "He is no longer a Kicker. He has become the *Fhinntmanchca* and requires nourishment that only the Orsa can provide."

Okay, Hank thought. Time to ask.

"What's the *Fhinntmanchca*? What's it do?"

"It is the Maker of the Way," Drexler said.

"Those are just words. What do they mean? How do you 'make' a 'way'?"

The One spoke without taking his eyes off Darryl.

"Cataclysm."

7. "In theory," the Lady said, leaning forward in the wingback chair, "when Opus Omega is completed, I will die."

Weezy felt a pang of dread as she stared at her. She'd

known the Lady before as Mrs. Clevenger, simply another of the town's eccentrics. But now she felt a deep kinship, an intimate connection.

"Why do you say 'in theory'? Is there doubt?"

"Of course there is doubt. Opus Omega has yet to be completed and may never be completed. So until it becomes fact, it must remain theory."

Jack leaned on the round oak table. "But those scars on your back . . . don't they mean that it's working, that burying those columns damages you?"

"They do."

"And that hole straight through you—"

"The Florida incident," she said with a curt nod.

Weezy was confused. "The Florida—?"

"Long story," Jack said, then turned back to the Lady. "Weren't you 'killed' then?"

"So it appeared. I cannot be harmed by anything of this world, but the creatures that devoured me were from the Other place."

. . . devoured . . . the Other place . . . what were they talking about? Weezy was dying to know the details.

"How did you come back?"

The Lady shook her head. "That I do not know. It should have been the end of me, but I survived. Perhaps if Opus Omega had progressed far enough along, I would not have come back."

Jack looked grim. "But the *Fhinntmanchca* is a product of Opus Omega. It might succeed where the chew wasps failed."

Chew wasps?

"True," the Lady said. "That is troublesome."

"But why attack you at all?" Weezy said.

"As the physical manifestation of the noosphere, I act as a beacon, proclaiming to the multiverse that this is a sentient planet. Should I be extinguished, this sphere will be seen as lifeless. The Ally, already rather neglectful, will lose all interest and turn entirely away."

"Giving the Otherness carte blanche."

An idea popped into Weezy's head. "What about an end run? Why doesn't it attack the noosphere?"

The Lady shook her head again. "By its very nature, the noosphere cannot be directly attacked. It is the product of all the interactions between the sentient beings on the planet. The only way to weaken it is to damage its population base—a deadly pandemic, a nuclear winter, that sort of thing. But that runs counter to the ends of the Otherness. The lower the population, the less fear and misery to feed on."

Jack chimed in. "But we know nothing about this *Fhinntmanchca*. Maybe it *can* disrupt the noosphere."

The Lady appeared to consider that. "I don't see how, but . . ."

"Let's just say it can," Weezy said. "What would be the result?"

"A disrupted noosphere would disrupt me. I would vanish."

"And the beacon would go out."

The Lady nodded. "Leaving the Adversary a clear field."

"That's got to be it," Jack said, straightening. "Suck the life out of you by disrupting the noosphere. Looks like someone's got to disrupt this *Fhinntmanchca* first."

"You?" Weezy said, her heart clenching.

He looked at her. "Well, yeah, I guess. Don't see that there's much choice. If you can think of someone else, I'll be happy to step aside."

"What about Mister Veilleur?"

"In case you didn't notice, Mister V isn't too agile these days."

"But you told me Diana said the *Fhinntmanchca* was dangerous and deadly."

He pointed to the Lady. "To her, we have to assume so. To us mere mortals . . ." He shrugged. "Who knows?"

"Do you know where it is?" the Lady said as Jack headed for the front closet.

"Got a pretty good idea."

Dread filled Weezy as she watched him take the pistol from the shelf and stick it in the waistband of his jeans at the small of his back.

"You don't really think that's going to be of any use against this *Fhinntmanchca* thing, do you?"

Another shrug. "Maybe, maybe not. But it works against people, and people brought that thing into this world, so maybe they can be persuaded to send it packing."

He disappeared into his room for a few minutes, then emerged stuffing things into his jeans pockets.

"You two wait here while I see what I can do."

Weezy had a sick, bad feeling about this. Something awful was about to happen.

"Be careful, Jack."

He gave her a tight smile. "Always."

And then he was out the door.

Weezy held back tears. "Will he be all right?"

"I cannot say," the Lady said, "because I do not know. This is all new."

"But why him? Why can't somebody else—?"

"Because there is no one else, and he knows that. So he does what needs to be done, or at least tries to. Though he hates it, though he wants no part of any of it, that is what he must do, because that is the way he is. That is the only way he knows, the only path he can see. That is why he was chosen as the Heir."

Jack . . . her Jack . . . skinny, funny Jack from Johnson . . . she still couldn't accept it.

The Tracfone started ringing. She saw Eddie's number

in the window. She thumbed the power off and put it back on the table.

"Your brother?" the Lady said.

Weezy nodded. "My brother, the Septimus." The word tasted like poison.

"Perhaps you should speak to him. He is blood, after all."

"I've spoken to him. And I'll speak to him again. But right now . . ." She shook her head. "I can't."

Possibilities and probabilities collided in her brain, producing an awful scenario: Eddie helping the Order track her through the phone. She opened its rear compartment and disconnected the battery. Just to be sure.

"Come, then," the Lady said, rising and patting her hair. "We will walk. The air will be good for you."

"But Jack said—"

"I am the Lady. I go where I please."

8.

Hank shook his head in silent wonder.

Whatever was in that stuff leaking from the Orsa, it had a miraculous effect on Darryl. At least as far as his strength was concerned. Ten minutes after lapping at it he got to his feet, but he didn't seem any less confused. He now stood, swaying slightly, before the One.

"Mother?"

The One showed a hint of a smile. "Yes. Your mother. You want your mother, don't you?"

Darryl nodded. "Mother."

"Do you know where she is?"

Another nod. "Mother."

He stepped aside and gestured toward the staircase. "Then by all means, go find her."

Hank watched Darryl move toward the stairs, leaving

wet shoe prints. He started with a shuffle, then graduated to a slow walk.

"What's all this about 'mother'?" Hank said.

Drexler shook his head. "I don't know. We've embarked upon an uncharted sea."

He gave the One a questioning look, but his attention was fixed on Darryl.

When Darryl reached the wrought-iron stairs, he hesitated.

Hank started forward. "Looks like he needs—"

Drexler thrust out an arm. "Don't touch. No contact. It's in the Lore."

"But—"

"Remember what happened to your coffee cup."

He remembered. Yeah, maybe a good idea to give Darryl some space.

He watched Darryl reach out and grasp the railing. Smoke rose from where his hand touched the wrought iron. He looked at it curiously, then released the railing and stared at his hand. Hank gasped when he saw that the iron he had touched was gone.

Darryl's gaze moved from his hand to the gap in the railing, then he started up, leaving a puff of smoke and a gap everywhere he touched.

Hank stood frozen, his tongue a sandbox. "Am I seeing what I'm seeing?"

"Yes, Mister Thompson," Drexler said. His eyes were bright, his lips parted with excitement. He looked ready to explode. "The *Fhinntmanchca* does not mix well with this world."

"Where's he going?"

"Only the *Fhinntmanchca* knows." He glanced over his shoulder. "And of course the One."

The One stood statue still, staring after Darryl, and smiling.

Drexler cleared his throat. "Sir, may we ask—?"

"You may," the One said without looking at him. "But if you wish an answer, you will have to follow him and find out for yourselves."

Drexler turned to Hank. "Then that is just what we will do."

Hank jerked a thumb toward the One, who hadn't moved. "He coming?"

"We need not worry about him. Come."

Hank followed him to the staircase. He waited as Drexler ascended ahead of him and checked out the gaps in the handrail. The iron appeared to have melted away but without leaving any slag. The free ends looked like they'd been cut with an acetylene torch. He gave one a quick touch but found it cool.

The damage to the handrails seemed to have destabilized the staircase because it wobbled as Drexler climbed. Once he was off, Hank hurried up after him. He glanced back and saw the One still standing by the shrunken Orsa.

When he reached the top and stepped out of the closet, he tapped Drexler's shoulder.

"Hey, how come the metal dissolved when he touched it, but his clothes are okay?"

Drexler shrugged. "I would assume because the clothes came through the Orsa with him."

Made sense.

Darryl had walked out into the main room of the basement. As they started after him, Hank heard a voice shout Darryl's name. He recognized it and heard trouble in the tone.

"Hey, I'm talking to you," Ansari said. "Not only do you look like shit, but what the fuck you doing here?"

Hank pushed past Drexler and found Ansari confronting Darryl.

"Mother."

Ansari's eyes blazed. "What you call me?"

He gave Darryl a two-handed shove to the chest. Darryl swayed, but Ansari wound up staggering back instead. His face purpling, he raised a meaty fist.

Hank shouted, "Hold it!" but not in time.

Ansari swung. His fist rammed forward, smashing against Darryl's undefended jaw—

—and dissolved in a cloud of red smoke.

Hank skidded to a halt as he watched Ansari stumble back, clutching his wrist and staring at the place where his hand had been. No blood sprayed the air—the stump was blackened, cauterized.

As Ansari screamed in pain and horror, Hagaman rushed up behind him, shouting, "What the fuck you do, asshole?"

"Mother."

"Goddamn!"

He bent and charged, as if to tackle, but Darryl put out a hand that caught Hagaman's arm above the elbow. Another scream, another spray of red smoke, and Hagaman spun and dropped to the floor—right next to his forearm. He writhed in agony as he clutched the stump of his arm.

Panic erupted as the other men in the room fell over each other in a headlong rush to get away from him. Darryl began to move toward them as they bunched up at the door.

"Mother."

"Get out of his way!" Hank shouted.

But either they didn't hear or were too panicked to understand.

Darryl reached them and put out his hands to push them aside. The result was more screams and more red smoke at they lurched away with chunks burned out of their backs and shoulders.

With the doorway cleared, Darryl stepped through and

headed upstairs. Hank and Drexler followed to the first floor. Word must have spread because everyone was pressed against the wall, staring in fear and wonder as Darryl walked toward the front entrance.

"The doors!" Drexler said.

He scooted ahead and opened one of the heavy oak doors, holding it for Darryl until he passed.

Darryl halted at the bottom of the steps and turned in a slow circle. He stopped, facing uptown.

"Mother."

He turned and began walking up toward Allen Street.

"Any idea where he's going?" Hank said.

Drexler shook his head. "No. But I believe the One does."

"The One . . . is he even human?"

"Yes, but something more."

Hank had figured that. "Can he be killed?"

Drexler gave him a sharp look. "Don't even think—"

"I'm not thinking anything." True. The question had popped out seemingly on its own. "Just wondering."

"Well, then, the answer is yes. But not by any such as us."

"Who then?"

"Another . . . like him."

"You mean there's *two* of him?"

If so, he wouldn't really be the *One.*

"Not exactly. The two are mortal enemies. And that is all I can say on the subject."

"I need more. Is the One going to be the head honcho after the cosmic shit hits the cosmic fan?"

Drexler's lips pursed. "You have such a way with words, Mister Thompson."

"You know what I'm saying."

"Yes, I do. And yes, once he defeats his counterpart, the Yang to his Yin, he will be the Lord and Master of this sphere." He glanced at Hank. "Don't tell me you had illusions of—"

"Hey, no way. You crazy?" But he had. He'd thought that with his Kickers at his back . . . "But we—you and me, that is—we're going to get to wet our beaks, right?"

He nodded. "When the Change comes, you and I will have places beside the One."

Well, that would have to do. Probably be fine. Just like Daddy promised—he and Jerry would be princes when the Others returned. Too bad Jerry wasn't around to join in.

Drexler pointed at Darryl's retreating figure. "We don't want him getting too far ahead."

As they began walking, Hank thought about how reality had begun doing slow cartwheels since his first dream about the stick figure known as the Kicker Man, becoming increasingly surreal until blossoming into the complete and total insanity of this past week.

Darryl . . . fucking Darryl, of all people . . . the *Fhinntmanchca* . . . the Maker of the Way . . . dissolving everything he touched. It was all going down, just as his daddy had said. In fact, it might be all going down today, and he was right here in the heart of it.

Hank's pulse raced—he felt cranked and scared. Made him want to pee, but he kept walking.

9. The man who was more than a man, who was known as the One to many, and as Rasalom to a few, who had numerous names, the most important known only to him, stood on the roof of the Lodge and waited.

In an hour or so, perhaps more, it would happen. He would know when it did. He would feel it.

And so would someone else.

You're nearby, Glaeken. I know it. When it happens you'll feel it and you'll know my time has come. And you'll be afraid.

Though difficult to imagine Glaeken afraid, Rasalom relished the thought. Glaeken would have good cause for fear when the Lady was gone. For the beacon would be turned off, the Enemy would abandon this sphere as lifeless and worthless, and Glaeken would be on his own.

What would that mean? Would he lose his power—his resilience, his immortality? Would he become just another mortal?

Wouldn't that be delicious.

You will pay for what you have made me suffer down these millennia. You imprisoned me, you even thought you'd slain me, but always I found a way back. And this time *you* will die, long after you wish to, and you will find no way back.

Rasalom's only regret was that success today would mean forgoing his vengeance on the transgressor. Slowly destroying that man's soul a second time would have been pure bliss. But he couldn't have everything. He'd see the man suffer like everyone else, but that universal fate lacked the élan of what he'd been planning.

Prepare yourself, Glaeken. The end begins today.

10.

The man who once had been more than a man, who was known as Mr. Veilleur to many, and as Glaeken to a few, who had had numerous names, stood at his window and stared out at the Sheep Meadow.

Far below, light traffic cruised Central Park West. A quiet, peaceful, sunny, summer Sunday morning in New York.

Why then was he so filled with dread?

The *Fhinntmanchca* . . . it could be only that. The Order, or perhaps Rasalom himself, had succeeded in bringing it into being.

And that meant . . . what?

He wished he knew. Perhaps then he might be able to head it off. But its purpose had always been a mystery.

He could only wait and see. But he felt something awful coming, something cataclysmic.

11.

"I really wonder if you should be out," Weezy said as she strolled along the sunny side of Columbus Avenue with the Lady and the dog.

Her long black dress and three-legged dog made it hard not to think of her as Mrs. Clevenger.

"You keep saying that. You think I should hide? I am the Lady. I do not hide. And besides, if the *Fhinntmanchca* is going to disrupt the noosphere, it will do so no matter where I am."

Weezy couldn't argue with the logic of that. The noosphere was all around, more ubiquitous than air. No one could protect it, no one could hide it, or hide from it.

Still, Weezy worried.

"But what if it's after you—personally, I mean?"

"Then it will find me eventually."

"Let's hope Jack finds it first."

The Lady nodded. "And for your sake—for everyone's sake—let's hope he can do something about it. But I fear he cannot."

A warm feeling rippled through her. "Jack seems full of surprises."

"A very capable man, but everyone has limits, even the Heir." She pointed to their left. "Let's head this way. We can walk along the edge of Taxidermy Park."

Weezy smiled. "Why do you call it that?"

"A piece of the city's wild past stuffed and mounted and put on display." As they crossed the avenue she said, "You love him, don't you."

The words startled her. "We're just old friends—dear old friends—and I care deeply for him, but I don't love . . ."

Or did she?

The wall of denial she'd built collapsed, and what she saw staggered her.

Yes, she'd fallen for him. But she'd been vulnerable. The void Steve left had never closed. She'd tried to fill it with her probings into the secrets behind 9/11, but that hadn't been enough. It wasn't just that he'd come back into her life, it was the *way* he'd come back—at full charge, with such *drama*. Vulnerable? She'd been a sitting duck.

Or maybe nothing was really new about this. She suspected now that she might have loved him back when they were teens, but her neurotransmitters had been too screwed up, swinging her moods back and forth, up and down, to let her notice.

Or were her feelings now just a manifestation of a new swing of her bipolar pendulum? Were these true emotions or just another hypomanic oscillation?

It sucked not to be able to trust your feelings.

The Lady suddenly gripped her arm and pulled her toward the curb. "Let's cross the street here."

Weezy sensed a sudden urgency. "Why?"

"I do not wish to walk past that place."

Weezy looked over her shoulder and saw a blue awning leading to glass doors. *Sitchin Clinic* was etched in the glass.

"What's wrong?"

"Their screams."

Baffled, Weezy looked again and saw *Women's Center*

in smaller letters. Women's center . . . the euphemism for abortion clinic.

"You can hear . . . ?"

The Lady nodded. "They linger."

After they'd walked a ways in silence, the Lady said, "His heart is taken, you know."

"Jack's? Yeah, I met her."

And liked her, damn it. Not the kind of woman she would have expected to be paired with the man Jack had become, but their differences seemed to strengthen their bond instead of weaken it.

"But we were close long before she even knew he existed. I can claim first dibs." When the Lady gave her a look, she added, "Only kidding. But who knows? They could split. Nothing lasts forever, right?"

She immediately hated herself for saying that. She didn't wish anyone pain, especially Jack, but relationships fell apart every day.

"They have a special bond . . . a child."

"Vicky? She's a doll, but—"

"No. Another child . . . unborn."

Weezy stopped walking and gawked at her. "Gia's *pregnant*?"

The Lady shook her head. "Was. I will explain . . ."

12.

The few Kickers on the front steps of the Lodge did not seem their cocky selves. They looked shaken.

"Hey, what's up?" Jack said, shaking out a cigarette and offering the pack to one of the hangers.

The guy waved him off, saying, "It's awful."

The *Fhinntmanchca,* maybe?

"What happened?"

"I didn't see it go down, but Hags and Ansari, man . . .

I got a peek at them. The others are bad, but they're just awful."

Something awful had happened to that creep Ansari? Well, that wasn't necessarily a bad thing.

Diana's warning popped into his head. *It's dangerous. It's deadly.*

"I'm not following. What—?"

"Darryl . . ." The guy shook his head.

"Darryl?" He remembered Ansari telling him about his HIV. "I thought he'd been kicked out."

"So did I. But he was back this morning and . . ." He shook his head again and looked away.

"Thanks. You've been a big help."

As Jack turned and climbed toward the entrance, he heard the wail of sirens. From the top of the steps he could see a pair of ambulances making their way down the street. He hurried inside where he found more shell-shocked Kickers milling around.

Where would Darryl and Ansari be? A group of guys were clustered around the stairway down to the basement. He headed in their direction. The basement looked like the place to be, and after following Thompson and Drexler yesterday, that made sense. If the *Fhinntmanchca* was here, that was where he'd find it.

"All right, everybody!" he called, clapping his hands as he approached. "Let's get clear! The ambulances are here. Let's let the EMTs through."

He began clearing a path down the steps, but a big guy at the door wouldn't move.

"Off-limits. And who the fuck are you?"

Jack looked him square in the eye. "One of your Kicker brothers. And I've got EMTs right behind me. You gonna keep them out while Hags and Ansari bleed to death?"

His eyes shifted. "Ain't bleeding."

No? Strange. Now he wanted more than ever to get past that door.

"You know what I mean. Come on, clear the door. You really gonna stand there and keep them from getting help?"

That last seemed to do it. With a grunt he turned the knob and shoved the door open. Jack slipped through and found a mess.

He counted eight Kickers, each seemingly damaged in a different way, lying or sitting on the floor. Moans and sobs filled the room. Half a dozen others stood and stared at them or tried to help. He spotted Ansari on his knees, tears streaming down his cheeks as he felt around on the floor with his left hand.

"Anybody seen my hand? Where's my fucking hand?"

What?

And then Jack saw the stump of his right wrist, but no blood there—it looked charred.

Hagaman sat on the floor, his back against the wall, his face a sick pale green. He clutched the stump of his left arm, charred as well. The rest of the arm lay across his lap.

He kept repeating, "You think they'll be able to sew it back on? Do ya? Do ya?"

Half a dozen other Kickers had deep, deep burns in their arms and backs. One lay facedown on the floor. He had a fist-size hole in his upper back, all the way through into his chest cavity. Except for the lack of blood, it looked like the kind of exit wound a Magnum hollowpoint would make. The guy's eyes stared at nothing and he wasn't breathing.

What the hell happened here?

"Where's the boss?" he asked one of the dazed-looking Kickers standing around and watching. The guy wore his sandy hair in a long mullet.

"Huh?" He blinked and focused. He seemed to have been in a trance. "He followed Darryl."

"Where'd they go?"

"The fuck should I know?" he said, his voice thick with the Deep South. "I just hope I never fuckin see that guy again."

"Who, the boss?"

"You fuckin kiddin me? Darryl!" He gestured to the fallen Kickers. "Look what he did!"

Jack stared at the guy. He seemed sober. His pupils looked okay.

Shock seeped through as he surveyed the devastation again.

"Darryl did this?"

"Fuck yeah!"

Jack tried to imagine it and failed.

"How?"

"The fuck I know? Like anything he touched turned to steam. Never seen nothin like it and hope to God I never see it again."

Darryl? This guy had to be on drugs. But then again, the wounds Jack had seen sort of fit with what he was saying.

But how? Could it have anything to do with the *Fhinnt-manchca*? Had to. What other explanation could there be?

Over the guy's shoulder and past his mullet, Jack saw the door to the smaller side room standing open. He needed to see what lay at the bottom of that circular stairway.

"How about Drexler? He around?"

"Who?"

"The dude in the white suit."

"Oh, yeah. That his name? He went with the boss."

The EMTs arrived then, and suddenly the focus was on them. Jack used the diversion to slip into the back room.

Inside, the closet door stood open, with the trapdoor up

as well. Looked like someone had left in a hurry. Jack closed the door to the main room, then stepped into the closet and listened for sound from below.

All quiet.

Okay. Make this quick.

He drew the Glock and started down at a quick pace, but the way the staircase wobbled slowed him. He spotted gaps in the railings. They looked melted . . . charred . . . like the wounds he'd just seen.

Darryl?

When he reached the subcellar he found the lights on. It smelled like the hold of a slave ship. A quick search proved it empty except for a leaking, gelatinous mass in an alcove at the far end. Jack approached it cautiously, wondering what it could be.

A close-up view was no help. He nudged it with a boot and the toe popped through the skin or whatever encased it. Thick, milky-white goo began to leak out onto the floor. Jack slapped a hand over his nose and stepped back. It stank like a rotten egg . . .

Diana had described the *Fhinntmanchca* as emerging from an egg. Was this it? If so, where was the *Fhinntmanchca*?

Darryl. Darryl had the *Fhinntmanchca*. That had to be it. He'd carried it up from the subcellar and whoever got in his way got hurt.

Had to find Darryl.

He ran up the wrought-iron stair, ignoring the wobble, and charged into the main room. The EMTs looked baffled as they tended to the wounded. Jack slipped past, made it up the steps, and out to the front entrance.

"Anyone see where Darryl went?" he called from the top step.

The dozen or so hanging about ignored him, but Kewan was just arriving from the right.

"Just saw him, Johnny," he said, jerking a thumb over his shoulder. "Crossing Allen. The boss and the suit weren't far behind."

I owe you, Kewan, he thought as he hurried down the steps.

"Thanks, man."

Kewan smiled and held up two fingers, scissoring them open and closed. "Got a cig?"

Jack pulled the pack from his pocket and pressed it into his hand.

"All yours, my friend."

"Hey, awright!"

Jack left him shaking one free as he trotted up the street.

Thompson and Drexler following Darryl. Only one reason he could think of for that confirmed his earlier suspicion: Darryl had the *Fhinntmanchca.*

13.

Mother . . .

The word breathed in his mind, filled it, flooded it, owned it.

Not his mother, not anyone's mother, just an idea of *mother.* And he wanted her.

She was a glowing speck in his vision, dead ahead, but far ahead, miles ahead.

He came to a wall. He could see the bright mother speck against the bricks. He turned and walked along until he cleared the wall, then he turned and faced the speck again. He continued his journey toward it . . . toward her.

For he *must* reach her. Nothing else mattered. His wants, his needs, his dreams, none of that mattered. Not even his name mattered.

His name . . . he was pretty sure it was "Darryl." He'd

heard people say that word to him. He remembered being sick and wanting a cure, but the memory of just what kind of sickness he'd had was lost to him now.

It didn't matter. Nothing mattered anymore but Mother. He had to find her, embrace her, clutch her to him.

And then he would be well. Then he would be clean and whole, and all the world would be renewed.

He picked up speed.

I'm coming, Mother.

14.

"Where the fuck is he going?" Thompson said in a peeved tone. "We must have walked ten miles already."

Ernst glanced at him. Sweat beaded his face. The hair at the nape of his neck was dark with moisture.

"More like half that," Ernst said, but he knew how Thompson felt.

The heat of the day was growing and he was not dressed for this sort of activity. He'd unbuttoned his vest and loosened his collar, but none of that had helped. Plus he wasn't used to physical activity. He wished he'd done more to stay in shape.

Darryl had led them up Bowery and then up Broadway through Times Square. Now he seemed headed toward Central Park. The stores weren't open yet, so car and pedestrian traffic were light. Good thing. Because Darryl did not stop for anything. He seemed to have a specific destination in mind and was relentless in his progress toward it. He paid no heed to WALK or DON'T WALK signals, simply stepped off the curb and into the street without breaking stride, sometimes to a chorus of shrieking tires, blaring horns, and screamed curses. He didn't seem to notice. His pale skin, sunken eyes, stained clothing, and stiff, plastered-down hair lent him a frightening look that caused the scattered Sunday morning pedestrians to allow him plenty of room.

As they neared Central Park South, the street and pedestrian traffic thickened. Something was going to happen. A collision with a car or a person seemed inevitable.

"Maybe we should walk ahead of him," Ernst said.

Thompson nodded. "Just thinking the same thing. Only a matter of time before—"

A woman screamed and fell away from Darryl, dropping to her knees and clutching her forearm as a teacup-size puff of scarlet smoke evaporated in the air between them.

"My arm!" she wailed. "He burned my arm!"

Ernst hurried past without looking at her, his eyes fixed on Darryl's back. He edged by those deadly swinging arms and positioned himself a dozen feet in front of him. He began waving his own arms as he matched his pace to Darryl's.

"Make room! Make room! Coming through!"

He didn't know how badly that woman was hurt, but had no doubt Emergency Services would be called. Police would arrive with them, and soon they'd be searching for Darryl. The last thing needed now was a melee between Darryl and the NYPD. He didn't think anyone or anything could stop Darryl, but they could impede him, throw him off course, perhaps make him miss a window of opportunity for whatever he was supposed to accomplish.

They'd have a much harder time finding him without a trail of wounded pedestrians to follow.

People seemed to be listening to him, because they were moving to the sides to let him pass. Ernst kept glancing over his shoulder to check on Darryl's position. He wanted to keep a safe distance between them.

He came to 58th Street. The orange don't-walk hand was lit. He knew Darryl would ignore it. He looked left and saw a black stretch limo racing his way, trying to make the light. Another backward glance shot Ernst's heart rate into the stratosphere: Darryl and the limo were on a collision course.

He stepped out into the street and began waving at the car, but it didn't slow. If anything, it picked up speed as it began to honk at him. Darryl was closer now. Ernst held his ground and waved his arms more frantically. The car never slowed. The honks became one prolonged blare. The maniac was going to hit him.

Ernst jumped out of the way just as Darryl stepped off the curb and into the street.

15.

"Oh, my God," Weezy said. "He's been through pure hell."

As they'd strolled through Central Park, the Lady had covered the past year or so of Jack's life—sketching the succession of betrayals and treachery, the circumstances of Kate's and his father's deaths, Tom's mysterious fate, but going into detail about what had happened to Vicky, Gia, and their baby just this past January. Eventually they'd reached the Turtle Pond and settled there.

They'd chosen a spot near the water's edge. The grass had been worn thin by the countless feet trampling it day after day, but that changed as soon as the Lady seated herself on the ground. Weezy watched in amazement as the anemic, beaten-down blades closest to her began to thicken and green and straighten. The rejuvenation spread in a slowly widening ripple until the grass for about a hundred feet in all directions looked like a carefully manicured lawn.

And then the turtles began to leave the water and approach. Soon a couple of dozen clustered around her, stretching their necks from their shells to stare at her.

But that didn't last. They'd had the lawn pretty much to themselves when they arrived, but now people were beginning to straggle in, bringing blankets and kids and food. The Lady shooed the turtles back into the water.

Weezy watched them swim with their heads above the surface toward the island at the center of the pond. Birds were circling and landing there. Not far away a snowy egret stood frozen in the shallows, eyes fixed on the water, waiting for breakfast to swim by. Nearby a man was trying to help his son launch a kite but the breeze was too gentle to keep it aloft.

Granite-walled Belvedere Castle with its conical tower loomed on the opposite shore atop Vista Rock, while the horseshoe of the Delacorte Theater sat empty to their right. She remembered dragging Steve there years ago to see *Hamlet* at the annual "Shakespeare in the Park" series.

A lump formed in her throat as she remembered how he'd said he'd hated reading Shakespeare in school and she'd countered that the plays were meant to be seen and heard, not read. He'd come away a fan.

If only he could be here beside her now, with the Lady, learning the secrets behind the Secret History.

Weezy gestured around her. "All this peace and beauty. It's all stage dressing, isn't it. Built to keep us from knowing about the dark turmoil that lurks behind it all."

"No," the Lady said. "It's real enough. It's simply not the only reality. And it is just as well that what is on the other side is hidden. Revealing it would cause only panic and misery."

"But people deserve the truth, don't they?"

She shrugged her thin, stooped shoulders. "Why?

Because you think knowledge is power? It isn't. Behind all this is an ugly truth they are powerless to do anything about."

Weezy couldn't—wouldn't buy that.

"Then why am I parsing the *Compendium*? Why is Jack somewhere out there trying to find the *Fhinntmanchca*?"

"You and Jack are not common folk. You are gifted, and he is . . . cursed." She pointed to a woman playing pattycake with a little girl on a blanket. "Look at that mother. Would she be better off knowing what fate awaits her child if the *Fhinntmanchca* destroys the noosphere? Would she be happier? Would she even be out here playing with her child if she knew?"

She thought about what the Lady had said about Jack.

. . . cursed . . .

From what she'd heard, it certainly seemed that way.

A spear has no branches . . .

Those words, and their portent, made her shudder each time she thought of them.

"How does Gia handle that?" she wondered out loud.

"Handle what?"

"Knowing that someone tried to kill her and Vicky and did kill her daughter just because the baby was Jack's?"

"She doesn't know," the Lady said.

"How can that—?"

"Jack hasn't told her yet."

"Oh."

Not good. She could see him looking and waiting for the right time to drop that bomb, but more than six months had passed.

"An odd tone in that syllable."

"Big, big mistake."

The Lady turned to her. "I agree. But you sound disappointed."

"Maybe I am . . . a little." She wasn't sure why.

"Because he is not perfect?"

Was that it?

"Maybe."

"Is that fair to him? He's never pretended to be perfect. Quite the contrary. He makes mistakes and he knows it. And though he may be the Heir, he's still only human. I know many beings who are perfectly human, but not one perfect human being. We should not expect perfection in anyone. If we do we shall be perfectly frustrated."

"We shouldn't expect even you to be perfect?"

The Lady smiled. "I'm only as perfect as the beings who feed the noosphere, and they are all imperfect."

Something occurred to her, and it made her uncomfortable.

"You know an awful lot about Jack. Are you that aware of everyone?"

She shook her head. "Because he is the Heir, I know where he is and I can find him. I pay special attention to Jack. That was why I moved into Johnson shortly after he was born. He was never aware of it, but I've kept an eye on him all his life."

Weezy shook her head. "I could have used some looking after."

"Your trials came from within and from the world around you, but they were always of this sphere. Jack has been an object of scrutiny from beyond."

" 'Watched keenly and closely by intelligences greater than man's.' " She winked at the Lady. "H. G. Wells, *War of the Worlds*."

"Perhaps not so 'keenly and closely,' but watched nonetheless. It is not for me to interfere in the natural course of events in this sphere." She nudged the dog with a foot and it raised its head. "My friend here is not so strict as I on such matters, but the fact remains that, despite how much we wish we could at times, we do not exist to influence human concerns and events."

"Except in Jack's case."

"His case is different. Forces from beyond this sphere have impinged and warped the trajectory of his life. Since they originate beyond the normal course of human events, I have on occasion felt justified in stepping in to nudge him onto a less hazardous path, or to ameliorate the effects of their intrusions. I have had varying success. For instance, I was able to save Gia and Vicky. I could not save their unborn."

Weezy thought again about Gia not knowing that the accident was no accident, and that it had been caused simply because of her relationship with Jack.

How would she react when Jack finally told her? Weezy didn't know her well enough to say. But she had a pretty good idea how she'd feel if she happened to learn from another source: furious, betrayed, devastated.

It might destroy their relationship.

Weezy suddenly hated herself for what she was thinking.

Don't. Go. There.

Ever.

The thought retreated, but it wouldn't die.

"You should convince him to tell Gia about what happened—ASAP."

"That is not my province. But you, as a friend—"

"Me?"

"If you love him, you will tell him."

"Is that why you told me all this? I could just as easily tell Gia and ruin things between them."

The Lady looked at her. "I don't think you would do such a thing."

"I'm even less perfect than Jack. And I'm not even supposed to know about it."

She almost wished she didn't.

"But you do. And you can tell him where you heard it. You may have an opportunity very soon."

"What do you mean?"

"He's coming this way."

16.

Jack squatted briefly by the woman who'd screamed—a young, pretty Hispanic with tear-streaked cheeks.

"Can I help?"

He doubted he could but he wanted to see what had happened to her.

A man standing beside her said, "I just called nine-one-one."

She showed him a charred area on her forearm. An area maybe four inches long and half an inch deep had been burned away.

"It hurts!"

"What did he burn you with? What did it look like?"

"Nothing! I just brushed against his hand."

"But he must have been holding something."

She shook her head. "No. I thought so too, but when I looked all I saw was his hand. It was like his skin burned me. But how can that be?"

"Good question."

But it dovetailed with what the Kicker in the basement had said: Anything Darryl touched dissolved.

Why? How? And if that were true . . .

He'd been trailing Thompson and Drexler as they followed Darryl, and had wondered all the while what had happened to him. He looked like he was on his way to an audition for George Romero, so people tended to get out of his way. This was the first time something like this had happened. Just lucky, he guessed. If Darryl's touch meant—

The blaring of a car horn and the squeal of skidding tires pulled Jack to his feet. He turned in time to see a limo plow into Darryl, sending him flying. He landed on his back on Broadway and rolled once. As he pushed himself off the pavement, the asphalt erupted in black steam where his hands touched it. He regained his feet, shook himself, then resumed his uptown trek as if nothing had happened. Jack watched in shock. That kind of impact should have broken at least one leg. Darryl wasn't even limping.

As he approached a gaggle of gawkers that stood in his path, he said something that sounded like, "Mother."

Jack started forward. If Darryl waded into them—bloodbath. But Thompson was ahead of him, shouting as he hurried toward the onlookers.

"Out of his way!"

Drexler did the same. "Let him through!"

They needn't have bothered. The knot was already unraveling at Darryl's approach.

Jack held back, stepping into the street and checking out the asphalt Darryl had touched. He found two perfect handprints, each about three inches deep, melted into the pavement. He stepped toward the limo where its driver stood looking back and forth between Darryl's retreating figure and the hood of his car. A hole had been melted through the steel.

Only one conclusion here: Darryl wasn't carrying the *Fhinntmanchca,* Darryl *was* the *Fhinntmanchca.*

And he was heading uptown.

Where Jack lived.

Mother . . .

The word rushed back at Jack like a bullet. He'd said "Mother." That could only mean the Lady. They'd assumed the *Fhinntmanchca* would be out to disrupt the noosphere, but it looked like he—or it, or whatever Darryl had become—was after the Lady herself.

He pulled out his phone and dialed his apartment.

No answer.

He tried the phone he'd given Weezy and the voice mail picked up immediately. She must have shut it off again.

He watched Darryl's retreating back. If he was heading for the Lady, then he was heading for the apartment. Jack had to get there first. Warn the Lady. Get her out of there. Tell her to move to the Wilkins ice shelf or someplace equally remote until he'd figured how to deal with this.

His first thought was to take the subway, but the Sunday trains ran few and far between. Something could go wrong and Darryl might beat him on foot. Best thing was to hoof it up there ahead of him.

Jack broke into a loping run, planning to bypass Darryl and his two handlers. He was just catching up when he saw Darryl step off the curb and stride into the middle of Columbus Circle. Drexler and Thompson stayed ahead of him, waving their arms, trying to prevent another collision. Amid screeching tires and blaring horns they succeeded—just barely—and Darryl entered Central Park.

Jack stood staring. If Darryl had been heading toward the apartment, he'd have angled left, staying on Broadway, following it into the Upper West Side. Instead he was taking a straight-ahead uptown course, due north.

But to where?

All Jack could do was follow.

He crossed into the park and quickly caught up. Darryl had left the path and was striding through the trees and bushes, with Drexler and Thompson close behind.

As he pressed into brush he would push it aside, dissolving whatever he touched. Jack tried to understand what he'd become. Not like he was antimatter, because when matter and antimatter collided, the result was mutual destruction. With Darryl, the destruction was only one-sided. Was that what the *Fhinntmanchca* was—some sort of human-Otherness hybrid capable of destroying any earthly matter it contacted? That was how it seemed. Except for his clothes. Why hadn't his clothes dissolved? Had to be a reason, and Jack was sure it wasn't modesty.

Darryl marched straight through the Heckscher ball fields, into the trees beyond, and then across the Sheep Meadow. Anyone who might have got in his way took one look at him and moved aside.

Where the hell was he going?

When he plowed into the trees at the north end of the Sheep Meadow and kept going, Jack had had enough.

Time for some answers.

He checked his pockets. He'd come prepared for various levels of conflict, close order and otherwise: a sap, a miniature stun gun, his backup piece, and an extra mag for his Glock.

Drexler and Thompson had been so intent on where Darryl was going they'd rarely looked back. Jack had stayed off to the side, following at a distance and at an angle, paralleling their course. As they entered the trees, he picked up his pace and closed the gap.

When he reached them he had his Glock and stun gun—a Firefly model, the size of a cigarette pack—ready. Thompson was on the left, Drexler on the right, so Jack held his weapons accordingly. Drexler had to know more, so that meant Thompson was going down.

They heard him at the last moment and turned. Jack pressed the Firefly against Thompson's upper arm, releasing 950,000 volts into his nervous system.

"Good morning," he said to Drexler, jamming the Glock's muzzle under his chin while he counted off five seconds of shock. Thompson jerked and spasmed, then collapsed as his muscles lost all tone. He lay in the brush, limp and dazed, as threatening as a puddle.

"Who are you?" Drexler said, on tiptoe now because of the upward pressure of the barrel. "Do you have any idea who I am, who you're dealing with?"

Jack pocketed the Firefly, grabbed the man's shirtfront, and wheeled him around so he could keep an eye on Thompson. Then he chose his words for maximum impact.

"Your precious *Fhinntmanchca*—where's it going?"

Drexler's eyes widened in shock. "What—what did you say?"

"You heard me. Your *Fhinntmanchca*—what's it up to?" He lowered the pistol to Drexler's gut. "Don't worry, it's not answer or die—it's answer or hurt a lot. An awful lot. Ever been gut shot?"

"*Nein!* Don't!"

"Then educate me. What do you expect it to do?"

"I have no idea, I swear!"

"Didn't the One tell you?"

That had been a shot in the dark, but it struck pay dirt. Jack hadn't thought Drexler's eyes could widen any further, but they managed.

"Who *are* you? How can you know—?"

Jack shook him and spoke through his teeth. "What . . . is . . . *happening*?"

"I swear I don't know. That's why I was following—to see. I swear."

Jack believed him. Rasalom was supposedly the only one who knew, and if he wasn't talking, then Drexler had to find out on his own, just like Jack.

But not *with* Jack.

He took a small step back and looked him up and down. His white suit was speckled with what looked like coffee stains.

"You fallen on hard times? What happened to your wonderful ice cream suit? You used to be such a neatnik."

The blue eyes bored into Jack's. "How do you know me?" The eyes narrowed. "We've met before, haven't we? The Taint is heavy upon you. I know you—"

Enough of that. Jack spun him around.

"What are you doing?"

He pulled out the Firefly and jammed it against the back of his neck. Five seconds later he joined Thompson on the ground. The Kicker king was stirring so Jack gave him another quick jolt, then went in pursuit of Darryl.

His trail of ruined vegetation made him easy to find. Jack followed as he skirted the lake along its west side, then passed behind the Delacorte. But instead of continuing uptown after clearing the theater, he stopped and looked around until his gaze fixed on something to his right.

He said, "Mother," and began to move in that direction.

Alarmed, Jack ran up behind him and scanned the area around the Turtle Pond. He let out a shout when he recognized two figures sitting on the grass.

17. *"No!"*

The raw emotion in the shout grabbed Weezy's attention. Something familiar about the voice too. She looked up and saw a scary-looking guy striding straight for them along the water's edge. His gaze seemed fixed just over her shoulder—at the Lady.

And then someone ran up behind him carrying a long club—no, a five-foot deadwood branch, thicker than a baseball bat. She didn't recognize his rage-contorted face at first, then—

"Jack!"

Without a word of warning he swung the branch

against the stranger's back. It landed with a loud *thunk!* that sent him stumbling ahead.

"Weezy!" Jack shouted. "Get her out of here!"

"Whatever is Jack doing?" the Lady said.

Weezy scrambled to her feet.

"I don't know, but I'm sure he had a very good reason for attacking that man."

"What man?"

Weezy turned to her. She was staring at Jack and obviously saw him, but . . .

"The man in the dirty work shirt." She pointed. "Can't you see him? He's right there."

The Lady shook her head. "No. I see Jack swinging a dead branch."

The dog sensed something. He was on his three legs, baring his teeth as the fur rose along his back.

Weezy turned back in time to see Jack thrust the branch between the stranger's legs. The man pitched forward onto his hands and knees. Weezy jumped as she saw the wet ground near the water erupt in steam and seem to dissolve where his palms landed.

"Ohmygod!"

"What just happened there?" the Lady said.

At least she'd seen that. And then Weezy remembered a remark she'd made earlier.

. . . certain doings involving the Otherness are hidden from me . . .

This strange man was somehow connected to the Otherness. That had to be it. Maybe he had something to do with the *Fhinntmanchca.*

As the man pushed himself back to his feet, Jack swung the branch again, this time at his head, but the end dissolved in a puff of smoke where it made contact. The man seemed oblivious. He straightened and started toward them again.

Weezy tugged the Lady to her feet. "We've got to get away!"

"I don't understand."

"Look," she said, pointing to the dog who had placed himself between the Lady and the stranger. "He does."

Weezy couldn't tell if the dog could see him or simply sensed a threat. She looked around. People had stopped what they were doing and turned to stare. A couple of men were hurrying over, probably coming to help the man Jack was attacking.

She turned back and gasped when she saw the pistol in Jack's hand.

He'd positioned himself with the man between him and the pond. He raised the pistol in a two-handed grip and fired. People all around began to scream and run. The approaching men did about-faces and ran to join the fleeing crowd.

Weezy held her ears as Jack pumped one bullet after another, at least a dozen, in rapid succession into the stranger. She saw holes appear in his work shirt, but instead of blood, only small gray wisps of smoke puffed out. The man barely seemed to notice. She saw Jack step closer, raise the pistol, and fire twice into the side of the man's head. The bullets disappeared into two puffs of smoke as soon as they contacted his scalp. The man didn't even break stride. It seemed whatever contacted his skin dissolved.

With a cry of rage, Jack tossed the pistol aside and picked up the branch again. Holding it like a medieval knight might a lance, he charged the man and rammed it into his side. This knocked him off balance but he did not go down. As Jack kept jabbing the branch into the man's flank, pushing him toward the water, the dog let out a howl and attacked.

Whether he could see the stranger or not, Weezy

couldn't be sure, but even if not, the way Jack was batting at him gave a pretty clear indication of where the threat lay.

"No!" Weezy screamed as the dog launched himself into the air, jaws agape, ready to bite. "*Don't!*"

The dog's teeth sank into the man's chest and the front of his head exploded in a red mist just as Jack rammed another blow to the left ribs with the branch. The combination of forces pushed the man off balance and he staggered to his right and tumbled into the pond.

The water exploded into jets of steam, shooting high and wide, its roiling billows blotting out the man and the pond and even the castle.

"Oh, no!" the Lady cried, rushing toward where the dog lay on its side on the grass. "What happened? What *happened*?"

Weezy grabbed her arm. "You can't stay here!"

She pulled free and knelt by the dog's limp form. His jaws were gone, his eyes too. What was left of his head and the base of his tongue weren't bleeding. It looked as if the flesh had fused. His gullet was still open and his chest rose and fell—still alive but just barely.

"What happened?"

The pond was still billowing steam like a boiling cauldron, enveloping Jack where he stood at the water's edge.

"The *Fhinntmanchca*!" he called from within the fog. "That guy was the *Fhinntmanchca*. He was here to kill you. You've got to get as far away as possible."

"Yes!" Weezy cried. "Listen to Jack."

"Not without him." She slipped her arms beneath the dog. "We stay together—always."

Weezy reached to help her. "Here, then. Let me—"

"No." The Lady shook her head as she rose with the limp form in her arms. "It can be only me. I—"

She heard Jack shout, "No!" as a figure in tattered clothing lunged from the fog with open arms.

"Mother!"

He threw his arms around the Lady and the dog in a needy embrace and the world exploded into darkness—a silent blast of anti-light that lasted only a heartbeat or two. No blast effect, no shock wave, but Weezy felt it suck the heart and heat out of her.

And then it was gone, letting the daylight return. Weezy blinked in the glare like someone who'd just spent days in a cave. When her eyes adjusted and she could see again, she cried out her loss.

The Lady was gone.

18. From his place on the rooftop, Rasalom heard the silent blast and raised his arms toward the vault of the sky, not in supplication, but in triumph.

Done.

She was gone. He could sense her absence. The *Fhinntmanchca* had done its job. Opus Omega had finally yielded fruit, though not in the originally intended manner. All those millennia of flogging generation after generation of the Septimus Order to keep setting those pillars, only to learn that they could not complete it. The Orsa had been the fail-safe, and that was why it had had to be secured no matter what the risks.

He had thought the Lady dead once before, when that little would-be usurper of his name had set the chew wasps on her. No one had been more surprised than he—except perhaps the Lady herself—when it appeared she had succeeded. The petty pretender had had no idea what she was doing, and only a unique alliance of circumstances had allowed her the means.

But she had merely appeared to succeed, for the Lady had reappeared elsewhere, wounded but alive.

Not this time.

The *Fhinntmanchca* existed solely for this task, and it had succeeded.

Now the Enemy will see this world as non-sentient and thus without value. It will turn away and devote its attentions to other worlds.

Your time has just ended, Glaeken, and mine is about to begin.

He wondered at his subdued feelings. Where was the exuberance, the joy, the ecstasy of victory after such a prolonged conflict?

Well, that would come.

He began planning his next moves. The first was a minor matter: dispose of that noisome girl and her unborn child. The child might have proved useful had the *Fhinntmanchca* failed. But now that the Lady was gone, he had no use for it; it might even prove a liability. Eliminating liabilities had been his credo since the First Age. It had served him well through the millennia. No sense in changing tactics now.

Dispose of her, then go to the mountain to initiate the Change. But first, the power.

He waited for the surge as the Enemy vacated—power to begin the Change—in himself and in the world around him.

But he felt nothing.

No . . . that was not right. He did feel something, a growing sensation in the back of his mind, slowly spreading across it. Strangely familiar.

It couldn't be . . . no . . . no . . .

"*NO!*"

19. "No!"

Glaeken squeezed his eyes shut and jammed the heels of his hands against his temples. He backed away from the window and dropped into one of the thick-upholstered chairs.

Something had happened, something terrible.

The Lady . . . it had to be her. He didn't sense her. Mortality had stripped him of certain abilities . . . awarenesses. The Lady's existence was like a scent in the air, and now that scent was gone.

The workaday world out there would not realize what had just happened. They did not know her scent, could not feel her presence, so they would be unaware of what they had lost.

But the Ally would notice and would turn away from what it perceived as a dead world.

Glaeken felt a sense of loss, a wave of sadness almost overwhelming in its intensity. She hadn't been a person, not in a true sense, just a physical manifestation of something much larger and more complex, but she'd been a personality, and thus a person to him. He'd grown fond of her over the millennia, perhaps even grown to love her. Not like he loved Magda, of course. More like a sister, or a dear, dear friend.

He'd had but two constants in his attenuated existence: Rasalom and the Lady. Now he had only Rasalom. And very soon Rasalom would—

He started at a crash behind him. He rose and saw a figure slumped facedown across the coffee table. A woman—naked, old, frail. For a moment he thought it might be Magda—it wouldn't be the first time she'd forgotten to get dressed—but then he saw the marks on her back and knew.

"You live?"

She raised her head and looked at him with bleary, pain-wracked eyes.

"Help me. Please . . . help."

MONDAY

1. Jack stared at the thin figure slumped in the wheelchair.

Not that he disbelieved Veilleur, but how could this wizened crone be the Lady?

Veilleur had called yesterday to give Jack and Weezy the good news, but suggested they wait till morning before visiting. He'd directed them to the furnished apartment below his own. Its floor plan was identical to Glaeken's, but the windows onto the park weren't as grand.

They'd found her propped up in a wheelchair by one of those windows, a frail old woman with tangled gray hair and rheumy, sunken eyes.

He looked around. "Where's Mister Veilleur?"

"Upstairs with his wife," the old woman said. "Magda is having one of her bad days. Every time he goes out, she suspects he's with another woman. This morning she found me there and became hysterical."

"Poor man," Weezy said. "Poor woman."

"The good thing is, she'll forget by this afternoon. The bad thing is, he won't."

Jack looked around again. Something else was missing. Then he realized what.

"Where's your dog?"

She shook her head. "He couldn't make it back."

"Oh," he said, feeling a stab of guilt. "I'm sorry. I did everything I could to stop—"

She lifted a gnarled hand. "He is not gone. He simply cannot be here. But you . . . you must not feel you failed. You could not have stopped him. No one could have."

He knew she was right. He'd done everything possible with the weapons at hand. And even if he'd had a grenade launcher or a surface-to-surface missile, the end would have been the same. But that didn't make him feel any better. Not after how she'd been there for him, intervening when he'd had nowhere else to turn.

Weezy stepped forward and laid a hand on her stooped shoulder. "What happened? You disappeared. Where did you go? Where did that strange awful man go?"

"Mutual obliteration. The three of us died. I was nothingness. I did not exist. And then . . . awareness returned. Somehow, for some reason, the noosphere was able to restore me. But only me. It should not have had the power to do that, but it did. It does."

Weezy frowned. "I don't understand. You aren't the noosphere, just a manifestation of it. Did your . . . 'obliteration' damage it?"

"Yes. But don't forget, I grew as the noosphere grew. When the sentient biosphere was small, the young noosphere initiated my existence. I began as a spark that became an infant, that became a child, and so on. It took millennia for the noosphere to grow, and as it developed, so did I, finally developing into adulthood at the dawn of the First Age. An unforeseen, profoundly tragic consequence of my matured existence was that it signaled the sentience of this world throughout the multiverse."

Jack said, "Attracting the attention of the Ally and the Otherness."

"Exactly. The Conflict was very much in the open then, much more head-on. After the Ally gained the upper hand

and the Otherness caused the Great Cataclysm, more oblique means were sought by the other side—such as shutting down the beacon. Thus I became a target, and Opus Omega was born."

Jack took his turn at the window and looked left. He couldn't see the Turtle Pond from here, but he could make out Belvedere Castle, which had overlooked everything that had gone down yesterday.

"So yesterday was the culmination of millennia of effort to destroy you. But if eliminating you wasn't going to hurt the noosphere that created you, why did they think the *Fhinntmanchca* would accomplish anything? The noosphere would simply re-create you and put you back out there as the beacon."

"It is not that simple. Obliterating me damaged the noosphere. It should have been forced to re-create me from scratch again—from that spark I mentioned. I can act as a beacon only when I am mature. My development wouldn't have taken as long as before, but more than long enough for the Ally to turn away and the Otherness to achieve a stranglehold."

"Why didn't it happen that way?"

"The only possible reason is that, even damaged, the noosphere is stronger and more resilient than I or anyone else ever imagined."

"But you're so . . ."

"Weak and old? Yes. But that the noosphere could do even this is miraculous. I am *here*—as an adult. And as such I remain the beacon. That is what is important. In the past, once I matured, I was able to appear at any age I wished. I often chose to be an old woman—no one feels threatened by an old woman. Now I have no choice."

"But at least you're back," Jack said.

She nodded. "Yes, I have returned. Barely. But I had to come alone. The noosphere did not have enough to send back my companion. I did not want to return without him, but I had no choice. I had to appear again, had to take human form, even if it is only this. I have just enough strength to keep the Ally aware of the sentience of this biosphere."

Weezy went to the window and gazed out at the city.

"They failed. Nine/eleven . . . the Septimus Order and R brought down the Towers, killed all those innocent people . . . for nothing."

"Not entirely for nothing." She fumbled with the hem of her cardigan, then lifted it to bare her belly. "I have been sorely wounded."

Jack saw what she meant: A second tunnel ran through her—this one to the left of her navel. Weezy stepped back from the window for a look.

"Ohmygod!"

The Lady lowered the sweater. "I shall not survive another attack."

Jack thought of that ruined, leaking, deflated sack of . . . whatever in the Lodge's subcellar. The "egg" in Diana's Alarm. Big enough to contain a man and hatch him as something else. But all the king's horses and lackeys weren't putting that thing back together again.

"There won't be another *Fhinntmanchca,*" he said. "The Orsa is dead. It's created its first and last."

Weezy said, "But you'll get stronger, won't you?"

The Lady nodded. "With time and an unbroken feed from the noosphere, I will soon return to my former strength."

Jack said, "How soon?"

"A year."

That long? pushed toward Jack's lips, then he realized that a century didn't qualify as an eye blink in her frame of reference. A year was barely measurable.

"I have never been able to influence the conflict itself,"

she added. "The Ally and the Otherness are far too vast. My importance has centered around my function as a beacon." She looked at Jack. "But as you know, now and again I have been able to intervene and provide assistance in earthly matters involving the Conflict."

Jack nodded. He'd never forget how she'd stepped between Rasalom and him during his darkest hour, yanked Gia and Vicky back from the brink of death. He owed her for all that—and for what else? He wondered what she'd done for him without his knowing . . . say, as Mrs. Clevenger.

"And I will be forever in your debt."

She shook her head. "No need. And no more from me for a while. Until I'm fully restored, I can play no part in what goes on about me. Nor can I move so freely among you as I used to. All my focus must be centered on simply existing. The beacon must remain lit."

Weezy dropped to one knee beside the wheelchair and gripped her hand.

"You said you won't survive another attack. How might they attack you again?"

"It must be with something from the Other side—like the chew wasps from the cenote at the nexus point, or the *Fhinntmanchca*. Nothing of this Earth can harm me."

Jack watched Weezy give a knowing nod. He'd explained what had happened in Florida last year.

"But Darryl was of this Earth," he said.

"No. He was no longer human. His very molecules had been changed to something Other, something from outside."

"What about R?" Weezy said.

"Even the Adversary himself is powerless in that regard. Though he has become something more than human, he is of this Earth." She patted the armrest of her wheelchair. "His minions could wire this chair with explosives and set them off, and I would not be scratched. So, unless they come up with something from the Other side—and I don't think they will—or complete Opus Omega—equally unlikely—I believe I am safe for now."

"So it's just a matter of time before you're back on your feet."

She nodded. "As long as the noosphere retains its present intensity, I shall be as new by this time next year."

Weezy smiled at him, and Jack did his best to return it. But he worried. Many signs pointed to a coming darkness, an endless darkness that would arrive next spring.

A year might be too long.

2. "Success?" Jack said as Russ opened the door.

He'd turned off his phone while with the Lady, and when he turned it back on he'd found voice mail from Russ Tuit saying he had something for him.

Russ shrugged as he stepped back to let him in. "Tough job. I don't know if it's accurate, but it's as good as you're going to get with available software. Better, actually, since I went into the code and added a couple modifications of my own."

Jack nodded without saying anything. He didn't doubt that Russ had done exactly what he'd said, but the extolling of his own efforts tended to act as prelude to the pumping of his fee.

"I approached it from every angle I could think of. I shaved each indi—"

"Shaved?"

Russ smiled. "Well, you wanted the beard off, right? So that required me to give him a shave. Get it?"

"Got it."

"Anyhow, I shaved each individual image, then assembled a composite. I also made a composite of the bearded ones, and shaved that."

"And the result is?"

Russ's smile faltered. "Well, they're not really the same face."

"How's that possible?"

He sat before his computer and began attacking the keyboard with machine-gun bursts of taps.

"Just the way the software works. Take a look. This is the one where I shaved the composite and it's probably the lesser of the two as far as accuracy goes."

A black-and-white image appeared on the monitor—the face of a dark-haired, dark-eyed, thin-lipped man who looked vaguely familiar, but not enough to trigger recognition.

"Let me see the other."

Another face replaced the first and sparked a cascade of memories, all of them bad.

"Shit."

Russ turned and grinned up at him. "I did it? You know him?"

"Yeah."

Jack couldn't take his eyes off that face.

"Well? Who is he?"

Jack continued to stare. "You don't want to know."

Jack too would have preferred not to know, but he did.

"The son of a bitch," he muttered. "The lousy—"

"You're looking a little scary, Jack. Who *is* he?"

He looked different from when Jack had seen him back in January—the nose was sure as all hell different—but not different enough to prevent recognition.

All so clear now . . .

Back in the nineties, after the Orsa became organic, the Order knew it was only a matter of time before it awakened, so they had to dig it up. To that end he'd infiltrated al Qaeda—probably not so difficult, considering his special abilities—and influenced the decision to attack America. Maybe he gave them the idea to use airliners as guided missiles. Perhaps they would have attacked the Trade Towers anyway—they'd already tried once—but he made sure they did.

He'd soaked his hands in the blood of three thousand innocent people and licked them clean.

Because during the attack Jack was sure he'd positioned himself close by, sucking up the terror, the panic, the chaos, the pain, the deaths, the grief and misery of loss. Same with the Madrid train bombings.

Him.

The man on the monitor screen.

The One . . . the Adversary . . .

He'd called himself Wahid bin Aswad. But he had a thing for anagrams, and that name didn't work as one.

Wait. Weezy had mentioned his full name: Wahid bin Aswad al Somar.

Al Somar . . .

That nailed it. No doubt now.

Rasalom.

"Can you copy that file onto a disk for me?"

"Sure."

"Good. And after you do that, I advise you to erase the files and anything connected with them."

Russ looked worried. "Why? This a bad guy?"

Jack nodded. "Real bad. The worst."

He didn't want Russ caught in the middle of anything that Jack might start. And Jack intended to start something.

As Russ made the copy, Jack looked into the eyes of the face on the screen.

So . . . you don't like your picture out and about? You send your Septimus flunkies around erasing all photographic evidence of your existence. What is it? Some First Age superstition? Afraid they contain pieces of your soul? Nah. You don't believe in souls. More likely you're afraid Glaeken will see through your disguises and decide to come looking for you. Yeah. Bet that's it. You want to stay behind the scenes, pulling strings and playing Dr. Mabuse with nobody the wiser until the Big Day when the Otherness shows up.

I can't seem to find a way to hurt you, but maybe I can find a way to distract you, annoy you. I know how to be really, really annoying.

Where are you now? Brooding and fuming about the failure of your *Fhinntmanchca*?

I hope to hell so.

3. Ernst watched the One stare at the lifeless husk of the Orsa. Its stink did not seem to bother him. But his silence disturbed Ernst. The command had come to meet him here, yet the One had spoken not a single word since Ernst arrived, when he'd found him standing just as he was now.

Ernst rolled his sore shoulders. Every muscle in his body ached from the Taser shock he'd received yesterday. A terrible experience. So helpless . . . completely at the mercy of that man.

His jaw clenched. Who was he? He knew much more than he should. It hadn't been Glaeken, he was sure of that. He'd never seen the legendary foe, but he was reputed to be a large man with flaming hair. This bearded stranger had been average in size and looks.

Whoever he was, he had to be found. Thompson hadn't seen him, but he was savagely intent on finding him. Ernst would add the Order and the Dormentalists to the Kickers numbers in the hunt. They'd find him. And when they did . . .

But that was the future. Ernst hoped the One would allow him a future.

He forced himself to speak, not simply to break the unbearable silence, but because he needed to know.

"How could this happen? How could the *Fhinntmanchca* have failed?"

A protracted silence followed, but finally the One responded.

"The *Fhinntmanchca* did not fail. It did exactly what it was designed to do. But what happened after its success . . . that is troubling. Her source recreated her almost instantly. It should not have been able to do that. In fact, it was considered an impossibility. Something has changed, something unforeseen has taken place within her source, enhanced its power. You must learn what that is and reverse it. Soon."

And then he turned and walked away, leaving Ernst alone with his thoughts and the remains of the Orsa.

The source . . . Ernst was familiar with the concept of another plane of existence engendered by the sum of human thoughts and interactions. In many circles it was considered a theory or a pipe dream. Ernst knew different. He knew it existed and was the progenitor of the Lady.

In and of itself, the übermind was no impediment to the Otherness. But its creation—its Eve, as it were—was. Through the Lady it trumpeted its existence to the multiverse, and thus to the Enemy. It was powerful and grew incrementally more so with each increase in the sentient population of the biosphere. But it should not have been powerful enough to reconstruct its instrument in a flash. That bespoke enormous power.

What was fueling that power?

And then . . . a flash of insight. He might be right, he might be wrong, but he saw an entirely new avenue of attack.

Excited, he hurried after the One to tell him. .

THE SECRET HISTORY OF THE WORLD

The preponderance of my work deals with a history of the world that remains undiscovered, unexplored, and unknown to most of humanity. Some of this secret history has been revealed in the Adversary Cycle, some in the Repairman Jack novels, and bits and pieces in other, seemingly unconnected works. Taken together, even these millions of words barely scratch the surface of what has been going on behind the scenes, hidden from the workaday world. I've listed these works below in the chronological order in which the events in them occur.

Note: "Year Zero" is the end of civilization as we know it; "Year Zero Minus One" is the year preceding it, etc.

The Past

"Demonsong" (prehistory)
"Aryans and Absinthe"** (1923–1924)
Black Wind (1926–1945)
The Keep (1941)
Reborn (February–March 1968)
"Dat-Tay-Vao"*** (March 1968)
Jack: Secret Histories (1983)

Year Zero Minus Three

Sibs (February)
"Faces"* (early summer)
The Tomb (summer)
"The Barrens"* (ends in September)
"A Day in the Life"* (October)
"The Long Way Home"
Legacies (December)

Year Zero Minus Two

"Interlude at Duane's"** (April)
Conspiracies (April) (includes "Home Repairs")
All the Rage (May) (includes "The Last Rakosh")
Hosts (June)
The Haunted Air (August)
Gateways (September)
Crisscross (November)
Infernal (December)

Year Zero Minus One

Harbingers (January)
Bloodline (April)
By the Sword (May)
Ground Zero (July)
The Touch (ends in August)
The Peabody-Ozymandias Traveling Circus & Oddity Emporium (ends in September)
"Tenants"*
Repairman Jack #14

Year Zero

"Pelts"*
Reprisal (ends in February)
Fatal Error (February)
The last Repairman Jack novel (ends in March)
Nightworld (starts in May)

Reprisal will be back in print before too long. I'm planning a total of fifteen Repairman Jack novels (not counting the young adult titles), ending the Secret History with the publication of a heavily revised *Nightworld.*

---

* available in *The Barrens and Others*
** available in *Aftershock & Others*
*** available in the 2009 reprint of *The Touch*

Turn the page for a preview of

FATAL ERROR

F. PAUL WILSON

Available now from Tom Doherty Associates

A FORGE HARDCOVER ISBN 978-0-7653-2282-1

I. Munir stood on the curb, facing Fifth Avenue with Central Park behind him. He unzipped his fly and tugged himself free. His reluctant member shriveled at the cold slap of the winter wind, as if shrinking from the sight of all these passing strangers.

At least he hoped they were strangers.

Please let no one who knows me pass by. Or, Allah forbid, a policeman.

He stretched its flabby length and urged his bladder to empty. That was what the madman had demanded of him, so that was what he had to do. He'd drunk two quarts of Gatorade in the past hour to ensure he'd be full to bursting, but he couldn't go. His sphincters were clamped shut as tightly as his jaw.

Off to his right the light at the corner turned red and the traffic slowed to a stop. A woman in a cab glanced at him through her window and started when she saw how he was exposing himself. Her lips tightened and she shook her head in disgust as she turned away. He could almost read her mind: A guy in a suit exposing himself on Fifth Avenue—the world's going to hell even faster than they say.

But it has *become* hell for me, Munir thought.

He saw her pull out a cell phone and punch in three numbers. That could only mean she was calling 911. But he had to stay and do this.

He closed his eyes to shut out the line of cars idling before him, tried to block out the tapping, scuffing footsteps of the shoppers and strollers on the sidewalk behind him as they hurried to and fro. But a child's voice broke through.

"Look, Mommy. What's that man—?"

"Don't look, honey," said a woman's voice. "It's just someone who's not right in the head."

Tears became a pressure behind Munir's sealed eyelids. He bit back a sob of humiliation and tried to imagine himself in a private place, in his own bathroom, standing over the toilet. He forced himself to relax, and soon it came. As the warm liquid streamed out of him, the waiting sob burst free, propelled equally by shame and relief.

He did not have to shut off the flow. When he opened his eyes and saw the glistening, steaming puddle before him on the asphalt, saw the drivers and passengers and passersby staring, the stream dried up on its own.

I hope that is enough, he thought. Please let that be enough.

But he was not dealing with a sane man, and he had to please him. Please him or else . . .

He looked up and saw a young blond woman staring down at him from a third-floor window in a building across the street. Her repulsed expression mirrored his own feelings. Averting his eyes, he zipped up and fled down the sidewalk, all but tripping over his own feet as he ran.

2.

"Gross," Dawn said, turning away from the window to pace the consultation room. "What is it with people?"

"Pardon?" Dr. Landsman looked up from where he sat behind his desk, scribbling in her chart. "Did you say something?"

Dawn Pickering didn't want to talk about some creep peeing in the street, she wanted to talk about herself and her baby. She ran her hands over her swollen belly, bulging like a watermelon beneath her maternity top.

"Can't you . . . like . . . induce me or something?"

She'd been reading up on labor and delivery lately, and was so not looking forward to it. A cesarean would be totally better—knock her out and cut her open. She wouldn't feel a thing, but then she'd have a scar. Well, a scar was a small price to pay for simply waking up and having it all over.

Dr. Landsman shook his head. "The baby's not ready yet."

A balding, fiftyish guy, he'd just done a pelvic exam, followed by her umpteenth ultrasound. Then he'd left her and waited here in his office for her to dress and join him.

"Isn't the ultrasound supposed to give you a clue?"

"It is, and it says he's not ready yet. But it won't be long. Your cervix is soft. Your body's getting ready to deliver."

"But I was totally due in January and here it is February." She rubbed her cold hands together. "Something's wrong. You can tell me."

"Ten months is unusual, yes, but nothing's wrong."

"Then why won't you ever let me see the ultrasounds?"

He did the scans himself instead of his tech, and never allowed anyone else in the room except Mr. Osala, her self-appointed guardian. The doctor had started giving her appointments on Mondays and Thursdays. Why? He had office hours and no staff at all those days. Was that what he wanted? And during the ultrasounds, he always kept the monitor screen turned away from her. For some reason, he never seemed to tire of looking at her baby.

"You wouldn't understand what you were seeing."

She resented that. She might be only eighteen—turning nineteen next month—but she was no dummy. She'd been accepted to Colgate and would be there right now if she hadn't screwed up her life.

"You could point things out to me."

"The baby is fine. You feel him moving, don't you?"

"Like crazy."

Some days she felt like she had a soccer camp inside her.

"Well then, I've told you he's a boy and you know he's healthy. What more do you need?"

"I need to see him."

"I'm not sure I understand your eagerness to see a baby you're giving up for adoption upon delivery. A baby you tried to abort, if I remember correctly."

She had nothing to say to that. She'd totally changed her mind about the abortion, but she was so not ready to raise a child—especially this child, considering who the father was. Someone else would give him a good home and raise him better than she ever could. No way she was ready for motherhood.

He pulled out an old-fashioned pocket watch and popped the lid.

"Your friend, Mister Osala, should be calling soon."

"He's not my friend."

"Well, he's very concerned about you and your baby."

Maybe too concerned.

The design on the lid of his watch caught her eye. Following the lines made her eyes cross.

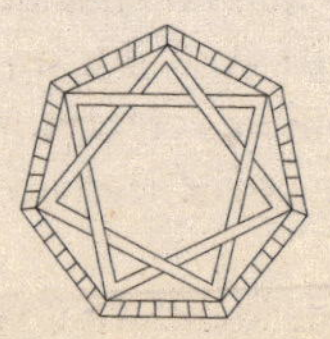

"That looks old."

He smiled. "It's been in the family for almost two hundred years."

"What's that design? It's weird."

"Hmm?" He glanced at it, then quickly pocketed it. "Oh, that. Just a geometric curiosity."

A phone rang. He dug out his cell and checked the display, then glanced up at her. "It's him. Excuse me."

"Sure." She knew who it was. "Don't forget to ask him how high."

He gave her a puzzled look, like he didn't get it.

"Jump," she said. "How high you should jump."

He still didn't get it. For such a supposedly top-notch OB man, he could be so dense at times.

Osala hadn't been around much lately. He used to come to all her appointments but now he was involved in some project down south that kept him away a lot. But he stayed in close touch with Dr. Landsman.

She felt the baby kick and shook her head. Sure felt like he wanted out. And she wanted him out. Not like she had back in the summer, when she'd tried to end the pregnancy. She'd been determined to get an abortion, and then Mr. Osala had told her, *You want this child . . . You will do anything to assure its well-being,* and everything changed, just like that. She couldn't believe now that she'd wanted to kill her baby.

But that was totally different from wanting the pregnancy over and done with. She simply wanted to be back to normal size. She'd never been skinny, but this was ridiculous. She couldn't seem to find a comfortable position anywhere, even in bed. She'd give anything for a full night's sleep.

And once her pregnancy was over and the baby born, maybe Mr. Osala would let her leave his home. She'd been a virtual prisoner there since last spring—almost her entire pregnancy. Could she complain about a Fifth

Avenue duplex penthouse where she wanted for nothing? Yeah, she could, because although she could have anything material, she couldn't have what she wanted most: contact with the outside world. Because Mr. Osala feared that might lead the baby's father to her. That was the last thing she wanted, too, but it seemed to her Mr. Osala had taken precautions to the extreme.

She wanted a *life*.

"Yes, I know it's overdue," she heard Dr. Landsman say. "I was just discussing that with Dawn when you called. But the baby's healthy and, frankly, how do we know this isn't perfectly normal? It's not as if we have any precedents to follow."

Those kinds of comments popped out every so often and never failed to sour her stomach. She'd learned not to ask about them, because Dr. Landsman only stonewalled her.

But she was convinced something was wrong with her baby. Dr. Landsman could tell her it was healthy till he was blue in the face, but that look in his eyes when he watched the ultrasound screen said he was looking at something he didn't see every day.

And then there was the thing about the ultrasound images—Mr. Osala made the doctor delete them after every session. And when he wasn't here, his driver Georges made sure they were history. Georges was almost as scary as his boss.

What was so different about her baby that no one else could know?

3. The phone was ringing when Munir opened the door to his apartment. He hit the RECORD button on his answering machine as he snatched up the receiver and jammed it against his ear.

"Yes!"

"Pretty disappointing, Mooo-neeer," said the now familiar electronically distorted voice. *"Are all you Ayrabs such mosquito dicks?"*

"I did as you asked! Just as you asked!"

"That wasn't much of a pee, Mooo-neeer."

"It was all I could do! Please let them go now."

He glanced down at the caller ID. A number had formed in the LCD window. A 212 area code, just like all the previous calls. But the seven digits following were a new combination, unlike any of the others. And when Munir called it back, he was sure it would be a public phone. Just like all the rest.

"Are they all right? Let me speak to my wife."

Munir didn't know why he said that. He knew the caller couldn't drag Barbara and Robby to a pay phone.

"She can't come to the phone right now. She's, uh . . . all tied up at the moment."

Munir ground his teeth as the horse laugh brayed through the phone.

"Please. I must know if she is all right."

"You'll have to take my word for it, Mooo-neeer."

"She may be dead." Allah forbid! "You may have killed her and Robby already."

"Hey. Ain't I been sendin' you pichers? Don't you like my pretty pichers?"

"No!" Munir cried, fighting a wave of nausea . . . those pictures—those horrible, sickening photos. "They aren't enough. You could have taken all of them at once and then killed them."

The voice on the other end lowered to a sinister, nasty, growl.

"You callin' me a liar, you lousy, greasy, two-bit Ayrab? Don't you ever *doubt a word I tell you. Don't even* think *about doubtin' me. Or I'll show you who's alive.*

I'll prove your white bitch and mongrel brat are alive by sending you a new piece of them every so often. A little bit of each, every day, by Express Mail, so it's nice and fresh. You keep on doubtin' me, Mooo-neeer, and pretty soon you'll get your wife and kid back, all of them. But you'll have to figure out which part goes where. Like the model kits say: Some assembly required."

Munir bit back a scream as the caller brayed again.

"No—no. Please don't hurt them anymore. I'll do anything you want. What do you want me to do?"

"There. That's more like it. I'll let your little faux pas pass this time. A lot more generous than you'd ever be—ain't that right, Mooo-neeer. And sure as shit more generous than your Ay-rab buddies were when they killed my sister on nine/eleven."

"Yes. Yes, whatever you say. What else do you want me to do? Just tell me."

"I ain't decided yet, Mooo-neeer. I'm gonna have to think on that one. But in the meantime, I'm gonna look kindly on you and bestow your request. Yessir, I'm gonna send you proof positive that your wife and kid are still alive."

Munir's stomach plummeted. The man was insane, a monster. This couldn't be good.

"No! Please! I believe you! I believe!"

"I reckon you do, Mooo-neeer. But believin' just ain't enough sometimes, is it? I mean, you believe in Allah, don't you? Don't you?"

"Yes. Yes, of course I believe in Allah."

"And look at what you did on Friday. Just think back and meditate on what you did."

Munir hung his head in shame and said nothing.

"So you can see where I'm comin' from when I say believin' ain't enough. 'Cause if you believe, you can also have doubt. And I don't want you havin' no doubts,

Mooo-neeer. I don't want you havin' the slightest twinge *of doubt about how important it is for you to do exactly what I tell you. 'Cause if you start thinking it really don't matter to your bitch and little rat-faced kid, that they're probably dead already and you can tell me to shove it, that's not gonna be good for them. So I'm gonna have to prove to you just how alive and well they are."*

"No!" He was going to be sick. "Please don't!"

"Just remember. You asked for proof."

Munir's voice edged toward a scream. "PLEASE!"

The line clicked and went dead.

Munir dropped the phone and buried his face in his hands. The caller was mad, crazy, brutally insane, and for some reason he hated Munir with a depth and breadth Munir found incomprehensible and profoundly horrifying. Whoever he was, he seemed capable of anything, and he had Barbara and Robby hidden away somewhere in the city.

Helplessness overwhelmed him and he broke down. Only a few sobs had escaped when he heard a pounding on his door.

"Hey. What's going on in there? Munir, you okay?"

Munir stiffened as he recognized Russ's voice. He straightened in his chair but said nothing. Monday. He'd forgotten about Russ coming over for their weekly brainstorming session. He should have called and canceled, but Russ had been the last thing on his mind. He couldn't let him know anything was wrong.

"Hey!" Russ said, banging on the door again. "I know someone's in there. You don't open up I'm gonna assume something's wrong and call the emergency squad."

The last thing Munir needed was a bunch of EMTs swarming around his apartment. The police would be with them and only Allah knew what that crazy man would do if he saw them.

He cleared his throat. "I'm all right, Russ."

"The hell you are." He rattled the doorknob. "You didn't sound all right when you screamed a moment ago and you don't sound all right now. Just open up so I can—"

The door swung open, revealing Russ Tuit—a pear-shaped guy dressed in a beat-up Starter jacket and faded jeans—looking as shocked as Munir felt.

In his haste to answer the phone, Munir had forgotten to latch the door behind him. Quickly, he wiped his eyes and rose.

"Jesus, Munir, you look like hell. What's the matter?"

"Nothing."

"Hey, don't shit me. I heard you. Sounded like someone was stepping on your soul."

"I'm okay. Really."

"Yeah, right. You in trouble? Anything I can do? Can't help you much with money, but anything else . . ."

Munir was touched by the offer. If only he *could* help. But no one could help him.

"No. It's okay."

"Is it Barbara or Robby? Something happen to—?" Munir realized it must have shown on his face. Russ stepped inside and closed the door behind him. "Hey, what's going on? Are they all right?"

"Please, Russ. I can't talk about it. And you mustn't talk about it either. Just let it be. I'm handling it."

"Is it a police thing?"

"No! *Not* the police! Please don't say anything to the police. I was warned"—in sickeningly graphic detail—"about going to the police."

Russ leaned back against the door and stared at him.

"Jesus . . . is this as bad as I think it is?"

Munir could do no more than nod.

Russ jabbed a finger at him. "I know somebody who might be able to help."

"No one can help me."

"This guy's good people. I've done some work for him—he's a real four-oh-four when it comes to computers, but he's got a solid rep when it comes to fixing things."

What was Russ talking about?

"Fixing?"

"Situations. He solves problems, know what I'm saying?"

"I . . . I can't risk it."

"Yeah, you can. He's a guy you go to when you run out of options. He deals with stuff that nobody wants anybody knowing about. That's his specialty. He's not a detective, he's not a cop—in fact, if the cops are involved, this guy's smoke, because he doesn't get along with cops. He's just a guy. But I'll warn you up front, he's expensive."

No police . . . that was good. And money? What did money matter where Barbara and Robby were concerned? Maybe a man like this was what he needed, an ally who could deal with the monster that had invaded his life.

"This man . . . he's fierce?"

Russ nodded. "Never seen it, and you'd never know it to look at him, but I hear when the going gets ugly, he gets uglier."

"How do I contact him?"

"I'll give you a number. Just leave a message. If he doesn't get back to you, let me know. Jack's gotten kind of distracted these days and picky about what he takes on. I'll talk to him for you if necessary."

"Give me the number."

Perhaps this was what he needed: a fierce man.